CW00411248

KARMIC DREAMS

Book One of the Karmic Paths Trilogy

Fiona J Ward

Proofread by Meredith Debonnaire

To

Hope you enjoy
the read!

xx

KARMIC DREAMS

Copyright © 2019 by Fiona J Ward

FIRST EDITION

Acknowledgements

I would like to thank the following people for their support

Mandy Morgan
Annabel Darby
Dr Jane Graham
June Plumb
Gill Walters
Erin Ward
Laura J of The South Devon Players
Dr Penny Sartori
Jonathan Newton of Let's Get it Shot Productions
Rebecca Fernfield
Amanda Skipp

And all my other friends and family who have
encouraged me …

Karmic Dreams

CHAPTER ONE

Katya knew a change was imminent on that cloudy Friday morning. A solitary white feather floated gently, landing at her feet as she sipped her coffee on the patio. She glanced upwards, seeking its origin. Nothing.

Bending down, she picked up the feather, feeling its clean softness. It was too white and pure to be that of a seagull. Returning her attention to her view of the harbour, she noticed grey clouds assembling, billowing with expectation. She held her breath as she felt a knot form in her stomach, and a quiet yet high-pitched singing began inside her ear. Katya had experienced the sound before, recognising it as subtle communication from the spirit world to take note. First the feather, now the singing; they were signs that something was happening. Finishing her coffee, she stood and took a deep breath. She placed the feather carefully in her cardigan pocket, and made her way indoors. She was intrigued to see what her cards had to say.

Katya always picked a card for the day ahead. Today, she avoided her angel cards as she had already received their message in the form of the feather. Intuition led her to the tarot deck instead. Taking the cards from their black cloth and giving them a quick shuffle, she pulled 'The Wheel of Fortune' - destiny, fate, events out of one's control. Should she be excited or concerned? Leaving her house with a sense of anticipation, she was disappointed to find everything as usual when she arrived for work at Eliza's shop.

Greeted as always by the heady aroma of incense, a permanent fragrance in the small shop, she was half-expecting to find that a phenomenon had occurred, or for Eliza to make a grand announcement. However, as the windchime above the door heralded Katya's arrival, Eliza appeared relaxed as she sat behind the counter and perused her diary. Sweeping her strawberry-blonde hair back over her shoulders, she straightened up to greet her assistant, her blue eyes sparkling beneath their black liner.

"Morning Katya!" She beamed, "I'm feeling the energy of the New Moon today. It's going to be a good one!"

"Morning," Katya held her breath, waiting for Eliza to say something more.

"Is everything okay?"

"Yes, fine … I think?" Katya turned to close the door behind her, then back to Eliza. "Has anything happened?"

"Such as?" Eliza shrugged.

"I don't know. Just anything?" Katya walked halfway through the shop, taking her coat off, "something?"

"No. Just an ordinary day." Eliza shook her head, smiling. "Is this one of your 'little hunches'?"

"Yes" Katya replied. Eliza referred to her nickname for the odd yet significant signals that Katya experienced, often a precursor to real events. At this moment, Katya's feeling of expectation was growing along with the knot in her stomach. She visibly jumped, startled as Eliza's phone rang.

"Daisy!" Eliza cried, glancing at Katya's reaction. "Why didn't you tell me …? Yes of course … give me half an hour… yes, don't panic…I'll be there."

Katya stood in the middle of the shop, her coat still in hand, as Eliza hurriedly swigged her coffee and reached for her handbag.

"I have to go!" She explained, grabbing her car keys. "Daisy has arrived!"

Katya was puzzled. "Daisy?"

"My old friend. Oh my, the poor thing, she has been through a terrible time. She needs me. She will be a mess. She has just arrived at the station and I have to collect her!"

"But what about the shop?" Behind her glasses, Katya's dark blue eyes were filled with worry and she began to play with her long black plait. Eliza made her way over to where her assistant stood.

"You will be fine. You can manage on your own."

"But …" Katya began.

"No buts, I have faith in you." Eliza squeezed Katya's shoulders and made her way to the door. "Luckily I have no readings booked in today, so all you need to do is look after the shop. I'll be back later … any problems just ring me."

Katya shook her head in disbelief as Eliza left the building, dreamcatchers fluttering in the breeze as she closed the door.

She stood for a moment, her heart racing. What if she did something wrong? She knew how hard Eliza had worked to build up this business. It was her pride and joy. Katya had worked here for just over a month, and had never been left alone for longer than half an hour. What if someone had a problem, or wanted a reading? What if she couldn't remember the price of something, or the till broke? Her mind began to spiral, creating scenarios that she told herself, logically, would never happen. Then she remembered the white feather landing at her feet. A sign from the angels. Her fingers touched her rose quartz pendant, its cool surface reassuring her. This could be a significant day. It might be her chance to prove her worth.

Her enthusiasm sparked as she remembered her lessons. Kneeling down, she furiously rummaged in her sequinned duffle bag for the now-tattered piece of paper she had read so many times. Folded in a plastic pocket, the hand-written note listed the karmic lessons she should fulfil in order to achieve her soul's potential. This was part of the reason why, at the age of thirty-six, she had moved away from the Midlands. Leaving her mundane job as an archive assistant and turning her back on her past, she had moved to Devon following what could only be described as an awakening. Two weeks later she had seen the notice in Eliza's shop window and applied for the job. Coincidence or fate?

She skimmed the page once again, re-reading the lessons. "Lesson One, finding your power and true voice. Lesson Two, facing and overcoming your fears. Lesson Three, to experience unconditional love." She had already completed lesson three, as she had a son, Liam.

Now nineteen years old and leading his own life, Liam was no longer in need of her maternal protection; yet she still experienced the ongoing, boundless love only a mother can have for her child. Yes, Lesson Three was definitely ticked off the list. The other two however, were still very much work in progress.

Since taking on this job in Eliza's shop, Katya was believing in herself more as each day passed. Perhaps today marked the next stage on her journey and a turning point? Her heart skipped with anticipation as she felt a glimmer of excitement. She stuffed the paper back into her bag and, with renewed determination, hung her coat up and switched the kettle on. As it began to boil, the noise sounded foreign within the silent room. She looked around and saw the eyes of the Green Man wood carving watching her reassuringly. Images of the Goddess on packs of cards and books inspired her to find her own magic. Yes, this was what she wanted. The chance to be herself, doing a job that she loved, learning all the time. Was this what this morning's 'signs' had been about? Eliza had said the New Moon energy was strong, and the New Moon marked new beginnings.

Unable to bear the silence that returned as the kettle stopped boiling, she switched on the CD player and lit an incense stick. The calming sound of panpipes and the magical aroma of white sage soon began to weave their way around the shop, cleansing its corners and bringing the spirits of the Green Man and the Goddesses to life. She was no longer alone. She could do this.

. . . . .

"Here it is!" Daisy exclaimed.

As the car approached the house, Daisy was already undoing her seatbelt and Eliza pulled up sharply, tyres screeching. She was worried that her impulsive friend might jump out while they were still moving. Daisy leapt from the car as soon as it stopped. For a brief moment, she stood still in her flurry to admire the façade of the building, exhaling an over-dramatic sigh. The grand, Victorian house stood proud and majestic on the cliff-top, although its walls were in much need of painting. The front garden was unruly with a tangle of spiralling weeds and suffocated plants. Turning to face Eliza, Daisy stood waiting impatiently for her friend to secure the car.

"Eliza, this is mine, all mine!" Daisy was waving the house keys, beaming with delight, and she proceeded to jump around like a child, her bobbed, dark curls dancing as she did so. Eliza joined her friend at the door with a slow smile on her face. Daisy was always rather dramatic, but it cheered her immensely to see her old friend so elated. She had been expecting Daisy to be depressed and tearful. Eventually, fumbling with nervous excitement, Daisy pushed the key into the lock and turned to Eliza, hugging her. "This is my new beginning! Finally!"

Eliza followed her into the empty property. The door opened into what would be a welcoming hallway, once it had been decorated. It had a proper staircase with balustrades and she could see that the parquet floor would come up a treat with some polish. "I love it," she complimented, casting her wise, blue eyes around the space.

"I love it too!" Daisy replied gleefully, gesturing for her friend to follow her into what she referred to as the drawing room. "Those are the original fireplaces" she pointed out, flouncing her hair and pouting proudly. Leading Eliza by the hand, she then scurried through another door. "Come and look at the kitchen!"

Room by room, Daisy gave Eliza a whirlwind tour of the whole building. They ended up in the attic, a large, well-lit space, and Daisy instructed her friend to close her eyes, leading her by the hand until she told her to look.

"Wow!" Eliza's eyes widened at the window's magnificent vista of the harbour and the wider bay.

"This," announced Daisy, holding her arms out to present the room as though it were a show piece, "will be my workshop and studio!" Daisy's background was in art, and it was something she intended to return to now she was divorced and in control of her life once more.

Eliza nodded, able to visualise her friend making this space her own; the view would offer great inspiration. "Great idea, yep. But what are you going to do with the rest of it? There are, if I am not mistaken, eight bedrooms …" she mused.

"Aha!" Daisy held her hand up in the air. "My grand plan!"

"What grand plan?" Eliza was worried. Daisy had a habit of allowing her artistic flair and romantic nature to cloud reasonable judgement.

"All will be revealed." Daisy fluttered her eyelashes mischievously, and led Eliza back down the stairs and through the kitchen to the back door, which opened onto a large terrace with steps and pillars. It was a sad, unloved space, complete with gnarled, spindly plants in cracked containers.

"I have plans to make this gorgeous." Daisy stated defensively, as Eliza stood with one hand on her hip, surveying the scene.

"Yes, you could make this really lovely, you could grow herbs out here and climbing roses or something," Eliza was trying to sound enthusiastic, but the underlying prospect of Daisy's grand plan was worrying her. "Please tell me about this plan."

"It's just perfect," Daisy said happily, leaning her slender frame against the wall, her brown eyes darting around the space.

"But what is it? Tell me!" Eliza was becoming infuriated by the intrigue.

"This," Daisy proudly gestured to the building that stood behind them. "Is my new business."

"Business?"

"My guesthouse and art gallery," Daisy enthused.

"What? But you can't even cook … how the hell are you going to run a guesthouse?"

Daisy ignored the comment, walking off, and Eliza followed as her friend's low heels tip-tapped lightly across the kitchen floor and into the dining room.

"I will hire a cook," she replied defiantly. "And a housekeeper." She turned to face Eliza, and stood elegantly next to the mantelpiece. "I will simply focus on running the business and making the place look beautiful." Daisy waltzed around, clearly imagining the end result as she told Eliza of the art exhibitions and evening soirees that would take place.

Eliza sighed deeply. "I'm sorry, but I honestly don't think you have thought this through Daisy. Do you know just how much work is involved in running a business?"

"Of course I do! I managed the art gallery in Paris before I married Christophe," Daisy replied.

"Yes I know, but that was not your own …"

"Not my own business I know, but fundamentally, it is the same principle."

Eliza could see she was fighting a losing battle. Daisy had already purchased this massive house, which needed much work, and was planning a venture for which she had no experience. In Eliza's mind, it was a recipe for disaster. "But, it is so …"

"Look I can do this. Okay?" Daisy snapped. "He might have treated me badly, but he hasn't broken me. Please try and understand."

As Daisy's eyes filled with tears, Eliza's heart softened. "I do understand, but this is why I am so worried. You have been through a difficult time."

Daisy began to sob, her slim body becoming concave as she perched on the windowsill.

"Hey, don't cry, this is a good day." Eliza placed her hand on Daisy's shoulder, feeling guilty that she had ruined Daisy's moment.

Daisy wiped a couple of tears away. "I know, it is. It's just a little over-whelming, that's all. After everything that happened."

"You still haven't told me exactly what did happen."

"It's a long story," Daisy murmured.

"What are you going to do about furniture? Is that arriving later?" Eliza frowned, worrying how this was all going to pan out.

A loud knock at the front door interrupted them and Daisy dashed lightly to answer it. A short man with suitcases and boxes presented Daisy with a clipboard.

"Luggage drop-off for Mrs Dupont." He spoke in a disinterested tone.

"That's me! There should be seven altogether," Daisy counted the items before she signed. The man stepped over the threshold, dropped the cases and boxes carelessly into the hall, then left as Daisy thanked him and closed the door.

"What's that?" Eliza pointed to the boxes.

"My belongings of course."

"When is the rest arriving then?"

"The rest of what?" Daisy asked, her eyes wide.

"The rest of your stuff."

Daisy looked blank. "This *is* my stuff. All of it. A lot of it is clothes of course."

Eliza slumped onto the stairs and shook her head.

"Oh those stairs are going to look so grand when I have finished," Daisy commented dreamily. "I have already chosen the carpet for the runner."

Eliza ignored the comment, frustrated by her friend's lack of practicality. "So let me get this straight. You are planning to stay in a huge house, on your own, with not so much as a kettle and a bed?" She reached towards a light switch and flicked it on. Nothing happened. "As I thought, you haven't even got the electric connected yet!"

"I've got my phone and my laptop, and they are both fully charged." Daisy protested. "I can get some candles!"

Eliza stared at her sternly.

"There was no point buying anything," Daisy continued. "You know I've been staying in temporary accommodation, since the split."

"How long have you got left on the lease?"

"I haven't, I'm fully paid up and out, that's why I asked them to bring my luggage over," Daisy explained.

Eliza groaned, scrunching her long hair as she buried her head in her hands. "Did you not think to even get some basics sorted out?"

Daisy pouted and her big brown eyes wore the expression of a lost doe; a look Eliza remembered from their college years when Daisy could not have something she desired. She looked as though she was going to cry again. "I was just so excited to get the keys. It's my new start." She murmured. "My freedom, my new life, without Christophe."

Eliza felt a little harsh. Her friend had been through a tough time. "Hey look, I know …I'm sorry. I just worry about you." She stood up and gave Daisy a tight hug. "It will be fantastic, I know it will." Eliza stood back and looked into her friend's eyes, her hands reassuringly on Daisy's shoulders. "But you must stay at mine until you get some stuff sorted out, okay?"

Daisy nodded, a forlorn expression crossing her face as she looked around at the empty shell of her new life.

"Come on," Eliza chivvied, "we'll go to mine, get online and sort all the boring stuff, and then tomorrow we can go shopping and get some basic furniture and appliances so you can move in. You can meet Brandon, my, er, kind of boyfriend."

Daisy looked curious. "Boyfriend? You never said …"

"It's nothing serious." Eliza felt her cheeks flush bright red, "you know, off and on sort of stuff." Eliza turned to look around the empty hall. "We need to get organised. I'm assuming you are alright for money to buy things?"

Daisy's face perked up. "Yes. Christophe has been quite generous," she looked down, solemn once more. "In his attempt to pay me off and get rid of me."

Eliza felt anger rising up as she saw the hurt on her friend's face. She was still not sure of the whole story behind Daisy's divorce, but seeing this normally exuberant woman so lost must mean that Christophe had treated her badly. "Then let's go and spend all his money!" She gave Daisy a high five and they began to move Daisy's few belongings into the car.

. . . . .

Glen's footsteps echoed through his now-empty home. The feet of an impostor, no longer belonging. Room by room, he took his final tour of the house, pausing here and there to say goodbye to his past. All he could see was a reflection of the emptiness he felt inside.

Yet his cavern of isolation was not because he had lost his wife Siân, as many assumed; but rather the loss of his own purpose and the realisation that his past was a sham. Insignificant, meaningless. Years spent building … what?

Pausing on the spacious landing, he looked through the open doors. One of the five bedrooms had been Siân's office when she worked from home as a successful magazine editor. That was, when she wasn't in London. Another bedroom had been her 'keep fit' room, kitted out with yoga mats and fitness balls. A walk-in off the master bedroom had been crammed with her designer clothes, the scent of her expensive perfume still lingering despite the garments having been sent away.

Descending to the ground floor, he walked heavily through the redundant kitchen, its sleek surfaces growing thick with dust. It had been designed for entertaining, yet there was no longer a hostess. Glen's married friends, once frequent social visitors, were now awkward with him and since the funeral, apart from one or two, their presence had been scarce. He had turned people away, unable to hear hollow words from the insincere. Funny, he thought, how life-changing events filtered the real friends from the fair-weather ones.

While he recovered from the accident, Glen had attempted to live in the house and make plans for his future, but despite its size he had felt suffocated and trapped. It was no longer a home, and he now wanted to be free of his old life and start again. He had questioned why he and Siân felt the need to buy such a large house, when they had no children. He now realised that it was a simply a reflection of their egos, a symbol of mutual success and the power of money. The same could be said of their marriage. Siân was successful in her own right, but his position in the property field was legendary. While her career was constantly threatened by the next upcoming talent, Glen's prospects were, on the contrary, extremely stable.

Glen's father had been a successful property developer and Glen had easily followed in his footsteps continuing to build the empire that was Heathstone Luxury Homes. Sian always got what she wanted, having a certain allure that commanded attention. Yet she was ruthless, playing hard-to-get when she wished, which bizarrely made her appeal even stronger. Glen, despite having no shortage of female admirers himself, had been completely sucked in by her charm. Looking back, he struggled to comprehend how a man as dependable and strong-minded as himself had allowed Siân to render him into putty.

He recalled that they actually spent very little time alone together during their marriage. He would often work late into the night and Sian would be working, exercising or networking. Their free time together was spent largely in social company. The large house was a property rather than a home – just like the investments that he had dealt with on a daily basis for the last fifteen years.

Only a small room downstairs actually felt like his own. His 'den' was filled with the books and music that he loved to escape to. He devoured fiction, non-fiction, history, myth, legend, and culture. His own private library. Siân had mocked this, caught up in her world of celebrity and high fashion. He often wondered whether he would have become a writer if his life had been different. Now, he supposed, he could do so if he wished.

The trappings of the material world no longer held any fascination and he was ready to move on to a very different life. He planned to sell the family business now that his career, once being his main focus, had shrivelled into triviality next to what he felt inside. Goals that had been his driving force now felt strangely shallow. His peers would never understand. They would say that bereavement can do strange things and he would soon be back to normal. What was normal? Rejecting everything he had once stood for, seemed perfectly normal to Glen, now that his spirit, his true self, was guiding his path.

Glen felt wiser. He felt that he had a special knowledge and a need to live his life with a purpose. In his heart and soul, his existence would never be the same again. Feeling the need to escape, he had initially been drawn to the coast and by bizarre coincidence, his attention was drawn to the same town several times. He then found out from his mother, Carmen, that it was the same area where he had enjoyed childhood holidays. Seeing this coincidence as a clear signpost to his new life, he purchased a static caravan near to the town, which reminded him fondly of a life more simple. He could live there during the holiday off-season and the location would allow him to process his experience while he decided what to do. He no longer wanted the traffic queues, the business suits or emails at ten o' clock at night. He only desired the sounds of nature, the views across the bay, and the scent of the sea.

In the aftermath of the accident, he had died and been resuscitated; and during the minutes of his clinical death he had visited the most wonderful place of harmony and peace. He had seen, felt, and heard joy of the highest and purest kind. Time and space had no meaning. Pain was absent and everything was more beautiful than he could ever have imagined. He wanted to stay there. Safe and happy, enveloped in pure love.

He was told to return, however. Told that it was not his time and he saw the image of a woman's face as he returned to life in his earth body with a harsh bump, once more aware of the monitors and the crash team around him. The bright lights and the unpleasant noise of emergency.

He was reluctant to talk about his experience. No one would understand, and when he returned home from hospital he felt empty. He knew there was a purpose to his continued existence. But what that purpose actually was left him at a loss. The image of the woman's face haunted both his sleep and his waking hours, and he knew that she was in some way linked with his return. He recalled meeting her briefly before the accident, but had no idea who she was or where to find her. He felt sure that she was the key to unlocking the answers. She was the catalyst. If he found her, he would understand the reason for his second chance and why his life had changed beyond recognition.

The way he had been guided to this coastal town, was this part of the plan? He was never a believer in fate and higher powers, but now he saw things differently. This was a new beginning, and a wave of excitement rushed through him as he prepared to leave his house. Pausing to look at himself in a mirror still fixed to the wall he thought he appeared older. His thick dark hair was greying slightly at the temples and he had lost a little weight from his cheeks, but he looked calmer. The stress was almost gone, and he had the hopeful glimmer of someone beginning a new adventure. He would find her, and this was the just the start. Smiling slightly at his own reflection and taking a deep breath, he carried the last of his luggage out to his four-by-four and, in what seemed to him to be a symbolic moment, he walked away from his past and closed the door firmly behind him.

CHAPTER TWO

Katya repositioned her glasses and placed her hands on her hips as she surveyed the shelves. A small flurry of customers had left a wake of disarray behind them. The Green Man was upside down and there was a sharp piece of amethyst jutting out amongst smooth tumbled stones on the crystal display stand. Two of the windchimes had become awkwardly tangled, and she was unsurprised to see the neat rows of books at the rear of the shop interrupted by sporadic spines.

Katya knew, however, that Eliza would be delighted when she saw the takings, and despite her initial fears she had managed well on her own. The last thing she wanted was to dampen her success by having Eliza return to an untidy shop. It had been a good afternoon, and she wanted to appear in control. She moved quickly, impatiently trying to restore the balance. To her annoyance the Green Man was still the wrong way up when Eliza burst in excitedly with her long lost friend, Daisy.

"… anyway Daisy, this is my shop." Eliza held the door open as an elegant young woman stepped tentatively over the threshold.

Daisy was glamorous with her dark, glossy hair, and her willowy frame dressed elegantly in a vintage day dress *Not exactly house-moving attire*, Katya thought. Quite the opposite of the bohemian Eliza, with her tie-dye vest and purple jumper. Katya self-consciously folded her arms across her old black cardigan, complete with bobbles and a couple of small holes.

"I can't believe this is all yours. It's amazing!" Daisy looked around in awe, visibly breathing in the mixed scents as so many of the customers did.

"Yep! All mine and it's going well." Eliza stated proudly, her hands on her hips. She reminded Katya of an ancient Celtic warrior woman.

Katya moved forward slightly, clearing her throat. "Er, sorry it's a bit of a mess. We ... you ... had loads of customers and they weren't very careful."

Eliza glanced around, her brow furrowing for a second. "Hey, it's fine. That's the nature of the shop. The free spirit."

Katya realised this statement was for Daisy's benefit. Eliza hated for things to be out of place.

"It's amazing," Daisy said again.

There was a silence as Katya felt too shy to introduce herself, not wanting to intrude on the bond between the two friends. Looking at the serene Daisy, with her pretty, slim face Katya wondered what terrible hardship she had endured to warrant Eliza's full attention. She had been expecting to see a broken and hollow woman on the edge of self-preservation, not someone who looked like a model.

"Oh, forgive me!" Eliza grabbed Daisy's arm and led her fully into the shop. "This is Katya, my wonderful assistant."

Daisy reached out and touched Katya's hand with cool elegant fingers. "Pleased to meet you," she smiled.

Katya nodded and returned the smile, feeling short and wide in comparison.

"Katya has been sent to me by the angels," Eliza continued. "She has been so helpful!"

Katya blushed and shook her head, uncomfortable with the compliment.

Daisy nodded, "I wouldn't know where to start with all this ... magic ... and stuff." She gestured around the shop, screwing her nose up slightly and Katya realised that she was one of the doubters, the dubious ones who thought it was all hocus pocus and fairies. She wondered if Eliza was aware of this, concluding that as they were such close friends she must do.

"Anyway, I was going to ask Katya to come and help me sage your new house before you move in." Eliza smiled.

"What to my house?" Daisy's brown eyes widened.

"Sage smudging. All new houses need smudging, isn't that right Kat?"

Katya hesitated, unsure whether her opinion was really welcome, and surprised to be included in the task.

"Yes, it's a good idea to get rid of old energy. It is better ... for a new start."

Daisy made no comment, merely looking at Katya with a confused expression.

Eliza nodded, "Too right. And a fresh start is exactly what you need Daisy."

"Now that I agree with," Daisy smiled. "Well, if you think it will help then by all means do it - as long as it's safe." She looked a little unnerved as she caught Katya trying to study her aura, and her alert reaction caused Katya to break contact before she had gained any insight. Katya reminded herself that not all meetings were appropriate for aura watching, except that now she knew how to do it, it was almost addictive.

"I have just got divorced." Daisy said, as though Katya needed some explanation.

"Oh, I'm sorry to hear that." Katya replied quietly.

Daisy nodded solemnly and sighed. "I need to be strong. To pick myself up and begin again."

Her words were delivered rather theatrically, yet they seemed to fuel Eliza's friendship trigger.

"That's what I'm here for, Daisy. To help you. We will get you back on track after what that idiot's done to you."

Daisy looked as though she was about to cry and clutched Eliza's hand. "Thank you."

Katya wondered just what had gone on before Daisy's divorce, conjuring images of a poor princess being locked in a tower. She quickly reprimanded herself - one never knew what went on behind closed doors.

"Christophe Dupont, my ex-husband is a concert pianist and composer. You may have heard of him?" Daisy pouted.

Katya shook her head, "Sorry, I am not familiar with the classical music field, Florence and the Machine is more my thing."

"Anyway. He swept me off my feet at a sculpture exhibition in Paris three years ago. His proposal was accompanied by a mini-orchestra playing a composition he had written especially for me and obviously I was bowled over." Daisy's eyes filled with tears again. "Once we were married, he changed. He was a different man. I can't believe I was so foolish."

"Hey, you are not foolish," Eliza said softly. "Who wouldn't be taken in by that?"

Katya nodded, thinking back to how easily she had been charmed on the night she conceived her son. Not exactly an orchestra though, more of a first-time drug and alcohol fuelled moment of over-confidence.

"Do you have any children?" She asked Daisy.

"No," Daisy replied sadly. "Although perhaps that is for the best, in hindsight." She looked as though she was still fighting back tears.

"Come up to the flat. I'll cook and we can have some wine," Eliza smiled, placing her arm around Daisy's shoulder. "I'll pop down later, Kat."

Katya nodded, disappointed that Eliza hadn't been a little more enthusiastic about her efforts. This old friend Daisy was obviously more in need of Eliza's support than she was.

. . . . .

Eliza's flat was above her shop - a fragrant haven of essential oils, decorated with bohemian throws and cushions. The living room was quite large but appeared smaller due to wall-hangings, woodcarvings, and candles that cluttered the room. Everything seemed to belong, however, creating a home and causing Daisy to feel slightly nervous as she pictured her empty new house devoid of embellishment. There was, she realised with a rush, so much to do. Eliza was right. As an artist, she knew only too well the trepidation of the blank canvas. This thought itself was daunting, as she couldn't remember the last time she had actually enjoyed painting.

Daisy's graduation from Art School had represented a grand finale to her studies, accompanied by a stunning and well-received exhibition. She had been commended on her 'contemporary twist on romanticism' and her work had reached the radar of the London art scene, boding well for her future.

She had then moved to Paris, successfully managing an independent gallery and selling some of her own artwork on the side.

Christophe, at the top of his game, and failing to remember the aspirations of a young creative soul, criticised Daisy's work as 'gimmicky'. He encouraged her to use her artistic flair to choose pieces for his London home instead. He paid for her to attend fashion shows so she could wear the right couture at social functions, and paid for the clothes. Daisy eagerly immersed herself in the novelty of expensive design, pleasing her new husband, and dressing correctly for Christophe's concerts and red-carpet events. At first it was sheer bliss and a dream come true. After a year it was tedious, and Daisy had lost the will or the inspiration to paint anything. Christophe forbade her trips to the London retro-markets she so adored. He did not want her seen to be 'resorting to flea purchases'. She could be driven to fashion houses, why did she need to go to a market? Daisy was now looking forward to being free to shop where she wished.

As Eliza went into the kitchen, Daisy perched on the edge of one of two mismatched sofas, becoming aware of a man sitting in the corner of the room, deeply immersed in his laptop. He had a certain style about him, as though he might be an actor or a poet. Noting a guitar propped against the wall, Daisy concluded that he must be a musician.

"You must be Daisy," he did not look up from the screen. "I'm Brandon."

"Hello," Daisy replied quietly.

His furrowed brow eventually relaxed as he firmly tapped a button on the keyboard.

"That's it. Finally," he muttered. "Done!" He shut the lid of the device triumphantly and looked over at Daisy, scrutinising her over the top of his glasses. Daisy looked away, feeling a little unnerved. He was very attractive with a short beard, dark brown eyes and lightly tanned skin. He had a nomadic look about him and Daisy suspected that if Eliza did try to formalise their relationship, he may just disappear into the night.

"Pleased to meet you Daisy," he smiled.

22

Eliza returned to the room with a tray of coffees and sat cross legged on the floor. "Make yourself at home," she said.

Daisy took this as an invitation to take her shoes off and curl her legs up on the sofa, retrieving her sketchbook from her handbag.

"Ooh, what have you been creating?" Eliza asked as Daisy opened the book.

"They are sketches … ideas for the house," Daisy explained. "And I have just realised how much there is to do in so little time."

"Well there's no rush," Eliza took the sketchbook from her.

"No there is! I want to be up and running within two months," Daisy announced.

"Two months?" Eliza looked shocked. "That is ambitious."

"Not really," Daisy replied, "there's no structural work to do; it's just decorating and getting all the furniture and the licences in place."

"What are you planning on doing?" Brandon asked.

"I'm opening a guesthouse, with an art theme."

Brandon plucked a business card from the pocket of his waistcoat and passed it to Daisy. "If you need a website, I'm your man."

"Brandon!" Eliza scolded.

"Hey, seize the opportunity. That's what you keep telling me, I have a business to run."

"Brandon designs and builds websites," Eliza explained as she leafed through the sketchbook.

"Well I will need a website, so thank you Brandon," Daisy tucked the business card into her handbag. "I'm outsourcing all the work to get everything done quickly. I can then build up some reviews over the winter ready for the holiday season next year."

"It sounds like you know what you are doing," Brandon nodded.

"It sounds expensive!" Eliza said, picking up a small wooden box from the fireplace.

Daisy looked tearful again, "Christophe paid me to get out of his life. I don't want that money hanging around like a sour smell. So, I am using the money to set myself up. I will be completely independent, doing something I love and never having to rely on a man ever again!"

Eliza had taken a deck of cards out of the box and was shuffling them, "I suppose if it does all go wrong, then you still have the house to sell…"

The comment injured Daisy's pride, "Why are you being so negative? It won't all go wrong!"

"I'm just being realistic, as your sensible side seems to be left in London. I don't want to see you struggling," Eliza pulled out a card from the pack, "oh …"

"What?" Daisy asked.

"Ten of Cups," Eliza said.

"What does that mean then?" Daisy rolled her eyes. "You know I don't believe in all that."

"Well, it means big, big love."

Daisy wrinkled her nose. "No!" She shook her head and waved her hand dismissively. "Never in a million years."

Eliza gave Daisy a cheeky smile. "Hey, it's in the cards."

"Maybe those cards are for you?" Brandon said to Eliza. "Maybe you are going to experience big, big love." He winked at her and Eliza blushed bright red.

Eliza wrapped the cards quickly in their cloth and stuffed them back into the ornate wooden box. "Anyway. More to the point we need to get your electric and gas sorted out. You can't run a guesthouse with no power." She took the laptop from Brandon and began searching for utility companies.

"Mind if I have a look at your ideas?" Brandon asked, "it will get me started thinking about the website."

"Please do!" Daisy eagerly passed him the sketchbook and he leaned back, put on his glasses, and began to leaf through Daisy's work.

. . . . .

Katya glanced at the time; it was five o'clock. Eliza often stayed open later on a Friday to capture the new arrivals for the weekend, so she wasn't sure whether to close the shop or not. She had seen Brandon leave the flat by the side door about two hours ago, but there had been no sign of Eliza. It had been a steady afternoon with a manageable trickle of customers and Katya was brimming with confidence having made several good sales, and sharing some enlightening and interesting conversation.

The windchime tinkled and two women entered, the first appearing quite flustered. She wore a bright ensemble of pink, and had several shades of red and blond in her thick, wavy hair. The other woman, couldn't be less colourful, dressed all in black, her short, greyish black hair neat and tidy. A large obsidian pendant provided the only embellishment.

"Thank goodness you are still open!" The colourful woman exclaimed, her cheeks flushed. "I need some rose oil and a pink candle."

"I don't know why you are even bothering at your age," scoffed the plain woman haughtily.

"It's never too late Jan. There is plenty of life in me yet," She turned to Katya and smiled widely. "Sorry, I haven't introduced myself. I am Sheryl, clairvoyant and one of Eliza's best customers."

"Pleased to meet you," Katya replied, instantly warming to the energy of this fun-loving woman. "I'm Katya, I've been working here for about a month."

"Are you from the Midlands?" Jan asked.

"Yes," Katya replied, stroking her long black plait nervously. "How do you know?"

Jan smiled a little, "The accent kind of gave it away."

Katya had to smile at the obvious explanation.

"You have kind eyes lovey," Sheryl smiled, "I think you will do well here."

"Are you going to hurry up and get these supplies?" Jan asked. "We have to be at the spirit group in an hour."

"Yes, yes, sorry," Sheryl threw a mock scowl at Jan, then turned to Katya. "Excuse my sister. She can be a little impatient."

Katya moved out from behind the counter to find the items for Sheryl. "Rose oil and a pink candle wasn't it?"

"Yes that's right lovey."

"She still thinks she can find true love," Jan laughed.

"And why not? Don't you want some passion in your twilight years?" Sheryl chuckled.

"I would rather have a cup of tea," Jan said sourly, "but each to their own."

As Katya wrapped the items extra carefully, Sheryl scrutinised her face. "You have a lot ahead of you lovey, a significant time for you I think."

Katya looked up, her interested piqued, following the signs she had experienced that morning. "Oh?"

"Sheryl you know we are not supposed to counsel people without their permission," Jan chided.

"Nonsense!" retorted her sister. "The spirits are giving me lots of nudges about this lovely lady. Especially your grandma dear."

Katya was caught off guard and gave Sheryl her full attention.

"She says it is time. The lessons are unfolding and she is guiding you all the way."

Katya's eyes filled with tears, and she took off her glasses.

"Don't cry lovey," Sheryl squeezed her hand. "She says you must be alert to the signals. It's not your imagination, this is indeed a magical time for you."

Katya, dabbed her eyes with a tissue, amazed by what Sheryl had picked up in just a few minutes.

"Come on sis," Jan nudged, "we have to go."

"Sorry, how much do I owe you?" Sheryl asked Katya.

"Oh, er, £4.99." Katya replied, her attention focused back onto her job. She wanted to ask Sheryl so many questions.

Sheryl paid for her goods and then fumbled in her bag, "here's my card. Sorry we can't stay and chat."

"Give our regards to Eliza!" called Jan as they left the shop.

"Bye lovey!" Sheryl waved as the door slammed shut.

Katya stood still, her mind going over what had been said and wishing Sheryl could have told her more. She looked at the card in her fingers. "Sheryl Stone - Clairvoyant Medium" was printed on a rainbow background. Katya placed the card neatly in her notebook. She noticed a text from Eliza instructing her to close the shop for the day and bring the keys up to the flat. Katya was relieved. Sheryl's impromptu connection with her grandmother and her confirmation of her 'little hunches' meant that all she wanted was to go back to her flat and read up on all her notes and jottings so far. She hurriedly cashed up the till, securing and locking everything before she made her way to Eliza's side door.

CHAPTER THREE

Eliza released the door via the intercom and Katya made her way clumsily up the narrow staircase, her duffle bag banging the bannisters as she did so. She slowed down as she neared the door, becoming aware of voices.

"I don't know where to start though … I haven't painted anything since I married Christophe," Daisy's voice sounded as though she was crying.

"But why?" asked Eliza.

"Christophe didn't like me to paint. He criticised my work," Daisy sobbed, "He said it was a waste of time. I had plenty to do being a wife, creating a home and attending his events."

"How antiquated!" Eliza sounded enraged.

There was a pause, so Katya knocked on the door. She did not want to interrupt the two friends' conversation.

"It's open!" Eliza called.

Katya turned the handle and walked tentatively into the lounge to see Eliza sat on a bean bag and Daisy with her feet curled up on the sofa, dabbing her eyes with a tissue. A half empty bottle of red wine stood on the carpet in between them.

"Katya, how have you got on today?" Eliza asked.

"Sorry, don't mind me, I'm just having a moment!" Daisy sobbed.

Katya was unsure what to say; it didn't seem the time to be cheery, but Eliza's hopeful face encouraged her.

"It's been great. There have been a lot of customers, and I have really enjoyed it."

"That's brilliant, well done! And thank you for covering at such short notice."

"It's fine, really it is!" Katya could not help smiling as she handed her employer the keys. "Oh, Sheryl and Jan popped in and asked to be remembered to you."

"Aha! So you have met the psychic sisters," Eliza laughed, "Quite a pair those two, but they are lovely. I have known them for years. It was Sheryl who got me into the tarot cards."

"Yes, she is pretty amazing," Katya nodded.

"Do you want a glass of wine?" Eliza offered the bottle towards her, "I'll go and get you a glass." She left the room.

Katya did not normally drink alcohol, but one wouldn't hurt. She was still reeling from what Sheryl had told her. She sat on the sofa opposite Daisy and took her coat off.

"I'm not normally like this," Daisy looked a little embarrassed, "I've just been through so much, and today it has all hit me, what with the new house and everything. I don't think I have ever been so stressed."

"It's okay," Katya replied softly. "I've seen worse, believe me." She thought back to the time when her mother had evicted her because she was pregnant, forcing her to stay with a less-than-trustworthy acquaintance.

"I am still heartbroken, if I am honest," Daisy murmured as Eliza returned with a glass for Katya and poured her a generous amount of wine.

"Thank you," Katya said, wondering how she was going to drink it.

Eliza put an arm around Daisy. "It will take time but you will get there. You are strong, remember?"

"He gave me everything," Daisy sniffed. "And then took it all away! He seduced me with his eyes and his conversation. He promised me the world."

"I know," Eliza replied quietly, "I remember when you first met him."

"He wouldn't even let me invite my friends to stay," Daisy sobbed.

"Or to the wedding," Eliza shook her head in disgust.

"That was our first argument," Daisy looked towards Katya, "Christophe only allowed me to invite my parents. Because of his celebrity status! I am actually quite relieved now that my friends didn't come," Daisy continued. "It would be so embarrassing, just drawing attention to my big mistake. I feel such a fool. Now I don't really have any friends." She began to cry again.

Eliza looked sympathetic, "You've got me," she reminded her. "And, hey who wouldn't be swept off their feet by it all? The red carpet, the mansion...? Not my cup of tea, but …"

"It was like being in a very expensive, luxurious prison," Daisy interrupted, her eyes fierce. "He wouldn't even let me have a baby."

"Well, that is probably a blessing in disguise now," Eliza pointed out, her blue eyes blazing between her black lined eyelids.

Katya nodded, "Children are wonderful, but can be hard work."

Daisy nodded, "Too much distraction from his bloody piano playing, apparently!" She scoffed. "But that didn't stop him getting little Sofia into trouble."

"Who is 'little Sofia'?" Eliza asked. "You stopped telling me anything in emails well over six months ago, I was worried."

Daisy looked at her apologetically. "Sorry. Sofia was a seventeen-year old piano student. A virtuoso apparently!"

"What? Seventeen! But he is so old?"

"I know," Daisy agreed. "Her mummy and daddy were delighted at the prospect of their daughter marrying into musical genius and money."

Eliza looked thoughtful. "Ah, I see …"

Katya recalled that she was seventeen when she became pregnant with Liam.

"I was in the way. A hindrance," Daisy sighed. "So I was divorced and paid off."

The two friends sat in silence and Katya did not know whether to speak or not. She found it difficult to feel empathy for Daisy, unusual for Katya, who empathised with most people. Daisy had airs and graces and seemed to expect the world to stop for her benefit. It seemed to Katya that Daisy was well shot of a husband who cared only for himself, and had come away with a small fortune and the rest of her life ahead of her.

Eliza however seemed to see things differently. "I could strangle him, for the way he treated you!" She said through gritted teeth.

Daisy sniffed, blowing her nose loudly on the tissue and the friends laughed, despite the seriousness of the conversation.

"This is a new beginning!" Exclaimed Eliza. "A fresh start and no one can tell you what to do! Except me of course …" She chuckled

"And it's the New Moon …" Katya added hopefully.

Daisy was still sniffing, but smiled. "I can do this," she said defiantly, "I know I can. I have to!"

"You don't *have* to do *anything*," Eliza protested.

Daisy shook her head. "I do though! I have to make this work. I have to prove that I can stand on my own two feet and make something of my life. I have to show that I am not a fool."

"I can relate to that," Katya nodded, taking a second sip of wine and wincing as the strength of it seemed to seep all around her head.

"You know, there was one night that made me realise how unhappy I was," Daisy recalled.

"Go on…" urged Eliza.

"You know when you see a couple and they are everything you want to be? They are in love, and both gorgeous and equal?"

"Not really, but carry on," Eliza looked puzzled, shaking her head.

"Well, the night, I found out about Sofia, me and Christophe were at one of these launch events," Daisy smiled. "We met this couple that Christophe knew … well he knew the woman. She was like a film star. She had blond hair and a red dress, and she just oozed confidence."

"As though she had an aura about her?" Eliza asked.

"Yes. Everywhere she moved people followed her with their eyes. I felt a bit sorry for her husband really. He took a back seat. I remember thinking how wonderful it was that he allowed his wife to interact with people, rather than just being an accessory on his arm."

"And that made you feel jealous?" Eliza opened another bottle and topped up Daisy's glass.

"Not so much jealous. It was more of a realisation of how I had become a background character in my own life."

"And that's certainly not you," Eliza smiled, "Being in the background I mean."

Katya had to smile to herself; this Daisy certainly did seem to enjoy being the centre of attention.

"Exactly! The old Daisy would never have put up with it, and that frightened me. In that moment, I realised just how much I was losing myself," Daisy took a sip of wine, and mopped her eye. "It was a turning point. So, when we got home, after the party, I told him, that I wasn't happy and that things needed to change."

"Good for you!" Eliza raised her glass.

"And then … then, he said that things would definitely change, because he was going to be a father, and I no longer fitted into his plans," Daisy sighed. "I suppose I should have been more careful what I wished for?"

Eliza paused. "Not really. I say the whole thing did you a favour. Everything happens for a reason, and meeting the couple was a catalyst," She took another sip of wine. "Personally, I think 'little Sofia' has done you a huge favour."

"Really?" Daisy asked, a little shocked.

"Really," Eliza confirmed, looking at Katya who nodded furiously to show her support. "You can get back to being the real Daisy Hartford again."

"I might change my name back, you know," Daisy mused, smiling.

"I would. And focus on what you have gained, rather than what you have lost," Eliza agreed.

"Yes, you're right. I have lost a grumpy old man and a stifling home, and gained my independence and freedom," Daisy paused. "He said I was naive, like a child."

Katya had to agree with Christophe on that one, but kept her thoughts to herself.

Eliza looked at Daisy. "Yes, you can be. But that is part of your charm. Your hopefulness."

"Do you think I am naive?" Daisy asked sadly.

"Yes, sometimes, you don't always think things through," Eliza hesitated, "you always expect everything to turn out right. You don't always live in the real world."

Daisy pouted. "Like you with your fairies and dragons! At least I don't believe in ghosts!"

Eliza smiled. "You would if you saw one."

Katya nodded, relieved that the conversation had lightened a little.

"Yeah right!" Daisy laughed.

"That's more like it," Eliza chuckled. "I'll do you a proper tarot reading tomorrow, if you like?"

"Like I believe in all that? I'll pass thank you."

Eliza laughed, "Okay, yeah yeah."

"However, now I think back, the last reading you gave me, before I went to Paris was spot on," Daisy recalled thoughtfully. "I don't think I really want to know what the future holds. I think I need to do this just by myself."

"Well remember where your friends are, you don't have to be a total loner," Eliza smiled and clinked glasses with her friend. "To new beginnings" she toasted.

"To new beginnings" agreed Daisy. She looked at Katya with slight suspicion, and Katya felt awkward. She was intruding. She also wondered if Daisy was really as helpless as she made out.

. . . . .

Glen finally finished unpacking his car and stood looking at the various boxes and bags that cluttered the caravan, thinking how strange it was that his entire life now fitted into this space. Yet, this was all he needed.

Turning his back on the boxes, he ventured outside and stretched, smiling as he took in the view and inhaled the sea air. He wanted to meditate here and try to reach that wonderful place again. Should he try now? No, he needed to unpack and clear the space first. But he could sit out here for a while on the decking.

He thought back, recalling that when he and his little brother Leo were very young they had lived somewhere near the coast. They had lived in an old draughty cottage with a real fireplace but no central heating. The windows would sometimes be frozen on the inside on winter mornings, old net curtains stuck to the woven ice patterns. He had truly believed it was the work of Jack Frost as his mother, Carmen, encouraged the magic of childhood beliefs, enjoying opportunities for storytelling. The cottage, he recalled, was full of his mother's creations. She was adept at sewing and painting and filled their home with hand-made love. Nothing matched, but it didn't matter. Carmen grew vegetables in the long rambling garden, and he and Leo would help to shell peas and dig up carrots and potatoes. Tea was home-cooked and their dog Boo would sit under the table waiting for scraps. Patrick Heathstone would arrive home for tea covered in plaster or brick dust and would devour his food after a day hard at work on the building site.

When Glen was around nine years old, things began to change. Patrick inherited a house and a large plot of land from an uncle and with his building knowledge, he went into partnership with a co-worker to develop the land into three small houses. Patrick worked long hours as he followed his dream and Carmen spent much time alone with the two boys. Glen recalled that one evening a man wearing a suit came to visit and had a meeting with his father. Patrick proudly told him that he was now in charge of building some more houses. Patrick worked and worked. When Glen was around fourteen years old his father announced they were moving.

They travelled in the car to a large, new house, in the middle of a building site. Glen remembered walking into the warmth of central heating. There were skylights and windows that didn't rattle when a lorry went past. There was new, plush carpet all the way through. The kitchen had a built-in oven and was smart and clean. There were two bathrooms and walk-in showers. Glen and Leo ran around the house excited and enthusiastic about all the modern features. After a long discussion with Carmen, Patrick announced that they would be moving into the house - the first ever Heathstone Luxury Home. Glen and Leo cheered with delight.

As time went on, Glen was encouraged to study, and when he left school Patrick insisted that he did a business degree rather than following the journalist career he wished to pursue. Glen was not happy, but his father pointed out that it would enable him to follow in his footsteps, with the chances he never had.

Now with a more mature outlook Glen realised that Carmen had never wanted to move. She was happy with the old cottage. She gave up her sewing and art as nothing she made seemed to fit the new house. The garden she loved to tend had been replaced by a large manicured lawn and slabs. Her only attempt at gardening in the new house was creating containers and hanging baskets and a small herb garden. Boo the dog passed away, and Carmen became withdrawn. She was frequently required to attend functions and events with Patrick, and was out of her comfort zone. Glen remembered her looking so beautiful before her dressing table mirror, yet sad in her reflection, unaware that he could see her. He now understood that she had sacrificed her simple life for her husband's dreams. Dreams that Patrick thought were making everything better.

As Glen immersed himself in his studies, graduating and joining the Heathstone business, Leo was given the freedom to travel and enjoy his love of adventure. Patrick reassured Glen by saying Leo did not have the temperament for business. It was a mark of his pride and faith in Glen that he had been chosen as his father's successor.

Then, tragedy struck. At age twenty, Leo was killed in a climbing accident and their world fell apart. Glen grieved alone, and his mother withdrew completely, becoming reclusive, drinking wine, and spending days at a time in her room. Patrick's way of coping was to immerse himself in his work, growing Heathstone Luxury Homes into a very lucrative company. When Patrick died of a heart attack two years later, Glen was thrown straight into his role as head of the company. Carmen moved away, but while Glen was concerned about his mother, he did not have the time to attend to her. He trusted that her regular letters confirmed she was well.

He now regretted the years when he had seen little of Carmen, and had enjoyed staying with her for a while at the animal sanctuary that she ran in Wales. She understood his need for change and to his relief, believed in his near-death experience. She had no doubts about his need to sell the business, and he wondered if it represented some sort of relief to her too. She told him that she had struggled when he married Siân as she had seen the woman for what she really was, as mothers so often can, but was unable to tell him. Glen now recalled seeing Carmen's face solemn and ashen at their wedding. He had not understood at that time, but his mother now explained that it was like losing another son.

Enough was enough. Glen had been shown a way forward while he still had a chance to live, purposefully and with love and hope in his heart.

Nothing else mattered. Not now.

CHAPTER FOUR

Katya stood outside her cottage, but she didn't seem to have the keys. It was night-time and the wind was fierce, powerfully driving the sea. The salt stung her face, sharp and cold. Her hair was torn loose from its braid, mischievously lifted and glued across her left eye so that she could not see properly. As another large gust of wind hit her, bringing with it a painful flurry of ice cold rain, she realised the keys were now in her hand after all. She could feel the coldness of the metal on her fingers. However, these were not the keys she normally used to unlock her door. These were heavy keys, attached to a large iron ring that weighed her hand down. *I would never be able to fit these keys into a pocket,* she thought. *How cumbersome and awkward. Why did they look so different?* Struggling to manoeuvre the keys in her cold, wet hands, she found the one that looked most likely to fit the front door. As she focused on the keyhole, struggling to stop her hand shaking, she noticed that the normally smart blue paint seemed grey and cracked. It looked all wrong and she grew concerned. Why did her house not look as it had done before?

She could hear people shouting loudly from the harbour area. What was happening? She was scared, the wind was too strong, and as she moved the key towards the lock the whole door rattled with the force of the wind. Just as she was about to insert the key fully, the door swung open from within, an oil lamp shining directly in her face. Momentarily unable to see from the glare of the lamp, which was swinging in the gale, she blinked until her eyes became accustomed to the light. Katya looked beyond the source of light to see a young woman's face, her features illuminated eerily by the glow. Katya was startled at her appearance. The woman stood on the threshold, her long dark hair plaited almost to her waist a shawl held tightly around her thin shoulders. Katya gasped out loud as she realised that the woman looked like a much younger and slimmer version of herself.

It was like looking at a very cloudy reflection. The woman's dark blue eyes mirrored her own as she stared at her, moving the lamp down slightly. Her vision was quickly blurred by the rain blowing into her face, and then the cry of anguished voices from the harbour seared through her very soul as she heard a crashing noise in the distance.

Katya woke with a start, gasping for breath, her nightdress stuck to her skin with perspiration. Sitting upright, she sat on the edge of the bed, disorientated as she fumbled for the lamp switch. As the bulb illuminated the space, she remembered that she was not in her old flat in the Midlands, but here in Devon in her cosy cottage apartment. It was not the first time she had experienced a vivid dream, but this was the first time a dream had been so intense. She thought back to what Sheryl had said about her grandmother's advice on seeing the signals and paying attention to them. Was this dream one of those signals? She reached for her notebook and jotted some words down – otherwise she would forget in the light of the morning. Replacing the book in her bedside drawer, she lay silently, trying to get back to sleep. She pondered over what the future may hold for her. Today had been a turning point, she was sure of that. It was all part of her progress, and she was certain that Daisy's arrival in town was something to do with it.

She could not help but think that Daisy seemed a little prissy and over-concerned. Daisy had everything going for her. Looks, style, money, and she was still young enough to make her choices and her way in the world. It wasn't so bad for her, surely? Katya had never had such opportunities before and she wondered if she had left it too late for her own fresh start. Did she have the stamina and confidence to make something of her life?

Katya bit back her frustration wondering if she was perhaps a little jealous that Daisy was receiving so much attention from Eliza. The more she tried to reason with her own mind, the more Daisy's arrival seemed to bother her, yet she could not understand why. Annoyed, she reached for her angel cards that always sat with her amethyst crystal on the bedside and took one. 'Patience - All will be revealed in good time' was the answer. Yes, she must stop worrying and trust that whatever her cause for concern may be, now was not the time for her to know.

CHAPTER FIVE

After opening the shop for a potentially busy Saturday morning, Katya sat at the counter, checking she had remembered to do everything as she waited for the first customers to arrive.

She smiled to herself. Over the last two weeks, Eliza had been so preoccupied with Daisy that she had placed increasing trust in her shy assistant, and as a result Katya had grown in confidence. Today was apparently 'pivotal' for Daisy as a team of workmen were arriving at the large house to bring Daisy's plans to life. Eliza had received several frantic phone calls over the last few days, and Katya had overheard repeated reassurance that everything would be fine, and to take lots of deep breaths. Eliza had voiced concerns over Daisy having a meltdown at the sight of stepladders and overalls. She wanted to be on hand to smooth any ruffled feathers.

Katya didn't mind. Sometimes, she liked to pretend that Eliza's shop was her own, and without the distraction of conversation, Katya had time to research and read about subjects that fascinated her when the shop was quiet.

Her interests centred on esoteric wisdom. She was inspired by New Age philosophies mixed with ancient traditions and her thirst for knowledge could not be quenched. Her now-unshakeable belief in the spirit world had absorbed her over the last two years, eventually guiding her to leave her old life behind. A competitive family who spent more time bickering than they did caring and her job in the archive office did little to fuel her soul as she plodded through her mundane life. The turning point was the death of her beloved grandmother, the only member of her family who understood her.

Lost in her grief, and perhaps the lowest she had ever been, Katya had been amazed to see an apparition at the end of her hallway. The being of bright light was quite simply hovering before her as she had turned to walk to the kitchen. Despite her surprise she felt no fear; instead, her heart filled with joy. Years of tears were unlocked, spilling freely as a heavy burden lifted. The next day she was given a carved box belonging to her grandmother, containing a deck of tarot cards and an amethyst set into a silver ring. Apparently her grandmother had wanted her to have it. Her older sister Ana had tossed the box towards her and rolled her eyes. It was behaviour like this that meant Katya did not even attempt to explain the apparition to her family; it would be futile. The box, the ring, and the presence of what she now believed to be an angel had given her hope and strength.

From that point, Katya grew from a shy and quiet cynic into a shy and quiet believer. While she said nothing about her experience, she found that people around her seemed more receptive, noticing her as though she had stepped forward from a shadow. She became aware of new sensations. People now had colours around them and she could pick up on how they were feeling. She felt great joy from small things she had once taken for granted. Life had changed significantly for her, but not for those around her, and it became even harder for her to relate to them.

Katya had her son, Liam, to consider, and drastic change was not an option. So, as a loving mother, she carried on as normally as she could, while quietly learning as much as possible about this new world that had opened up before her. She attended spiritual events, sat through numerous psychic readings, and explored many books. She was seeking answers which resulted in more questions, forming an ever expanding spiral path she never tired of walking. Liam was now grown and making his own way in the world, leaving her with a gaping, aching void in her heart which needed to be filled with something else. Finally allowing her spiritual beliefs to guide her, Katya viewed this separation positively as an opportunity to change her own life and to find herself.

Now, she sat before the shop computer, browsing all the spiritual and holistic training courses she would love to do. She silently asked the angels to manifest the resources for her. A movement caught her eye and she glanced up from the screen. Nothing there. The singing sensation began in her ear again.

They really were trying to get her attention lately! Something was happening and the familiar knot in her stomach reaffirmed itself. Taking a deep breath, and focusing on the gentle music coming from the stereo behind her, she tried to relax.

Katya often sensed subtle changes, yet pin-pointing this intuition to certain people and places was something she found more challenging and as such she was keeping a journal of events to try and make sense of it all. She now reached for this diary from her duffle bag and scribbled down the time, date, and a quick note of the sensations. She closed her eyes, asking the angels for more guidance and was subsequently startled as the little windchime above the door tinkled and a male customer ventured in through the doorway, where he hesitated.

"Morning," she called quietly, self-conscious that the man may have seen her sitting with her eyes shut.

"Hi," the man replied. "Is it okay if I have a look around?" He looked awkward, as though he had never been in a shop like this before and his tall, well-built frame made the shop doorway appear smaller.

"Yes, yes, of course," replied Katya. She noted the man's attractive appearance, but was not swayed by it; her days of being wooed by a handsome face were well and truly in the past. "Feel free to have a look around," she attempted to disguise her Midlands accent, as the man spoke in well-educated tones.

"Thank you," he proceeded to look at the crystals on display in the centre of the shop.

She tried to busy herself with the computer, attempting not to watch him as he looked around the shop, yet she was intrigued by him. He made his way over to the literature section on the rear wall and stood for some time reading the backs of the books before replacing them. She could not ignore him, and found her eyes watching his back and tuning in to his aura. She saw the colour field enlarge and expand as he absorbed the books. He was searching for something, and she could sense a hunger eating away at him and a feeling of desperation. He was seeking answers.

He turned, and Katya dropped her eyes quickly, reluctantly relinquishing the connection she had made with his ethereal body. Making his way to the counter with two books, he seemed thankfully unaware of her curiosity. As well as the books he placed a clear quartz and an amethyst crystal on the counter.

"What do these stones do then? I don't know much about all this." He seemed apologetic for his lack of knowledge.

Katya was naturally shy and found small talk difficult, however when someone wanted to know about something she was interested in she spoke easily. She took a deep breath to guard against nervous waffling.

"Crystals all have different properties which you can use for many things - clearing and boosting your chakras, manifestation, and to focus meditation," She began to stroke the long black plait that hung over her shoulder.

His green eyes widened as he studied the amethyst in his fingers and she allowed herself to look at him while he was distracted. He returned his attention to her, "I do that. Meditation, I mean. I'm really not sure what you mean about all the other things."

Caught off guard she blushed, "sorry. I have a tendency to waffle. I mean, I say stuff … I am … well, to put it plainly, the crystals can balance you. The clear one helps with focus and the purple one helps psychic work and offers protection."

"Ok, I'll take both of these then. Any others that are useful?" He asked, still looking a little confused, as Katya wished she had the gift of calm and confident eloquence.

"Well, they are all useful in some way, but these are good all-rounders, so start with these and see how you get on," Katya smiled inwardly at his innocence in such matters. Her eyes found his and she immediately felt the need to look away as a rapid and powerful feeling of recognition shot through her, stimulating her solar plexus like a fairground ride. Fight or flight adrenalin.

Thankfully, he failed to notice her reaction and breathed in deeply, letting out a relaxed sigh. "What is that smell and that music?" He asked thoughtfully, looking around, "it is so calming."

She smiled, relieved that he had broken eye contact.

"The smell is Nag Champa, authentic Indian incense, and the music is a meditation CD. They do go rather well together."

"I need something to help me meditate," the man looked uncertain as he told her this, his voice lowering slightly, "I have been to a couple of groups, but I want to meditate at home too and I can't relax enough. Are the CD and the Nag Champa for sale?"

"Yes, of course," replied Katya, climbing down from her stool and moving her rounded body out from the counter to get the items, "Where have you been going to meditation classes?" She pulled her old, black, cardigan defensively around her curves. She preferred being safely hidden behind the desk.

"It's over the other side of the bay and it's really helped me, but I have so much I need to find out, about myself ... I feel I need to progress a little deeper," he replied quietly, "Plus, I prefer to be private, I'm not sure about the whole group thing."

Katya warmed to his willingness to talk openly and forced herself to make eye contact again as she returned to the counter. There it was again. The feeling. Simultaneous elation and emotional pain. The feeling was so deep that she felt she might cry and she looked down. "So, are you looking to connect with your higher self?" She asked, as she focused on the wood grain pattern of the counter.

"Yes, I want to contact my soul, if that makes sense?" She could sense him trying to regain eye contact. "It's hard to blank out the real world most of the time."

She glanced up at him quickly, so as not to appear ignorant. "I know exactly what you mean. I meditate too," Katya had a thought, and made her way back over to the CDs and began sorting through them. It offered a useful distraction too. "I think there may be one in here that will help you."

"Thank you," he was looking through the leaflets on the counter, "Do you do these tarot readings? Maybe that would help me?" He asked, putting one of Eliza's leaflets into his pocket.

"No, Eliza does the tarot, but she's not here today," Katya explained as she returned to him, "Here, this CD is more appropriate for what you want, rather than the other one." Her heart was pounding as she handed him the CD and he looked at the cover, reading the words on the back.

"I've never had my cards read before," he confessed as he looked through his wallet.

"Well, you need to speak to Eliza," She passed him one of her employer's business cards, not realising he had already taken a flyer, "Have a look at the website or pop in and have a chat with her." Katya's stomach knot tightened deeply at the prospect of this man returning to the shop. She wanted to look at him, but feared her own reaction.

The man smiled. "Thank you," he said.

Katya smiled back, glad that she had been able to help. She was expecting him to leave now the transaction was complete. He loitered. The air felt expectant, as though he were about to say something and she held her breath as he walked to the door. She knew there was something more he wanted to ask. She was almost willing him to return, yet simultaneously desperate for him to go. As his hand rested on the door handle it seemed that he sensed her indecision, and he turned, boldly making his way back to the counter. Katya gasped, thinking that the goddess was working very quickly today.

"Sorry." He looked vulnerable for a moment.

"Yes?" She asked.

"You seem to know a lot," He gestured around the shop, "about this sort of stuff."

Katya nodded and blushed. "I read a lot of books."

"Do you know much about near-death-experiences?" He blurted this out, and she realised that being this open was foreign to him. His general manner suggested that he was a man used to being in control. He probably had no one else to talk to.

"I know a little bit from reading, and I am happy to listen," She took a deep breath, knowing she must regain her composure. He was a customer after all and she had a job to do.

. . . . .

"Careful of the floor!" Daisy screeched, holding her hands up, as two workmen dragged their ladders audibly across the hallway, "It's original!" She looked very much the lady of the house, wearing an elegant vintage dress, her dark hair immaculate.

One of the workmen rolled his eyes at the other and they pointedly lifted the ladders further from the ground.

Daisy hovered like a small bird protecting its nest, her eyes darting from one man to the other, and visibly holding her breath as the top of the ladder swayed precariously close to the chandelier. Letting out a huge sigh as the ladder cleared the ornament she then watched in horror as they nearly bumped into the bannisters.

"Let's go in the kitchen and have a coffee," suggested Eliza, from the end of the hall, unable to watch Daisy's fretful disposition for any length of time.

"But I need to ..."

"You are paying them, they are professionals. Let them get on with it and keep out of the way. Besides, you have invited Brandon to show you his work on the website," Eliza reminded her, smiling through her frustration.

Daisy stood, rooted to the spot for a moment, then followed her friend into the kitchen, which now looked quite cosy thanks to the addition of a large vintage table and chairs. Brandon had already made himself at home with his laptop and a large mug of coffee. Daisy sat down, while Eliza poured them both a cup.

"Thank you," Daisy smiled gratefully as Eliza set a steaming hot beverage before her. "I don't know what I would do without you both sometimes."

Eliza shrugged as she sat opposite her friend. "It's no trouble, we just want you to be happy," She placed her hands around her own mug. It did seem quite cold in this kitchen.

"So what's the grand plan for all this work then?" Brandon asked, leaning back slightly on the chair and tucking his pen behind his ear. As usual he sported a shirt, tie, and waistcoat with his jeans and sneakers.

Daisy sipped her coffee. "Well, it's the painting and decorating this week and next. Furniture is arriving the week after. Then it's the final touches and the checking everything, and getting ready for the launch," Daisy smiled anxiously, "There is so much to do!"

"I did say that two months was ambitious," Eliza commented, avoiding Daisy's eyes. She did not want to come across as the 'I told you so' friend.

"It is, ambitious, yes, but I can do this," Daisy said firmly. "And I have Stella Prince coming over in a while to discuss the PR," Daisy paused and smiled at Brandon, "which will help you with the website, so I am really glad you are here."

"Not Stella Prince from college?" Eliza gasped, slamming her coffee mug down.

"Yes. She runs her own consultancy now," Daisy smoothed her hair, "Apparently she is doing very well for herself too."

"But after what happened at college? How can you trust her ...?" Eliza was wide-eyed and wondered if Daisy actually remembered.

Daisy cleared her throat, as some of her coffee went down the wrong way. "I would like to think that now, as grown women, Stella and I can put all that behind us."

Eliza raised her eyebrows and frowned a little, "a leopard never changes its spots, Daisy. She tried to destroy everything you worked for!"

For a moment Daisy looked as though she had found a sour sweet in a bag of bonbons, then she found her smile again. "As I said, we have moved on. I bumped into her in London, at one of Christophe's events and we swapped details. She is a lot less ... erm ... volatile now."

"Volatile? The woman was unhinged!" Eliza cried, then looked apologetically at Brandon, who was now alert with curiosity.

Daisy lowered her eyes and voice, as though they were being listened to. "It wasn't her fault really though, was it? It was him."

Stella Prince had started out at college as the darling of the student social scene and the tutors' favourite. A femme fatale from a wealthy family, she rocked designer Boho-Chic, and only attended the best parties. Much to the annoyance of her family she became obsessed with Rick Rockley, a photography student who was delving into the dark side of designer drugs as part of his 'art', and he played her for every penny he could get. Unfortunately for Daisy, Rick was attracted to her 'old-fashioned English beauty' seeing the brunette as a magnet for 'vintage style camera work' to add to his portfolio. While Daisy actively discouraged his advances, Stella saw her as the root of his lack of interest, and sought to destroy Daisy's reputation with rumours and accusations. Coincidentally, three of Daisy's end of term canvases were brutally slashed, causing Daisy much grief and stress.

"Hmm, Rick Rockley," Eliza smirked, "What a state he was, and what a fool our Stella made of herself."

"Did she though? Really?" Daisy mused, "Love can make you do foolish things. I should know."

"Including trying to destroy someone's work out of jealousy?"

"You can't prove it was her," Daisy retorted.

"Yeah right," Eliza shook her head.

Daisy dismissed her doubts with a wave of her hand, "Well, that's in the past. I'm sure she has moved on, just as we all have."

Brandon yawned and stretched, nearly causing his chair to topple. "Girls, come on, give her the benefit of the doubt," He looked at Eliza with a smirk, "I bet you were no angel at college?"

Eliza chuckled half-heartedly as she recalled trying to balance her textiles course with two part-time jobs. She had been forced to support her mother and younger brother, following her father's departure. "Yeah, I was wild," she murmured dryly.

"Anyway!" Daisy clapped her hands together. "Today is important, the work is starting. The new me. The new business and my new future - and never falling in love ever again!"

Brandon lifted his coffee mug in a toast. "To the new Daisy!"

Eliza nodded, not quite believing Daisy's words. She had been her friend for too long.

. . . . .

"You must miss her very much... your wife?" Katya asked after he told her about the accident and Siân's death.

He paused, awkwardly, a guilty glance crossing his face. "If I'm honest, no." He swallowed hard, and Katya sensed a weight lift from him as he admitted the truth, "She was, well, how do I put it politely...?"

"Go on ..." Katya relished listening to the honest stories of others.

"We were on our way back from a large business launch connected with Siân's magazine. She had been all over this guy, who was some big shot and it was so obvious, it was embarrassing to be honest. She was normally a lot more subtle, so I could never be sure," he hesitated, "She was making a fool of herself and of me."

Katya could not imagine this man being made to look a fool. He had a gentle way of commanding respect.

"Anyway, I watched from a distance, and kept my ear to the ground, you know. Until ..." he looked upwards, as though still feeling a moment of futility, "I heard what I had suspected for some time. They were having an affair and she was planning to divorce me."

Katya shook her head in disbelief. As he focused on his own story, recalling events, he had made little eye contact. She was able to study him without the intense and peculiar sensations she had experienced earlier. His voice was compelling and she felt relaxed as she listened to his story.

"I confronted her in the car on the journey home, and she tried desperately to defend herself, telling me one lie after another," he laughed half-heartedly, shaking his head, "She did not realise how she was becoming tangled and trapped by her own words. Years of manipulative engineering of our relationship, and a misplaced sense of her own importance. She set her own trip-wires and they were all being activated one by one."

"Well they say what goes around comes around," Katya said without thinking, immediately worried that she had spoken out of turn.

To her relief, he nodded in agreement. "I lost my temper. I couldn't listen to the string of shallow excuses and attempts to justify her behaviour. I can't even remember what I said…" He broke off rubbing his chin and frowning.

"Go on," Katya urged.

"Well, that was it. The moment it all happened. I hadn't seen the other car, because of my anger. I was mad, and I wasn't looking as closely as I should have been. The other car was travelling way too fast. The last thing I saw was the glare of the headlights and I heard her scream. Then, I came round in hospital … having had the most wonderful experience."

"The near-death-experience?"

"Yes," he paused, "I would feel foolish trying to tell anyone else about this, but I have a feeling you will understand," he smiled.

"I will try," Katya wanted to hear about this experience. She had read several books on the subject, but had never met anyone who had actually been through it.

"It is difficult to find the words, as I was in another dimension, if that makes sense?" He glanced at her, "Everything was light. I mean not just light, but an *amazing* light. It felt like love. That's the only way I can describe it."

It reminded Katya of how she had felt when she had seen her angel.

"I think I know what you are trying to say."

"The colours were brighter, colours I have never seen before. They were just so … and the music. There was music. My father embraced me with so much love and told me he was proud of me. My brother Leo stood next to him and he looked so peaceful and happy. I could feel their love all around me," The man's eyes began to well with tears, but he swallowed and continued, "Sorry. It was emotional."

Katya nodded, and touched the back of his hand, her natural empathy taking over as she visualised what he was telling her. Feeling the warmth of his skin and the reality of the touch, she pulled her hand away quickly. She should not have done that.

He did not seem to mind however, as he continued. "I wanted to stay. I wanted to stay in that place. It was incredibly beautiful. But I was shown an image and told it was not my time. I was told to go back."

"You were shown an image? What like a vision?" Katya asked, still embarrassed that she had just reached out and touched his hand.

"I met a woman that night."

Katya felt another, very different knot in her stomach. "Oh?"

"She was beautiful, like honesty shining out through a room full of fakes," His eyes wandered across his imagination as he recalled the event, "I can't explain how she made me feel. We didn't even speak, but seeing her, made me see Siân for what she really was."

"Do you know her?" Asked Katya, avoiding his eyes as he looked back at her.

"No. Well, I didn't, and I don't, but now I feel that I do know her, because she was the vision in my near-death."

"What do you mean?" Katya was confused.

"The face of this beautiful woman was before me, and I was told I had to return. I came round, back in my body, to find out that Siân had died and I had died for several minutes. Everything had changed," he shook his head, "It was a shock, but everything was different. All the things that had once mattered, didn't matter anymore. It was so intense."

Katya nodded slowly. "You think this woman is the reason for your return?"

He looked into her eyes and she noticed with an uncomfortable feeling of disappointment, how they softened as he recalled the woman in his vision. "I know she is the reason for my return. I have to find her!"

Katya was surprised by the depth of his conviction, her heart sinking. "Do you have any idea where she may be?"

"No. But something will guide me, I am sure. This is why I have started the meditations. I want to connect with the world where I encountered my experience. I can't just carry on as normal and forget about it … what else can I do?" He looked at her with so much feeling that she nearly cried. Why was she feeling so much intensity?

She must remain calm. This was not her story, she was just feeling his vibes as any empath would.

"It may not be easy." She replied softly as she decided that she must try to help him. Her own spiritual journey had been life changing and had been less rapid than his. She could not let him flounder in a world he did not understand. "I may be able to help you. I don't yet know how, but do keep in touch. Please."

"I will," He said, quietly yet certainly, "I didn't catch your name?"

"Katya," She replied.

"Glen," He took her hand, gently, "I had better let you get on with your day. Thank you … Katya," He spoke her name with purpose, as though he wanted to remember it. He left the shop, closing the door quietly behind him and she watched as he walked past the window and out of her world. Her heartbeat was too fast and the frequency of the singing in her left ear had tuned up a notch. She was not sure what had just happened.

CHAPTER SIX

Eliza was the first to spot Stella arriving like a diminutive whirlwind as she marched up to the doorstep in a steel grey dress suit. She was five minutes late, her phone on speaker as she loudly instructed someone called Marie to use her imagination for once and get a result. Switching her phone off as Daisy opened the front door, Stella flashed her straight white teeth in a dazzling smile and stepped over the threshold in heels that for some would pose a serious health threat.

"Daisy, Dahling!" Stella gushed, kissing her new client on each cheek, "You look amazing!"

"I love the hair!" Daisy enthused in response. "It's so … so … you!"

Stella swished her long, thick, blonde locks - the only hint of the bohemian, artistic soul that Daisy had known at college. The two old rivals' heels clicked across the parquet floor as they made their way to the kitchen where Eliza was preparing more coffee.

"This place is fantastic!" Stella cried, as she removed her jacket, flicking her hair back over small, tanned shoulders.

"I know! I am so excited," Daisy agreed, gesturing for Stella to sit and join them all at the table, "This is Brandon, my web-designer."

"Pleased to meet you Brandon," Stella was obviously taken by him, her eyes widening as he stood to shake her hand, which did not go unnoticed by an already defensive Eliza.

"And, you must remember Eliza from college?" Daisy gestured to her friend who was too far away from the table to shake hands. Eliza smiled reluctantly.

"Yes, I think I do remember you," Stella, screwed her nose up, "You had a thing about cushions if I remember rightly?"

"Interior design and textiles – and I was researching natural dyes, hand stitching and batik," Eliza replied without smiling, "Sugar?"

"No thank you, and no milk. Got to keep in shape," she patted her flat belly and cast a cursory glance over Eliza's more relaxed figure. Stella turned her attention quickly back to Daisy, not missing a chance to flash a charming smile at Brandon as she sat down.

"So," Stella clasped her hands, resting her chin on her manicured forefingers and looked at Daisy with penetrating grey eyes, "how are things going?"

"It's all going to plan!" Daisy replied enthusiastically, "I am hoping to have this place up and running by the end of the month."

"Good, good," Stella nodded, opening her notebook. She then shook her head and pouted, "Terrible, the way things turned out with Christopher, you must be very upset."

Daisy smiled politely, "Christophe, not Christopher. At first, yes, but now it's time to move on and leave the past behind. This is a new beginning!"

Stella's phone rang, "Excuse me …Yes, it's all in progress Marie. Yes, yes, nothing for you to do until we go live. Yes, ok then. Speak soon."

Eliza placed a tray of fresh mugs of coffee on the table, rolling her eyes at Brandon as she did so. Placing her phone on the table, Stella apologised for the interruption and turned her attention back to Daisy, "Don't you miss the old lifestyle?"

Daisy shook her head, "No, not at all. It actually became terribly boring after a while."

"Oh My God! Really?" Stella appeared surprised and frowned a little.

"Yes, really. The red carpet is not all it seems and I have this business to launch now. My new beginning!"

"You are amazing! It must be so hard to move on and leave it all behind. The mansion, the parties, the clothes!" Stella, glanced at her phone then looked back at Daisy, "I mean how do you follow *that*?"

"I want to do something completely different, that's how I follow it!" Daisy snapped, "That is what this guesthouse is all about. My future. That is what we are here to discuss."

Brandon cleared his throat, and turned his laptop round to face Stella, "These are my ideas for the website."

"Thank you Brandon," Daisy looked relieved.

Stella's eyes widened, "that looks amazing. You certainly have a flair for design," She pouted at him as she sipped her coffee and Eliza willed the coffee to burn her top lip a little. "I love the website, but the art theme thing?" Stella frowned, "It is *interesting* but I honestly don't know how well it will work." She looked apologetically at Daisy. "It's a fantastic idea but there are already several excellent galleries in the area. You would be up against a lot of competition from square one."

"I know that, but this is not a gallery - it is an art-themed guesthouse. I am planning to hold events and soirees. High class stuff," Daisy argued.

"I totally get it Hun, but from a business perspective it is very ...how would you say ... idealistic?"

Eliza nodded silently as she found some washing up to do in the background, acknowledging that much as she hated to admit it, Stella was vocalising concerns that she didn't have the heart to broadcast.

"Excuse me, I'll let you two discuss the details. Feel free to have a look around the website," Brandon stood, and taking his cigarettes from his pocket, went out of the back door.

"Look! Stella! I know art. I know quality. I ran a gallery in Paris for goodness sake. And I have resources," Daisy began to tap her finger on the table.

Stella smiled softly and sympathetically, "Look Hun, I know it sounds harsh, but you would rather I was honest, wouldn't you? I just don't know who your audience is and that makes the PR a lot harder."

"Well," Daisy waved her hand theatrically, "people who are looking for somewhere to stay, who have an interest in art. People who might be interested in investing in unique pieces that will be on display. That's the audience."

Stella opened her mouth to speak, but Daisy got there first. "There must be a way of promoting it so it will work? That is what I am paying you for!" Eliza sidled over to the table, sensing that Daisy's artistic temperament was about to blow up.

Stella raised her hand abruptly to silence Daisy, "Think about it for a moment. There will be masses of set up costs, then the overheads, then the marketing, then the competition, then the inevitable slump. I think you should start with something far simpler. Just a basic guesthouse, or, if you are dead set on the art theme, capitalise on what you already have," Stella explained.

"I don't know what you mean, what I already have?" Daisy sighed, glancing at Eliza "What is your idea then? I'm all ears. Tell me."

Stella reached into her bag and smiled as she produced a folder.

"This is how it could work. This would be your PR angle," she began to open the folder and Eliza sat down at the table, curious to see what Stella had in mind.

Eliza felt Daisy's horror as Stella took magazine cuttings from the folder, and laid them across the table. Daisy's eyes filled with angry tears as an array of photos of herself and Christophe were set before her. Eliza shook her head, as the face Daisy most wanted to forget stared out at them. Daisy looked numb. Stella continued, "You still have the Dupont name. We can capitalise on Christopher's celebrity status to re-launch your identity as an artist," Her phone rang again, and with a glance at the screen she quickly rejected the call, "This would provide guaranteed publicity … news coverage. You would be trending everywhere in the art world and get your exhibitions in high profile galleries."

Daisy opened her mouth to speak, but merely shook her head in disbelief.

Stella waved her hands theatrically, "Imagine the stories in the Arts columns … 'Dupont Makes Creative Comeback' … 'Divorced Daisy Delights Once More' … We can get some high profile people to stay for a weekend, through your contacts with Christopher. They can give some reviews and we have a very marketable product."

"No!" Daisy cried, slamming her coffee cup down so hard that some of its contents splashed onto her new table. Eliza rushed to get a cloth.

Stella froze, shocked by the outburst.

"I don't want to use his name! I am an artist in my own right. Or I *was*." Daisy hissed, her eyes wide with defiance, "I had successful exhibitions, as 'Daisy Hartford', in *my* name. And that's how I intend to go forward," She pointed at herself, "Me! On my own!" Daisy stood up, her face pink with rage, "And it's Christophe, not Christopher! You can't even get his name right!" She picked up one of the cuttings and screwed it up, throwing it towards a bemused Stella and totally missing her, ruining the moment.

"Excuse me!" Daisy said firmly, as she flounced from the table and stormed out through the back door onto the patio.

Eliza shot a stern look at Stella, who now looked very small on her own at the table. "Well that was really sensitive wasn't it?"

"But it would work?" Stella looked surprised, "why can't she see the benefits of using her connection to him?"

Eliza rested her hands on the table and leaned forward towards the small executive, her blue eyes blazing.

"Because she wants to do this on her own, without a man, and to give a final two fingers to Christophe bloody Dupont and his damn ego trips!"

Stella lowered her voice to a whisper. "But her idea, this art thing, I can't see how it will work."

"I know that! So think of something that will work, if you are so good!" Eliza hissed. As she turned to follow Daisy through the back door, something caught her eye and for a split second she thought she saw a figure in the corner of the room. "Damn, we never did sage the house." She whispered to herself as she walked out to the patio.

Stella picked up her phone. "Hi, Marie, yes. Get me as many contacts as possible in the art world," She scooped up her folder and her handbag and made her way to the front door, "Yes, photography, sculpture, painting, design. I need a list of good names and quickly! Get in touch with photographer Rick

Rockley as well. I think he is in London at the moment. He owes me a favour." Stella let herself out through the front door.

. . . . .

Katya returned home to her flat, tired and yawning. Her day in the shop had turned out to be quite busy, which was frustrating as she wanted to find out as much as she could about near-death experiences. Wearily glad to be home, she locked the front door to the shared hallway. At least now she could dig her books out and get online. She also wanted to research the strange feelings of recognition she encountered when she looked into Glen's eyes. Thoughts of him had haunted her whole day.

As she turned her back on the door, she saw a small black kitten sitting on the stairs. It looked at her curiously and squeaked, its head cocked to one side. Unable to resist the lure of the small, inquisitive animal, Katya climbed the stairs quietly, crouching as she beckoned it to come. Tentatively, the kitten padded towards her and, after flinching slightly, allowed Katya to stroke its fur and tickle its ears. As the kitten became used to her, he stood on his hind legs and nibbled her hand, digging tiny pinprick claws experimentally into her skin.

"Aw, you're a playful little thing," Katya whispered, smiling.

The door to the upstairs flat opened a little, and a woman's voice rang out, "Merlin! Puss, Puss, Puss."

Katya stood up, taking the kitten in her hands and approached the doorway. "He's here," she called.

The door opened further and a kind looking woman with long brown hair and spectacles peered out.

"Merlin! There you are," she smiled with relief as Katya passed the bundle of black fur to her, and Merlin squeaked again, "Sorry, he must have escaped when I came home from work. He is so small and dark that I sometimes lose him," the woman chuckled.

"It's okay," Katya replied, "I love cats, if you ever need me to babysit. I live downstairs."

"My name's Josie," The woman shook her hand, nodding and smiling broadly. "Come on in."

"Oh, thank you, but I've got a lot to do…" Katya replied. Seeing the bright eyes of Merlin looking at her, and Josie's warm expression, Katya decided that she would accept the invitation after all. Much as she wanted to settle down for the evening and study, she still didn't know many people in the area, "But it can wait."

She followed Josie into her flat and was delighted to see a large shelf unit full of books. Josie obviously enjoyed reading as much as she did. Katya wanted to scan the spines and see what treasures sat on the shelves, but as the kettle whistled, Josie emerged from the kitchen before she had the chance. Merlin began to wriggle furiously in Josie's hand as he saw that the door was still open, and Katya quickly closed it before he could explore again.

"Thank you," Josie said, placing the kitten down onto the rug, "Take a seat." She gestured over to two upright armchairs that sat in the bay window, "Excuse the old-fashioned kettle, I just like the noise. Do you take sugar?"

"One please," Katya replied, seating herself in the armchair. The view was better than the one from her flat; being that little bit higher up, the eye could see further. She watched as the boats bobbed about, the lights pretty in the dusk harbour.

Josie returned with two cups of tea, and placed them on the small table between the armchairs, "I can sit and watch the boats for hours," she smiled, "I waste a lot of time staring out of the window."

"I can relate to that," Katya replied, still transfixed by the vista, "You have a better view than me."

"But you have the patio!" Josie winked cheekily, and pointed at her windowsill in the adjoining kitchen, which was crammed with plants, "That doesn't stop me trying to grow things though."

"Well you are welcome to use the patio," Katya suggested, "Just go in through the side gate." She referred to a small, iron, gate that opened off steep steps running up from the harbour. Katya had found them quite challenging at first but she was now getting used to the daily climb.

"Thank you," Josie replied, "That is very kind. You didn't tell me your name."

"Katya."

"Ah, Russian, meaning 'pure' if I am not mistaken," Josie nodded.

"Yes, that's right," Katya replied, "How did you know?"

"I read a lot," Josie sipped her tea, and nodded towards the bookshelves. "Mostly history and random useless information. I work at the museum over the other side of the bay."

"Oh wow, that must be fascinating. I love finding out about old times and ancient legends," Katya liked this lady already.

"It keeps me absorbed and the day passes quickly," Josie smiled, "What do you do?"

"I work at a shop in town. The one selling all the crystals and tarot cards."

"Oh I love that shop!" Josie replied, "I've not been in for a while though. I must pop in and book a tarot reading."

"It's my boss Eliza who does them," Katya smiled.

"I love all that sort of stuff. As well as history of course, and historical fiction." She smiled and patted a well-thumbed copy of Pride and Prejudice" on the table, "Got to love Mr Darcy."

"I read a lot, but mine is mainly New-Age research rather than fiction."

Josie nodded thoughtfully, "It's good to meet someone else who appreciates books; everything is getting too technological for me and I'm only in my forties. I like old things, old buildings. That's why I love this cottage. Did you know it's over two hundred years old?"

"I suspected as much, but I don't know the history," Katya replied, "It would be interesting to find out."

"Believe me, I am looking into it," Josie smiled, "I have the advantage of having access to many resources at work." Josie stood quickly to scoop up Merlin as he began to try and scale the bookcase with his tiny kitten claws, his eyes wide with the prospect of adventure. "You are not allowed to read mommy's books," she told him firmly, "No."

"I would be interested to hear what you find out," Katya replied, sipping her tea thoughtfully. She knew there was an energy in the cottage, nothing sinister, but it held memories and stories and she was curious. Right at this moment in time however, she was more interested in finding out as much as she could about Glen's near-death experience. As Josie was giving Merlin some food in order to distract him from the furniture, Katya finished her tea.

"I'll be off then, I do have a lot to do this evening."

"Pop in again soon. If you want to that is?" Josie smiled warmly.

"I will, thank you and I meant what I said about the patio."

"Thank you," Josie replied.

Katya knelt down to give Merlin some fuss and made her way back to her own flat, looking forward to a quiet evening alone with her books.

CHAPTER SEVEN

Katya was standing once again outside her cottage, fumbling with the same heavy, iron keys. The wind had gained power, even stronger than the last time, and the rain beat down hard, sharp and cold, the wind blowing it into her eyes. She could not see the keys or the keyhole properly and she was uncomfortably cold. Her pyjamas were soaked, clinging to her, and made colder by the force of the strong blasts. *This wasn't a summer storm; it was the middle of winter* she concluded. She inwardly criticised her choice of clothing as totally inappropriate, except that as she was asleep what else would she be wearing?

She could smell smoke from the chimney, and it evoked feelings of longing for the comfort it offered as she imagined the logs crackling and spitting in the kitchen fire. She knew that Mama would be inside, tending to the hearth and caring for little Arabella, her sister. Arabella had been ill with a fever. She was still not fully recovered and Mama would be fretting.

There it was again, the noise of shouting and cries from the harbour; the voices were carried away by the wind, and she could not hear what was being said. Something was wrong. Very wrong. Her stomach was tensed up and she had a sense of dread, but at this moment all she could think about was being inside the house, *her* house, but again it didn't look like her house. Although it was dark she could see that the paint on the door was peeling, and looking across the front of the cottage she noticed that there was a small hole in one of the panes of glass. Could that have been from this wild weather? It was rattling the door again.

This was fierce, she had never endured weather like this. Casting her eyes around, she realised that there were no cars parked along the road and there was no pavement. She felt herself sway as a huge gust of wind pushed against her, and her fingers gripped the wall, cold bricks digging into her fingers. Two young women were running towards her, their faces stricken with anguish as their long skirts billowed out behind them and they pulled shawls tightly against the cold. Their hair was unkempt; once neatly fastened it had become unravelled by the wind. They almost collided with Katya as one of them began to beat loudly on the door with her fist.

"Annette!!! Annette!!" the woman cried, hammering on the door. Katya looked at her, to see if she knew her but she was unfamiliar. However, in the darkness and rain it was difficult to see properly.

Katya tried to show the women the keys that she held, to demonstrate that she could open the door if they wished her to, and then wondered if they actually realised she was there, as they completely ignored her.

The second woman began banging the door. "Annette!! Open up!" She shouted. Her face angry with frustration.

Eventually, the door opened inward and Katya saw once more the woman who resembled herself, her shawl pulled tightly and her long hair plaited just as hers was.

"Annette!! Come on!" The women shouted, impatient, already making tracks towards the steep steps that ran downwards.

"Wait! I'm coming!" The woman from the house almost screamed, leaving the door open and ushering a younger girl back inside and telling her to stay with Mama.

The door of the cottage was still slightly open, providing a peek of the fire that glowed within, and Katya could just about make out the shapes of another woman and two more children huddled next to it. The warmth was calling Katya inside, but although she felt she belonged, she was highly alert to Annette's sense of urgency. She must follow her immediately. There was something Annette was trying to show her. She must go and see. She heard the ship's bell toll again and that loud crashing noise that she had heard before. It was his boat. She just knew.

Katya awoke, her heart beating and her skin sweating as she heard the sound of rain hammering on the windows of the cottage. Relieved it was a dream, she surmised that the noise of the rain outside had triggered her subconscious into dreams of storms. However, she desperately felt the panic and urgency of these women, rushing through the wild gale. It was so real and vivid. What was going on at the harbour? How did she know about Mama and Arabella and who were they? His boat, whose boat? She quickly switched the lamp on and scribbled notes on a piece of paper. Unable to make any sense of it, and feeling exhausted, Katya tried to push the thoughts out of her mind as she drifted back into an uneasy sleep.

CHAPTER EIGHT

"Oh do you think this all looks perfect enough?" Daisy looked anxiously at Eliza as she surveyed the newly decorated drawing room.

"It looks fine," Eliza reassured her, thinking that the decorators had done a fantastic job in a short space of time, not only to get the drawing room finished in tasteful, vintage grey and white, but also to decorate the other rooms and to repaint the outside of the house. Daisy had also employed a gardener to trim back the jungle in the front and tidy up the rear terrace. The furniture, a mixture of Victorian, modern and shabby chic gave the whole house a beautiful and welcoming finish. Eliza felt a burst of joy at her friend's achievements, "You've worked wonders, they will be so proud of you!"

Daisy let out a dramatic sigh and checked her hair as she pouted in the over mantle mirror. "I cannot risk hearing their criticism. I am too fragile and it will just about finish me off if they don't absolutely love it."

"I really don't know why you are worrying so much," Eliza shrugged and slumped onto the chaise longue, "It looks brilliant!"

"Don't crumple the cushions! At least not until they have had the entrance effect."

Eliza stood up immediately, looking for something she could lean against that would not result in a dent or a dirty mark. "How much has all this cost anyway?"

Daisy straightened a flower stem in one of the vases. "You really don't want to know. Enough," she raised an eyebrow, "I might as well do this properly while I have the chance."

Eliza nodded, thinking that if she had an influx of money she would definitely buy out the empty retail unit next door and extend her shop. "Yes, you are lucky to have the opportunity to do this. Not many people have such a chance to follow their dreams."

Daisy looked at her and smiled broadly, as the autumn sun gave her a radiance in her red dress. "I am so lucky to have you as a friend. I couldn't do all this without you."

"Hey I'm just me. I just roll up and do what I can," Eliza blushed.

Brandon appeared in the hallway with a case of wine. "I hope these are the right ones, I'm not great with white wine. I'm more of a Jack Daniels' guy personally," he said. Daisy rushed over and scrutinised the box.

"Yes, perfect, thank you Brandon. If you could put the bottles next to the glasses over there …"

He walked over to the table, sporting his usual waistcoat and tie with trousers and shoes rather than jeans, then sidled over to Eliza who was wearing a dress for a change; a floral maxi with a cropped cardigan. "Is the Queen coming?" He whispered.

Eliza felt reassured by his presence and the warmth of his breath against her ear. She did not know whether she could cope with Daisy's drama by herself today. "No not the Queen. We are entertaining Daisy's family," Eliza rolled her eyes.

"Hmm," Brandon nodded and pulled a face that made Eliza want to giggle.

Eliza followed Daisy through to the kitchen where some small, elegant snacks were laid out on the table. "I hope they're not too hungry. These are tiny!" She commented, lifting a canapé.

"Put that back!" Daisy tapped Eliza's hand, "We're going out for lunch - this is the appetiser that I ordered from the caterers. I haven't hired a cook yet."

"You should have said," smiled Brandon, "we could have brought over a big pot of veggie chilli."

Daisy looked at him as though she were not sure if he was joking or not.

"It was just a suggestion," He responded, as Eliza shook her head at him behind Daisy's back.

Two cars pulled up outside.

"They're here!" Daisy beamed while wringing her hands. She rushed to the door, a flurry of nervous excitement as Eliza and Brandon hovered awkwardly next to the wine.

Harry and Felicity Hartford walked in, kissing Daisy on the cheek and commenting on how lovely the entrance hall was. They were closely followed by Daisy's sister Heather, her husband Simon, and their four-year-old daughter Fleur.

"Hi sis," Heather beamed radiantly, "How's it going? You are looking good considering everything."

"Oh thank you!" Daisy sighed theatrically, "I'm surviving. You look fabulous."

"Well, one has to try," Heather appeared quite ordinary compared to the extravagant style of her sister. She was attractive in an understated way, less flamboyant, and wore traditional clothing.

"Daisy, lovely to see you," Simon gave her an awkward peck on the cheek and Daisy recoiled slightly, her smile on the verge of a grimace. Simon was a successful accountant, part of the old boys' network, and far removed from Daisy's world of art and fashion.

Closing the door behind her guests, Daisy knelt to greet little Fleur, who was looking in awe at the staircase and the chandelier that hung in the hallway.

"Does a princess live here?" She asked.

"You could say that," Brandon muttered under his breath. Eliza dug him in the ribs and stifled a laugh.

"No, darling. Just me, your old Aunt Daisy," she kissed Fleur's cheek gently and the child took hold of her aunt's hand, still looking up at the chandelier as the family walked through to the drawing room.

"Quite impressive!" Harry exclaimed as he examined the room, looking dapper in a blazer and crisp shirt. Daisy breathed a sigh of relief as he examined the chaise longue that Eliza had almost disturbed, "Ah, original Eastlake. Perfect. You seem to have inherited my eye for detail Daisy," he smiled at her, raising a dark grey eyebrow, "You could have asked me to help though."

"I wanted to surprise you dad," Daisy gave him a doe-eyed look. "I still need some accessories and ornaments. I was hoping you could help me with those?"

Harry Hartford was an art and antique dealer. His profession began at age sixteen in the mid 1970's, following the chance purchase of a music box for his mother, from a junk shop – only to discover it was worth a great deal more than he had paid. He began to research and to attend auctions, his enthusiasm fired by each good deal he made. Eventually, with a habit of being in the right place at the right time, Harry built a successful business.

"The colours looks lovely," agreed Felicity, "I wouldn't have chosen grey myself, but I think it works. The wallpaper and textiles lift it. You have done a good job."

"Let me get you all some drinks, and then I can give you the grand tour." Daisy walked over to the table and Brandon passed her a glass which he had already filled. Eliza followed cue and filled several more, making sure that she took a large sip from her own. It was going to be a long lunchtime.

. . . . .

Katya was disappointed. Mainly with herself and her own lack of understanding. She sat behind the counter, staring into space as she wondered what the future held. She had been so sure she was on the brink of something. There were all the signs she had been receiving and the meeting just two weeks ago with Glen, a meeting that continued to play on her mind. She felt so certain it was all connected with her lessons and what she had been preparing for over the last two years. The knot in her stomach still persisted, yet now it was annoying; a constant reminder that her world was about to change, yet being given no further clues as to what those changes might be. She read through the lessons again. The words she had read so many times were now becoming less inviting and more confusing as she became sadly aware that she did not actually understand their meaning.

She had been so excited when she had first received the numerology reading, feeling that she held the key to unlocking her destiny. Everything would fall into place and she could become mistress of her own universe, manifesting great spiritual happenings. Katya shook her head and laughed at herself and her own naive hopes and dreams. Who was she? She was not some great sage or wise-woman. She was just a woman, still a girl at heart, who had run away to the seaside and worked in a shop. She screwed up the paper in bitter frustration and threw it across the floor. The green man looked at her and seemed to frown, and regretting her actions, she stood and retrieved the paper.

"Sorry," She said aloud to the wood carving, then laughed at herself once more, for talking to an inanimate object.

The windchime above the door tinkled, and Katya braced herself for customers wanting to know which crystal would bring them true love. She was relieved to see Sheryl, the charismatic clairvoyant, standing in the doorway, today dressed mainly in shades of orange and ochre.

Sheryl smiled broadly, about to launch into a greeting, then paused. "Oh lovey, what's wrong?"

Katya's eyes filled with tears, as so often happened when someone demonstrated genuine concern.

"Huh, is it that obvious?" She placed the ball of paper on the counter and began to unscramble it. Wiping a tear from her eye, she passed the page to Sheryl who patted Katya's arm and donned her reading glasses. The older woman scanned the jottings on the page. Katya held her breath, waiting for Sheryl's response. She had never shown the report to anyone, not even Eliza.

"Aha, numerology. You are a Pisces. That doesn't surprise me dear," smiling, she carried on reading, "Oh, yes, I see."

"Do you understand what it means?" Katya asked.

Sheryl removed her glasses and looked at her. "No. No one knows what it means, other than your higher self," she placed the paper onto the counter and attempted to smooth some of the creases from it, "Did the reader not give you any more information?"

"Yes, he told me all sorts of things, but I couldn't take it all in. This was what I wrote down to take home, and then I lost his card so I couldn't ask him about what he said."

"Then you were not meant to know at that point in time," Sheryl smiled, removing her orange scarf, "It's warm in here dear. My age you know."

"Then what was the point in me having the reading?" Katya was not feeling any better.

"Lesson One, finding your power and true voice. Lesson Two, facing and overcoming your fears. Lesson Three, to experience unconditional love. Hmm," Sheryl took Katya's hand, "The spirit world and the psychic realm will only provide us with a certain amount of information. Sometimes, we have to work the rest out for ourselves. It's part of our learning and growth."

"But what do I need to learn?" Katya shook her head in desperation.

"What it says lovey!" Sheryl sighed, waving the piece of paper, "Look, do you want to make me a cup of tea? I'm not in a rush, we can go through it."

Katya was elated by Sheryl's suggestion. "Really? Oh you are so kind, yes I'll stick the kettle on," she gestured for Sheryl to follow her to the back of the shop, to a curtained area where Eliza did her tarot readings, and made them both a cup of tea.

"Thank you lovey," Sheryl put her glasses back on and read through the report again, "Okay, your lesson one, finding your power and your true voice. What does that mean to you?"

Katya was blank; she had been asking herself the same question and out of the three, she found this lesson the most confusing. "I don't know? Being myself I suppose? Which is what I am trying to do."

"What is your power?" Sheryl sipped her tea.

Katya had never felt power. Others had constantly taken advantage of her good nature and she was usually the underdog in most relationships, workplaces and especially in her own family.

"I don't have any power," she replied sadly.

"Nonsense," Sheryl scolded, wagging her jewelled finger, "Everyone has power. It's how you use it that counts. Power isn't about the ego, or control. It can be simple – such as the ability to listen. By using your power you can empower others. It's all about intention and balance."

Katya nodded. "Well, I can sense how others are feeling. Strongly."

"Empath?" Sheryl looked at her knowingly and Katya nodded, "That's your power. You have an amazing ability to connect with others and this is something you should work on. But it isn't all about giving, and this is where finding your true voice comes into it. Ah it's starting to make sense now!" Sheryl nodded, pausing to sip her tea and Katya was keen to hear what she said next, "Empaths are like sponges. I am one too," she confided, "We feel, we help, and we get drained. I have gone home with other people's baggage so many times. So you need to find your true voice to balance your power. Learn to say no. Set your boundaries. Learn your craft and be confident."

Katya nodded. Saying no to people, was one thing she had never mastered. "Yes, that makes sense."

"Also, learn to protect yourself – spiritually I mean," Sheryl became serious, "Jan, my sister, is the expert at that and it is important," she glanced back at the sheet. "Right, onto facing your fears."

The windchime signalled the arrival of another customer, and Katya reluctantly departed from the small table and Sheryl's warmth, rather like cake and afternoon tea, to deal with them.

· · · · ·

"Who is paying for this meal?" Brandon whispered to Eliza as menus were passed round, "Have you seen the prices?"

"Don't worry. Apparently Daisy's dad gets offended if he isn't allowed to pay," she squeezed his knee under the table and he winked at her as he grabbed her hand and moved it higher up his thigh. Eliza felt her cheeks starting to flush.

"Good, good," he smiled, "Then I might just go for the steak."

Eliza laughed and topped his glass up, "You are doing quite well on the wine, considering you're more of a JD man."

"And I could get used to this," he murmured, looking into her eyes and squeezing her knee back. Eliza blushed as bright as her hair and secretly longed to go back home with him rather than enduring this meal.

Felicity Hartford folded her menu and placed it flat. "I'll have my usual Harold," she said to her husband, who nodded and rolled his eyes slightly. She fidgeted with her napkin for a moment and then leaned forward towards Daisy, who sat opposite her, "So, how are you after all that terrible business with Christopher?" Felicity had managed to ask the question quite loudly, just as the chatter around the table had reached a natural hush.

"His name is Christophe mother, and I'm fine," Daisy looked annoyed as all eyes turned to her.

"Well if you will run off with a bloody foreigner!" Harry snorted before summoning a waiter.

"I am fine dad," Daisy looked defiantly at her father and then at her mother, "I am a businesswoman now and I will make something of my life, with or without a husband."

Simon choked slightly on his drink as Heather nodded enthusiastically at her sister.

"Daisy, dear, you have to remember you are not getting any younger," Felicity chided, pursing her lips, "Don't leave it too late to find a husband if you want children."

Brandon felt Eliza's body tense in response to the comments and squeezed her hand. "Shush," he whispered, "Now is not the time for your feminist, goddess stuff."

"Well perhaps she doesn't need a husband?" Heather spoke up, unexpectedly, "Perhaps she is perfectly capable of managing her life as a single woman?"

"Heather dear, there is no need to be antagonistic," Felicity snapped.

"I'm not being antagonistic mum, but perhaps you should look at how well Daisy is doing with her own plans rather than focusing on her lack of a husband?"

Their mother rolled her eyes. "Yes, I am well aware of this independent woman trend, I don't live in the dark ages Heather," she took a sip of wine, "I don't hear you complaining about your lifestyle though." Felicity gave Simon a smug grin and he looked momentarily reassured.

"Mummy…" Fleur piped up. "Why doesn't Aunt Daisy have a husband anymore?"

Heather was lost for words for a moment. "Because … because, darling, she is so special that she doesn't need one now." Simon shot Heather a 'What?' glance and Daisy smiled to herself.

"Is Daddy still going to be your husband Mummy?" asked Fleur, her wide eyes looking innocently at Heather.

Heather paused for a moment as an awkward silence fell. "Yes of course sweetheart. Because Mummy loves Daddy very much."

The answer seemed to satisfy both the young and old around the table and Eliza decided to refrain from commenting, totally distracted by Brandon's hand moving up her inner thigh.

"So what's next with the guesthouse?" Brandon tactfully steered the conversation, "I need to update the website."

"I am so glad you asked about that!" Daisy exclaimed, looking relieved. "It's mainly arranging the launch now. It's getting really exciting."

"I think you are being too ambitious," Felicity shook her head. "There are so many guesthouses …"

"It's going to be an art gallery too," Eliza chipped in, becoming annoyed with Daisy's mother.

"Yes, it's not just an ordinary guesthouse, the drawing room – the room you saw today – will be hosting exhibitions, soirees, and will be a cultural hub," Daisy's eyes looked to one side, as though imagining her creative project coming to life, "I need to use the space for events to bring the customers in."

"That really is good business sense," nodded Simon, glancing at Heather as if for approval, "Adding something unique – however don't forget that the basics are important. Good food and accommodation are still essential, no matter how arty the whole place is." He gave Daisy a sheepish smile and, for once, Daisy smiled back at him.

"Business sense? What do you know about business?" Felicity addressed Daisy, "You are a divorced artist."

"Mother, I will learn. I have people who can advise me," Daisy looked at her dad for support.

Harry patted his wife's hand. "Darling, perhaps just enjoy the meal? Yes?" He looked at Daisy and stood, raising his glass, "To my daughter and her new start," he smiled, and the others around the table joined in.

Felicity, however, continued the tirade across the table. "I don't know why you feel the need to do this Daisy," she shook her head as though she were ashamed, "Why couldn't you be content with being a wife? Where has all this need to run a 'business' come from?" Felicity had made a career out of being a successful wife and mother, supporting Harry's business activities through being seen in all the right places, ladies' lunches, charity events and head of the PTA when the girls were young.

Daisy stood up, her hands clenched on the edge of the table. "It has come from in here!" She said, pointing her finger at her heart. "This is my plan, this is me. Husband or not. Get used to it!" Daisy stormed away from the table towards the back of the restaurant.

Harry looked at Felicity. "Well done Fliss!" He said, sarcastically.

Heather moved quickly from the table, following her sister across the room, while Simon attempted to distract Fleur from the unfolding family drama.

. . . . .

Jayne was distracted from the conversation between Glen and her husband, Stefan, as she caught sight of a glamorous woman striding past their table; seemingly quite angry and closely followed by another, plainer woman who seemed to be trying to console her. She wondered what that was all about. Other people's dramas had never previously interested her, but she was taking far more interest in the lives of others since being at home with Leo, her six month old son, named after Glen's late brother. Daytime television, magazines, social media. She could not concentrate on anything substantial anymore. Reading a book was a challenge. She would get half way through a page, and then the inevitable crying would start because she wasn't giving him her full attention.

She had tried inviting the work girls over two weeks ago, for some real, grown-up conversation only to be reduced to a stressed wreck as her boss ended up finishing the cooking when Leo decided to have an unusual and unexpected meltdown. Not the impression she had wanted to give her colleagues. Now, she was trying to focus on what Stefan and Glen were talking about. It was important, to do with Stefan's job, but she had one eye on the sleeping child that lay in the carrier, waiting with baited breath for him to awaken.

"Anyway," Glen continued, "I can't keep the business going as I have been."

"Do you not think it's a little hasty to sell up though?" Stefan asked, his brow furrowed with concern.

"Sell up?" Jayne was now attentive. They had purchased their dream home two years ago. A large cottage in the middle of nowhere, an idyllic representation of the perfect family home. It needed all sorts of work doing and they were mortgaged up to the hilt. Having given up on the prospect of being able to have children following two failed IVF treatments, they had plunged their savings into the house. Leo had arrived as a welcome surprise and Jayne had opted for a career break, knowing that they could rely on Stefan's employment as head architect at Heathstone Luxury Homes.

Glen's father, Patrick, had taken the young Stefan under his wing, seeing his potential early on. He invested in him, perhaps as some sort of therapy after losing his own son, also called Leo. Stefan had been Leo's best friend and the name had been passed on to his and Jayne's child in remembrance. Stefan had blossomed and grown under Patrick's guidance, and this had continued when Glen took over Heathstone Luxury Homes following Patrick's death. Now, here was Glen talking about selling. Jayne willed the young Leo to remain asleep, nervously watching his face moving, as she wrestled with her mind, determined to hear the rest of the conversation.

"Look, I know how it must seem, but without sounding patronising you really don't understand what I have been through," Glen's eyes clouded for a moment, "No one does. I don't even understand it myself."

"So you are going to throw away everything your father worked for, over a vision?" Stefan was twitchy, Jayne noted. Not good. He wanted to say more than he could, "Do you not think it is just a reaction to Siân's death?"

Glen paused, glancing at Jayne. "No, it is not just a reaction to Siân. And, it was not just a vision – it was a whole experience. My life has changed beyond belief. I cannot begin to explain it."

Jayne nodded, trying to look as though she was taking it all in, but the words swam around meaninglessly. Despite her usual quick-thinking nature, she felt as though her brain was filled with sand. Coloured sand with shapes. New shapes that Leo had learned to match this week.

"So ... this is irreversible – not open to negotiation?" Stefan asked.

Glen nodded. "I will not change my mind. I am negotiating a good deal with Helena Sharpe who is the main contender for taking over the business. She has assured me that if I sign over to her, all chief staff will be taken on as part of the arrangement," he looked firmly at Stefan, "You are not going to lose your job."

"But ...." Stefan interrupted, "what if she has her own people...?"

"You *are* Heathstone Luxury Homes, Stefan – it's your designs that have shaped the business."

Stefan's blonde hair and beard were illuminated as his face became flushed, embarrassed by the compliment, and Jayne was reminded of how he had looked when they had first met and they had completed a climb together.

Jayne put a hand on Stefan's arm. "Glen's word is good, it will be fine," she felt proud as Glen nodded at her words and smiled at her. She could get back in the driving seat again if she really tried. She was not lost.

"Let's just hope Helena Sharpe thinks that too," Stefan replied, raising his eyebrows at Jayne, "We cannot afford risk at the moment, however much we used to thrive on it."

Jayne and Glen both realised the sentiment behind Stefan's words, as he referred to his past with Glen's brother, and their love for risky, adventurous pursuits – which was how he and Jayne had met. Now, as a family, the risk taking was something they had chosen to leave behind. Jayne often wondered if Stefan missed the old lifestyle. The freedom, the wind flowing through his hair as he abseiled or the heart-quickening buzz of the rapids. She knew that *she* did. Stefan had got seriously into cycling as an acceptable form of adventure for a father but she no longer had the energy. She yearned to be out at the top of a mountain, hearing the rush of a river or feeling the weight of a rucksack as she pushed her body to climb just that extra step.

Now her arms ached just from the weight of her son, she spent much of her time in the house and her brain seemed scrambled. Things that had never even occurred to her before now seemed of paramount importance. Was the kitchen clean enough? Were there germs in her nails that could infect him? She clipped her nails every few days to make sure. She washed her hands with soap and sanitising gel, she cleaned the sink furiously as his bottles and bowls touched it. No germs allowed. She thought back to camping-out with Stefan on their tour around the Americas; she hadn't washed properly for a week then. How had she become so fixated with germs? She looked at the sleeping Leo, and her attention turned to the table top. When he inevitably awoke she would be holding him near its surface. She began to move the cutlery backwards towards Stefan and Glen and moved her glass of lemonade further away.

"What are you doing?" Stefan asked her, his brow furrowed.

It was so obvious, why was he even asking? "For when he wakes up," she replied.

"But he is asleep, just relax." Stefan smiled, but she could see the tension in his jaw. It was forced. He was sick of her and it was her fault. She wanted to cry. No it was his fault. If he didn't go off cycling all the time and spent more time at home, perhaps she would be more in control?

"So how is fatherhood?" Glen smiled.

Stefan smiled proudly. "Its hard work, but just great. I love being a dad!" He clinked glasses with Glen and Jayne wanted to rip his beard off.

Oh yes, just like that, she thought. *The man – the father. So much hard work, like you would know.*

Stefan excused himself from the table.

Glen turned to Jayne, his pleasant smile momentarily smoothing her edges. "And how are you?"

"Oh I'm good," she lied, "it's such an adventure being a mother."

"You're not missing work then?" He asked, smiling, taken in by her words.

She wanted to cry there and then, to tell him that yes, she was. She was missing her identity as a woman and she missed her independence. To tell him she missed the ability to make clear decisions that didn't revolve around feeding times. That her outside world no longer existed.

"Hey are you okay?" Glen reached forward and touched her hand lightly.

She looked down as the tears threatened to well up. "Yes, sorry, I'm just tired. I don't get as much sleep as I used to," she laughed as if to make light of the fact, wiping her eye with her finger as Stefan returned to the table. She was not going to cry. Not here. She had endured physical pain on expeditions and not cried. Stefan looked annoyed and she wondered what was going through his mind after Glen's announcement. She knew he would be in a bad mood when they got home.

Perhaps sensing the tension, Glen announced that he needed some fresh air and left the table.

. . . . .

78

Katya returned to join Sheryl after the customer had left the shop. "Sorry about the interruption."

"Stop apologising! That was a lovely cup of tea, and you handled those customers expertly," Sheryl smiled.

"Really?"

"Yes, really; you seriously underestimate yourself you know."

Katya wished she had a pound for every time she had heard that phrase. "I know. Perhaps that is part of finding my power?"

"That is everything about finding your power. Empowering yourself and believing in yourself. It will come lovey. Give it time."

"Time? I'm thirty-six!" Katya laughed.

"Confidence building takes longer for some people than others my dear. I was a late starter too."

Katya warmed to Sheryl's understanding of her. The bright eyed older woman's aura was full of rainbow colours and she exuded something that both cheered and comforted Katya. "I don't know if I can be that person?"

"You will lovey. Something will click, and you will feel comfortable in your own skin."

"I feel so on edge. It feels as though something is happening," Katya shifted, "things … feelings …"

"You have had signs?" Sheryl pre-empted her.

"Yes! I had lots of signs, I was so excited! Then Daisy moved to town and everything seemed to shift. I have had a knot in my stomach for weeks. Then I met Glen and that was so amazing, as he is so lost and I want to help him and I keep getting singing in my ears. I thought something was happening, then it stopped, but it hasn't …"

"Whoa, Katya, slow down. Take a breath," Sheryl breathed in and out deliberately, and Katya followed suit, "start at the beginning. Who is Daisy and who is Glen?"

"Sorry. Daisy is an old friend of Eliza's who has returned. She has gone through a divorce and is setting up her own business with her settlement," Katya paused and frowned, reluctant to admit the truth. "Try as hard as I might, I can't take to her. I don't know why; it's a gut thing."

"Hmm, it's always best to follow your instinct."

"But Eliza loves her, so she can't be a bad person?"

"Different dynamics lovey. Just because Eliza gets on with her, doesn't mean you have to. Besides there may be an underlying reason why you don't connect with her."

"That's what it feels like – she hasn't done anything to upset me, it's like there is something behind the scenes, something I know about but don't know about,"

Sheryl nodded. "Then it's primal and subconscious. Don't fight it, there must be a reason. Who is Glen?"

Katya's eyes drifted to one side and she smiled. "Glen is a lost soul trying to find his purpose."

"Oh? That sounds intense."

"It is. And fascinating. Do you know I could listen to him talk all day. He has this way of explaining things that just absorbs my attention, you know?"

"Your aura grew massively while you were talking about him lovey. Pink shades too."

Katya laughed. "Stop it! It's not like that."

"The aura never lies!" Sheryl smiled.

Katya blushed. "Am I imagining it all? I see auras too. Although I haven't been watching them lately."

"Since all this started?"

"Yes. I am losing sight of my own quest."

"Take a break dear. Just a few days out. Relax and adjust. Work out what these lessons mean to you."

"Will they happen in order? The lessons? And when will it all start?" Katya felt as though she may cry, she was so overwhelmed.

"It's started already lovey. And it may all happen simultaneously, not one answer at a time," Sheryl smiled, "you have so much ahead of you, but until you realise your full potential you can't move forward. I think I now understand what this reading is about."

"You do?"

"Yes. It's like this," Sheryl stared into Katya's eyes, "you are on the way to finding your power and voice, as we have discussed. Then facing your fears will be easier. But prepare for it. Write it down. Identify the fears. Then once you have overcome all of that and you learn to love yourself, the unconditional love will arrive."

Katya laughed. "You know that is the only one I have already experienced. The unconditional love is the only one I understand. That's my son, Liam."

Sheryl smiled, taking Katya's hand and she shook her head. "No. Tell me of any mother who doesn't love her child unconditionally. This is something bigger."

"What? What could be bigger than that?"

"Trust me. You will find out. I can't say anymore," Sheryl smiled to herself as though she had a secret knowledge, and nodded at Katya, "Work on the other two lessons and the rest will follow."

"I am not interested in a relationship or anything like that."

"Perhaps not dear, but you may not have a choice," Sheryl gave her that knowing look again and passed Katya her empty cup, "Now, what did I come in for? I have quite forgotten," she walked back into the shop and made her way over to the incense.

Katya watched Sheryl's aura as she browsed, relaxed and full of many colours. Although she was doubtful about this promise of unconditional love, she trusted this woman. She just wished Sheryl would tell her more.

CHAPTER NINE

Daisy clenched her fists tightly around the edge of the sink in the ladies' washroom, as Heather crept in through the door.

"Don't let her get to you," Heather said softly, placing a hand on Daisy's shoulder.

Daisy turned to face her. "That's easy for you to say! You live in domestic bliss. You fit into her picture of what the perfect daughter should look like."

"If you say so," Heather shrugged, scrutinising her face in the mirror, "what makes you think it's bliss?"

"Sorry. I didn't mean to snap at you," Daisy felt bad, seeing Heather's uncertainty.

"It's okay."

"I just don't understand why she can't be proud of me, most parents would be pleased that their daughter had pulled herself back from the brink of despair," Daisy opened her clutch bag and re-applied her lipstick.

"It doesn't fit neatly into her world though does it? She is from a different generation," Heather pointed out.

"Well, I've always been the disappointment, the strange one, the arty one. You've always been the favourite, the sensible one." Daisy laughed, "I should be used to it by now."

"Hmm, yes. Good old sensible Heather," She stood next to her sister and they looked at each other in the mirror, "Do you know I have turned into one of those women who always has a postage stamp in her purse, and a plaster and pack of tissues?"

"That really doesn't surprise me," Daisy shook her head, chuckling.

"I envy you," Heather said, looking down.

"Why?"

"Because you are free. You have a blank canvas to do what you want."

"But you have a husband and a beautiful daughter?"

"I know. But I sometimes wonder who I am?" Heather looked as though she might become emotional, but like the true stalwart that she was she held it together.

"Is everything okay sis?" Daisy asked.

"Of course it is," Heather laughed, "I am the sensible one remember?"

Daisy nodded, although she was not convinced by Heather's performance.

Checking her appearance once more in the mirror, she turned to Heather. "Right, I'm fine now, ready to take on round two. Thank you."

The sisters embraced and Daisy felt reassured by the scent of clean washing on Heather's clothes.

"What's that perfume you are wearing?" Heather asked, "See I am envious of your exotic perfume too!"

"It's very expensive!" Daisy laughed, "My new statement fragrance now I am an independent woman."

They made their way back out into the dining room, when Heather stopped suddenly.

"Oh, I think I'm going to be sick," she said unexpectedly, looking horrified, and she ran back into the toilets. Daisy followed Heather's line of vision to a table where a bearded man and a woman with a baby were sitting. While looking at them, she failed to see a tall man walking quickly in her direction. At the same moment, a waiter laden with a tray of drinks hurtled through swinging doors from the kitchen. The tall man collided with the tray, and Daisy's red vintage designer dress was splattered with a combination of wine and water.

"What the hell do you think you are doing?" She shouted.

"Sorry! I am so sorry!" The man held his hands up, as the waiter ushered them to one side, attending to the broken glass.

"Can't you look where you are going?" Daisy snapped, surveying the front of her now ruined dress.

"Could we have a cloth please?" The man said to the waiter.

Daisy saw from the corner of her eye, the woman with the baby and the bearded man turning to stare. She looked up at the clumsy man who had been responsible for the spillage, and felt an overwhelming and unnerving sense of familiarity.

"Have we met before?" She asked eventually as his eyes studied her face, as though waiting for some sign of recognition.

"Briefly," he replied, his moss green eyes making her feel as though the world were about to end, "You probably don't remember."

She felt giddy, a strange combination of both elation and sorrow overwhelming her and a sensation deep in her stomach, telling her to move as far away from this man as possible. "I don't remember, no," she avoided his eyes as he was about to speak further, and then the waiter appeared with a cloth and she busied herself with trying to wipe the worst of the liquid away.

"It was in London, several months ago," he said as she ignored him, "I have been looking for you ever since."

She stopped wiping and did not dare look up. Was he some sort of stalker? "Excuse me," she muttered, "I must return to my guests." She walked quickly back to the table, her heart beating fast, aware of the horror on her mother's face as she neared her seat.

"Oh my god," Eliza said, "What happened?"

"Some idiot knocked a tray of drinks over me," Daisy sat down, taking a large swig of wine.

"That won't come out dear," her mother said, "It will stain."

"I know that!" Daisy snapped. She turned to Simon, "How's business going?"

Simon looked flabbergasted to be spoken to by Daisy of all people, and as Heather re-joined the group he was busy explaining the effect of the stock market on his current investments. Daisy watched as the strange man returned to his table, thankfully sitting with his back to her. She tried to think where she had seen him before, but she couldn't place him. He turned round as he was in mid-discussion with the man and the woman with the baby, and the woman looked directly at Daisy, a blank expression on her face. So she was being discussed. They were all weird, the three of them, Daisy decided. She kept her eyes lowered for the remainder of the meal, and let the rest enjoy their small talk as she waited patiently for the dinner to end.

As they were about to leave, the man came over and placed a business card before her on the table. "I do apologise, and I didn't mean to disturb your meal. Please contact me so that I can pay for the dry cleaning bill."

"That won't be necessary," Daisy replied curtly, "It's ruined, and it was a one off piece. Paris, 1940's." She refused to look up, and the man sheepishly made his way back to his own table.

"There was no need to be so rude," Daisy's mother scolded, "It was only an accident."

"You wouldn't understand mother," she replied, watching the man's back as he walked away. What was it about him that unnerved her so much and why did he look so familiar? And that feeling? She had never felt that way before. Part of her longed to follow him, to ask questions. Another part of her wanted to move as far away as possible.

"Is everything okay?" Eliza asked, squeezing her arm, "You look really upset."

"Hmm, I'll talk to you about it later," Daisy replied, finishing her wine swiftly, "Now is not the time or the place. I just want to get out of here."

CHAPTER TEN

Katya was walking up the cliff path towards the large house, frost crunching beneath her feet as the sun tried to break through the white, winter clouds. Looking down at her long, woollen skirt and cotton pinafore she knew she was dreaming again. She was Annette.

The coarseness of her shawl was uncomfortable, but she was grateful for its warmth. Her hands were turning numb in her woollen mittens, not helped by the weight of the basket that she carried. It had panniers and she recognised her own neat stitching on the cotton covers, made from the same fabric as Mama's Sunday dress. She could see her warm breath hovering in small clouds before her and she hurried towards her destination. She knew there was a large open fire in the kitchen and while the housekeeper inspected her delivery of sewing she may get a chance to sit next to its warmth.

As she neared the front door, something at the top of the house caught her eye, and she saw the pale face of a woman with dark hair looking out of the attic window. She could not see her clearly, and the woman retreated from the window as Katya climbed onto the doorstep and rang the bell that hung in the porch. Taking a moment to place the basket on the floor and blow warmth onto her fingers, she was relieved when the maid came to answer it.

"Annette," she cried, "Come on in, you look perished."

She retrieved her basket and gratefully entered the doorway, following the maid through to the warm kitchen at the rear of the house. The housekeeper looked stern as always, but her face softened when she saw the basket that Katya placed on the large table.

"Ah, My Lady will be so pleased," she pulled the covers from the panniers and pulled out two beautiful hand-stitched, lace-trimmed cotton table cloths with matching napkins. Katya now remembered Mama sitting by the oil lamp each night stitching until her fingers were sore. *Mama was clever, she really was,* Katya thought with pride. The housekeeper gasped as she admired the handiwork.

"Perfect," she said, smiling primly.

Katya was standing as close to the fire as was polite. The housekeeper gestured to the maid who scurried to the dresser to collect a bundle wrapped in cloth, which the housekeeper placed into Katya's empty basket. She placed three shillings into Katya's hand.

"Three shillings?" Katya gasped.

"With Season's Greetings," the housekeeper smiled. Katya was now excited that the bundle the maid had placed into her basket may be candied fruit or mincemeat tarts. The extra shilling would be most welcome at home. With a spring in her step she bade them farewell and wished them a Merry Christmas as she skipped out of the door, her hands warmer and her hopefulness piqued by the bundle in the basket.

It was then that she saw him, standing under the tree, watching the attic window. Why was he here? What business did he have with this house? He worked on the boatyard, he would have no reason to visit this home. He was aware that she had noticed him and he avoided her eyes as he threw something angrily to the ground before he walked away quickly, out of view. Her heart ached. She rarely saw him now, as their once frequent meetings had ceased. Something had changed. Her eyes filled with tears and she looked back up at the attic window, but the woman was not there. Was it she that he looked for? Was it she who had taken the place in his heart? Katya felt an ache in her chest as she realised his turning away was an act of dismissal. He did not want to see her.

Running all the way home took longer than she wanted it to. She could not run fast enough. Her legs felt like lead. The basket was cumbersome and she wanted to throw it over the edge of the cliff. She wanted to scream at the ocean thinking how blissful it might be to allow herself to fall over the edge and drown in the deep water. To be swept away into the suffocating peace of the tide forever. What did the festive season matter when his affection was lost? For so long she had dreamed of their love, thinking that one day they might be wed. There had been no other since their childhood. Part of her very soul was now missing.

Katya awoke, tears streaming down her face as her heart ached with the sadness that Annette had felt. Who was the man that had broken her heart and soul in two? Who was the woman in the window? And who was Annette?

Katya wiped her eyes and took her journal from her bedside, jotting down notes furiously before she lost the thoughts that remained from the dream.

CHAPTER ELEVEN

"Thank you so much for coming with me!" Daisy smiled at Brandon as he drove over to the main town, "I will get a car sorted out soon, but I have had so much to do."

"Hey don't worry, I want to hear what Stella has to say about the launch plan, so I can put it on the website," Brandon glanced over at her, "Eliza doesn't trust her you know?"

"I know, but Eliza doesn't trust anyone!" Daisy laughed.

Brandon did not reply. His face set into a frown as he concentrated on the road.

"I mean she trusts you, but she is defensive all the time, you know. She's been through a lot. She's a tough cookie."

"Yes, it can be difficult sometimes," Brandon replied quietly as he parked the car in expert fashion outside the restaurant where they were meeting Stella.

Getting out of the car, he paused to light a cigarette. Daisy put her coat on and pulled it tightly around her, feeling the chill of the autumn breeze. She was worried she had offended him, with her comment about Eliza.

"She does love you, you know."

He raised an eyebrow over his glasses, his dark hair flopping over his forehead in the wind. "I hope so. I really do," his voice faded as he turned his back on Daisy and looked out to sea. Despite her concern, Daisy was annoyed. She did not want to stand in the wind, becoming ruffled before her meeting with Stella, but she could not ask him to hurry when he had been so kind. She was relieved when he stubbed the cigarette out and picked up his laptop from the back seat.

"Come on then," he said more enthusiastically as he walked briskly towards the buildings. Daisy struggled to keep up with his long stride in her kitten-heeled boots.

Stella was not there when they arrived.

"Bloody late as usual." Brandon shook his head, and rolled his eyes as he perused the menu.

"Yes, I hate it when she is late, I get nervous," Daisy was panicking.

Brandon looked sternly across the table, his brown eyes quite serious. "Look, Stella is a jumped up little madam from what Eliza has said. You on the other hand, are a bona fide business woman. There is no comparison and you don't need to be nervous. You have the upper hand."

Daisy felt reassured by his words. "Thank you, that means a lot." He continued to look at her and she felt uncomfortable holding his gaze for a moment, as in that instant his reassurance made him seem very attractive. She looked away as the tension was broken by Stella's arrival.

"Yes. Just get it sorted please!" Stella spoke loudly into her phone as her heels clicked sharply across the laminate floor. She joined them at the table, placing her over-sized handbag on the seat as she removed her coat and scarf, "Sorry I'm late! Please forgive me. So many people to see and so little time!"

Daisy smiled at her while Brandon frowned, glaring at Stella.

"You should make it a priority to meet all your clients on time," he stated.

Stella was thrown off guard by the comment. "Yes, yes, of course. I do! All my clients are my priority," she flashed a white smile at Daisy as she seated herself and summoned the waiter, "I'll get the food, by way of an apology."

As the waiter arrived, Daisy resisted the urge to smirk as Brandon took full advantage of her offer and ordered grilled sirloin steak and a small glass of red wine.

"So how is the guesthouse coming along?" Stella asked, smiling at Daisy.

Daisy did not need an invitation to launch into her favourite subject. "It's looking amazing!" She enthused, "All the furniture is in place, the decor is done and it's almost ready to go. I am so excited I can hardly breathe!"

"We need some photos of you for the press and your social media," Stella explained, "I have set up your accounts ready, but without some photos there is little point in posting anything."

Brandon cleared his throat. "Yes, we need some photos on the website too."

"Let's organise a photo-shoot this week then," Stella seemed eager to get back on side with Brandon.

"Okay," Daisy was already imagining what clothes she should wear "which room? The drawing room looks amazing now."

"No, we need one of you outside the front of the house. You welcoming guests in, with the sign clearly displayed."

"Then we need photos of all the rooms for the website," Brandon added, "I can take those, that's not a problem."

"Once the room photos are available we can get some trial guests to stay and leave reviews on the travel sites," Stella smiled.

Daisy nodded, and smiled at the waiter as he brought their food. "Thank you both of you, I am so nervous. I am interviewing cooks and housekeepers at the moment, so we are nearly ready for people actually staying."

"Nice steak," Brandon murmured, glancing at Stella as he bit into a forkful, "How are the launch plans going Stella? So I can update the website?"

Stella looked momentarily lost as the piece of lettuce she was about to eat fell from her fork. "Sorry?"

"The launch. The big event?" Brandon prompted.

"Yes it's in four weeks," Daisy joined in, wiping some pate from the corner of her lip. Daisy became aware that Stella was no longer listening, her eyes were focused on the end of the table.

"Oh my god, that is Glen Heathstone!" Stella replied in a hushed tone as a tall man approached them.

Daisy looked up to see the man that had spilled the drinks at the family meal.

"I am so sorry to bother you," Glen said politely, touching Daisy's arm gently, and casting a defensive glance at Brandon.

Daisy looked at him with fierce eyes. "What do you want? I am in the middle of a business meeting."

Glen looked awkward. "I wanted to apologise for the incident the other week and to give you my card again regarding the dry cleaning... as I haven't heard from you," he held his card out, and Daisy felt that same uncomfortable intensity, forcing her to look away.

She glanced at Brandon for support but he was busy tucking into his steak. Looking up again at Glen, a heady mix of pain and happiness struck deep down in her heart. These were feelings she did not understand. She did not want to understand them as she knew it would hurt. She recognised him, obviously, from the restaurant a week ago but this was a familiarity she couldn't describe. When she looked into his eyes it was akin to falling into an abyss, an unknown darkness, and her stomach reeled. Was it excitement or fear, or both? It made her feel slightly sick with adrenaline. She wanted him to stay and to talk, but simultaneously willed him to go. Such was the paradox that when she opened her mouth to speak, her throat was too dry and she almost choked. She took a sip of water as he placed a gentle hand on her shoulder. The touch startled her and she pushed his hand away. "Thank you, you are most kind, but I do not need the dress dry cleaned; as I said it was a one-off piece."

The man thrust his card in front of her anyway. "It was an accident. But I understand why you are upset."

Daisy picked up the card. "It's okay. Honestly."

"Do you have another one of those cards?" Stella piped up, standing and holding one of her own cards out, "I run a PR company, Daisy is one of my clients, and she is opening a new guesthouse. You may be interested in the launch being as you have an interest in property?"

Glen shot her a tired look. "I am actually retiring from the property business, but thank you for asking," he paused, glancing at Daisy, who was pointedly ignoring him, and changed tack, "thinking about it, an invite to the launch would be interesting," he smiled and took Stella's card.

"I am Stella Prince, and this is Daisy Dup ... Hartford, Daisy Hartford," Stella gushed.

"Daisy," He spoke her name slowly with deliberation, "I am sorry. And if there is anything I can do to help your business take off, please let me know," he touched Daisy's shoulder briefly once more before moving away. Daisy felt a surge of energy from his touch. He had touched her before, she did not know when or how but she knew she had felt this previously. She felt dizzy and out of control, needing to take another sip of water. Glen left the table and the restaurant and despite her intense discomfort around this man, she also resented him leaving.

"Are you okay?" Asked Brandon.

"Yes," Daisy lied, "I am just stressed. Forgetting to breathe, you know that sort of thing."

"Well, now we can invite him to the launch!" Stella enthused, tucking Glen's business card into her wallet, "retiring or not, he has a huge business presence, and his wife was an executive on a top magazine."

"Wife?" Daisy asked.

"Yes, Siân Heathstone. She died. He is devastated of course," Stella wiped her mouth with her napkin, "So sad."

"So who else have you got coming to the launch?" Brandon asked.

"Sorry?" Stella replied, "Oh yes, well, the Mayor is already booked for that date, but is sending a deputy and we have some reps from the art college and the other local galleries."

"What?" Daisy looked surprised.

"Look, it is short notice Daisy. The high profiles have rates, they cost money. They don't just attend for free."

"Then what do I do? How do I have an opening night or event that will make people want to come?" Daisy was panicking, "It's great that the mayor can send someone, and obviously I assume you will invite the press, and yes I need to get on side with the local galleries, but I need something, something unusual, that will draw people in?"

Stella appeared dumbfounded.

"What is the history of the building?" Brandon asked, "People like a tale, and you have already restored a lot of the original Victorian features."

Stella nodded furiously. "He has a point. That could really work."

Daisy cocked her head slightly with interest.

"It was a convalescent home. Wealthy people from the city retreated to the coast to recover from TB and scarlet fever."

"So we could work with the retreat angle?" Stella waved her hands as her imagination came into play, "A haven of rest and relaxation. Enjoy the views, the artwork and the great accommodation…"

"Hmm, I'm not sure. It's not exactly what I had in mind," Daisy was doubtful.

Stella looked at her phone and draped her coat and bag over her arm. "I have to go. This should cover the bill for your steak." She thrust a twenty pound note towards Brandon, "Daisy please give the launch ideas some thought, I need something more to work with, and quickly, if you want to achieve your deadline. "I wish you would consider using your connections with Christophe, it's a ready-made market. It would make life so much …."

"No! I have already told you, this has nothing to do with him!" Daisy's eyes were defiant.

Stella nodded uncertainly and made her way swiftly to the door, her hair flying out behind her.

Daisy slumped, pushing her half eaten lunch away from her.

"What's the matter?" Brandon asked.

Daisy's eyes filled with tears. "It's all going wrong! This is going to be a disaster."

Brandon smiled reassuringly. "Perhaps you need to be a little more flexible and consider some other ideas?"

Daisy frowned at him. "Look, Eliza's really worried that you are trying so hard to prove a point and do all this on your own, when you can let people help you," he looked at Daisy as her bottom lip began to quiver, "There is no need to get upset. You have achieved a great deal already. Just maybe think about some alternatives."

"Perhaps you are right," Daisy admitted reluctantly, dabbing her eye with a napkin, "I just had this vision, you know …"

"Daisy, no one is knocking that. The best entrepreneurs sometimes have to change their vision," he stood, picking up the notes that Stella had thrown on the table, "I'll go and settle the bill."

Daisy nodded, her eyes still filled with tears. For the first time since she had received her divorce settlement, she felt out of control. She was no longer sure her big idea was going to work and everyone seemed to be against her. If she wasn't sure it was going to work, then why should anyone else believe in it? The prospect of failure now entered her mind like a dark cloud.

She could not fail. She had too much to prove. To herself, her family and to Christophe. She had to make this work. Wiping her eyes defiantly, her thoughts turned to Glen as she saw his card still on the table next to her plate. Another self-absorbed millionaire, probably just as controlling and selfish as Christophe. She would phone Stella and tell her not to invite him to the launch. She did not need him to bring his posse of followers to her party. She would find her own guests. She screwed the business card up and put it on her plate with the remains of her lunch.

"Feeling better?" Brandon asked as he returned to the table.

"Yes. Thank you," Daisy replied, forcing a smile as she picked up her bag and followed him out to the car.

. . . . .

Jayne watched Stefan absent-mindedly as he sat by the wood-burner, talking quietly to someone on his phone. She was trying to get Leo to sleep for his afternoon nap and she was planning to check and reply to some emails if he settled down. Just a few more gentle rocks and he would be off and she might get an hour or so to herself.

Leo's breathing was steady, his little hands relaxed and his face peaceful. Jayne gently lowered him into the travel cot that stood in the corner of the lounge, holding her breath as she let go of him carefully so that he did not realise she had put him down. Walking slowly backwards, she breathed a sigh of relief and returned to the sofa, clicking her laptop into life. As it fired up, she dashed into the kitchen to load the dishwasher and then remembered she had washing to do as well.

Like a dervish, she grabbed handfuls of baby clothes and towels and stuffed them unceremoniously into the washing machine, before returning her attention to the dishwasher. She might not get another chance today and although Stefan was at home, he was working, and she did not want to bother him with the household tasks. This was why she was on maternity leave. She had been thinking about returning to work, liking the idea of part-time hours. To start with anyway. She would tell Stefan when he was in a good mood.

She ventured quietly back into the lounge, hoping that the noises of the machines in the kitchen did not wake Leo.

"What do you mean, you've met her?" Stefan spoke into the phone loudly. He looked troubled, his brow furrowed. Jayne paused with baited breath, wishing he would talk more quietly.

"Glen, I'm sorry but this is making no sense!" Stefan exclaimed. Jayne moved into his field of vision and gestured frantically for him to be quieter, pointing at Leo. Stefan rolled his eyes at her, which was infuriating. He didn't understand. It was easier when he wasn't working from home.

"Look, you've been through the mill, and things are bound to be different. But really, do you actually trust Helena Sharpe?" Stefan was becoming irate and Leo made a small noise. Jayne froze. No. Please don't wake up just yet.

Stefan was looking angry now, and Jayne was gesturing for him to cut the call short or speak more quietly.

"Look, I have to go," he said, "Just don't rush into anything. Please, this is my livelihood we are talking about."

He threw his phone onto the sofa and strode towards the window, his hands on his hips and his face scowling as he looked out over the garden.

"What's the matter?" Jayne asked quietly.

"Bloody Glen and his new life. That's what!" Stefan snapped, "The man's lost the plot!"

Leo stirred a little at the sound of his father's voice.

"Shush!" Jayne whispered, "Come into the kitchen."

Stefan followed her into the half-finished farmhouse kitchen with a face like thunder. She put the kettle on while Stefan reached for the gin. Her gin. Her special gin, two glasses on a Saturday night if she was lucky, if Leo settled down. She felt resentful, wanting one too as he poured a measure.

"So what's going on?" She asked.

"He has signed the documents to hand over the business to Helena Sharpe. That's it! I am at her mercy. *We* are at her mercy!" He took a large swig of gin and slammed the glass down.

Jayne flinched and then held her breath waiting for Leo to wake. "Look, I am sure it will be fine. Glen is an honourable man, he wouldn't sell to someone he didn't trust?"

Stefan raised the glass and drained it with another swig. "Do you know what Helena Sharpe's nickname is? Eh?" He glared at her, 'Helena Shark'." He hunched his shoulders, leaning on the table and shaking his head, "Glen is just not thinking straight. Siân's death has sent him doolally. He thinks he has seen God and now he has met this woman - this Daisy Hartford, who he thinks is the answer to all his prayers …after everything his father built up. Patrick Heathstone must be rolling in his grave!"

Jayne walked towards him and touched his arm. He shrugged her away quickly and she flinched.

"Do you know what will happen if I lose my job? Eh?" He pointed at her, his finger nearly touching her face, "You lose this house! We lose this house! We will be back in a rented terrace with our camping mats on the floor."

It crossed Jayne's mind that she would at least have some company, and be able to take a stroll to a corner shop instead of living in the middle of nowhere.

"I could go back to work? Well, I might have to, my maternity pay finishes soon."

Stefan laughed. "Yeah right. You going back to work. You can't even string a sentence together lately. And no offence but your job doesn't cover the childcare costs, remember?"

Jayne could have easily smashed the gin bottle over his head, but instead she took it from him calmly before he could refill his glass. "That's my gin," she heard herself say, trying desperately not to cry, "I want to go back to work. I need to!"

The sound of Leo crying echoed from the lounge, and Jayne's tears spilled over, the knowledge that her hour of peace and quiet was now gone, was too much for her. She wanted to sleep. She wanted to be hugged and reassured.

"I need some air!" Stefan picked up his car keys and stomped out of the kitchen slamming the door behind him, as Jayne rushed to her son, tears streaming down her tired face.

. . . . .

"You've been very pensive today Kat," Eliza commented as Katya cleaned the shelves, reorganising the books as she did so.

"Hmm?" Katya heard Eliza's words through what seemed like a veil, and not quite reality.

"You seem deep in thought. You have hardly spoken," Eliza prompted.

Katya adjusted her glasses and sighed wearily, casting the duster to one side. "I have been having some strange dreams," she replied, "You know those dreams that seem so real you can't forget them when you wake up?"

"Ah, the ones that seem to infiltrate your whole day," Eliza nodded.

"I am just trying to work out what it all means," Katya wrinkled her nose, her hand moving to her long plait for way of comfort.

"Do you want to talk about it?" Eliza asked.

"Yes. I do. It is in the past because I am in old-fashioned clothes, I mean I am an old-fashioned woman, like living in those times … in the dreams …" Katya began as Eliza nodded.

Eliza's phone rang. "Excuse me," she picked up the phone, "Hi you ok?"

Katya returned to her bookshelf, deciding that perhaps she was not meant to discuss the dream just at the present time.

"What do you mean?" She heard Eliza say, "Look, stop panicking, we will think of something. Do you want me to come over?"

Katya had already guessed who was on the phone, before Eliza jumped up and announced that she was leaving for the afternoon.

"Sorry, I have to go, Daisy is having a meltdown. I knew this would happen, Brandon was with her earlier and texted me to say she may be upset."

"Then you had better go and make sure she is okay," Katya smiled slightly, but did not turn to look at her employer, "I will be fine on my own. As you have said I am in a quiet mood anyway."

Eliza paused. "Look, I don't mean to keep dashing off, but she really is in a bad way, despite the front she is putting on. We will talk about your dream another time. I promise."

Katya smiled and nodded. "I totally understand," she said. As Eliza left, she felt resentful. What was it about this Daisy that had everyone running around in circles and dropping everything? She had been through a divorce, yes, she was hurting, yes. Nothing unusual about that. Katya began to clean the shelf more furiously. Daisy wasn't destitute, she had no dependents. She was young and beautiful. Katya fought back angry feelings of resentment and jealousy. Her research had taught her to let go of such emotions and focus on her positive energy. She was only hurting herself by feeling like this.

The windchime signalled the arrival of a customer and she turned to see Glen standing in the doorway. She stopped breathing for a second. It had been weeks since their first meeting, yet she thought about him so often that he seemed almost like a celebrity entering the shop.

He was wearing business clothing, and it made him seem less accessible to her than the open and vulnerable man she had encountered the last time. With a surge of déjà vu the image of the man under the tree in the dream flitted through her mind but she dismissed the thought. The man in the dream had not looked like Glen.

"Sorry, I didn't mean to startle you," he said.

Katya became aware that she was standing rooted to the spot, holding her breath like a deer in the headlights. "Oh, no, it's okay, you didn't! It's just me. I mean I am in a … just cleaning you know. I have been sorting these out," she gestured at the bookshelves, hearing her waffling words and watching his face become confused. She turned her back, placed the cloth down and silently asked the angels to guide her as made her way over to the counter. "How can I help you?" She smiled, "How's the meditation going?"

He looked instantly relieved at her recall of their previous conversation and he removed his tie, placing it into his pocket. She could smell traces of alcohol on him. A business lunch perhaps.

"Well, something is definitely happening," he announced, smiling broadly. His eyes were lighting the whole of his face and her heart quickened, hoping to share his joy.

"What has happened?" She waited for his reply as the world seemed to move in slow motion. His aura was huge today she noted, he was happy, and the feeling spread to her, her empathic tendencies soaking up his elation.

"I have met her," he stated proudly.

"Who?" Katya asked, unable to stop smiling, such was his happiness.

"The woman from my vision. I have her name. I know who she is. I have found her."

"Oh that's wonderful!" Katya was genuinely pleased for him, "Perhaps now you can begin to put the pieces together?"

"Yes, that's how I feel, it is all falling into place. This is the second time I have met her in as many weeks," he looked into Katya's eyes, "I think this is the work of the universe."

"It sounds like it," Katya agreed, understanding that this was of paramount importance to him and wishing that she didn't experience these strange feelings she could not comprehend when he looked at her.

"It is fate, destiny. I was meant to meet her. This is so amazing. I knew you would understand."

At that moment in time, despite him being in his thirties, he seemed almost teenaged, like her son, and her heart warmed to him, wanting to be part of his happiness. "I do understand. It's like an illumination when the universe shows us a path," she wanted to hug him, but refrained.

"She doesn't realise though. I need more guidance to understand how to approach this and let her know we are meant to be together," he seemed desperate, "I need one of those tarot readings, or something."

"The Universe will only give you the information you need at the present time," Katya warned, remembering her conversation with Sheryl. A reading will not always provide answers."

"I don't care, I just need to hear something. I need a way forward, a sign," he spoke quickly as though propelled by a force beyond his control.

"I don't do the cards. Eliza does."

"But I bet you can?" He asked, "I would rather you did them. I feel … I don't know, a connection with you. I have never met Eliza."

Katya's feelings were piqued in such a way that she could not let him flounder. Of course she could read his cards. She didn't have to charge him, it wasn't a business transaction. Noting the feelings she had recalled about the dream, she thought perhaps her connection with him was to be encouraged in order to seek out her own answers. "I have the day off, on Thursday," she replied, "Here is my address." She quickly scrawled her address and phone number on the back of one of Eliza's flyers before she had a chance to change her mind.

CHAPTER TWELVE

Daisy opened the door to Eliza, who had stopped off on the way to buy a bottle of wine. Eliza was sad to see that her friend had been crying.

"Aw, what's the matter?" She asked, as Daisy walked down the hall towards the kitchen, blowing her nose gently. Eliza closed the door behind her, frowning as she followed. Despite the new decor and the expensive furniture, the old, large house echoed with emptiness. She imagined Daisy sitting night after night alone in this place, probably not relaxing at all. Had she even created a space just for herself in this mansion or was it all about the business?

As Daisy sat down at the kitchen table, Eliza found two large wine glasses and poured them both a drink, seating herself opposite her friend.

"Okay, tell me what's going on in that head of yours. I don't like seeing you so upset."

Daisy looked grateful as she sipped the wine. "It's all going wrong!"

"Why do you think that? The place looks fantastic!" Brandon had mentioned that the meeting hadn't exactly gone to plan and she suspected it was something to do with Stella.

Daisy began to sob again. "Because hardly anyone is coming to the launch and the art theme won't work because apparently my ideas are a load of crap!"

Eliza took her hand. "Is this Stella's doing?" She asked.

Daisy looked at her doe eyed. "The lack of launch guests yes, but even Brandon said that I might need to change my vision... to come up with an alternative."

Eliza smiled inwardly. He had spoken the words she wasn't brave enough to say. "He doesn't think your ideas are crap, no one thinks that. He just thinks you need to be more flexible," Eliza took a sip of wine, "As do I."

"What you too?" Daisy cried, "See I might as well forget the whole thing!"

"Sshh," Eliza took her hand again, "Look. You want this business to work. You have to choose a theme that is going to pull people in, not set yourself a small niche market. Start basic, the rest can follow once you are established."

Daisy nodded. "You mean I don't have to lose my ideas?"

"Not at all," Eliza smiled, "But you don't have to do it all at once. Take small steps to your big dream."

"Really?" Daisy took another large sip of wine.

"Really," Eliza confirmed, "I started off with a market stall before I had the shop. Now I want to buy out the shop next door and get Katya qualified in holistic therapies and run courses and stuff, but I don't think I can afford it. It's always there in the back of my mind though," Eliza squeezed Daisy's hand, "You don't have to give up on your dreams, but sometimes you have to wait for them."

"I think I see what you mean," Daisy relaxed a little, then let out a sigh, "There is another thing."

"What's that then?" Asked Eliza.

"You know that man who spilt the drinks over me at the meal?"

Eliza nodded, smiling. "You mean the really attractive one who offered to pay for your dry cleaning?"

"That's the one," Daisy nodded and frowned, "He was in the same restaurant as Brandon and I today. And he came and spoke to me!"

"What's so bad about that? He seems very pleasant and polite."

"Well Stella has only gone and invited him to the launch," Daisy replied, "Apparently he is some big shot and she was gushing all over him. She is so obvious sometimes! Why would I want him at my launch anyway?"

"Although I hate to say it, maybe she has a point – you wanted high profile people at your event? If he is a big shot, then he will have contacts and that can only help," Eliza shook her head, "I don't know why you are so concerned about it."

"He unnerves me. I feel… distressed… almost nauseous when I am with him."

"Eh?" Eliza was confused.

"I know. It sounds totally crazy but I get this weird feeling, like I know him – yet I don't know him. I have never met him before the day at the restaurant," Daisy lowered her voice to a whisper, "He may be dangerous."

Eliza could not help but laugh. "What makes you think that?"

"It's just this feeling I get. My stomach tightens up and I don't want to be near him. It's really strong. I think I am scared of him."

"Maybe this is just a defence mechanism after Christophe. Maybe you are just wary of men?"

"No, because I am okay with other men… Brandon for example. It's just that man," Daisy drained the rest of her glass, "And, as much as I don't want to be near him, I hate it when he walks away too."

Eliza was lost for words. "But you don't even know him."

"Exactly!" Daisy refilled her glass and topped up Eliza's, "Why would a complete stranger have that much of an effect on me?"

"Unless he isn't a stranger?" Eliza mused.

"I don't get what you mean."

"May be you know each other from a past life?"

Daisy nearly spat her wine out. "Oh Eliza, you do make me laugh. It's always spiritual and mysterious with you!"

Eliza looked at Daisy sternly. "I'm being serious. Have you been having any strange dreams since you met him?"

Daisy continued to laugh. "No," she said, "Other than dreaming about how this house probably looked in Victorian times and the harbour. But that is natural – all I am doing every day is dealing with the house and looking out over the harbour. I really must get out more often."

"Which reminds me – you have spent so much time creating the guest areas, have you made a space for you? Do you have your own chill out room?"

"Oh yes!" Daisy smiled, "I have the attic. Come and look."

She took Eliza's hand and led her up three flights of stairs to the attic door which already had a 'Private' sign affixed to it. "It's so basic compared to the rest of the house, but it's mine. I love it up here."

Daisy opened the door and Eliza followed her into what had once been an empty room with bare floorboards. Now it was divided into sections with vintage screens. There was a seating area with two small sofas and a TV, a sleeping area with a double bed, lamps and a clothing rail. Then Daisy led her through to the area by the window. This was still an empty space except for some cupboards, an easel and an armchair. A desk in the corner was full of Daisy's sketchbooks and there were some blank canvases leant against the wall. Daisy's paints, Eliza noted, were still in a box. *I must encourage her to start painting again,* she thought.

"Wow," Eliza looked around, amazed at how Daisy had used the space.

"See this is my den. I can paint, relax, sleep, and before the guests move in I am having an en-suite fitted – This floor is mine. A self-contained flat."

"I love it," Eliza nodded, taking it all in, "No wonder you haven't accepted my invitations to come round for dinner."

Daisy smiled. "You know, I think you and Brandon are right about the whole vision thing. Maybe I should just go one step at a time," she stood and looked out of the window, watching the harbour in the sunset. Eliza saw the spirit of a Victorian nurse walk up behind her friend, placing her hand gently and protectively on Daisy's arm. Daisy rubbed her arm.

"I must get some allergy cream. My arm keeps tickling."

The nurse walked into the wall and Eliza decided there was no need to sage the house. Someone was looking after Daisy; her friend had been here before.

CHAPTER THIRTEEN

Katya was anxious as she surveyed her living room again. It was a mix-and-match of things she had collected, mainly from charity shops, and furniture included in her rent. No one had ever set foot in this flat, apart from upstairs' Josie popping in for a cup of tea and Eliza calling in to drop the shop keys off. This space was however, now she thought about it, sacred and totally her own. It was just as she wanted it to be and she had never given any thought as to how someone else may view it.

Waiting for Glen to arrive she was already nervous, not only of his views on her humble abode, but about the reading too. The cushions were plumped, the kettle was full, and her tarot cards sat expectantly on the dining table filling her with a feeling of dread. This would be the first time she had ever given a reading to someone other than close friends. She closed her eyes for a moment, absorbing the calming sound of the rain pouring relentlessly against the windows, trying to block her self-doubt.

The buzz of the doorbell signalled his arrival and she glanced at her grandmother's clock noting that he was exactly on time. She loved that old clock. Despite its age, it never faltered.

"Hi," he said, smiling as she answered the main front door. He was soaked, water dripping from his hair and his jacket, his face shiny with raindrops. "I walked, rather than driving. Perhaps in hindsight it was not such a good idea." Katya closed the door behind him as he crossed the threshold, the fresh scent of the outdoors accompanying him.

Hearing a familiar squeak behind her, she turned to see Merlin, curious and slightly bigger now, sitting on the stairs. She climbed up and stroked him, wondering whether to take him into her flat until Josie returned home. No, she had promised to read Glen's tarot. She couldn't do that with a kitten running around.

"Is he yours?" asked Glen, removing his wet coat.

"No, my neighbour's. He is rather mischievous," she took Glen's coat and draped it over a small radiator.

"Thank you," he smiled, wiping water from his dark hair.

Katya nerves rose again. What if she could not read for him?

"About the reading…" she began.

"Are you sure it's okay?" He asked.

Katya thought of her chat with Sheryl, about being true to herself and finding her power. This was something she needed to do. If it didn't work then it was not meant to be.

"No. Yes, I mean it is fine. It's just I'm out of practice. I am not a professional at this."

Her heart leapt a little as he looked deeply into her eyes.

"But you understand me, you understand my problem." She looked away, overwhelmed by his sincerity. "Besides, I've never had my cards read before. I have nothing to compare it to."

Katya smiled and opened the door to her flat. "It's not much," she said, "but it feels like home to me."

He stooped his neck slightly as he walked through the low doorway and she sensed that he seemed at ease as soon as he entered. His eyes were drawn straight to her bookcase, crammed with books and magazines.

"Do you want a cup of tea?" She asked, making her way to the kitchen.

"Coffee please," he replied, "You have a lot of books."

"That's just some of them," she replied as she poured the kettle, "The rest are in storage at a friend's house. I really need one of those houses with a wood panelled library," she mused, "Do you take sugar?"

"No, just milk please," he replied as he read the spines of the books, "Wow, is there anything you haven't researched about the supernatural?"

She carried their drinks through and placed them neatly on the dining table, settling herself on one of the chairs, reassured by the way he was so interested in her book collection.

"I am fascinated by it all, I never stop reading. The only thing you won't find on there is witchcraft."

He turned to face her, an amused smile on his face. "Why is that?"

"It freaks the hell out of me. I don't know why," she shuddered and gestured for him to sit at the table, pulling her cardigan around her.

"But aren't the tarot cards a little bit witchy? And the shop?"

"I suppose, but I won't have books about it in the house. Pentagrams, spells, all that stuff, it scares me." She recalled the horror films her sister Ana had made her watch as a child, and while she knew that white witchcraft was nothing to do with those themes, the symbolism still associated with it in her mind.

"Thank you for the coffee," he smiled. Glancing at the cards wrapped in their silk cloth and Katya's large clear quartz crystal, he asked, "Is there anything I need to do?"

Katya took a deep breath. This was it, the moment she had been dreading since they had arranged this. "No, just relax and think about anything you want guidance on," she removed her glasses and looked across the table at him as she unwrapped the cards.

"Wow," he stated, his green eyes wide across the table.

"What?" She asked nervously.

"Your eyes. They are a really unusual blue. I never noticed with your glasses on."

She blushed, looking down. "I don't need the glasses to read the cards. My third eye does all the work." Her grandmother once told her that the unusual deep blue of her eyes was an indication of her spiritual connection, but she had always been shy of showing their beauty. Her need for spectacles created a useful barrier in her opinion.

She passed the cards to him and asked him to shuffle and to concentrate on the questions he needed answering. She watched his hands as they had no difficulty managing the large cards. *Man's hands,* she thought. Yet they were soft, no sign of labour. *Not like Robbie's hands,* she thought. *Who was Robbie?*

Where had that come from? Pushing the thought aside she took a deep breath and closed her eyes, asking the angels to guide her with the reading. The singing soon began in both her ears and she knew they had heard her. Glen passed the deck back to her and she placed the cards back onto the table, hearing her own voice asking him to cut the pack into three and for a moment she felt quite detached from her body. She became warm as though hands were caressing her cheeks and holding her shoulders and she knew that Spirit was with her. She was supposed to be doing this.

She concentrated on the images illustrated on the cards as she turned them over. First 'The Star', crossed by 'The King of Pentacles'.

"You are full of hope," she gestured to the naive image of the woman on the first card, "Yet you are blind in your faith, you are seeking answers and relying on the universe to present them. It is positive however, and signifies that yes, you are meant to be on this path for a higher purpose."

Glen nodded.

"The King is crossing you. Sensibility and practical matters, financial arrangements and property are holding you back from your goals."

"Ha!" Glen smiled, "Yes, I have many things to finalise before I can truly follow my heart. Property being a main part of it."

She glanced up at him and the word 'Stef' came into her mind, or was it Steven?

"Who is Steven or Stef?"

"Stefan," he replied, the corners of his mouth turning down.

"He doesn't understand. He is fearful."

Glen nodded but remained silent, his brow furrowing slightly.

Katya turned over the next card, the crowning card.

"Aha, The Fool," she smiled.

Glen looked worried by the image of the young man skipping blithely.

"Fool?"

"Not in the way you might think," she smiled, happy that she could appease his concerns, "The Fool represents new beginnings, following dreams without concern for the outcome. Unknown territory and hope. Like a birth, being reborn."

Glen nodded, "Yes that figures, my near-death … it was like a re-birth."

Katya turned the next card: 'Death'.

"This is the root of the matter, what has brought you to this point. The ending of a situation, closure, the end of a chapter."

He looked serious. "Do you think she is at peace?"

Katya was surprised. "Your wife?" she asked.

"Yes."

"I don't know, but from what I have read, most souls are at peace when they cross over. You saw it yourself in your own experience. The light and the joy?"

He nodded. "Yes, if she is in that place then she will be happy. Finally."

Katya noticed relief cross his face. Despite his realisations about his wife, she could tell he felt bad about moving on without her. She wanted to hug him but instead she turned the next card.

"Okay, this card is about the recent past. You have The Ace of Cups."

He nodded, looking at the image of a naked Aphrodite standing in the ocean, her long, black hair flowing as she held a single golden cup in her hand.

"You are ready to receive love. Again, this marks a new beginning and relates to your near-death experience. Your heart is open and you have been guided by feelings rather than logic. Love is now more important to you than it once was," she glanced up at him, noticing his aura expand and his eyes soften, "Your feelings are very real and you have been right to follow them. This is a new path. Embrace the changes and don't fight them."

Katya, in her highly attuned state, could almost feel his emotions touching her and she fought the urge to reach out and caress him. To tell him it would all be okay. That she was here for him and she loved him. Her eyes filled with tears as she saw for the first time the depth of feelings that this normally rational man was experiencing. Oh he was so lost. She had to guide him.

"Are you okay?" He asked, looking at her, "Do you want to stop?"

She blushed, the warmth from her angels enveloping her more. It was intense. "I am fine. It's just my spiritual connections working." At that moment she felt as if she had always known him and could tell him anything. Her fear was diminished and she felt a rush of joy, her face tingling.

He looked at her intensely for a moment, and time stood still, an acceptance of truth across his face, and a seriousness in his eyes. She looked back at him, daring herself to linger with the gaze, and she took in his image fully. A fleeting nuance flickered across his eyes and she saw his aura swell and move. As though an invisible energy ray linked them she knew that he trusted her completely and she trusted him. She no longer felt any uncomfortable sensations and was finally able to look at him clearly, almost confidently. She knew him.

Returning her attention to the cards, her heart pounding and her face growing warmer she turned the next one.

"The Wheel of Fortune," she announced, "Fate, destiny," she looked at him, "matters over the next few weeks may be out of your control."

He ran a hand through his dark hair. "The last six months have been out of my control, so that's not surprising."

"This reading is reinforcing the fact that everything has happened in the way that it was meant to. None of this has been an accident. The Universe is at work and you should not fight it. Just let events unfold as they are meant to," Her words were flowing as if oiled by the goddess herself and as Katya turned the next card she felt no surprise at seeing The Three of Cups". "You will experience joy. There will be a cause for celebration, perhaps even a family connection or an announcement. There may be an engagement or a wedding. You can look forward to a happy time."

He did not look up, but merely stared at the image of joy and unity of love depicted on the card.

"The next card is how others see you, and unfortunately at present, others are not quite understanding you in the way you would have hoped. The Moon shows people with more than one face. Be wary of those who present themselves as allies. They may not be as they seem. Only trust your intuition and your gut, don't listen to false words and forced smiles."

Glen tensed. "That's the trouble – the business is stopping me moving forward. I have so many loose ends to tie up and not everyone approves of what I am doing. Especially Stefan."

"Ah! Here is your meditation," Katya smiled as she turned the ninth card over, "Four of Swords. Evaluation. Take the time to connect with yourself and stay single-minded. This is about you, not everyone else. As the rest of the reading indicates, fate is at work, everything has changed and you have strong emotions. The meditation and the solitude you have found are perfect and necessary for your outcome."

"Which is?" He asked, curious, "What does this reading predict ultimately?"

Katya turned the final card over to find that there was another stuck to it. "Oh, you have two cards!"

"What does that mean?" He asked, looking excited.

"It means there are two parts to the outcome. The first is success, you have The Four of Wands, recognition and reward. Others are going to come round to your point of view eventually if you stick to your beliefs. The second is The High Priestess," Katya gasped, it was her favourite card, the one she most resonated with.

"And she is …?" He asked, looking at the image of Persephone, dressed in white with long, black hair to her waist.

Katya's eyes filled with tears. "She is your guide. A person, who will help you on your path, or she can represent your intuition. That is important. You must follow your spirit and listen to your guide."

"Is she you?" He asked innocently, not realising Katya's own connection to the card, "After all, you are the only person who has come close to understanding all this and helping me."

Katya struggled to speak as she focused on holding her tears in. She wanted to hold him, to kiss him and reassure him. As she looked at the vulnerability on this strong man's face her heart seemed to break in two. All his pain and all his confusion were hers too. She loved him. "I don't know."

He looked at her and a tear rolled down her cheek, so immense was her connection with him. Perhaps she should not have done this reading?

"Are you okay?"

"Yes, yes, I'm fine. It's just such a wonderful reading. It confirms you are doing the right thing," she wiped the tear away feeling embarrassed and already feeling the spiritual connection diminish, her skin becoming cooler as the reading came to a close.

They sat looking at the cards spread out before them, the rain still pouring hard. The silence between them seemed to swell with an expectation of conversation, yet there were no words to say. The sound of the clock ticking and the rain beating on the glass were the only sounds as they sat, his eyes studying the cards. Katya was worried he may hear her heart beating.

Eventually, he spoke. "I will never remember all this, not properly."

"I'll type it up for you," Katya replied. She felt drained and tired. It was like an afterglow. The come down after the high. Reality was seeping back in and her spiritual connection with him was disintegrating.

"Thank you ...Katya," he looked at her deeply and she noticed his eyes dilate, the deep greyish green around his irises becoming more intense.

She smiled, his words meaning the world to her, touching her heart. The way he spoke her name in his soft yet clear voice seemed to echo through her and she felt almost lost, wanting to take him into her arms and feel his soul as she knew they had been once before. In that moment her heart was his again, if only for an instant in a place of joy. Would she ever tell him how much he meant to her? How could she, knowing that he was obsessed with the woman from his vision? It was futile. Yet surely she had not imagined the way he had looked at her?

Feeling once again awkward under his gaze, she put her glasses back on and wondered what was going through his mind. Did he mean to look at her the way he had? Was he even aware of the effect he had upon her? It felt as though their connection was now lost and she fought the urge to cry again. No wonder Eliza felt exhausted when she had done a lot of readings.

He sat for a few moments, staring at the cards.

"Do you do other things?"

"Sorry?" She asked.

"I mean other spiritual things. Healing and all that sort of stuff?"

"I am attuned to Reiki, but I never got my certificate so legally I can't practice. And I did a course in hypnotherapy but again, not qualified," she sighed, "There are so many things I want to train in. But it all costs money."

He nodded and smiled. "You should give it some thought. I think you have a gift for helping others."

"Thank you," she smiled back, "Eliza, my boss wants to buy out the empty shop next door and turn it into a therapy room. Maybe if she did that I could learn more?" She was waffling again and willed herself to be silent and relish the moments she had with his presence.

"Don't give up on your dreams," he said as he stood and stretched a little, "You probably have a lot to get on with on your day off. I should go."

"You don't have to go!" She blurted out. Why had she just said that? "I mean, don't feel you need to rush off."

"Katya," he took her hand and she felt chills run through her, "You have done so much for me today. Thank you. But I need to go and think about the reading and maybe meditate. I don't expect you to give up any more of your time to help me."

"It's okay. Really," Katya replied, knowing that a dormant energy for love had re-awoken and was now bubbling away beneath her skin.

When he left, she ran straight back to her flat despite Merlin's noises. She needed to be alone for a long time to process what had just happened.

On re-entering her flat, she noticed that something was missing. She looked around. It was the noise of the clock. For the first time ever, her grandmother's clock had stopped. The air was still and she heard what sounded more like a whisper in her ear than the usual singing sound. Her mind interpreted this as a need to take note. Something significant was happening.

. . . . .

After waking from a fretful sleep, feeling exhausted rather than rested, Daisy decided to spend the day painting. She had dreamed yet again, of watching a violent storm take place from her attic window. It was devastating, and she saw distressing scenes of boats being dashed against the rocks. It was not helping her stress levels and she considered that taking a day off, doing what she loved, and using the dream as inspiration may help. She unwrapped one of the large, blank canvases, feeling excited as she fixed it to her easel, eyeing her array of acrylic paint pots just waiting to be opened. She wanted to fill the guest area with large paintings that would add to the effect she had created with the decor and furniture. Her stomach somersaulted as she realised that the addition of the paintings would mark the final finishing touches to the guesthouse and her true new beginning.

She mixed a dark base colour to begin with. The familiar feeling of the paintbrush in her hand was so natural and as she dabbed the first colour, diluting and blending the paint to form a stormy background, her mind seemed to empty as she focused on the movement and mixing of the colours. She worked quickly, adding darker areas, intending to highlight pockets of colour with white once she had created some depth. Loud drilling from the workmen in the bedrooms startled her and her hand skidded, leaving a harsh line of dark grey down the middle of the canvas. Not the effect she was hoping for. Annoyed, she placed her brush in water and quickly tried to blend the sharp line of paint before it dried. Smudgy and wrong. She tried again, adding a lighter colour, and just about salvaged her work. It wasn't the same. The feeling had gone.

Growling inwardly, she fiercely replaced the brush back in the water pot and stomped over to the window folding her arms. There was no point trying to paint until the workmen had gone. She wondered how she would feel when the guesthouse was full of strangers. That would be different. She would have her housekeeper, Siobhan, and her cook, Penny, who she had recently hired to work for her. All she would need to do was meet and greet, and then she could escape into her attic. It would be fine. The guests would not start drilling and hammering, she reminded herself. They would probably all go out after breakfast. She imagined herself painting all day and selling her work at local shops and online.

As she stood by the window, she felt as though someone had placed a gentle hand on her shoulder, a strange sensation that she had experienced before when she was standing in this spot. Today it felt particularly reassuring. The sound of the rain beating down and sight of the sea a little wilder than usual, reminded her of the dream, and she wondered how it would feel to walk in the rain. She imagined it blowing into her face, washing away her cares and worries, and this appealed to her dramatic nature. The fresh air and the views might inspire her, and put an end to her creative block once and for all.

Once she had decided on her course of action she hurriedly found a bag of clothes that she had retrieved from her parents' house, digging out a pair of old wellies and a waterproof coat. That was something she had never needed with Christophe. He was not a lover of the outdoors, and they travelled everywhere by car, usually chauffeur driven. She felt a small sense of rebellion as she stepped outside, allowing the wind to sweep her dark curls upwards before the rain then plastered them across her face. Pulling her hood up she proceeded to walk towards the coastal path and the woodlands. She felt anonymous, venturing out with no make-up, wearing her old denim shorts and the wellies. But nobody noticed. Nobody cared, everyone was keeping their head down. She was just another person braving the weather.

CHAPTER FOURTEEN

Glen walked back out into the rain, leaving the warmth of Katya's cottage behind, and the thought of returning to his caravan was unappealing. He desired solitude, needing to be on his own, yet the thought of being indoors was claustrophobic. Better to be out in this wild weather, feeling the power of whatever force was behind all these events he was experiencing. He had no doubt now that there was indeed a higher power – 'The Universe', Katya called it. Was it God? He did not know. He simply knew it was a beautiful light, one that made him feel great joy and the ultimate sensation of love. To walk in nature was surely the best way to communicate with this power, to feel its strength and glory and refresh his soul once more.

As he walked, he thought about the reading that Katya had given him, hearing her voice in his mind, recalling her wise words and her warm empathy extending to him across the table. He had felt an energy from her. She had confirmed that he was doing the right thing, to follow his gut instinct and listen to his intuition. His heart leapt as he heard her voice in his mind, saying that the universe was at work and fate was busy behind the scenes.

His thoughts turned to Daisy Hartford, the beautiful woman from his vision. Their chance meetings were no coincidence, Katya was right. This was all happening as it was supposed to be. He thought about the image on the final card, 'The High Priestess'. A woman standing between two pillars, long black hair down to her waist and the image had reminded him of Katya, if her hair were unplaited. She had cried when he asked her "Is this you?" and he wondered, not for the first time, why he found it so easy to talk to her and how readily she seemed to understand him when all others thought he was suffering some sort of mental breakdown. He desperately wanted to give her something in return for helping him, yet she had no idea just how much of a difference she had made, actually listening to him and making some sense of what he was feeling inside.

As he approached the coastal path, he paused to take stock of the cloudy skies, feeling the salt water against his face. He was in awe of the vastness of the ocean; he was so small in comparison. Everything he had once stood for, worked for, thrived for, was trivial and pointless. A minor fragment in the workings of the universal forces. The power of the sea, the strength of nature, the unstoppable cycle of the tide, that's what was real. The man-made world of machines, money and politics – what did it all matter, really? Who cared? He didn't. Love was all that mattered. He had been brought back in order to love. Something he had not encountered before his experience.

Had he loved Siân? He was in love with the idea of being with her and being the envy of other men. Had he viewed her as a possession just like his properties? The inauthenticity of his old life made him laugh out loud. A man scuttling past him on the path cast him a glance as though he suspected that Glen may be slightly mad. This thought too, made Glen laugh. It crossed his mind that perhaps he was insane. He could totally understand why people such as Stefan were finding his new way of life difficult to comprehend.

Thinking of Jayne and baby Leo, he reminisced on days gone by with Stefan and his own late brother. He felt deep concern. Katya had pointed out that Stefan may be a spanner in the works, and he understood why. He had a responsibility to them as a family. Jayne was clearly struggling with her new role as a mother, despite the front she tried to put on, and Stefan was fearful of losing his job. Glen decided, that out of loyalty he must, as a matter of priority speak to Helena Sharpe and ensure that Stefan's job was safe. He owed him that, at the very least.

Sighing and realising that he was not yet quite done with the business world, he began to walk some more. He headed towards a cove he had visited as a child with his parents and Leo before Heathstone Luxury Homes had even been a spark in his father's eye. He recalled them playing with Boo, their dog, digging in the sand with sticks while his mother sat on the rocks reading a book, and his father had helped them to explore the rocks. He remembered a thunderstorm breaking up the day however, and a small girl who had been watching them being led away by her brother in tears. The recollection of the memory confused him, returning as a powerful image in his mind. He shook his head and continued walking, his eyes filling with tears as he remembered seeing his father and Leo in the place he had visited when he died. It was so peaceful. He had told Carmen, his mother, this, and she had cried with relief. She had never recovered from Leo's untimely death. Glen now realised, with his new spiritual insight just how sad and alone his mother had felt. Hopefully, one day he would take Daisy to meet her.

. . . . .

Daisy made her way along the coast path, venturing into the woodlands, inhaling the rich aroma of the wet trees and bracken. The ground squelched underfoot, splattering droplets of mud upwards onto her bare legs. There was hardly a soul around other than the odd dog walker and she felt humble in her solitude, surrounded by a treasure-trove of nature. The tangle of tall trees, punctuated by clearings here and there. Places where travellers had perhaps once rested, branches forming natural seats and sheltered spaces. These trees and rocks had stood here for centuries. This was so different to the world she had shared with Christophe. Here, it didn't matter that she looked a mess, her hair drenched with rain. There were no red carpets, no one else to see her, and no judgement. It was bliss and it was real. She breathed in deeply.

Inspired by the beauty of the woodlands she took her phone from her rucksack and took some photographs of the trees. She doubted that the photos would capture the colours or the richness that she saw with her naked eye, but it was worth a try.

Eventually she reached some steps leading down to a cove she remembered from her childhood. On a fine day this cove would attract several visitors, but today it was almost deserted; the only noise was that of the waves crashing onto the rocks and lapping the shoreline. Daisy carefully picked her way across the pebble strewn sand and found a large rock to perch on, watching the way the wind and the rain whipped up the sea, creating foam. Picking up a pebble she skimmed it across the water enjoying the mild disruption it created to the ebb and flow of the water. Nothing ever stopped the tide. Pulled by the gravity of the moon and affected by the wind and temperature. She remembered the times she had come here as a child with her father and Heather. Life was so simple then, yet she hadn't realised at the time. How had she become so embroiled in a false world that, in reality, meant very little?

She became mesmerised by the water as she stared out, the rain soaking her to the skin even through her jacket. She did not care and gratefully allowed tears of relief to roll down her cheeks as she felt the final clutches of Christophe and her old life slipping away. Eliza was right, she did not have to follow all her dreams at once. She had already achieved a great deal and this was just the beginning. Feeling her heart lift for the first time in months, she concluded that she was happy. It did not matter what her mother thought, or her peers in Paris and London. This was home. She could now, finally, be herself. Her own house, her own business, the time to paint and her best friend living just a few minutes' walk away. It was perfect.

Smiling to herself she wiped her tears away and stood holding her arms out, letting the wind and the rain hit her even more. She picked up another pebble and threw it hard so that it skimmed across the surface of the water, and squealed with joy. Taking a step backwards she picked up another and did the same, and again. This was fun. On her next step backwards she stumbled, and twisted her ankle, falling against a rock. She heard footsteps rushing towards her.

"Are you okay?" A hand touched her arm reassuringly as she tried to rebalance herself.

"Yes I'm fine, I just caught my ankle, no broken bones …" She looked up to see a familiar face, momentarily feeling relief, until he pulled his hood down and she realised it was the man who had spilt the drinks over her. Glen Heathstone.

Her relief dissipated as a feeling of dread crept through her and she experienced a sensation of having been in this exact same moment before. It felt like a re-enactment. For a split second, just a tiny fragment of time, she knew exactly what was going to happen next. He was going to speak to her and she knew what he was going to say, feeling as though she could join in with his words. This impression of repetition and a consciousness of knowing what was about to happen felt foreign, yet strangely reassuring.

"So, we meet again," he said quietly, the very words she knew he would speak. Her precognition meant that she was unsurprised when a seagull landed on the rock right next to them, yet it still made her jump as her prior knowledge was now alarming her, and she was beginning to feel nauseous.

It seemed like long minutes, but was in reality just seconds, as though time itself were passing more slowly. Every movement and sound happened as she expected, as though she had experienced it before. Except she hadn't. Daisy finally felt her body and mind lurch back into the real world with a jolt. Yet, the past minutes had not seemed unlike reality at all. It had been very clear and present. She shook her head in disbelief.

"Are you okay? You look really worried," his face was kind and his voice soft, but she felt again that disarming power of discomfort around him. He took a step towards her, as she had anticipated he would do, and Daisy felt his hand touch her waterproofed arm again. Despite the plastic layer, there was an odd feeling when his fingers touched her and her solar plexus knotted up with anxiety. It was too intense and she was fearful. She was trapped. There was nowhere to hide, and no way to escape, unless she ran back into the woodlands.

He looked at her, concern spreading across his face as he looked into her eyes and she felt as though she was drowning, forced to look away. Not understanding her own reactions, there being no reasonable explanation for any of these extraordinary emotions, there was only one obvious solution; and that was to flee.

Daisy picked up her rucksack and put it back over her shoulders hastily. "I have to go! I have a meeting to get to!" She lied, already walking away from him briskly towards the steps, her wellingtons feeling heavy and cumbersome in her stride. Her ankle was still very tender, too.

She looked over her shoulder, seeing disappointment clouding his face.

"Wait! Please!" He began to follow her, "I am not going to hurt you."

Daisy ignored him, continuing to walk. Not only did her legs feel heavy but with the rain beating against her, and the shingle underfoot, she felt as though she was not moving anywhere near fast enough.

He was catching her up. "I *need* to talk to you. Please!" He called.

Daisy did not reply. Her heart was beating fast and she realised that if he followed her into the woodlands, she would be at his mercy. She momentarily visualised the headlines the next day, 'Lone Female Rambler Left for Dead,' and people questioning why on earth a woman had chosen to walk alone in the woods with a complete stranger. Telling herself quickly that she was being melodramatic and that no such thing was likely to happen, she had nevertheless unnerved herself enough. She climbed the steps as quickly as she could, the stone surface supporting her pace better than the sand. When she reached the safety of the first landing point, she checked over her shoulder, pausing slightly. He had made no effort to follow her but simply stood at the foot of the steps, his hands in his pockets, and his deep mossy eyes pleading for her to wait.

"Just let me talk to you," he begged.

"I told you," Daisy replied firmly, "I need to go!" She felt sick.

He walked to where he could reach up and she flinched half expecting him to grab her ankle, but he merely placed a card at her feet. "This has my details on," he shrugged, "In case you have lost the other two cards I gave you." He turned his back on her and walked away, with hunched shoulders.

Daisy watched him, wondering whether to run but the danger seemed to have passed. Thinking logically she picked the card up. If something happened to her, it would be evidence. Her cold hands screwed it up tightly, within her pocket, feeling angry as she walked the rest of the way up the steps. What had just happened? What did he want with her?

Once out of sight she walked so quickly that she was almost running back through the woods, her heart pounding, and her breathing fast. She tripped over tree roots, her boots slipping in the mud. She did not even pause until she was back to the safety of the open gardens, where, once sure he had not followed her, she stopped to lean against one of the benches. Her twisted ankle was throbbing. An old man with his dog walked past her, and asked if she was okay. His voice sounded as though it were a recording, being played in slow motion, through a fog. It felt as though the real world did not exist. She nodded to the man, still out of breath, and thanked him as he went on his way. She needed to speak to Eliza.

CHAPTER FIFTEEN

Katya entered Eliza's shop, feeling odd to be a customer for a change. She had decided to treat herself to some dream stones to keep by her bedside and a new journal for her awakening thoughts. The dreams were intriguing and she felt they were connected with Glen and her cottage. Following the intensity of the reading and the realisation that she was, whether she liked it or not, falling in love with him, she now wanted answers of her own. She concluded that her dreams may provide the key.

"What are you doing here on your day off?" Eliza grinned, as Katya emerged from the outdoors, squeezing raindrops from her long plait.

"I need a couple of things," she replied, "And I want to talk to you about something. I need your opinion."

"Okay!" Eliza jumped down from her stool, "I'll put the kettle on."

Katya removed her wet coat and made her way over to the journals, choosing one that had caught her eye during the last week, with an angel on the front cover. Picking up the bag of dream stones, she placed them on the counter as Eliza returned from the back of the shop.

"Ah, dreams. You mentioned this the other day. Then I had to dash off. Sorry. You said you were in old fashioned clothing if I remember?" Eliza recalled.

"Yes. I am dreaming I am in the past. I am in my cottage, but I have dealings with a large house on the cliff top too."

"Is it a recurring dream?" Eliza asked.

"Not as such – each one is different, but I am the same person in each dream."

"You are not you then?"

"Well I am me, I look like me, but younger and slimmer and I am called Annette. And I know all the other people in my dream. There is Mama and Arabella, my sister – she has been ill. Papa is missing in the storm, and then there is the big house. I know the staff, and there is a man under the tree, but I don't know him."

"Whoa, slow down!" Eliza cried.

"Sorry. It's just that I have been dying to tell you about this, to make sense of it, but you have been so busy with Daisy we haven't had a chance to talk."

"Yeah, I know," Eliza said apologetically, "I don't mean to keep disappearing, but I do worry about her."

"I know. It's okay," Katya smiled, "There is something else as well." She hesitated unsure whether to tell Eliza about Glen.

"What?" Eliza asked, concern spreading over her face.

"Well," Katya paused, "I wasn't going to tell you about this, but I think I should."

"Go on."

"There was a customer that came in a few weeks ago. A man. A very nice man, very charming and very attractive."

"Oh I see," Eliza replied with a smirk.

"No, no, no, I don't mean that. He is lovely, but he is lost. He talked to me for ages about an experience he had and I think I can help him, and – don't hate me for this – but I read his cards for him this morning."

"What?"

"I know, I'm really sorry! I tried to encourage him to come to you for a reading, but he wanted me to do it. I didn't charge him though. It wasn't a business thing."

"No, I didn't mean that. I had no idea you could read the cards!"

Katya was relieved. "Well I don't. I mean I didn't – just for friends when I lived in the Midlands."

"But this is fantastic! You can help me out. Sometimes I have days when I have too many readings. We could share the work," Eliza was beaming at her.

Katya shook her head. "No, I am not good enough, I mean I have never read professionally before."

"Did it work today?"

"Well, yes, it was amazing. I felt a real connection to him."

"Have a think about it," Eliza smiled, "No pressure, but it would help me out a lot if you could do a couple of readings a week."

"I will have a think," Katya replied, feeling more confident, and pleasantly surprised by Eliza's reaction.

"Are you attracted to him?" Eliza asked.

"Well I do feel some kind of ..."

The door flew open and Daisy burst in. "Oh my god you have to help me!" She cried.

Katya's heart sank as Eliza's attention switched immediately to the drenched, out-of-breath woman that stood in the doorway.

"What's happened?" Eliza shrieked, rushing towards her friend and placing a protective arm around her, steering her towards the counter.

"That man again! The one from the restaurant and the meeting with Stella and Brandon. He is stalking me I swear!" Daisy was out of breath and her words rolled out quickly.

"Okay, what makes you say that?" Eliza frowned.

"Well I went for a walk in the rain, along the coast path to clear my head, and then I was on the beach at that cove. You know the little one, and he was there and I knew exactly what was going to happen next, it was so weird. I freaked out and ran away through the woods."

"Did he try and follow you? Did he hurt you?" Eliza asked.

"No. But he could have done. I was all alone and he appeared from nowhere. He could have been watching me for ages, he was right behind me. Then he looked at me, and I felt all weird like I always do when I see him, then I knew exactly what was going to happen next. I knew what he was going to say, I knew he would touch my arm. I even knew the seagull was going to land on the rock next to me. It was so weird."

"Déjà vu," Katya said quietly.

"What?" Daisy asked, looking at her as though she was an alien.

"Déjà vu. The feeling of having been somewhere before and pre-empting exactly what will happen next."

"Yes, that's what it was," Daisy nodded, "But what does it mean?"

"Well, some say it can be an indication of a past life," Eliza replied, "Although there are other more scientific explanations."

"Oh not the past life thing again!" Daisy shook her head, "I was so scared. Every time I see him I feel so strange, so intense. I don't understand it."

Katya was uncertain whether or not to add to the conversation, but could not resist. "That too could be an indication of a past life connection – strong feelings about someone that you don't know very well."

Eliza nodded; "Kat's right. What did he say to you?"

Daisy sighed. "He asked if I was okay, as I had stumbled and hurt my ankle, and then he told me that he really needs to talk to me."

"Well, maybe you *should* talk to him?" Eliza suggested, "At least then you might have more idea what is going on?"

Daisy shook her head. "No. I have enough going on without all this. Put this in the bin would you?" She took a crumpled piece of card from her pocket and thrust it onto the counter next to Katya's dream stones.

Eliza left the card where it was. "I think you are over-reacting."

"No I'm not. There is something about him that makes me feel uncomfortable. When he looks at me I feel fear and this overwhelming recognition, like something bad is about to happen."

"Past life again!" Eliza smiled.

"Stop it!" Daisy cried, "I don't want my past life, I am enjoying my current one."

Katya was becoming annoyed by Daisy's dismissal of Eliza's help. "Look, I had better go," she reached for her purse to pay for the items.

"Have these on me, Kat," Eliza said, scooping the items into a bag. "You have been so helpful over the past few weeks, it's the least I can do."

"Thank you," Katya replied, taking the bag, "I'll see you tomorrow." As she walked out of the shop she felt sad. She felt anger towards Daisy, but was not sure exactly why. Yes, the woman was annoying, dramatic and wouldn't listen even to her best friend. But this was deeper. Katya hated to admit it, as she tried to see the good in everyone, but she really didn't like Daisy Hartford. She walked home in the rain, now desperate to return to the safety and comfort of her cottage and leave this whole Daisy charade behind. Perhaps little Merlin would still be on the stairs. She called into the small supermarket and bought some milk and kitten food.

. . . . .

Glen wondered if he was being intrusive returning to Katya's cottage so soon and without an invite. He had taken up enough of her time already today but he could not think of anyone else who would understand or listen to him. Stefan was certainly not someone he could confide in at the moment, nor any of his old friends. They were too far away, and it would mean explaining everything again. He was losing enough face as it was, among peers who were now shaking their heads at him as a lost cause. He could picture their reactions. The false smiles above their suits, smug at his apparent downfall. The success that had turned to catastrophe following a spiritual awakening. He was probably a laughing stock amongst the old boys. Weak and emotional. A failure. He did not care.

He walked briskly now, anxious to tell Katya about the meeting at the cove, how Daisy had run from him, and his fears that she would never listen to him. This was the only problem he had. The knowledge that Daisy was connected to his return from the brink of death was clouded by her continuous dismissal. If there was no purpose for his life then he would gladly go back to the beautiful place where he had encountered his father and Leo. He knew he was meant to meet Daisy for a reason, but getting her to stand still and listen was another matter. She appeared to be terrified of him.

He reached Katya's cottage and rang the doorbell hoping she wouldn't mind his interruption. Eventually he heard the sound of footsteps, and Katya opened the door. She looked shocked to see him.

"Sorry!" He wanted to explain his presence quickly, "I have to talk to you, but if it's not convenient please say."

"What are you sorry for?" She asked.

"To turn up again. On the same day."

"Are you okay?"

"No. Not really."

Concern crossed her face. "Is it because of my reading?"

"No. No! The reading was great. It's something else. I actually came here because you are the only person who I can talk to," he was relieved to see her face soften, and realised that her defensiveness stemmed from her own lack of confidence,

She opened the door wider for him and he was surprised at how much he longed to be in her flat once more, away from his isolation and to be with someone who actually cared. He followed her through the door, which she shut firmly behind him. "Sorry I didn't mean to slam, but Merlin might run out."

"Merlin?" He asked, then nodded as Katya emerged from the corner with the black fluffy creature in her arms.

"He is a live wire. Here, you hold him while I put the kettle on."

"Do you have anything stronger to drink?" Glen asked, flinching as the kitten patted his cheek with its paw.

"I have a bottle of white wine in the cupboard that Eliza gave me. It's unopened, I don't drink."

"That'll do. If you don't mind?" He found the softness of the kitten comforting as Merlin nestled against his chest; Glen could feel the small animal purring as he stroked him, "I might get a dog you know …"

Katya nodded, uncorking the bottle and pouring him a glass, making herself a cup of chamomile tea. "Pets are good for the soul. Very calming," she ushered him to one of her two armchairs, switching on her lamps as the clouds outside were now mixing with the threat of winter's early dusk.

He sat down, feeling immediately at ease in this small, cosy flat with its books and cushions. As he sipped the wine and looked at the patient and kind woman sitting opposite him, he was grateful beyond belief to have this new friend who was prepared to listen to him.

"Thank you," he said softly.

"What for?" Katya looked surprised and adjusted her glasses.

"For being here and allowing me to come and talk to you again."

"It's fine. Your story fascinates me."

"Really?" He was surprised, no one else seemed interested in his experience.

Katya nodded as Merlin jumped down from Glen's lap and proceeded to play with a feather that must have blown in from outside.

"What have you been buying from your own shop?" Glen pointed to the familiar purple paper bag that sat next to Katya on the coffee table.

"Oh, it's not my shop. It's Eliza's," Katya proceeded to open the bag and took out the journal and the dream stones. A small crumpled card fell from the bag as she did so, and Merlin made a beeline for the new plaything as Glen leaned forward to retrieve it, "I have been having a few interesting dreams, so I bought these to assist me in understanding them."

"Why is one of my business cards here?" Glen attempted to pull the card straight and he was surprised, not only by the card, but also by the expression on Katya's face. She looked at him in complete shock as though something very drastic had happened.

"Your card…?" She asked, her eyes wide, as she began to twirl her long, black plait in her fingers.

"What's the matter?" He was worried now, he had never seen her look this way before. She was normally so calm.

· · · · ·

Jayne drove carefully along the country lane, cat's eyes lighting the way. She hated driving alone in the dark and it took all her concentration. However she would soon be clear of the country and safely back in more populated areas with streetlights, shops and houses. Stefan was still at work. She had left a note telling him she was going to her mother's for a few days. He would not mind as he knew she had a strong bond with her mother. There was nothing unusual about it.

What he didn't know was that she had also arranged a meeting with her manager to discuss returning to work and a meal with two of her girlfriends to catch up and relax. Jayne smiled to herself as she reached the turning from 'the middle of nowhere', as she called it, and civilisation began to emerge at the roadside. A row of shops, people walking on pavements, a bus and traffic lights. She was no longer alone, and she needed this break. Just a few days where she could be Jayne again. The old Jayne who was good at her job and had a sense of fun and adventure. She might even get a decent sleep if her mother would be kind enough to care for Leo.

She glanced at the sleeping babe safely strapped into the carrier on the passenger seat. He was so peaceful now. Only two hours earlier she had been unable to stop him crying. She had felt out of her depth. Everything she had tried to do to console him had failed. Other mothers didn't seem to have this problem. Apparently their babies were in perfect routines and they suggested that Leo was picking up on Jayne's own anxiety. Their sideways glances told her, that these women – this clan of fantastic mothers – considered her to be the root of the problem. Their babies were content. Their babies slept. Their babies would become advanced neurosurgeons and barristers, because they were so amazingly ahead in their development. *Well good for them!* Jayne thought with a feeling of rebellion. Perhaps Leo, *her baby,* would turn out to be an intrepid explorer, guided by herself, once he was old enough to enjoy the outdoors. She would have bet that none of the mums at the horrible baby and toddler group had ever climbed the Three Peaks or gone white-water rafting. If they had known that level of excitement and adrenalin, they would surely not find the mundane world of baby mash and omega three so exhilarating.

Stefan did not understand this part of her life. He did not have to endure the comparison conversations, and would not take them so personally if he did. It did not matter to him how many hours of sleep his son had during the day, or what brand of formula was being used. When Jayne tried to talk to him about her worries, he would laugh them off, and tell her to go and have a bath and relax. That was all very well, but Jayne had never been a bath type girl; she was more of a shower-on-the-go woman. Why now, just because she had become a mother, would she want to lie in a bath full of bubbles, still on edge because she could hear Leo crying downstairs? And the bathroom was less than idyllic. They had plans to rip out the old suite and replace it with a modern one, with new tiles and heated towel rails. As it was she sat in a scuffed avocado green bathtub looking at chipped brown patterned tiles. She could think of nothing less relaxing.

That afternoon, unable to bear the crying any longer, she had called her mother to check she was in. She had quickly packed a bag for herself and Leo, and called her boss and her best friend to arrange both the meeting and the meal. Amazed at how quickly she had managed to alter her routine for the next few days, she had hurriedly scribbled a note for Stefan. With lightning speed, before anything could possibly thwart her plan, she had thrown the bags into the car, strapped Leo in safely and started the engine, knowing that Leo would sleep once the car was moving.

Returning to work would be the key, she decided in her new-found optimism. Just a couple of days a week to start with. The drive wasn't too long, and she was sure her mother would help out with Leo. It would all be fine. She would be back to the old Jayne in no time. That would show Stefan. She smiled angrily. Let him miss her. Let him come home to an empty house and see just how isolating it could be. That would teach him for taking her for granted and forgetting her identity as a woman. He had forgotten her as his lover and his companion. She thought back to their travelling days, hours spent in each other's company, pushing their bodies to the limits as they explored and adventured together. They saw great sights, wonders of nature from the highest peaks, before tired and aching, they made love under the sunset or the stars.

Now he saw her differently. She had crossed the line from his youthful sexy soul mate to become his burden of responsibility. A woman who could not cope with her own child, a woman who snapped at him because she was so tired, a woman he no longer wanted. Her eyes filled with tears and she gripped the steering wheel tightly as she recalled the email she had read by accident. The real trigger for the events of the day.

As she slowed down to enter the twenty mile zone of the housing estate where her mother lived, Leo stirred and his eyes began to open, taking her attention away from herself again.

"Sshh baby boy," she whispered, "We are nearly at Grandma's." He gurgled putting his small fist in his mouth and waggling his feet gently. He was hungry.

"Nearly there," Jayne cooed in a soft voice, relieved to see the entrance to her family home and looking forward to a long weekend with her mum.

· · · · ·

Katya was lost for words and she felt as though time was frozen. The card was, she realised, the card that Daisy's 'stalker' had passed to her. The same card that Daisy had screwed up and slammed onto Eliza's counter, and somehow it had ended up in her bag of shopping. This meant that Glen was the man that Daisy was so unnerved by. The man that she claimed was following her. The one Eliza felt she had a past life connection to. As her mind processed the facts, her intuition told her that Daisy must be the woman from Glen's vision. The woman that he was desperate to be with.

"Are you okay?" He asked.

She couldn't answer him yet, she needed time to think. "Yes I'm fine," she answered, shaking her head.

She then tried to focus on what Glen was talking about as he sat opposite her, but he became out of focus. She was too warm and felt sick, her stomach sinking like a sharp stone. She zoned in and out of what he was saying, talking about his father, his guilt over the business and his experience which was so amazing, so enlightening. While she would have usually been all ears and listened intently to his conversation, at this moment in time all she wanted was an answer to the burning question – was Daisy Hartford the purpose of his whole being?

She focused once more, his image becoming sharper as she tuned in to his aura, wanting to see just how much he was feeling. It was full of colour, which was good for him, and all over the place. But she could not concentrate until she knew the truth. Had he come round here purely to tell her he had met Daisy this afternoon and that she had run away?

"Why did you come round tonight?" She interrupted him abruptly, and he looked surprised.

"Sorry?"

"Just why did you come over tonight? To talk about your experience or to ask about something more specific?"

"Well, I er… wanted to tell you about …"

"Cut to the chase Glen and tell me what has happened since you left this morning," Katya was as surprised as he was at her direct approach.

"I went for a walk after my reading. I wanted to feel the rain and..."

"…Where?"

"The coast path, but what does it matter where?" He frowned as though Katya had stepped into some forbidden territory.

"Did you meet the woman from your vision while you were walking?" She asked, her heart beating fast and her head beginning to hurt.

"How did you …? I mean, yes I did … I was just getting to that."

"So … Let me guess. You met her. Again. It didn't go to plan, in fact she ran away from you."

Glen shook his head; "How did you know?"

"So she runs off and you just turn up here again to tell me all about it and hope that I have the answers!"

He took a large sip of wine. "Yes. Sorry, I didn't mean to upset you."

Katya wanted to cry. Daisy was the woman. The object of Glen's obsession, his purpose and his mission. She had so wanted to help him, she still did – but Daisy? Did she really want to help him get together with this drama queen with her airs and graces? She was not sure.

"Katya, what is it?"

She could not speak. She did not know what to say. There were no words to explain how she was feeling, as she did not understand how she was feeling herself. "Excuse me, I just need a minute," she walked into the kitchen and closed her eyes, listening for a message, listening for the singing. She heard nothing, other than her own heartbeat. Her throat felt choked, too tight to let out the questions she wanted answers to. She wanted to scream or to cry but she could do neither. Her face was hot and her mouth dry.

What did Daisy have that was so amazing? She had Eliza running around after her and now Glen was shaping his whole future based on an image of her face. Her own dreams had started the night Daisy had arrived, and the feelings Daisy had described when she was with Glen were not dissimilar to those Katya had experienced herself. What was going on? Daisy's arrival had created a ripple effect and Katya was caught up in the tide whether she liked it or not. Were they all linked in some way?

She had a gut feeling that destiny was in motion, remembering the cards in Glen's reading; she knew she now had a choice to either walk away from it all, or continue to help him. The image of 'The High Priestess' in his cards returned to her. It had represented herself. She knew it and he knew it. But what was the connection? She must stand by her offer to help him, and, for her own peace of mind, she needed to understand this. Taking a deep breath she returned to the lounge.

"Sorry. I don't know quite what came over me. Forgive me please," she sat down and refilled his glass, "Tell me what happened Glen."

"Are you sure? I didn't want to upset you," his eyes looked genuinely concerned.

"It's fine. I am trying to work some stuff out for myself, and it may be linked to you and Daisy. I want to help you, but I also need to know what is happening."

"You know Daisy?"

"Yes, she is friends with my boss, Eliza," Katya sighed and fetched another glass from the kitchen; she poured a small amount of wine for herself.

"You don't drink," he looked at her quizzically.

"I do tonight. Tell me what happened."

As Glen described almost exactly the same scenario as Daisy – including the feelings of déjà vu, Katya became convinced that this was no ordinary meeting of two people. This was something significant, and could not be ignored. She needed to speak to Sheryl.

Eventually Glen left, and when she returned from seeing him out she discovered that Merlin was nowhere to be seen. Panicking, she called him and looked under all the furniture. She stood silently, waiting for a noise to signal his presence and was rewarded by a scuffling sound from under the wood burner. Kneeling down, feeling thankful that it was not lit, she scooped the small creature out from under the tight space beneath. As she pulled him out, something was dragging along the floor in his paws. She cuddled him, relieved that he was safe, and prised the item from his tiny claws. It looked like a very thin pendant on a broken chain. On closer inspection she could see that it was an old coin, but that the usual markings found on a coin were mainly worn away. The thin chain, threaded through a hole in the top, was dirty.

Taking the item into the kitchen, she found a cloth and began to polish the coin gently to see if any markings appeared. They did. Engraved roughly into the metal were letters that looked like 'R & A' and there was something underneath it, very small. It looked like a series of four numbers, but she could not make out what they said.

A knock at the door interrupted her, and she went to answer it, still holding the coin.

It was Josie. "Do you still have Merlin?" She asked, "Sorry, I've only just got in from work, and saw your note."

"Yes, he is fine. Come on in," Katya opened the door wider, and Josie walked in, making a beeline for the kitten who was sitting on Katya's armchair.

"Hello little one. Did mummy lock you out again?" She picked him up and nuzzled his fur, "Sorry Katya, and thank you for looking after him."

"It's no trouble, I love cats, and he is a delight," Katya sidled over to Josie, "and look what he has found," she showed her the coin pendant, "It was under the wood burner."

Josie, holding Merlin in one hand, took the coin in the other and held up to the light.

"What do you think it is?" Katya asked.

"Hmm, at first glance I think it is an old love token."

"A love token?"

"Yes, you see the initials have been carved into a coin, and there is what appears to be a year underneath it."

"But why would anyone give an old coin as a love token?"

"In olden times, working class folk would not have been able to afford jewellery, so they would make their own. A coin etched with lovers' initials would have been a way of presenting someone with a token of their affection."

"Wow," Katya sighed, "That is romantic."

"It would have been given to someone who was almost engaged, like an unofficial betrothal, perhaps in secret. There would have been many working class people living around here in Victorian times due to the fishing. This town has always been associated with the fishing industry, and while the affluent would have been few, many men would have worked as fishermen or boat builders."

"What about the women?" Katya asked with interest, thinking of her dreams, "What would they have done?"

"Mainly sewing and stitching, perhaps making nets and baskets. It would have been a good job for a working class woman to be a seamstress or to do repairs and decorative sewing for the more affluent."

Katya's heart skipped a beat as she made the connection between this information and the dream of visiting the large house.

"Oh, how fascinating! I wish we could find out more about the coin."

"If you would allow me to borrow it, I can take it into work and have it analysed. They may be able to identify the date, and find out more."

"Yes please!" Katya clasped her hands together, excited. This was reassuring after the day's turn of events.

"I have found out more about this cottage too," Josie smiled, "It was built in the early 1800's as housing for the fishermen and their families. I am looking into census data to try and find out who actually lived here. However, census data from the Victorian era was not as comprehensive as it is today."

"I would be interested in anything you can find out, about the cottage, or the coin," Katya smiled.

"I will keep you posted," Josie agreed, "Anyway, I had better get this little rascal back upstairs, thank you again for looking after him."

"It's a pleasure. Always," Katya smiled.

CHAPTER SIXTEEN

Katya was walking along one of the small alleyways that led out from the harbour. It was becoming dark even though it was still the afternoon as it was winter, and it was cold, freezing cold. She waited as always in the doorway that was hidden from view, waiting for the familiar sound of his boots on the cobblestones. Wrapping her shawl around her and holding her breath, she heard nothing but the wind howling through the narrow street. Had he found her note? She had been bold and passed it to him quite directly as she walked past him on purpose at the market. It was possible that someone had seen her, and she knew it was forward behaviour, but she needed to know and had thrown caution to the wind. Since seeing him standing under the tree at the big house, she had been thinking of him, wondering what had caused his change of heart. They had been so close, for so long.

As it grew a little darker, she feared that he may not come, but then she heard the boots and him clearing his throat to signal that it was him, and not to be afraid. At least he had remembered that.

Eventually he stood before her, his face shielded by the shadow of the walls. She could feel his breath warm in the cold winter air. As he spoke, his voice plucked every string that held her soul together, and she could feel her resolve crumbling before him. She had intended to be restrained, to await his explanation first, but she still felt a deep, deep cord uniting them. She could feel it in her heart, her stomach, her womb. Her face was tingling as she heard herself ask

"What is with you that ye do not wish to meet no more? Do I not please you?" Her heart was pounding, her yearning so deep for his love it brought tears to her eyes. The pain of knowing he was about to tell her he had found the arms of another.

"Annette," he began, and at the sound of his voice she felt reassured.

"Yes?"

"Annette, we are no longer children. It is time to grow up."

"What do you mean?"

"I have seen a new world. One that I would never have dreamed of."

She did not know what he meant. But she pleaded to his heart. The heart that had once loved her.

"Then take me too."

He put a gentle finger to her lips;

"Sshh, you are not wise in the ways. I have a journey now. A purpose."

"I don't understand? We were to be…"

"Yes, we were childhood friends and that turned to love, and I still love you, but I have been shown a different way."

"Is it someone at the house? The big house?" His silence told her it was, "What is she to you? And who is she?"

"You need not know. Annette, I have a journey ahead."

"Where?"

"There is a boat sailing tonight with a promise of good work and money," he coughed, "I am to be on that boat."

"No! Stay here, I implore you," Annette felt her heart rip into two.

"I need money. I have plans when I return."

"Plans?"

"I cannot talk of them. It is a secret."

"We never had secrets. Is it her? At the house? Are you to be wed?"

"She is educated. She reads poetry to me. And she will teach me to read once she is recovered from her fever. She is to make me a gentleman."

Annette was numb, lost and silent. She wanted to scream. Instead she cried. He pulled her towards him, probably to muffle the sound as footsteps and voices were approaching, and she could feel his heart beating through the thin linen shirt, smelling his warmth and relishing this just-for-a-moment poignant feeling of safety. She could stay here forever, with no need of any other nourishment. When she desired no other, why was he so enamoured with this educated lady? Once the passers-by were gone, she pushed him away, feeling cold as his arms released her and she was empty for a moment until his voice sounded once more.

"Annette, please understand. Tonight I must go."

"No!" It was unbearable and she heard herself say, "You will be killed. Don't go."

"I will not be killed, I am with men of the sea, men who have travelled before. Tonight we set sail."

Annette felt sick, not just from the loss of her love but from a feeling of premonition. She wanted to hold onto him and never let him go and her arms took hold of him.

He pulled her hands from him and she realised her fingers were almost digging into his flesh.

"Annette. Let Go!" He commanded, pushing her away.

"As you wish," she broke free and ran, defiantly, wishing that she had never heard his voice, or felt his embrace, or ever kissed his lips. But she had, and the pain seared through her heart. Tears streamed down her flushed cheeks, and she could feel his eyes watching her run from him, his words like swords in the soft flesh of her back leaving scars that would never heal. She ran until she reached the cottage, her mama stood at the hearth wringing her hands on her apron.

"Annette, where the devil have you been?"

"Just leave me mama," she cried, attempting to run past her mother, but the woman was too quick, taking her firmly by the shoulders, and tilting her daughter's face up to look into her eyes. Mama's face softened.

"And so there it is" her mother said quietly, "The love is in your heart."

Annette was shaking, the tears now spilling at the warmth she felt from her mother. "Mama?" she cried.

"Annette, you are not the first and you won't be the last. Alas for you the time is not right, and your heart will mend," she took her daughter into her arms as her slim body quivered like a small, broken animal. The quivering turned into heaving sobs, each one racked with a pain that was unrelenting.

"My heart will never mend. Never!" Annette sobbed, her words muffled by her mother's body. Her head was pounding, his touch still in her veins, his words still in her ears, her heart beating as though it may explode. Her stomach felt ripped into pieces, her legs ached. Her energy was lapsing, and she began to feel dizzy and faint. She would never mend. Never heal. Never. No more.

Katya awoke in tears, and in her half-sleep she scrawled on the notepad beside her before drifting back into her slumber.

CHAPTER SEVENTEEN

Brandon sat at Daisy's kitchen table and fired up the laptop. "Wait until you see this," he smiled proudly.

She pulled her chair closer to him, her arm and shoulder resting against his, and he shifted slightly, as he showed her the homepage of her new website. He had used the sign above the door which was simple and displayed the name of the guesthouse as the header for the site and used neutral colours to make it stand out. A moving, changing gallery of beautiful photos of the exterior and communal areas set the scene perfectly for what Daisy had wanted to create.

Daisy gasped. "It looks so professional!"

"Of course it does! I did it," he smiled, scrolling onto the next page, "Here are the photographs of the bedrooms with a link to the booking page and here is your team page." He clicked onto the next page to display a photograph of Daisy and her two new employees, Siobhan and Penny.

"Oh, I actually look quite good," Daisy smiled and smoothed her hair, "You are a good photographer."

He laughed. "It helps when you have people who know how to work the camera."

"Well I had a lot of practice with Christophe," Daisy became a little subdued at this recollection, and although her proximity and need for compliments were annoying him, he put up with it a little longer.

"This is the only page that now needs more work, and this is for your reviews and testimonials. Stella is right that you need to get some guests to stay and leave some comments that you can post."

"Well Stella is working on that as part of the launch," Daisy nodded, "Thanks to your firmness with her at the last meeting, I think she has chivvied up a little."

"Well, someone needed to give her a kick up the backside," Brandon shrugged.

"I don't know how to thank you. This is amazing!" She touched his hand and he moved it away slowly, not wanting to be rude, but also concerned that Daisy was a little too close to him lately. She had kissed him on the cheek after the photo shoot, and stood leaning against him quite intentionally as she had been trying to see the photos on the camera. Not having known Daisy for very long, he wondered if it was just her way, but he did not want to encourage her if she was making subtle advances towards him. He was, despite his outward appearance, a very private person and she was Eliza's best friend. Perhaps Daisy saw him as the safe dependable male in her life at the moment, the no-threat flirt and validation for her attractiveness following her divorce. He did not want the responsibility and with Eliza's defensiveness around relationships in general, following her own father's desertion, he did not want to give her any cause for concern.

"I have also listed you on all the travel websites and put all the links in," edging a little further away, he showed Daisy what he had done.

"This is perfect, just perfect!"

"I have sent all the photos to Stella too, so she should have set all your PR up."

"Hey, let's check," Daisy took the laptop from him and logged in to her email. Sure enough there was an email from Stella with links to the social media accounts and confirmation that tonight a press release would be published. She followed the links and beamed as she saw what Stella had done, "Oh wow, this is real! This is finally happening."

"You already have forty-five followers," Brandon pointed out.

"Oh my," Daisy grinned, clicking on one of the photos that Stella had posted, "and over sixty people already like this photo and there are three shares!" She clicked again and scrolled down the list of likes, "Oh, I might know he would have to get involved!" She grimaced.

"Who?" Brandon asked.

"Glen bloody Heathstone. He has liked it and shared it."

"Who is that? Is it that guy who spoke to us in the restaurant?"

"Yes. He is everywhere," Daisy frowned, "He's doing my head in."

"Hey, don't knock it, all publicity is good publicity, remember. His sharing could gain you a lot of business," Brandon reclaimed his laptop and logged out of the site.

"Yes but the last thing I need is another wealthy man trying to control me," Daisy sighed and touched his arm, "But I suppose you are right Brandon, it is positive."

"Well, if he gets too in your face, I am sure Stella will be able to take him off your hands!" Brandon laughed, and so did Daisy.

"Ah you make me laugh Brandon. And I need laughter at the moment," her hand was on his arm again and she was leaning so close he could smell her perfume, "Laughter is good for the soul, and you are just amazing!" She kissed him quickly on the cheek, very swiftly, but the action crossed a boundary that he was not altogether comfortable with.

"Hey it's nothing," he pushed her away gently, closing the laptop and standing up. It was time to leave.

"Are you going?" She asked, her face disappointed.

"Yes, I have a lot to do today," he lied.

"Okay," she also stood.

"Look, you should go and paint or something, or better still, get on your social media and reply to your comments and likes." He put the laptop in its bag and donned his coat.

"You can't go without a hug," Daisy pouted, pulling him towards her and wrapping her arms around him. He reluctantly put his arms around her too and allowed another kiss on the cheek before moving swiftly towards the front door. It was not that he didn't like her. He just didn't want to be in such a compromising position with someone who was not Eliza. No woman could ever be Eliza.

. . . . .

Luckily Jayne's mother had been more than happy to look after Leo, relishing time with her grandson and enabling Jayne to attend the meeting with her manager, Nina.

It felt oddly familiar as Jayne walked through the office, saying hello to colleagues she hadn't seen properly for almost a year. Everything was exactly the same, give or take a change in hairstyle or two. Everyone commented on how well she looked and asked cheerily after Leo. She could feel the old Jayne returning with each step she took across the grey carpet that led towards Nina's office. Smiling, she knocked on the door before opening it, expecting to see Nina with a large mug of coffee and her pen behind her ear, typing away. Instead she saw Nina sitting still, the coffee in a pot and Stan, a senior manager next to her.

Nina gave her a broad smile before standing to greet her.

"Jayne, it's so lovely to see you," she said.

This felt wrong. If Stan hadn't been there Nina would have launched into a diatribe of what had been happening, and how stressed she was.

"Nina, Stan. It's good to see you," Jayne smiled nervously.

"Take a seat please," smiled Stan.

Jayne sat down and was relieved when Nina poured her a coffee.

"Two sugars isn't it?"

"Oh no, not anymore," Jayne replied, "I am trying to lose the baby bulge. Just milk please."

Nina smirked at her in a kind way and Jayne relaxed a little; perhaps Stan was here to offer her some flexible working patterns? After all she had hinted to Nina on the phone that she wanted to discuss her working arrangements, it would only be sensible to have someone from HR present.

"So, how's motherhood suiting you?" Stan asked.

"Ah it's great. Sleepless nights, lots of washing, you know," Jayne laughed, "Which is partly why I want to return to work. A bit at a time. I need to get a routine again – apart from Leo that is."

"Yes, my wife was exactly the same after our children were born," Stan smiled.

"Have you been keeping up with your emails?" Nina asked, raising an eyebrow.

"No, that is one thing I have not really had time for."

"Ah. Okay," Nina frowned.

Stan shot Nina a look before returning his attention to Jayne.

"There have been some changes. We are going through a restructure to enable 'Empowered Working'."

"Sounds interesting," Jayne nodded.

Nina rolled her eyes behind Stan's back.

"It is called 'Empowered Working' because each employee can now shape their future with our streamlining activities."

"Oh? Okay?"

"We want business operations to be more efficient for everyone and empower staff who really make a difference. We are asking each employee to complete a form about their strengths and aspirations."

Jayne's brain crumbled; maybe she wasn't ready for this.

"I am sorry, I don't understand?"

"We are asking you to highlight how you could contribute to a tight functional team of highly motivated staff."

"So what are you asking me to do?" Jayne asked.

Stan passed her a form. "Take this home and have a look. This is your chance to shape your future!"

As she studied the form, the questions that were being asked and the references to streamlining and restructure unnerved her. Wasn't this a way of assessing her to see if she could still do her job?

"Are you saying that I have to apply for my own job?"

Nina nodded furiously behind Stan's back.

"Consideration needs to be given to the future and how staff fit in with our proposed business model. Recent cuts mean that we cannot function in the same way as we once did."

"And what if … what if I don't make the grade?" Jayne asked solemnly.

"There will be a chance to discuss options and packages," Stan smiled.

Nina looked down at her coffee and Jayne was deflated, her energy zapped.

"I will… go home and look at the form then…" She waved the piece of paper and stood up, collecting her handbag and feeling awkward as she left the room, "Thank you."

As she left Nina's office and walked through the team room there was no chatter, and it seemed all eyes were upon her. Her legs felt heavy, moving in slow motion as she walked back to the lift which thankfully arrived quickly, allowing her some privacy and space to breathe. She looked at her reflection in the mirror, expecting to see the old Jayne, and realised just how tired she looked. Her face was thin despite her still round belly; perhaps she needed to eat more and be patient for the rest to diminish. She hardly looked like the vibrant employee Stan had described. She wondered if there was any point in even completing the form. The organisation had plenty of highly skilled employees, ready to work all hours and jump through hoops. Why would they want someone who would need time off for childhood illnesses and school performances? As for her ideas about flexible working, well, she could see now that just wasn't going to happen.

She managed to hold back her tears until she reached the car, and then cried like she hadn't cried in ages. She contemplated phoning Stefan and unlocked her phone, ready. No. That would be admitting defeat. She had imagined going home and telling him proudly that she was going back to work two or three days a week. Now what was she going to do? She needed to rethink.

. . . . .

"Well, I think that went rather well," Glen said to Stefan as they left the Heathstone Luxury Homes' office.

"Yes, thank you. I really appreciate it," Stefan gave Glen a slap on the back.

"I told you there was nothing to worry about. Helena knows a quality employee when she sees one, and your designs have been the backbone of Heathstone since I took over. She knows she would be a fool to lose you."

Stefan nodded. "I guess so. I just needed to see it for myself."

"Which is precisely why I set up this meeting," Glen smiled, "Come on let's go for a drink."

Stefan breathed out a long sigh, and Glen realised just how much this had been weighing on him. "Yes please!"

They made their way to a pub around the corner from the office and Glen ordered them both a pint as Stefan perched on a bar stool, taking his tie off and putting it in his pocket. Glen followed suit.

"I don't miss wearing all this garb," Glen smiled, "My jeans are just so much more me lately."

"Just don't get into the whole trackie bottoms look though eh? Unless you are doing sports," Stefan laughed, and Glen once again saw the relief on his face.

"I can walk away now." Glen said, gazing into space.

"What do you mean?" Stefan asked.

"Well that's it. The papers are signed, you are sorted out. I can walk away from Heathstone Luxury Homes without a shred of guilt. I have tied up all the loose ends. This is my release. The start of my future."

Stefan shook his head at him, rubbing his blond beard. "I still can't believe you are doing this. I think you will regret it."

"Not at all. I am almost the happiest man alive at the moment."

"Only almost?"

"Yes. I still need to talk to Daisy. She refuses to hear me and I suppose it is a little unnerving when a complete stranger turns up in your life and begs you to talk to them."

"Is this the woman you are obsessed with? She probably thinks you are some sort of stalker!" Stefan laughed, "Maybe you should take a holiday now you are free. Take some time out to clear your head. You may see things differently?"

Stefan's laughter annoyed Glen. "Why would I do that? When I have only just found her? No. I may lose her again. I need to stay close until she understands."

Stefan's face recoiled and Glen could see that he was really not interpreting this as he intended. "Look I know I sound obsessed, I know I sound ridiculous. But just imagine if your whole life changed. If you saw yourself as you really were, without all the baggage and the responsibilities and the assets. Just imagine if all you wanted was love," Glen took a swig of his drink, "Because you had felt so much love, and understood that everything else was trivial?"

Stefan looked at Glen. "I don't understand, sorry."

"What I saw, when I went to the… other side… when I died, was love." Stefan looked blank. "It is so hard to put into words. Okay, imagine… think back to the first time you and Jayne met, when you were with my brother. Think back to your times of adventure. Seeing new things, completing challenges. Experiencing total excitement and lack of responsibility. What did it feel like?"

Stefan paused, taking a sip of his pint as he thought back. "It was joy and elation. Nothing else mattered."

"Exactly. That is love. Only, imagine that times one hundred thousand and tell me you could go back to normal?"

Glen saw that Stefan was now listening to him properly.

"I don't know whether I could ever feel like that. Or even begin to understand," Stefan said.

"Yeah, I know, I don't even understand it all myself sometimes. But I have to try."

"So how are you going to convince her?"

Glen shrugged and sighed. "I don't know. I have a friend, Katya, who is helping me. She knows Daisy and Daisy's best friend so she may be able to persuade where I have failed?"

"How did you meet Katya?"

Glen shook his head. "You wouldn't understand, but she is like minded. She is kind and a beautiful person. And at the moment the only person who can help me."

Stefan raised an eyebrow, "Perhaps you should be chasing after Katya rather than Daisy?" He said.

"No it's not like that. Our relationship is purely platonic. And spiritual," Glen could see Stefan trying not to smirk, "Look, I know you don't get it, but it's real. I saw a different dimension when I died."

"I can't believe how flippantly you can say 'when I died'."

"Because it happened, and it was real, and Katya understands. She can help me with Daisy," Stefan nodded but Glen could see that he still didn't get it. He didn't expect him to, "So how is Jayne? I am sure she will be relieved when you tell her about the meeting today?"

Stefan sighed. "Jayne is not in a good place at the moment. I don't know what to do."

"What do you mean? She seemed fine at the restaurant. A little tired perhaps."

"She has become obsessed with details. You know, like she keeps washing her hands all the time. She keeps cleaning the kitchen. I mean not just once or twice, but frequently. She won't sit still. She is on edge all the time. It's as though she is trying to prove she is a superwoman."

"Do you think it's because of Leo?"

"Yes, I do. I think she feels under pressure to prove, for whatever reason, that she is the world's most amazing mother and has the cleanest house and the result is some sort of neuroses."

"Has she seen a doctor?"

"No. She had a health visitor who used to come round. That was a whole drama in itself. She was convinced that the health visitor was trying to find flaws and so she used to clean frantically before the woman arrived and get so agitated," Stefan shook his head, "I try and encourage her to relax. I mean I even ran her a bath with candles and everything the other week and she went mad at me, saying she was more than just a mother, and that she has a brain, and a bath wasn't going to make everything better."

"Did she take the bath?"

"Yes, and then she spent an hour cleaning the bathroom," Stefan laughed half-heartedly, "I want to help her, but she keeps pushing me away. I feel like a stranger in my own home. She doesn't want me anymore. If it wasn't for…" He broke off.

"For what?"

"It doesn't matter," Stefan took a swig of his beer, "She has gone to stay at her mother's for a few days. I think it will do her good, so I am giving her some space. I will tell her about the meeting with Helena Sharpe when she returns."

Glen nodded. "You could make an occasion of it? A meal or something."

"Yes that's what I was thinking. And then I need to sit down with her and talk and try to help her," Stefan sighed and the two men sat in silence for a few moments.

"You will keep in touch won't you, now we are no longer business colleagues?" Glen asked.

"Of course," Stefan smiled, "I really don't understand what you are going through, but we go back a long way."

Glen nodded. "You know I saw Leo, when I died? As in my brother, not your son."

Stefan smiled. "You did?"

"Yes, he was with my dad and he looked so happy. He is at peace."

Stefan held up his glass. "To Leo."

"Yes, to Leo," Glen joined him and they clinked glasses.

"This Daisy, is her surname Hartford?" Stefan asked.

"Yes, why?"

"No reason, I just wondered."

CHAPTER EIGHTEEN

Katya was nervous as she looked at the clock. She had invited the psychic sisters, Sheryl and Jan, to the shop without telling Eliza. She was worried that Eliza may see it as an excuse to dash off to Daisy if she knew Katya had company, and she desperately wanted to include Eliza in the conversation. She had felt edgy all day, knowing that she was about to tell Eliza all about Daisy and Glen, Glen's experiences, and the connections with her own dreams. Something was going on, and she was caught in the midst of it, but she could not do anything alone. She needed support from people who had the expertise to understand it. This was it. This was the time she had been preparing for. At three o'clock the windchime rattled as the shop door opened.

"We're here!" A familiar voice called.

"Hey, what a surprise! Good to see you both!" Eliza exclaimed moving out from behind the counter to embrace the sisters as Katya made her way over to the front of the shop.

Sheryl was wearing red today including lipstick, and Katya noted that she had a very vibrant energy about her. Jan was dressed in her usual black and, as always, appeared very serious.

"I invited the ladies over for a chat," Katya informed Eliza, her hand playing with her long plaited hair, "I hope that's okay."

"Of course," Eliza nodded, "but it's not like you to take charge?"

Katya glanced at Sheryl for support. "It's important"

"I think Katya may be finding her true voice," Sheryl smiled, casting Katya a wink.

Eliza shook her head, chuckling; "Have I missed something?"

"Yes, because there are things I need to tell you. I want you to join us," Katya replied, hardly believing that she was controlling this situation, "Can we use the tarot room?"

Eliza looked worried. "You're not about to tell me you're leaving or anything are you?"

"No! Oh my, far from it," Katya looked directly at Eliza with what she hoped was a knowledgeable expression, "Something is going on, and I need all of you to hear me out."

"Okay. I am now officially intrigued!" Eliza put the door on the latch, and turned the closed sign before following the three others to the back of the shop.

"Well done," Sheryl squeezed Katya's hand, "This is just the start."

"What's with the red?" Katya whispered.

"Oh just a bit of online passion," Sheryl winked.

Once they were all seated, Katya became nervous, especially of the stern-faced Jan, with whom she was not familiar. She was also unsure how Eliza would react to what she had to say. Her eyes naturally moved towards Sheryl for an opening, hoping that she could pick up on what Katya was trying to do.,

She did of course. "Katya lovey, what is it? Fire away."

Katya took a deep breath and cleared her throat. "Okay; one, Daisy; two, Glen Heathstone; three, Me. We are all linked. I think. I just don't know how or why, but I have an intuitive feeling about this."

"What do you mean?" Eliza appeared to be the only one who was surprised. Jan was always poker-faced, and Sheryl of course already had an insight.

"You know I told you about the man who came in to see me? The one whose cards I read?"

"Yes," Eliza nodded.

"That was Glen Heathstone. The same Glen who is freaking Daisy out. You know when she ran into the shop that day?" Katya felt lost for a moment as she did not know which bit to tell them next.

"Go on," Eliza was intrigued but she was frowning.

"He is not a stalker. He is a very lovely man. Glen had a near-death experience about six months ago, during which he saw Daisy's face and he is convinced she is the reason for his return to life and his whole existence. He is besotted with her."

Seeing a doubtful and worried look cross Eliza's face, Katya felt compelled to defend Glen. "Yes I know how it sounds, but he is genuine. I know he is telling the truth."

"It seems a little obsessive?" Eliza pointed out, "And you do see the good in everyone Katya."

"I know, but you know when Daisy described the déjà vu and the strange feelings?"

"Yes…"

"Well Glen visited me that evening and relayed exactly the same encounter, it was almost the same story from each of them individually."

"So where do you fit in?" Eliza asked.

"I have the same intense feelings about him that Daisy does, except I have learned to trust him."

Eliza shook her head; "So you are saying that you are in love with him and Daisy hates him? Is that what you mean?"

"No!" Katya felt her cheeks colour. Of course she was in love with him. She had never felt so comfortable yet so uncomfortable with anyone in her life. It was a new feeling. Her jottings from the last dream confirmed her suspicions. The man she yearned for in her dreams as Annette could be Glen in a different guise. Katya felt as though she was about to cry; she had not expected Eliza to be so defensive, yet she was not ready to admit the entire truth of her feelings. "I think I have a spiritual connection to him."

"I think what Katya is trying to say is that she, Glen, and your friend Daisy are intertwined either in another existence or in a different dimension," Jan chipped in.

Katya nodded, surprised that the stern-faced sister had backed her up. "I have dreams, which I have tried to tell you about."

Eliza nodded: "Are they about a storm?"

"Sometimes. But mostly they are about me as a woman called Annette. But yes the storm was in my first few dreams."

"Daisy is dreaming about storms too. In the harbour. She dreams she is watching it from her attic window and then wakes up to find herself standing there, sleepwalking," Eliza frowned, "I am worried about her."

"I didn't know that?" Katya replied, feeling a little harsh at the way her mind had been judging Daisy Hartford. Then remembering the feelings and raw emotions in the dream and the woman at the window of the big house, she wondered if Daisy was the woman who had taken her love interest from her.

"Why are you crying?" Eliza asked.

Katya's tried to hold the tears in. "I don't know, but this feels so intense."

All four women sat silently, and Katya felt extremely self-conscious; as though Jan and Eliza were judging her. She could see, out of the corner of her eye, the little pink cloud her fellow empath, Sheryl, sent across the table to her to boost her aura.

"So what do you suggest we do?" Eliza said eventually.

It was Jan who came forward with the suggestion. "Regression for all three."

Eliza shook her head. "Daisy doesn't believe in anything like that. She fears it. She doesn't even realise she has spirits in her home."

"Does she?" Katya asked.

"Yes, but they are two nurses ... the ones I have seen so far anyway. One in the attic and one in the kitchen. They are protecting her."

"Glen would be willing though surely? With his new-found beliefs?" Sheryl suggested.

"Except there is only one person he will trust," Jan said as all three women looked at Katya.

"Me? I have never regressed anyone fully?"

"What do you mean fully? I have never regressed anyone at all!" Eliza exclaimed.

"I did a training course, but I never qualified," Katya admitted.

"Why?"

"I ran out of money. And Liam was doing his exams and I couldn't get to all the lessons," Katya shook her head,

"Is there anything else you can do that you haven't told me about?" Eliza smiled, "First tarot reading, now regression."

Katya thought. "Well I did Reiki, but I never got my certificate because the teacher emigrated. Then the crystal healing which I started…"

"So you could safely regress Glen?" Sheryl asked.

"Yes, I could. But wouldn't my own feelings get in the way?"

"Not if you are resolute that they won't," Jan advised, "If your intention is purely to help him and you can manage to keep your own feelings separate, then it is possible. However, if you are going to try and project your own memories and feelings – even unintentionally – you could influence his experience."

"But we can do something to protect you against that beforehand, lovey," Sheryl said.

As the three others stared at her, Katya felt that at that moment, they all believed in what she could do. She began to feel strength from their eyes and hearts.

"You can do this Katya," Eliza's blue eyes were fixed on her face, "We must help Daisy."

"And Glen," added Sheryl.

"And you! It may help answer some of your own questions," Jan's face softened slightly, almost a smile.

A loud knocking signalled that a customer wanted to come into the shop and Eliza jumped up as the meeting disbanded.

"We'll see you later then lovey," Sheryl stopped to admire a new crystal ball in a carved wooden box that sat on the shelves.

"Come on, you haven't got the money for that at the moment," Jan pulled her sister's arm.

Eliza saw Daisy standing outside the front door and unlocked it and changed the sign back to 'Open'.

"Why were you closed?" Daisy asked, looking bewildered as the sisters walked past her, "You never close."

"We were having a meeting," Eliza gestured for Daisy to come in, "and you couldn't have timed it better."

Daisy looked Katya up and down, as if she did not approve of Katya's old purple gypsy top. It was, however, one of Katya's favourite garments. She was about to pull her black cardigan around her defensively, when something stopped her. Why should she feel ashamed of her own wardrobe? She didn't particularly like Daisy's navy blue vintage trouser suit if she was honest. She stood and returned the woman's gaze and it was Daisy who looked away first.

"What was your meeting about then?" Daisy asked Eliza.

Eliza glanced at Katya.

"Oh, we were, er, planning a psychic evening." Katya lied.

"What in here?" Daisy laughed, "It isn't big enough."

Eliza looked a little insulted. "Well we need to find a venue."

"What about the guesthouse?" Daisy became excited. "You could be my first event after the launch!" Eliza looked at Katya again.

"We are only in the early stages of planning. But that's a great idea!" Katya smiled.

Eliza nodded. "When we have more concrete plans, we'll discuss it further."

"Okay," Daisy grinned, "Anyway I'm live! Your wonderful man Brandon has finished my website, and Stella's posted lots of things. Look." Daisy showed Eliza the website on her phone, and then produced the local newspaper from her handbag and turned to page six, where a photograph of Daisy outside her guesthouse was emblazoned across the pages. "Look I'm in the press!"

"Oh!" Katya could not prevent her reaction to the photograph. The house was the big house that had featured in her dream.

"What?" Eliza asked.

"It's just so amazing… that's all. It's a really good photo of you Daisy."

"Why thank you Katya. That is so kind of you!" Daisy looked impressed.

"It does look good. I have to say Brandon is really good at what he does," Eliza replied proudly, her cheeks flushing.

"He is a star!" Daisy cooed, "You are so very lucky."

Eliza smiled, and folding the newspaper, passed it back to her friend. "Anyway. You need to speak to that Glen."

"Eh?" Daisy looked confused, "What has he got to do with anything?"

"I have been thinking," Eliza glanced at Katya who nodded, "I think he is harmless and that you should agree to meet with him and hear what he has to say."

"But he scares me …"

"If he intended to harm you, then he had ample opportunity when you met at the beach the other day."

"We didn't meet! It was a …"

"Accident? Coincidence? Fate?"

Daisy laughed. "Oh now you are going to tell me that the universe is at work and that the meeting was prearranged by some higher force."

Feeling uncomfortable, Katya busied herself with looking at the crystal ball that Sheryl had been interested in, and looked at the price. She wanted to buy a gift for the lady to thank her for helping her.

"And that could quite possibly be the case, but I know you don't think like that, so let's keep it simple," Eliza smiled, "He has been polite, not hurt you in anyway, the spilled drinks was an accident and he is a well-respected business man. What is the harm in meeting him to find out what he is so desperate to talk to you about?"

"He could be weird?" Daisy argued.

"But if you meet in a public place, say a pub or restaurant, then he can't do anything because there will be others around."

"Hmm, I don't know."

"Look, at least you will know what he is on about, and then you can tell him to leave you alone and put it out of your mind," Eliza insisted.

"Okay," Daisy replied, "I will call him tomorrow."

"Promise?" Eliza smiled.

"Promise" Daisy squinted suspiciously at her friend, "What are you up to?"

"Nothing. Absolutely nothing," Eliza replied firmly.

CHAPTER NINETEEN

While her mother was enjoying looking after Leo, Jayne decided to take an impromptu trip to speak to Glen Heathstone himself. She had Glen's address from a letter he had sent to them when he moved, which she had put in her contacts list. It wasn't too far to drive and, following the meeting with Stan and Nina, she was more concerned than ever about Stefan's future. Their security now depended on his ability to provide an income. She was also becoming worried about Stefan's personal reaction to the changes at work, as she watched him become more distant, his anger rising easily and making him volatile.

Perhaps she, as a woman, could gently persuade Glen that he should consider the impact of his crazy decision and talk him out of it. As she drove to the caravan she imagined returning home to tell her husband the good news that she had saved his job, that she had been able to reason with Glen and encourage him to see that his new life choices were foolish and unreasonable. She envisioned a grateful Stefan embracing her, his face beaming with pride and delight at his clever wife.

As she pulled up outside the caravan, the evening was already dark, and she felt very alone as she tentatively knocked on the door of the mobile home. There was no answer, so she knocked harder. Eventually she heard the movement of someone inside and Glen appeared behind the glass door.

"Jayne?" He frowned and appeared surprised to see her.

"Glen, sorry to descend on you without warning. I, um, just wanted to have a chat," she smiled uncertainly. Perhaps this had been a mistake.

He invited her in and offered to put the kettle on, but she declined and he poured them both a glass of water instead. He gestured for her to take a seat and she sat on the L-shaped sofa, cleverly designed to fit the compact space.

"This is lovely," she stated as she looked around the caravan, "It's really not what I expected."

"I haven't truly made it my own as I am only staying here until the spring."

"What will you do then?" Jayne asked.

"Who knows? It all depends on what happens next."

"I can't believe how different it is from your house old though. Stefan and I used to love your parties. Siân was such a great hostess," Jayne bit her lip, worried she had said the wrong thing. She had not intended to be so direct.

"She was, and the house was amazing, but that lifestyle is no longer for me. My whole outlook is now different, as I have tried to explain to Stefan."

"What happened Glen? Why have you changed so much?"

Glen sighed. "Has Stefan not told you?"

Jayne, looked down. "No, we don't really talk much lately. The baby and everything you know."

Glen nodded and smiled gently at her. "It is hard to put into words, but I experienced something that has made me realise that my whole life's work was inadequate. That love is more important. That happiness is more important. Money, possessions, property and power are trivial in comparison to what lies in my soul."

"That's quite a statement from someone who used to work until eleven o'clock at night and buy a new car every year."

Glen nodded proudly. "I know."

"So, that is why you are selling Heathstone's?"

"Yes. I have no choice."

"No choice? I would argue with that. It's your business."

"No, it was my father's business and he made sure I followed him. It wasn't necessarily what I wanted to do with my life."

"But you were so successful; most people would cut their right arm off for the power you had."

"People who are shallow, short-sighted and ignorant of what truly matters," Glen added.

Jayne shook her head. She could see she was fighting a losing battle.

"I'm sorry, but I am struggling with this. You really have changed haven't you?"

"And for the better," Glen smiled.

"Is it for the better though? You are losing an empire and part of that process will be good honest people losing their livelihoods when this Helena Sharpe takes over. Do you know how desperate Stefan is to keep his job? Do you know how much is at stake?" Jayne's voice shook as she held back her tears, "It's all very well you saying love is the most important thing but what of the real world? We have a large mortgage you know, and a son to provide for!"

"Jayne, calm down. Stefan is not going to lose his job okay? We had a meeting today with Helena. Has he not told you?" Glen reminded himself of the conversation earlier and Stefan saying he was going to keep the news as a surprise. He had just blown that one.

Jayne shook her head; "What meeting?"

"Look, he didn't want to say anything until you got home, so pretend you don't know, but Helena is very impressed with Stefan and has guaranteed him a future at Heathstone. He is not going to be made redundant. I can assure you of that."

A single tear rolled down Jayne's cheek, and she wiped it away self-consciously. "Really?" She asked.

"Really," Glen paused, "Jayne is everything else okay?"

It was one question Jayne did not want to hear as she saw the sympathy and genuine concern in Glen's eyes. Her lip began to quiver and before she knew it she was crying properly.

"No. It's not."

"Can I help?"

"No," she shook her head as Glen passed her a tissue, "I think Stefan is having an affair. I saw an email, and I am so tired all the time with Leo. Stefan thinks I can't cope at being a mother, he thinks I am useless. I don't know what to do when he cries, and all the other mothers I know seem to be fine. They all seem to know what they are doing. And now I can't even go back to work because I'm not good enough."

Glen waited until she had finished talking. "I don't think Stefan is having an affair; it may be your imagination. But perhaps you need some support. Have you been to the doctor?"

"What and reinforce his belief that I can't cope? It's not my imagination. I have seen emails."

"Emails can be misinterpreted. Especially if you are already under pressure and feeling tired."

"No. I know what I saw. I am not going mad if that's what you think," Jayne stood, feeling that she had said far too much. Of course Glen was not going to tell her the truth. He was on Stefan's side, "I had better go. I am sorry to have wasted your time."

"Hey, Jayne, it's okay," Glen followed her to the door.

"I'd appreciate it if you didn't say anything about this visit to Stefan," she said quietly.

Glen nodded. "Of course."

She almost tripped in the dark as she stepped down from the caravan and Glen caught her arm.

"Thank you. Sorry," feeling foolish she walked as quickly as she could to the car.

"Jayne."

She turned to face him; "Yes?"

"Try not to worry eh? The old Jayne was carefree," he smiled.

Easy for him to say, she thought, *with his vast fortune and his new beginning*. She sat in the car and sighed as he closed the door of the caravan. She wondered whether to call Stefan and tell him about the meeting and decided against it. She still had her meal with her friends to look forward to. At least that may take her mind off everything else.

. . . . .

Daisy's painting was gathering momentum. Inspired by her dreams of the storm, she was now well on her way to finishing the piece she had started several days ago, enjoying adding depth and dimension to the crashing waves and electric sky. She could picture this painting in the alcove of the drawing room, perfectly complementing the grey and white colour scheme. She had also made some sketches of the cove she had visited on her walk and was planning to use this scene for her next piece. As she surveyed her work, she decided a short break was in order and made her way downstairs to the kitchen for a coffee. It crossed her mind that coffee was perhaps not the best drink for the evening, but she didn't mind if she was up late; she could do more work.

As she waited for the kettle to boil she heard a noise from the terrace. It sounded as though something had been knocked over and she froze, switching the kettle off again so that she could hear. She waited for another noise, but heard none and then wondered if she had imagined it. This was the only drawback to living alone; if anything untoward was to happen, she was isolated and vulnerable. She decided to open the back door to see. She was scared and needed to put her mind at rest if she was going to carry on with her painting.

Her heart beat fast as she moved slowly to the back door, unlocking it and pushing it open gingerly, peering out into the dark night. As a cloud moved and revealed the light of the moon, she noticed that one of her terracotta pots had fallen onto its side, a slight crack on its rim. It must have been the wind, or a stray cat. There was nothing more to see and she closed the door hurriedly and firmly, locking it and pulling down the blinds in the kitchen. She was about to switch the kettle back on, but realised that the noise it made would drown out any other noises she might need to hear. She poured a glass of wine instead and then stood still, listening. She could hear nothing. Shrugging, she was about to walk back up to the attic when she realised there was no wind that evening. There was no way the container could have been knocked over unless something or someone had bumped it or tipped it up. Wouldn't a real terracotta pot be too heavy for an animal to dislodge?

Rooted to the spot, too unnerved to make her way back up to the attic, she tried to remember if she had locked the front door. Picking her phone up, just in case, she edged her way nervously along the hall, switching the light on so she could see the front door. She breathed a sigh of relief that the bolts were firmly in place. She would not have bolted it without locking it first. Walking back to the kitchen to retrieve her glass of wine, she laughed at herself for being so paranoid.

There was a strange noise from the drawing room that sounded like something scraping the glass on the window. Had she really heard that? She stood silently, her hand now shaking, and she took a large gulp from her glass to steady her nerves. She gasped. There it was again. It was a definite crack and scrape on the glass of the bay window. Too scared to move, she wondered whether to call the police. What would she say to them? That she heard a noise? She needed to see what was happening. She edged her way into the dark drawing room, her heart beating fast. She could see from the dim light outside that there was something on the outside of the glass, but she couldn't work out what it was. Before she could investigate further, a loud crash and the sound of broken glass sounded from the other front room, across the hall. It sounded like the window had been broken. Her stomach tightened and she felt dizzy yet highly alert, her nerves full of adrenalin. She was too scared to walk into the lounge to see what had happened behind the closed door. Hiding in the darkness of the drawing room, she phoned Eliza.

"I think I have an intruder," Daisy whispered.

"What?" Eliza asked, "I'm in the middle of a reading. Are you okay?"

"No! I'm terrified, someone has just broken my window," Daisy could feel tears beginning to form as panic became set into her heart.

"Phone the police. I'll send Brandon over," Eliza hung up.

Daisy phoned 999 and explained that she thought she had an intruder and was a lone female. She waited, too scared to move, for what seemed a long time, until she heard a car pull up outside. Peering through the non-smashed window of the drawing room she saw Brandon arrive, and rushed to the front door to let him in.

"Oh Brandon thank you for coming," she cried, flinging her arms around him and sobbing onto his shoulder.

He pushed her away slightly and made his way back out to the front garden as a police car also arrived. When she followed him outside, she could see clearly that one bay window pane had been smashed, and the bay window on the other side of the front door, the drawing room window, was covered in smashed eggs.

"Oh my god!" Daisy cried, "Who would do such a thing?"

"Is the back door locked?" Brandon asked.

"Yes."

The police got out of their car and one officer checked over the front of the house and then round the back, while another officer sat in the drawing room with her taking a detailed description of what had happened. She found this difficult as she was not really sure what had happened. They took photos of the damage and made a call to get someone round to board the window up.

"It could just be kids messing about, but do you know anyone who you might have upset recently?" The police officer asked.

"No," Daisy tried to think. There was of course Christophe and Sofia, but they would not bother stooping to such levels. She thought of all the people she had seen recently. Katya, she was sure, was not very fond of her, but she could not imagine Eliza's assistant throwing eggs at her window. Then she remembered Glen, "Well, there is a man who keeps following me around."

"Is he harassing you?" The police officer asked.

"Well, he keeps turning up in the same places and is desperate to talk to me," Daisy shook her head.

"Has he made any sexual advances or threats of violence towards you?"

"No," Daisy replied.

"Has he ever visited the property?"

"No, but he knows where I live as my website went live today. I am opening a guesthouse."

"So this man has not attempted to gain entry to the property nor has he made any violent or sexual advances, nor any threats to harm you?"

"No," Daisy felt a little foolish.

The officer looked at her, appearing exasperated. His cohort emerged from the hall.

"I've checked round the back and there's nothing," he said.

"Look, Ms Hartford, at this moment in time there is nothing more I can do other than log the incident, but I urge you to contact us immediately should anything else occur. At this stage there is not enough evidence to make any further investigations," he turned to Brandon, "Are you able to stay with your girlfriend until the window has been secured?"

"She's not my girlfriend," Brandon corrected, "but yes, I can do that."

Daisy remained close to Brandon, clinging onto his arm as the police officers got back in the car and drove off.

"I can't believe this!" she cried as they stood outside looking at the two front windows, "Why?

Brandon shook his head. "I don't know. Like the officer said, it's probably just kids messing about."

"I'm scared," she said, falling against him and putting her head on his shoulder. Brandon touched her arms gently and she felt safe and reassured, "You are brilliant Brandon. Thank you." She looked up at him and standing on her tiptoes kissed him gently on the lips. She gasped as he let go of her quickly and took a step backwards. She realised that she had crossed a line. "Sorry!" She cried, "I don't know why I did that. It's just that…"

"Look, I know you are scared, but I am with Eliza. You have to stop all this Daisy," he rubbed his brow, and then reached into his waistcoat pocket for his cigarettes.

"I know, I just… I mean, you just made me feel safe that's all, I'm sorry."

He nodded to her, turning his back as he smoked.

"Don't go until they have secured my house will you?"

"No, of course I won't," he replied, still with his back to her.

"I didn't mean to…"

"I know."

"It's just that I am so …"

"You are so... fragile and dramatic and needy!" He turned to face her, stubbing his cigarette out, "I love Eliza more than I have ever loved anyone in my life and I need her to trust me. You are her friend, so I want to help you, but don't put me in this position, particularly when Eliza has done so much for you."

Daisy was taken aback by his words. They stung and hurt, perhaps because she knew he was right.

CHAPTER TWENTY

Daisy awoke the following morning, after a fretful sleep. The previous night's events pervaded her dreams and she felt shaken and sad as she emerged from her disturbed slumber.

Half an hour later she stood with a mug of strong coffee in her hand as she scrubbed furiously at one set of bay windows, while a glazer repaired the other one. She thought back to the awkwardness with Brandon. His words of truth had caught her off guard and she wondered whether this had anything to do with Eliza's insistence that she should meet with Glen Heathstone. Did her oldest friend now see her as a threat?

Daisy was still convinced that Glen had something to do with the disturbance. She could not think of anyone else who would try to intimidate her, other than Stella. However, Stella was less unstable than she once had been, and Daisy was a paying client. She had no reason to doubt Stella.

Daisy decided that she had no choice but to call Glen, if she was to find out exactly what was going on and attempt to appease Eliza. The prospect of contacting him filled the pit of her stomach with dread, but it was now or never.

She had thrown away all the cards he had given her, but she private messaged him, following the links from his share of her page. Within five minutes he had responded and suggested they meet for lunch.

He had given her the address of a hotel restaurant just out of town and when her taxi pulled up outside the venue, Daisy was impressed. It was a large old building with wisteria stems climbing across its stone walls and an old English garden to the front. She entered the doorway to find herself in a wood panelled hall, decorated with imposing suits of armour and well preserved portraits of monarchs and gentry from times gone by. Turning into the doorway on her right she walked into a wonderful red-walled banqueting hall, lined with more paintings and collections of medieval weaponry. The atmosphere conjured up images of Tudor times, one of her favourite periods of history. The beautiful beams along the ceiling drew her eyes to the bar at the end of the room where Glen stood, casually watching her reaction to her surroundings. Her nerves began to creep in as it occurred to her that she could not simply walk off and make an excuse to be somewhere else. She had come here with the sole purpose and intention of meeting him. What if he was behind last night's attack? What if he was dangerous? Feeling stuck to the spot she contemplated running away, wondering why she had arranged this, but she needed to get to the bottom of what was going on. There was no turning back. Untucking her feet from their imaginary roots she made her way slowly towards him.

"I thought you might like it here, being an artist," he cast his eyes around the room.

"It is breath-taking. Yes. I love it."

"What can I get you to drink?" He asked.

Daisy was about to ask for a red wine, but reminded herself that she had hardly touched her breakfast and was already concerned for her own safety. "I'll have a lime and soda please," she instructed.

Glen ordered their drinks and ushered her towards a table. "So what has changed your mind?" Glen asked, "I didn't expect you to contact me this quickly."

"I need to know where you were last night."

He looked confused. "I was in my caravan, very tired after travelling back from London from a business meeting. But why do you want to know?"

As she heard his calm voice she felt foolish. Of course, throwing things at a window would not be Glen's style. If he wanted to attack her then it would be more subtle, more sophisticated.

"I had a disturbance at my house and some criminal damage, and with the media for the business going live and everything I ..."

He looked shocked. "You don't think it was something to do with me?"

Seeing from his reaction that he clearly had nothing to do with the incident, she realised how irrational she must sound.

"Well, I, er… I don't know who else would want to hurt me?"

He appeared to be deeply offended. "Not me. Believe me. That is the last thing I would want to do."

"Okay. Sorry," Daisy looked down at her drink.

"Are you okay?" He asked, looking at her with concerned eyes.

She looked away. If he wasn't responsible for the attack then who was? "I don't know," her voice shook a little.

There was what seemed like a long silence and now strangely Daisy felt a lot safer with this man than she had done when she arrived. She looked up at him wondering what to say next. He really was very polite and attractive, why was she so dismissive of him?

"You wanted to talk to me, anyway?" She prompted.

He looked a little apologetic. "Yes, but if you are upset, then perhaps this isn't the best time?"

She avoided his eyes again, defensively. She knew from previous experience what happened when she looked into them. "No, it's okay. Go on…"

"Where do I begin?" He sighed.

She took a sip of her drink, wishing she had chosen something stronger.

"At the start?" She half smiled.

"Okay then. Here goes. Please be patient and hear me out," he cleared his throat and straightened the collar of his shirt, "It all started back in February. I was at a party, with my late wife. It was a launch connected with her company in London. You were there."

Daisy thought back to all the various events she had attended with Christophe, but could not recall seeing Glen at any of them. "Sorry. I don't remember. What did your wife look like? What was her name?"

"I thought you might ask that. Her name was Siân." Glen pulled a photo from his wallet, passing it to Daisy. As Daisy looked at the picture the events began to reform in her mind. It was the woman who she had admired so much, on that fateful night when she had found out about Sofia. The couple who had made so much of an impression on her that she had even mentioned them to Eliza. Siân was a woman so in control of her own world, her doting husband allowing her to take centre stage, while Daisy had almost cowered in Christophe's shadow. This beautiful woman had inadvertently been the catalyst for the end of her marriage and her release back into freedom. Now she was dead.

"I remember her!" Daisy gasped, "I did not really notice you though, sorry," Daisy said quietly.

"Siân had that effect on most people. Memorable... striking... that was what she did. That's how she worked." Glen said softly his eyes focusing on the photograph.

"I am sorry for your loss," Daisy murmured.

"Thank you for your sympathy," he replied, "A death can also make you see the real picture. I faced up to the truth, just moments after I saw you." He paused, as though reflecting, "You are everything that Siân was not. You are also beautiful, but you are so natural, so free-spirited. Almost childlike."

"Are you saying I am naïve?" She asked.

"No. I didn't mean that, I mean that despite your designer clothes and your sophistication there is something so real about you Daisy. You are like an English rose. Strong and vibrant but also fragile and delicate."

Under normal circumstances, Daisy would have wanted to laugh at such an analogy, but there was so much sincerity behind his words that she could not speak. He looked at her intensely and she became awkward under his gaze. She had allowed herself to look back at him and felt lost in a myriad of what she could only describe as some form of torment. She could not think of words to pinpoint her emotions. This happened every time.

Glen's face turned to a frown. "That night, you were standing behind a very arrogant man. You looked like a powerless soul trapped in a world where you didn't belong. You looked so unhappy. Believe me I have thought about nothing else. I have gone over and over that moment in my mind."

Daisy felt a lump appear in her throat as Glen described that time in her life almost perfectly. He had managed to put into words exactly how she had felt with Christophe. A trapped and powerless soul. She simply nodded, speechless, as her eyes filled with tears.

"That night, perhaps because of you – well at the moment I saw you – I also saw Siân for everything that she was. The honest truth, no illusion, no airbrush, no lies. And to be honest, I didn't like what I saw. Siân was her own product if you like. Everything she did was engineered meticulously. She 'created' herself, her brand. The world of Siân. To be completely blunt, well... she was a bitch and a liar," he said, looking at her directly.

Daisy struggled to hide the shock from her face. How could he speak like that about his dead wife? "But, she must have ..."

"She was having an affair," he explained, "She was planning to divorce me, and take me for every penny I had. That had been her plan since we first met," he looked down, his pride clearly affected by this realisation.

Daisy did not know what to say and simply looked at him. She could see the hurt in his eyes, recognising the same emotion that she had felt when she had learned of Sofia's pregnancy.

Glen continued. "I finally realised. I found out the truth, just moments after seeing you. You were vulnerable and hidden, controlled by someone else's ego," he sighed, "Just as I was being controlled by Siân's. Then, we had the accident..." He looked down.

"...And she died," her words seemed to ring out as a hollow echo in the quiet room.

"Yes," he replied, looking up again. He leant forward, his eyes fixed on hers intensely, "You see, from that night, that moment when I met you, everything changed. Everything. My life, my whole outlook on life. It sounds so clichéd, but you were the catalyst."

Daisy once again thought back to that evening. She herself had been so inspired by Siân's presence and envious of her self-assurance that it had caused her also to look at her own situation and demand changes with Christophe. Then she had found out about Sofia. "My life changed that night too," she admitted, a tear finding its way over her eyelid.

"Are you okay?" he asked tenderly, as she wiped the tear.

"Please could I have a glass of wine?" She asked, "Red?"

Glen went over to the bar to grant her request and Daisy sat quietly trying to compose herself and to absorb what he had told her. From her point of view on that night, Siân was the catalyst and not Glen. But one thing was clear; events on that evening had changed both their lives significantly with little intervention from each other.

Glen returned, placing a large glass of Merlot before his companion.

"Thank you," Daisy gratefully accepted the glass, taking a sip as he sat down. "So what happened next?" Her suspicion and fear had subsided, and she was curious to know more, seeing now that there did indeed seem to be a link between them.

"Well," Glen paused, "I died too, in the accident."

"I don't understand?" She shook her head.

"I was resuscitated. I died for about nine minutes and had the most amazing experience."

Daisy was trying to make sense of what he was saying; she had heard of this sort of thing before.

"What you mean one of those near-death experiences? Is that what they are called?"

"Yes, an NDE."

"What was it like?"

Glen hesitated, then; "It is hard to find the words... I saw colours that we have no names for. Time was not important and there was this immense feeling of love, everywhere. I did not really want to come back if I'm honest."

Daisy would have normally scoffed at such an account, but there was something very vulnerable about this man describing something so personal, and she felt her eyes filling up again at his emotion.

"My life has changed. You know things that were once important now seem so trivial... I was weightless, and free. I wanted to stay there. It was golden. Nothing hurt and nothing could touch me. I saw my father, but he said it was not my time, and to go back but I didn't want to."

"But you did …"

"And… I saw your face so clearly before my eyes, and then I was back in my body." He looked at her and she was sure of his truth.

"You saw my face?" Daisy asked, "How?"

"I don't know, it was all out of this world. It was real but in another dimension, so I don't know how I saw your face – obviously you weren't actually there, it was more as though I was shown a picture of you," he looked frustrated by his own explanation, "I know this sounds so weird."

"Do you think it was because you saw me before you...?"

"...Died?"

"Yes... perhaps I was just in your mind at that moment?" Daisy asked hopefully, trying to make some sense of it all.

"I don't know?" He sighed, "I saw many people that night. Some of whom I knew well. I just think it's strange that out of all the people I know, and all the faces I saw that night, it was your face that was presented to me? The experience has totally changed me. I realised once and for all what Siân was about, how trivial and worthless my business was and just how important all the other things were."

"Such as?" Daisy asked thoughtfully; this man was making her curious.

"Well, I remember stuff from my childhood, before my dad became successful and when life was simple. When life was about what I loved to do rather than being a successful business man," he said.

"Isn't that just growing up and leaving childish things behind?"

"I don't know… perhaps… but how sad that we are forced to grow up," he looked at her with that gaze that seemed to search her very soul for answers that she couldn't give.

She laughed uncertainly, "And here's me finally growing up and just starting out with my business."

"But you haven't lost sight of yourself, you still have that fire and passion for what you do. It's different," he argued,

"Answer me one question. Why are you setting up your business?"

Daisy thought for a couple of seconds. "Because I want to find my identity again, and be self-sufficient, doing what I love."

"You see that is different," Glen smiled, "That is what it should be about. I now know I have a purpose. There is something I should be doing that means more. But until I find out why we have been brought together, I cannot even begin to think what that might be."

"So what do you want me to do?" Daisy asked.

"I need you to allow me to get to know you. To be a friend first and foremost," he paused and his eyes clouded a little, "However, my attraction to you is beyond anything I have experienced... on earth that is."

Daisy did not know how to answer. Her self-preservation was telling her to walk away, not to get involved, it was his quest not hers. She had too many other things to deal with. There was her business, the launch and then the incident last night. But Glen's experience was unusual and there was, whether she liked it or not, a definite link to herself. "I don't know what to say," she replied honestly.

"Well, it is a lot to take in," he agreed, "And I appreciate that from your point of view, I am a stranger, asking you to consider something that is of no concern to you. In reality, why should you help me?"

"But I seem to be involved whether I like it or not," Daisy replied, reluctant to lose the connection and wondering why she was arguing, when she could have simply walked away. She shook her head, "Supposing we find out the answers and you still don't know which way to go, what then?"

"Believe me, I have thought about that – my life is an open book, for the first time ever. But until I can get my head around why we have been brought together, I don't feel I can even begin to think about the rest of it," he looked at her, and again she turned her eyes away.

"Yes I see," she nodded.

"I really don't know what else to say," Glen replied. He now looked lost, and her heart went out to him.

"Well we have at least talked, I suppose that is a starting point. But I need to think about this. I don't know whether I am able to help you," she replied, "Or whether I want to, yet. Like I said, I have other things to do as well."

"That is perfectly understandable," Glen nodded.

There was a pause as Daisy sipped her wine.

"There was one more thing," he added, "You know on the beach, when you ran away from me?"

"Yes?" Daisy said, surprised.

"Well, firstly I want to apologise for scaring you, as you were obviously pretty freaked out, but did you feel strange while we were talking?"

"How do you mean? Strange?" Daisy asked.

"Well, like time stopped. As though you had been there before?" He looked at her deeply now, and she felt that awful emotion once more. Instead of turning away she challenged herself to accept it and looked back. It was like losing herself in a deep well of pain, love, hope and regret all at the same time. Where did this come from?

Daisy decided there was no option other than complete honesty. "Yes, I did feel it," she paused, knowing that she must look away now, or she would reach out to him and touch his hand, or stroke his face which would be wrong. "It was disturbing. As is the feeling now."

"Yes, wasn't it? Isn't it?" He rubbed his brow, "I get this each time we meet. It is a strange sensation. You are so familiar, and yet I know nothing about you. I don't understand it."

Daisy was speechless, as he identified the exact same sensations that she herself had been experiencing. "I think," she said calmly, despite the feelings that were churning up inside, "that we both need to go away and consider everything. Well I need to go away and get my head around it all anyway... If I can."

"Yes. I respect that, in your own time. But please keep in touch," his eyes begged her, "If we can't resolve this, then so be it and I will leave you alone. But please give me a chance, and thank you for hearing me out."

"Agreed," Daisy replied, not entirely sure exactly what she was agreeing to.

"I'll give you a lift back into town," he said, "That is if you trust me to?"

Daisy nodded, contemplating that her insecurities around his physical presence had now gone, and it was only their spiritual connection, if there was such a thing, that now bothered her.

She finished the last sips of her wine and her head lurched a little. As they walked out into the garden towards Glen's car, she swayed slightly and he caught her arm.

"Are you okay?"

His hand felt reassuring on her elbow and she had that same sensation she had experienced when he touched her arm on the beach.

"Yes, I'm fine. I haven't eaten."

He looked at her. "You should have said, I could have bought you some lunch."

"No. I can't eat. I couldn't eat. Not at this moment."

They stood and she dared herself to look at him properly again, knowing the feelings his eyes would evoke, but wanting to feel it all the same. His hand moved from her elbow to the top of her arm and she felt as though she was swimming or drowning under his gaze. She realised that her physical body was on high alert as her stomach somersaulted with an adrenalin rush and her skin began to tingle as he moved a little closer and she could smell his scent mixed with his aftershave.

As his lips touched hers tenderly, she swayed again from the intensity of what was a very soft and simple kiss. His hands stopped her from falling as he gripped the small of her back gently. He moved his face away.

"Sorry, I shouldn't have … that was …"

"No, you should have," she replied, wanting him to kiss her again. She touched the side of his face and he responded, this time his kiss deeper and more fervent. She was falling into an abyss that she never wanted to climb out of; as the outside world merged into a blur of abstract colours and shapes, all she could feel was the sensation of his lips on hers, the smell of his skin and the touch of his hands around her waist.

CHAPTER TWENTY-ONE

Eliza had given Katya the day off and, following the joint decision of her peers that she should attempt to regress Glen, Katya had spent all morning excitedly researching her notes, books, and anything she could find online about past life regression. Sheryl was right, she could do this. She was capable of doing it and she was the only person Glen would trust enough. Yet she was still unsure. Was it the right thing to do? What if she opened a can of worms? What of herself? She was involved in this for some reason, and although she had only hinted to the others of her connection with Glen, she was sure that she also had a past life link to him and perhaps Daisy. What if she discovered something that upset her?

Her tired mind pictured a spiral of never-ending repetition. How did she break the spiral, and was she meant to break the spiral or was it part of her destiny? Sitting quietly she tried to meditate, to ask for guidance but nothing would come. She felt alone, as though her spirit guides had left her. She had heard of this happening to others; maybe she needed a break?

She thought of her son, Liam, and wondered how he was getting on in France. He was travelling with friends, working in vineyards and bars to earn money. She knew he was sensible and that no news was good news, but she wished he would get in touch more often. He suffered from the natural arrogance of youth, oblivious to the fact that she worried about him frequently. Just a quick email or private message would reassure her. She checked his social media and was happy to view a photo he had posted the night before, enjoying food and drink in the Loire. She wondered whether he would return to the Midlands upon his return to the UK or whether he might come here to Devon – the main reason she had rented a two bedroom cottage, just in case.

While she was online, she searched for Daisy Hartford, out of curiosity, and found links to Christophe Dupont, the classical pianist and composer. Scanning the pages, she saw Daisy looking fabulous but forced at various events with her ex-husband. Now here was an interesting one. A photo of Christophe shaking hands with a striking woman who reminded her of a 1940's film star, a blonde siren full of feminine vitality. Glen stood in the shadow behind her, only just visible but it was clearly him. She followed the links until she found a photo from the same event, with the same woman in focus, and this time Daisy was in the background of the picture, unaware that she was being snapped as part of the scenery for this starlet. So Glen and Daisy's paths had crossed before. Upon reading the captions, Katya discovered that the blonde woman was Siân, Glen's late wife. She thought back to her first conversation with Glen where he had told her that he had seen Daisy shortly before the accident. Were these photos taken on the night of Siân's death? The night of Glen's near-death? She shuddered as she viewed the image of this glamorous woman so close to her end, yet totally unaware. The image disturbed her and she wanted to get away from the screen and get some fresh air.

As she put her black fake fur coat on, the one Eliza said made her look like a teddy bear, she wondered where she could walk to. She let her mind wander and thought of the tree in her dream, the one where the man who had broken Annette's heart had stood, his eyes dismissing her. That tree was outside the big house, the one she now felt sure was Daisy's guesthouse. She decided to take a slow walk up to the high ground where the guesthouse stood. If Daisy was at home, she might even be bold enough to knock on the door and say hello.

Refreshed with a new enthusiasm at her mission to find out more, Katya enjoyed the gentle uphill climb. Compared to the steep steps from the harbour it was an easy walk, and one filled with the exhilaration of nature as she took the cliff path. As she emerged from the public footpath and re-joined the road, she could see the house up ahead. And there was indeed a tree. The same tree she had seen in her dream, an old oak. Walking up to it, she touched the bark, closing her eyes and trying to recall the dream. As he had dismissed Annette, he had cast something to one side, thrown it on the ground. Her instinct was telling her to dig, but she obviously had no spade so she kicked gently at the mud and grass with her heel making a small indentation in the ground. A leaf fell and tickled her nose and a white feather fluttered past her. Her angels were here! She was no longer alone. Finding a stick she began to poke around beneath the tree, where whatever he had thrown may have landed. It was clear to her now, the key to the puzzle may be buried in the earth.

After no results, she decided to walk up to the house instead and get a proper look at the attic window and the front doorway that she had dreamed of. It felt surreal as she approached, and with her eyes focused on the window at the top she saw a woman's face. It was not Daisy, nor was it the dark haired woman in her dream. This woman's face was calm and serene. As she approached the house a little more, she saw a car pull up and Daisy herself got out. Glen got out of the driver's side and accompanied Daisy to the front door, where to Katya's sheer horror they began to kiss and embrace one another. She felt her heart descend into her stomach; it was just as she had felt in the dream. Her eyes burned as she fought to hold her tears in, the cold wind now feeling icy rather than refreshing. Once again the image of the never ending spiral came to mind and she turned her back on the amorous duo as Glen was about to return to his car. She did not want him to see her.

A robin was now pecking at the ground beneath the tree and she stood still, waiting for the small bird to finish what it was doing. The bird cocked its head towards her and looked at her with a beady eye and she thanked it before she slumped down on the tree's large roots and sobbed.

She searched her memory for the meaning of a robin. It was a symbol, she remembered, of patience and faith; to believe in oneself and trust that all would be well. But just how patient did she have to be? She was losing sight of her own goals, as Glen and the dreams seemed to get deeper and deeper into her subconscious. Perhaps this spiritual stuff was becoming too much for her? She sighed and ran her fingers through the earth where the bird had been digging, enjoying the feel of the soil and the scent it released as she felt that she opened up the earth itself. Hearing the car drive off, she felt relief that Glen had left and that he and Daisy were no longer in each other's company.

She became alert as her fingers found something buried in the mud where the robin had been pecking. It felt like something metal and round and she dug her nails in and pulled it out to find that it was a coin, with part of a broken chain threaded through it. Just like the one in her cottage. Wiping the dirt from it and rubbing it against her jumper, she could see that this one too had been roughly engraved with letters and numbers, but she could not make out what it said. The robin had been a messenger. She silently thanked the bird and her guardian angel, and, placing the coin in her pocket, made her way home. She was anxious to speak to Josie and see what she had to say about the latest clue.

· · · · ·

Jayne returned home just as the sun was setting. It had been a quiet drive, considering it was rush hour, and Leo had slept for the whole journey. Despite the difficulties she had experienced over the last two days, she had caught up on some sleep and just getting out of the house while her mother cared for Leo had given Jayne the energy boost that she needed. Taking the baby carrier from the car and approaching the house, she felt a mixture of uneasiness and excitement. She had decided to confront Stefan about the emails she had seen. It was now or never, before her fatigue set in and wound her down again.

Her mother had comforted her following the meeting with Nina and Stan, pointing out that she could get another less demanding job that was nearer to home. This was something Jayne had not wanted to consider initially, but the thought of applying for her own job was something she simply did not have the energy for. Stefan's job was safe, according to Glen, and whatever happened to them as a couple, Stefan had a responsibility to ensure that his son was financially supported.

She took in a sharp breath as she opened the kitchen door, expecting to walk into a mess and instead seeing the kitchen table set with candles and place mats. There was a bottle of wine and a bouquet of flowers in the centre. Stefan was cooking something that smelt deliciously warm and spicy and he rushed over to take the heavy baby carrier from her.

"Welcome home," he placed the carrier safely onto the floor and took Jayne in his arms kissing her tenderly, "I am so sorry," he whispered as he ran his fingers through her hair.

"What for?" Jayne asked nervously. He had caught her off-guard, throwing these unexpected romantic gestures at her when she was about to accuse him of having an affair. 'Start worrying if he suddenly buys you flowers for no reason.' One of her friends had warned. *Was Stefan that complicated?* Jayne wondered. He had always been so straightforward, certainly not a game player. She wanted to believe that the flowers and this show of affection were genuine, that he truly was sorry.

"I have been a complete arse," he said, "Worrying about the job, when I should have been here for you and Leo."

"Hey it's understandable," Jayne shrugged as he poured a glass of wine and handed it to her, "You have put years of work into your career at Heathstone."

"But I have been angry and stressed. I can't have been the easiest person to be around."

"Well, yes, I shan't argue with that," Jayne smiled.

A gurgle and some arm waving signalled that Leo was waking and Jayne moved immediately to set her wine down, but Stefan stopped her.

"I can deal with him, enjoy your drink."

Jayne fought back the urge to rush to her son, trying to push aside thoughts that Stefan would do something wrong, making Leo cry. She held her breath as he unbuckled the carrier strap and lifted the sturdy baby boy, holding him against his chest and kissing his forehead. Leo reached out and tugged his dad's beard, his eyes smiling and his mouth turned up at the corners before his fist went into his mouth as it usually did when he was hungry.

"Aw little man, are we hungry?" Stefan carried him to the high chair, passing him a spoon, which Leo put straight in his mouth, and took a pot out of the microwave.

"What's that?" Jayne was worried. It might be too hot or heated unevenly and she craned her neck peering, trying to see.

"A mixture of baby rice, pureed mash and broccoli," Stefan said proudly, "I prepared it ready."

"Is it cool en...?"

"Yes, just relax."

Jayne remembered that she was not meant to know about Stefan's meeting with Glen and Helena Sharpe, and so should be curious about why he was in such a good mood.

"So what's all this about? Why are you so cheerful?"

"I have my wife back home, and my son. I have missed you both."

Liar, thought Jayne. *This is all about the job and covering his dirty secrets.* It dawned on her that she no longer trusted him. Perhaps he *was* more complicated than she had given him credit for. Playing along with the game, she continued. "No, don't be daft, it must be more than that. I haven't seen you look this happy for a long time."

"Well," Stefan paused to help Leo guide the spoon into his mouth, "Glen and I met with Helena Sharpe yesterday and she wants me on board. She has guaranteed that I am part of the new team and has stated that she cannot envisage running Heathstone Luxury Homes without my support and input."

Despite her annoyance with him, Jayne felt a surge of pride and was genuinely pleased about his news.

"So, there is no need for you to worry about going back to work now, you can enjoy being at home with Leo," he grinned at her.

If only it were that simple. He would never understand her need to have an identity apart from that of a wife and mother. He would not get the fact that she wanted to earn her own money, even if that money purely paid for childcare. It wasn't even worth explaining. She decided not to tell him about her meeting with Nina. She would look for something local and part-time and let him think she had willingly resigned from her old job. She could pretend too. She could also stall for time while she made her own plans. No need to rush into anything, she could play the game and find out more in the meantime.

CHAPTER TWENTY-TWO

As she stood looking on, the wind and rain practically biting at her, she felt that she may just get blown over the side of the wall and into the harbour. She was frightened, but the proximity of the others offered safety as the women held each other and stood firm against the weather. The howling of the wind was unrelenting, and drove a chill through even the bravest heart. It seemed as though the noise of death itself was swooping into their small world. She felt her heart sink at the noise of another boat tossing and turning against the breakwater, its bell ringing as it swung back and forth. What if that was his boat? She did not know what time he had set sail, or even if he had set sail, and she could only hope and pray that he was clear of the storm before it arrived. After all, the evening had been calm. Who would have known that this beast of a storm was to arrive?

A vicious strike of lightning ripped the sky as it hit the beacon, accompanied by the loudest crack of thunder she had ever heard. As a thick darkness descended, cries and screams sounded all around her. The brightest light was gone and she felt the same heart-wrenching despair as the others. The beacon had gone, its light lost and unable to guide the boats into the safety of the harbour. The women's collective hope seemed to vanish.

A large woman that she knew by sight stepped up onto the harbour wall, holding onto some ropes. Her sisters held onto her legs as the wind swayed her dangerously.

"We can build a fire!" She cried, her voice fighting with the noise of the gale. "Bring what ye can burn! Let's light their way home!" Her words were echoed along the crowds of women that lined the harbour, the noise of sobbing overtaken by words of renewed possibility.

The frightened lull of moments before gave way to intense activity as women scattered to their homes and the boatyard to find fuel for the fire. Annette ran with the others heading towards her cottage. She burst in through the door to find Mama still by the hearth consoling Arabella and the baby.

Annette gathered up one of the straw filled mattresses from the back room and ran outside.

"What are ye doing?" Mama called, running to the door with the baby in her arms.

"The beacon has gone! We need to build a fire to guide the boats into harbour. Mama please! Think of Papa."

A tear rolled down Mama's cheek.

"Go, Annette, take what ye need!"

Annette ran as fast as she could, the weight of the mattress and the force of the wind slowing her down, but she must keep going. Eventually she reached the pyre that was being built and waited as attempts were being made to set light to it. The wind and rain were hindering the flames from starting and urgency was increasing as the women heard the noise of yet another boat being smashed against the rocks.

The large woman who had instigated the fire looked up at the heavens.

"Come on, let us be. Give us a chance to light this!!"

Moments after her words, the flames took hold and the pile of household items, mattresses, blankets, clothing, furniture and rags began to burn. "Keep 'em coming!!" Shouted the woman, "Bring more to burn!!"

Katya ran back again to the cottage to find Mama now at the rear window watching the harbour fire with Arabella and the baby. She placed a hand on her mother's shoulder.

"He's gone. I can feel it," Mama said.

"You don't know that," Annette replied.

"I know. I can tell."

"Papa?" Arabella looked up at her Mama.

"Sshh," Mama replied huddling the frail child to her body.

"I need more to burn."

"What is the use?" Mama sobbed,

"Because he may still be out there, the fire might just bring him home!" Annette picked up anything she could carry and ran back out of the cottage, this time throwing the items down the steep steps to others waiting to take them to the fire, then returning for more.

The wind grew into a billowing power that engulfed her, taking the air right out of her lungs, and causing her to sway enough to seek shelter by the wall of the cottage. She was exhausted and leaned against the bricks for a moment sobbing. The pain hurt too much, her Papa and her love. They could not die. She would be lost forever. She wondered whether Mama was right. Was it futile? Were they already lost?

She could not take the chance. She had to go on. Hearing the cries of the women on the harbour rallied her, and she returned to the cottage taking the last straw filled mattress, much to the dismay of her mother, and made her way back to the harbour walls.

Katya awoke with a start, and quickly turned on her lamp, grabbing her journal and jotting down notes before the events of the dream faded.

CHAPTER TWENTY-THREE

Daisy sat in her kitchen, sketching ideas for her next painting, as thoughts of yesterday's lunch meeting with Glen haunted her. She had never intended for that kiss to happen. Now, in the cold light of reality, with no heart-rending tales to cloud her judgement and unable to surrender to his eyes, she was annoyed with herself for allowing the liaison to go so far. She had a suspicion he would now be unable to leave her alone. While the depth of the kiss had taken her to another place entirely, she was not ready for another relationship. As she sketched the cove, this too brought back memories of Glen and how strange their encounter in the rain had felt. She was puzzled as to how someone she had met only a few times had already formed memories and associations for her. She tore the page and screwed it up, angrily wishing that she could shake him out of her mind.

The doorbell rang loudly, startling her, and for a moment she was rooted to the spot, remembering the events of two nights ago. It rang again, and she walked tentatively to answer it. Peering through the gap held firm by the door chain, she was both relieved and surprised to see Heather, her sister. Quickly unfastening the chain and opening the door fully, she saw that Fleur, her niece, was also on the doorstep.

"Sis! What a lovely surprise," Seeing the look on Heather's face told her that perhaps these were the wrong words for the situation. "What's the matter?"

Heather ushered Fleur in and they followed Daisy into the kitchen. Fleur immediately made a beeline for Daisy's drawing materials.

"Oh Fleur, no. Those are Aunt Daisy's pencils."

"It's okay, they are only for sketching."

"Sorry to descend on you like this, but are you okay to mind Fleur for a couple of hours? I have something I need to sort out and mum's at her Ladies' Club today." Heather rolled her eyes.

"Yes, of course, I might need to take her into town to get some food, as I don't have much in the cupboard."

"That's not a surprise!" Chuckled Heather, "You have never been able to cook."

"Can we get an ice-cream?" Fleur asked hopefully.

"Oh I should think so," Daisy smiled. She turned to Heather. "Is everything okay sis?"

Heather sighed and grimaced. "Not really, but nothing I can't sort out. I can't tell you at the moment," She nodded towards Fleur.

"Well you know where I am if you need me."

"Thanks."

"I have lots to tell you too," Daisy raised her eyebrows.

"We need a girls' night out," Heather embraced her sister and, after telling Fleur to behave herself and giving her a kiss, she left.

Fleur looked up at Daisy showing her a rag doll that she had brought with her. "This is Poppy."

Daisy bent down and looked at the doll. "Hi Poppy."

"She is very brave, because grandma had to sew her eye back on."

"Oh that is brave," Daisy replied, smiling, "Do you and Poppy want to come up and see my magic attic where I do my painting?"

Fleur's face lit up as she eagerly jumped off her chair and, holding Daisy's hand, followed her aunt up the stairs. "Can *I* do painting?"

"Yes I should think so."

Daisy led Fleur into her attic room and found an old shirt to cover her niece's clothes with. Then, sitting her at the work table, she squeezed out some blobs of paint and gave her a paintbrush and some sheets of paper.

Smiling as she watched the little girl's face scrutinising the paints and deciding which one to use first, Daisy was annoyed by the sound of the doorbell.

"Are you okay to carry on while I go and answer the door?"

Fleur nodded, too engrossed in her artwork to speak.

Daisy ran down the stairs, wondering why it was so busy today, and saw the familiar red uniform of the postman through the frosted glass.

"There's one to sign for." He passed her a brown cardboard envelope as she signed and closed the door, absent-mindedly opening the letter as she moved towards the stairs. She pulled out a thick glossy piece of card. It was a photograph of her and Brandon outside her front door on the night of the broken window. The photographer had managed to capture the exact moment when Daisy had lost all reason and kissed Brandon on the lips. She gasped in horror. She checked inside the cardboard envelope for a note but there was none, so she turned the photograph over to see words scrawled in red marker pen; 'Is one man not enough for you???'

Looking at the photograph again, she felt nauseous. This meant that whoever had been outside her house two nights ago had taken the photograph and had then printed it out and posted it yesterday. Whoever had broken her windows had been watching the house the whole time while Brandon and the police were there, and none of them had had any idea.

She wanted to go and talk to Eliza, but how could she show her the photograph and the words when she was quite blatantly kissing Brandon? Her mind began to spiral that if the photographer had done this, then what was to stop them finding out Brandon and Eliza's identities and sending a copy to them also? And what about social media? Photos could end up going viral nowadays. Eliza would wonder why Daisy hadn't told her about it and it would look far more suspicious than it was. Especially when both Daisy and Brandon knew that there was no reason for the kiss other than Daisy feeling insecure. Brandon had been more than appropriate in pushing her aside, and reminding her that he was with Eliza. She would have to visit them and come clean. There was no other option.

Hearing a bump from upstairs, she dashed up the stairs to find Fleur still happily painting.

"Are you okay sweetheart? I thought I heard a bump."

"Oh that was just the lady," Fleur said, "Look at my painting. It's you!"

Daisy looked at the patches of colour on the paper, the black splodge that was supposed to be her hair and an over-pink face with a garish red smile. "That's lovely Fleur. But what lady?"

"The lady who shut the door. That's what the bump was."

"Which lady who shut the door?"

"She came from over there." Fleur pointed to the window that overlooked the harbour.

"Then what did she do?"

"She smiled at me and touched my head."

"Did she hurt you?"

"No, she is kind. She smiled and went out the door."

Daisy felt faint and her stomach lurched. Her phone started to ring. It was Glen. She dismissed the call.

"Come on Fleur, let's go and grab that ice-cream you wanted." Daisy needed to get out of the house and get some fresh air.

. . . . .

Katya tried to keep herself busy in the shop, but there didn't seem to be much to do today. The image of Daisy and Glen kept flitting through her mind, unsettling her. She tried to focus instead on the excitement of finding another coin pendant. She had already passed it on to Josie for analysis at the museum and wondered if the two pendants were linked or whether it was merely coincidence. It did not work as a distraction from her thoughts though and she was relieved to see the friendly face of Sheryl appear in the doorway.

"Morning lovey!" She beamed as her array of indigo and violet bustled in. "How are you today?"

"I'm okay, I suppose," Katya sighed.

"Oh dear, that doesn't sound convincing. We are coming up to the full moon you know, it can make things seem more intense."

Katya chuckled. "I think it's a bit more than that, but yes you are right, it might be a factor."

"Have you done anything yet about Glen's regression?"

Katya shrugged. "I don't think there is any point."

"Why?"

"Well he already seems to have convinced Daisy to be his girlfriend. What is the point of regressing him when he already knows that they are meant to be together?"

"That is not the point of the regression lovey," Sheryl chided, "If you remember, we are trying to find out what the purpose is between him and Daisy, and where you fit into all this. Not just to prove that they are pre-destined."

"Do you think they are pre-destined?"

"I really don't know. But we will know more if you do the regression."

"I'm not sure whether I want to. I saw them kissing yesterday and it felt so odd. I never knew I would react this way."

"Ah sweetie, you really are smitten aren't you? Well there must be a reason for that too."

"Yeah right," Katya frowned, "to get my heart broken, again."

Sheryl for once seemed lost for words for a moment and paused.

"Look, you are seeking answers yourself. If Glen's regression does not answer your questions, perhaps you would let me regress you?"

"Then why can't I just do that and forget about Glen?"

"Because Glen seems to be the common link in the whole situation. If you regress before he does, you may become aware of something and unintentionally influence him."

"Then why don't you regress Glen?"

"Because he trusts you, not me. You are the only person he feels comfortable with."

"Okay," Katya replied reluctantly, "I'll go and see him tonight."

"That's better," Sheryl replied, "Now, you mentioned the last time we met that you had been having dreams. Why don't you tell me all about those?"

Katya tried her best to describe the dreams to Sheryl, particularly the last one in which the storm was so vivid.

"Ah, that sounds like 'The Great Gale'," Sheryl replied.

"The what?"

"Back in Victorian times, 1866, I think, there was a terrible storm. Many boats were wrecked and the beacon was destroyed. The women of the town rallied together and gathered all that they could find to build a fire, in order to guide their men safely into the harbour."

"I didn't know about that?"

"Well you probably wouldn't, you're not local are you?"

"Daisy has apparently been dreaming of storms in the harbour too," Katya made a mental note to ask Josie about the Great Gale. She would undoubtedly know all about it.

"Exactly. If Glen's regression reveals the same, then this is probably where the link comes from."

The windchime tinkled and Daisy walked in with a small child. "Is Eliza around?"

"No, she has a day off today." Katya found it difficult to speak to Daisy as she recalled the image of her and Glen in their embrace.

"Oh," Daisy looked worried.

"Can I help you at all?" Katya swallowed her pride, her face burning as looked at Daisy.

"Not really no. I need to speak to Eliza. In person," Daisy replied, "However there is something you may be able to help with," She knelt down and spoke to Fleur, "Tell these nice ladies about the lady you saw in my attic."

"She was very kind," Fleur said, her mouth bright blue from the bubble gum ice cream she had enjoyed.

"What did she look like lovey?" asked Sheryl.

"She was very white. Her dress was white."

"Anything else?" Asked Katya.

"She had a hat."

Daisy shook her head. "I don't know what to think, there was no one else in the house."

Katya glanced at Sheryl. "I think you know what it was Daisy," Katya did not want to say too much in front of the child.

"The spiritual world does not have to be frightening dear. Children can often see things we are not aware of," Sheryl smiled.

The colour drained from Daisy's face.

"It's nothing to worry about," Katya turned to Fleur, "Did the lady say anything to you?"

Fleur shook her head. "She was very smiley."

"See?" Sheryl nodded, "Nothing to worry about. She may even be helpful."

Daisy did not look any more reassured. "Hmm, well I don't like things I don't understand."

"Aunty Daisy," Fleur piped up, "I really like these." She was picking up some little fairy figurines from one of the shelves.

"Would you like one for your bedroom?" Daisy asked.

Fleur nodded, "Yes please."

"I'll take one of those please," Daisy said to Katya.

Sheryl went over to the crystals and found a piece of dark amethyst.

"Here lovey, have one of those too, they are only one pound."

"What's that for?" Daisy asked, turning her nose up at the small stone.

"Protection," Sheryl replied, "Not that you need it, but it might make you feel a little better."

Daisy smiled a little as she looked into Sheryl's kind eyes.

"Okay, thank you."

Katya wrapped the items, passing them to Daisy as she checked a message on her phone. She led Fleur to the door.

"Come on Fleur, we need to meet your mummy so she can take you home."

Katya nodded and then once the door had firmly closed breathed a sigh of relief. "Well that was interesting."

"Eliza said she has two spirits in that house, both nurses. That would tie in with what the little one said," Sheryl reminded her.

"Do you ever get a feeling that something big is about to happen?"

"Yes I do," agreed Sheryl, "And all the more reason to get this regression done now!"

"But the shop ..."

"I'll mind the shop. You never know I might meet someone interesting."

"What about ...?"

"Katya lovey, I am quite capable of running a small shop for a couple of hours. Eliza has prices on everything! I have been a customer for many years. Just go, before you think about it too much."

. . . . .

Eliza lay in bed looking into Brandon's brown eyes after a rare relaxing morning together.

"Hmm," she twirled his hair around her finger, "Why can't every day be like this?"

He kissed her softly.

"It could be."

"I have a business to run, we have to earn a living."

He began to kiss her neck. "You could take more days off, and spend them with me?"

"And then we would quickly be destitute," She smiled, reluctantly pulling her body away from him, and pulling on her robe.

"Are you saying I cannot provide for you?" He gave her a look of mock sadness, and she wanted so much to return to his warmth and his touch, but she had a meeting later about the empty shop next door.

"Of course not! Your web business is growing all the time," she watched longingly as he emerged from the bed, stretching his limbs, "But..."

"Ah, I knew there would be a 'but'..." he pulled his jeans on and splashed some aftershave on his neck, his eyes playful in the mirror.

"I have that meeting this afternoon about the shop next door. I need to prepare."

"All work and no play..." He teased.

"Shut up," she said, throwing a pillow at him. She padded down the stairs to collect the post. There was a bill and an A5 brown card envelope with a handwritten address. Expecting it to be junk mail, Eliza was absent-minded as she opened it, walking back up the stairs as she did so. As she reached the landing she gasped as she pulled out a photograph of Brandon and Daisy kissing. She slouched against the wall, her knees weak as the image hit her. She felt sick. It couldn't be. But it was there in print real as the light of day.

Brandon emerged from the bedroom. "What's up?"

"This!" hissed Eliza, throwing the photograph at him. She stormed off to the kitchen and switched the kettle on.

Brandon was silent as he looked at the photo and walked slowly into the kitchen.

"Well?" She looked at him, her hand on her hips and her eyes defiant.

He shook his head. "It's not what you think."

"Oh please. If you are going to cheat on me, then at least spare me the excuses and have the balls to admit it!"

He flung the photo down on the kitchen table, and moved quickly to stand so close that he was almost pressing her against the worktop.

His eyes blazed into hers, his jaw firm. "There is a reasonable explanation for that!" He gestured at the photo. "It is not as it appears. I love you! If you don't know that by now, then you never will." He moved away, smoothing his hair and reaching for his cigarettes

"But you are kissing her."

Brandon began to laugh as he lit a smoke. "No. Correction. She is kissing me. And if whoever took the photograph had taken another shot, they would have snapped me removing her hands from me and pushing her gently away."

"But why would she kiss you?"

"Because she is vulnerable. She is lonely and she is losing the plot."

Eliza wanted so much to believe him. She did believe him. Daisy had always been volatile and impulsive and she loved to play the damsel in distress.

"Think about it. She is all on her own, she has just been badly hurt, there is this weirdo following her around and then there is you. Strong, dependable Eliza, the loyal friend who always comes running to help. Except you are not a man. And Daisy needs a man in her life whether she likes to admit it or not. She needs to feel desired and I must have fitted the 'safe male' role quite nicely. Her best friend's boyfriend. No danger, no risks. Because she knew I would say no."

Eliza was not sure what to say. His words rang true, but as someone who was reluctant to allow anyone into her life, she had always struggled with the way some women needed male attention. After all these years however, she was used to Daisy. It wasn't unsurprising behaviour that Brandon had described.

The sound of the doorbell interrupted them and Eliza stomped off to answer it, avoiding his eyes as she passed him.

Opening the door to see Daisy was the last thing Eliza wanted to do.

"Hi. Have you got a minute?" Daisy asked. Eliza stood defensively, as Daisy made her way in and up the stairs.

"Oh, just come on in why don't you?"

"Sorry?"

"What is it? I am busy. I do have other things going on in my life besides you."

"What? You are still in your dressing gown."

Eliza followed Daisy up the stairs.

"Look, sorry to drop in unannounced, but I really need to talk to you about something," Daisy bit her lip, "It affects Brandon too." She reached into her bag and pulled out a brown envelope as she made her way into the kitchen. She stopped in her tracks.

"Is this what you wanted to speak to me about?" Eliza picked the photo up from the table and waved it in Daisy's face. Best friend or not, Eliza felt that she could actually slap Daisy's pretty face as it contorted into a helpless and tearful expression. "Go on then, explain!"

Daisy glanced at Brandon, presumably for moral support, and Eliza watched his reaction, pleased to see that he simply stared at Daisy with stern eyes.

"It's not how it looks, that's why I wanted to talk to you," Daisy pleaded.

"So go on then. What happened exactly? Tell me," Eliza folded her arms.

"It was the other night, when my windows got smashed, I was so scared. And I got carried away because Brandon helped me and I kissed him," Daisy looked down.

"Ah so the poor little, damsel Daisy was frightened and big strong Brandon rescued you. Did he arrive on a white horse too?"

"Don't be silly," Daisy looked embarrassed.

"Silly? Me?" Eliza walked up to Daisy and prodded her sharply on the shoulder. "You are the one who is silly! Your airs and graces, the drama. Oh my god, how terrible it all is."

"I ..."

"Don't interrupt me!" Eliza continued. "What happened to you being Little Miss Independent? I thought you were going to stand on your own two feet and get this business running. But no! You faff around with business lunches here and dramas there. What have you actually done to set up your guesthouse eh?"

"Well I have made plans for ..."

"What exactly? Stella is doing your PR and your launch, the decorators did the hard work on the house and Brandon has built your website."

"I made the investment," Daisy fought back.

"With Christophe's money!" Eliza realised that this was a hard nail to throw, but her friend needed to hear it.

"What?" Daisy's eyes filled with tears.

"When you have actually got round to doing any work towards running your own business, rather than paying other people to do it for you, then tell me you are a business woman. Because at the moment you are playing a game and expecting everyone else to rally round when you need them."

"But ..." Daisy protested.

"And you can save the tears! It won't work with me anymore. I have a real business meeting to prepare for today. One that *my* future dreams depend on!" Eliza picked up the photo and pointed at it, "This has not helped to put me in the right frame of mind."

There was silence apart from Daisy letting out the odd sob.

Eliza was still angry. "Do you know what you need to do?"

"What?" Asked Daisy.

"Go back to your guesthouse and get your hands dirty doing some real work for a change. Get the door open, get some guests in. Get some reviews. Feel what it is like to really push yourself, to work all hours and hopefully earn enough to cover the overheads. Then come and tell me you run a business, because at the moment you are running a circus!"

Daisy shook her head and ran out of the kitchen, almost stumbling down the stairs, slamming the front door as she left.

Eliza stood, her heart beating, her eyes blazing.

"Wow," Brandon said softly, "I have never seen that side of you before."

"I would say sorry, but I am not," Eliza replied, taking the cigarette from his hand and taking a drag, "It was all true."

He pulled her into his arms and kissed her fiercely and for a few seconds she responded, before she pushed him away.

"I need to get ready for my meeting," she walked out of the room and went into the bathroom, locking the door.

"As you wish my warrior woman," Brandon murmured.

CHAPTER TWENTY-FOUR

Katya stood outside Glen's caravan, pulling her coat tightly against the cold. She felt isolated on this blustery cliff top, her dark hair escaping in thick strands from its braid, flying around her head. Her anxiety was heightened as he was not expecting her and she had not seen him since the night he visited her cottage. She had no idea how he was going to react. Feeling awkward, she knocked on the door; the noise sounded intrusive and foreign in this secluded landscape.

She heard movement inside the caravan, and, after what seemed like ages, he opened the door.

"Hello," she said quietly, looking up at him over her glasses. Her stomach felt knotted and she held her breath.

"Katya," he replied. He looked surprised but opened the door wide, "Come in out of the cold, you must be freezing."

"Thank you," she replied, pulling her coat around her as though it were a blanket as she climbed the shallow step into the mobile home.

"Did you get the cat sorted?" He asked.

"Cat?"

"Sorry I haven't been in to see you since you gave me that reading and then I turned up and drank all your wine. You were looking after the kitten."

"Oh, yes, Merlin found his way back home," she replied, relieved that Glen was not angry at her arrival.

"Good, good," Glen replied, "So what brings you here today?"

"Well," Katya bit her lip, wondering just how to begin, "I might just as well come out with it, as there is no easy way to explain all this."

"Explain?" Glen looked confused.

"Okay. Here goes," Katya took a deep breath, "It has to do with Daisy and your connection with each other and the déjà vu and her dreams."

He looked highly interested at the mention of Daisy's name, but also confused. "I don't think Daisy is going to be part of my life," he frowned.

"But..." Katya could not tell him she had seen their kiss, "You were so hopeful?"

"And things were going well; we met up and she began to believe me. But this morning, in fact just now, before you arrived, she called to say she thinks it is better if we no longer see each other."

Katya did not want to let this opportunity pass. She needed answers. Sheryl had her under a protection spell so that she could shield her own thoughts, and her crystal pendulum was charged and ready to guide the regression. She would never find the confidence again, it had to be now. "I may be able to help... both of you. If you want me to that is?"

"How?"

"Have you heard of regression?"

He looked slightly amazed and worried at the same time. "Take a seat," he gestured to the L-shaped sofa, "Would you like a coffee?"

Katya spied the array of herbal teas in the compact kitchen.

"Please could I have a chamomile instead? I don't do caffeine. Sends me a bit loopy, you know."

"That's fine," he replied, making his way to the kitchen and preparing her drink.

"I hope you don't mind my coming to see you?" Katya asked.

"Katya, if you can shed some light on the mysterious goings on that have been plaguing me since my accident, then you are my guest. I have no problem with anything you can help me with," he turned to face her, "Besides, I trust you."

He trusted her. This admission made her feel confident. She sat down, removing her coat as she was now too warm after coming indoors out of the cold. She took in the surroundings, feeling the energy of the room. "This is lovely, but it's not you," she said breaking the silence, "If you don't mind me saying so."

"You mean the caravan?" Glen asked.

"Yes. You have so much… what's the word… depth. This is beautifully modern, but it is not a reflection of your soul."

"Well, I am only here until March. It is serving a purpose at the moment, while I find what *my* purpose is." He poured the contents of the kettle into two mugs that were obviously new, "It has been brilliant for giving me solitude and the view is amazing."

"You are lucky you have so much choice," she said quietly.

"Sorry?" He looked over.

"I live in that small, rented, cottage, and that is as much as I will ever have. It is lovely, enough for me and my books and my stuff. But," she sighed wistfully. "I sometimes wish for something a little grander, you know, a bit more space, for a desk and more books – like a wood-panelled library or something."

He sat down next to her, placing the mugs on the coffee table. "Property was my world. I lived and breathed it, but recent events have taught me that a house is merely a set of walls and a roof. All that we need is in here," he tapped his chest.

"Oh, yes, I totally agree with you, but hey, if I won the lottery or something, I would have a library." Katya looked down and picked up her mug; she had said too much. Waffling.

"So, what's all this about regression?"

"Okay. Taking everything into account, your vision and experience, Daisy's dreams, the sense of familiarity and the déjà vu, I think you two may have been together in a past life," she explained, watching Glen's face closely for a reaction.

He simply looked at her, blankly.

"Sorry, have I offended you?" She asked.

Glen shook his head slowly. "No. I am just absorbing what you have told me and it does seem to make sense. If anything does?"

"There is an ancient concept around a spiritual form of record keeping, called the Akashic Records," Katya began, "Every word, action, thought and deed is recorded. Past, present and future. Nothing that happens is an accident."

"That would be pre-destination," Glen frowned.

"Yes. And to a certain extent, I believe that pre-destination exists, but that we have choices that go alongside our destiny, to…" Katya hesitated as she sought to find the right words, "…learn the lessons we agreed to experience before we were born."

Glen nodded, but looked a little confused.

"Let me give you an example," Katya smiled gently "A man in his past life took many taxes from poor people and made them suffer. He may have decided in between lives, that in the next life he will learn the lesson of what it means to be poor in order to restore his karmic balance."

Glen looked at her. "So we choose our lessons?"

Katya was feeling more confident now she was talking about a subject she understood. "In essence yes. It is theory that has been backed up by research through regression and channelling.

"Wow," Glen looked at her in admiration.

"So, perhaps you and Daisy have been brought together by pre-destination in order to learn a lesson you have both agreed to fulfil?" Katya looked up, once more sure of her own knowledge. "Maybe you have some sort of karmic issue to resolve. That's why the pull is so strong."

Glen smiled, and looked deep in thought. "What would happen, do you think, if we both ignored this calling and went our separate ways?"

Katya was about to speak, but Glen gestured for her to wait and continued. "I know that for Daisy it would probably be far easier for her to forget she had ever met me. But I strongly believe, like you, that we have been brought together for a reason. It could have taken me years, decades to find her. But I found her right here in this town. I only moved back this way because it reminded me of childhood, and simple ways. I never for one moment thought that the woman from my vision would be living here."

Katya smiled. "And Daisy has only returned here because she and Christophe got divorced. Otherwise she would still be living near London."

Glen stopped and looked startled. "I lived near London. Why didn't we meet there?"

Katya thought back to the photos she had seen.

Glen stood up. "Wait, we did! That night – there was a party we were both at, and that was the night both our lives changed, Daisy and I have talked about this already," he looked excited, and was talking quickly, "Then within hours we were both single and within months we had both moved on, for different reasons, to this town."

"See," Katya said, "that is the pre-destination. Your paths have been intertwined, gradually getting closer."

Glen sat down again, silent appearing to be in awe of the revelation.

"You could choose to ignore it, but you would then probably have to repeat all this in the next life." She looked down, playing with her amethyst ring and feeling a little sad as she imagined him and Daisy together; why was she being brought into this? What part was the universe really asking her to play?

"What's the matter?" Glen asked.

Katya shrugged. "Nothing," she replied, "I just sometimes struggle to make sense of the path that has been set for me."

"Do you want to talk about it?"

Katya shook her head. "Not now. That's for another time," she looked back at Glen, "This is about you and Daisy and this is why I am here. If you will let me help?"

Glen looked a little hopeful. "Please. What do you want me to do?"

. . . . .

Daisy re-seated herself at the laptop in the kitchen feeling determined. Following Eliza's outburst, she had stomped all the way home at a fast pace, pouting and trying not to cry. Who was Eliza anyway? She ran a little shop selling weird stuff. Not like running a guesthouse. She herself had run an art gallery in Paris of all places! She would show Eliza, Brandon, and her mother that she could do this and prove once and for all that Daisy Hartford was capable of great things. As she walked, she rejected a call from Glen, then almost instantly decided that the new Daisy would take charge of the situation, so she phoned him straight back and told him that it may be better if they didn't see each other while she got the business up and running. He began to protest so she simply cut the call short, saying she had to go. It was so simple, so easy. So decisive.

The stomp turned into a springing step as she neared the guesthouse and upon arrival she turned the radio on loud. She was not going to be spooked by creaks and bumps as the walls isolated her from the real world. Soon this place would be full of people and she would not have to endure the silence anymore.

She had got straight to work, phoning Stella to arrange a meeting that afternoon, then phoned Penny and Siobhan to do the same, and visited her social media pages to post some positive comments about how excited she was about opening. Now, enjoying the buzz of being busy and realising she had emerged from a mist of apathy, she looked at the website Brandon had created and proudly viewed the photos of the bedrooms and the drawing room. How could she get the rooms occupied to get some reviews? Swallowing her pride, she phoned her father and also invited him round for a chat. Harry said he could be there by six.

Penny was the first to arrive, standing anxiously on the doorstep, as Daisy welcomed her in.

"Come on in Penny, thank you for seeing me at such short notice," Daisy led the cook through to the kitchen, "Let me get you a coffee."

"Thank you." Penny smiled, her round face quite pink, perhaps from years of working in kitchens.

Daisy dashed out as the doorbell rang again, this time signalling the arrival of Siobhan, the housekeeper. The slim Irish girl followed Daisy into the kitchen and seated herself next to Penny.

"So we meet again. It's great to see you." Daisy smiled, placing their drinks down as she joined them at the table. "Right, let's get to the point. Are you both okay to start work next week?"

The two ladies glanced at each other, smiling and both nodding.

"We were wondering when you were going to ask us." Siobhan replied.

"Oh, sorry, yes I've had a lot going on," Daisy blushed, embarrassed that she hadn't contacted them since the photo shoot, "Well, I am looking at getting some trial guests in next week and seeing how it all goes, and some reviews."

"You will need to finalise your menu then," Penny piped up.

"Sorry?" Daisy asked,

"You haven't decided on a menu. At my interview you said it was a crucial part of running the guesthouse but …"

"Please, forgive me. Yes you are quite right Penny."

"Anyway, I hope you don't mind, but I've put together some ideas," Penny reached into her handbag and pulled out a sheet of paper with a menu neatly hand-written.

Daisy scanned the list, impressed by Penny's ideas. "Thank you, that is so helpful."

"Do you have your catering suppliers ready?" the cook asked.

Daisy panicked; she had not even thought about that and wondered about asking Penny to organise it. No, she must do this herself. "It's on my list to do for next week. Do you have any recommendations from work you have done before?"

Penny nodded and borrowed Daisy's pen to write the company names on the sheet of paper.

"I will need to make all the beds up and clean everywhere the day before the guests arrive," Siobhan pointed out.

"Oh the beds are already made up – me and my friend Eliza did them for the photo shoot," Daisy paused, "Actually Eliza did most of them, come to think of it…"

"But that was over a week ago. They will need freshening up and new linen and towels," Siobhan looked down, "If you don't mind my saying?"

"Yes of course," Daisy replied. These two women knew far more about running a guesthouse than she did.

The sound of the doorbell interrupted the meeting as Stella arrived. As usual she was in a hurry and her heels echoed through the hall. She talked as she walked. "We are almost ready to go with the launch. The Mayor can now come, press will be here, the owners of the galleries in the area, the Head of Art from the college, some other local business owners, and Glen Heathstone."

Siobhan and Penny looked startled as Stella arrived in the kitchen and flashed her smile at them.

"Glen Heathstone? What have you invited him for?" Cried Daisy.

"Contacts! He has hundreds. You could fill your rooms with his email list alone."

"But he is retired. You should have confirmed this with me Stella."

"Look, I don't know why you are getting so uptight about it. Trust me, having him at your launch is no bad thing."

"Do you want me to plan a menu for the launch Ms Hartford?" Penny asked.

"Yes please do. Nibbles, buffet, sophisticated food, that sort of thing."

Stella looked impatient. "Do you have an itinerary for the launch?"

"What?" Daisy asked, "I thought you were doing that?"

"I need some pointers though. What is happening when? Do you have any music organised? Where do you want the press to stand?"

Daisy felt three pairs of eyes staring at her. She needed to sound like she knew what she was doing. She did know what she was doing. She just hadn't done all this for a long time. She thought quickly. "Music needs to be classical. I will arrange it.

Of course, I have a draft itinerary; I just need to finalise it and then I would love your feedback Stella, as you are a pro at this." Daisy smiled.

"Is that all then?" Stella asked, "I have to go."

"Yes that's all. But keep in touch."

Stella looked a little smug. "I do keep in touch. If you had checked my emails over the last three days, I could have saved the trip," she kissed Daisy on the cheek and then left, slamming the front door on her way out.

It dawned on Daisy that Eliza was right; she had not been hands on at all with this business and if it was a complete disaster, it was her own fault. She had to turn this round. She looked at the eager faces of Penny and Siobhan and her shoulders slumped. "Do you have any ideas for the grand launch or the trial guests?"

"Not off the top of my head," Siobhan shook her head, "but I will have a think."

"You could do a special offer?" Penny suggested.

"Oh!" Siobhan smiled, "you could have a theme evening. The launch could have a theme, with the music and the food."

"Or with the trial guests, have a theme evening and a quiz night or something?" Penny suggested.

Daisy was not sure that a quiz night was in keeping with the style she wanted to create, but she was liking the idea of a theme and enjoying the way these ladies were so keen to help her.

· · · · ·

Katya had managed to hypnotise Glen quite easily. His leanings towards meditation and his current open-minded state lent themselves well to linking with his subconscious. He relaxed on the sofa as she sat next to him, watching him carefully. His eyelids were closed and his face peaceful.

"I ask you now to walk towards a set of doors. Just two to start with. Each door will lead to a former life, and it is up to you to choose which one you take," she waited as she noticed some slight movement in his facial muscles, "When you go through the door of your choice, look down at your feet and tell me what you are wearing."

"I am wearing sandals," he said slowly, "I have bare legs and I think I am wearing a tunic."

"What colour is the tunic?" She asked.

"Brown," he replied, "It's not fancy but I have a nice belt. It is precious to me. It was my father's."

"Do you know where you are? Can you look up and tell me about your surroundings?" She waited for him to process the instructions.

"I am in a courtyard. It is beautiful. There are pillars and a fountain. Other people are wandering about," His face was relaxed as he indulged in the location.

"Do you know any of these people?" She asked.

"I don't think so," he shook his head.

"Okay, that's good. Now travel forward a little in this life time. Tell me what happens," she waited as he progressed.

"The ground is rumbling, and I am holding a woman's hand. She is my mother. But not my mother in this life, this is an unknown mother."

"Your mother, is she talking to you?" Katya asked.

"She is telling me to go, to leave her," he frowned.

"Do you want to?"

"No. But I have to. I have no choice."

Katya watched as his eyelids began to move.

"Now I am with a younger woman. I am telling her to come with me. But she doesn't want to leave," he looked a little anguished, "She must come with me."

"Why do you both need to go?" Katya watched him with concern.

"It is coming. It will kill us all." He was clearly upset.

"What is coming?" She asked.

"The fire is coming up into the sky and rocks are falling. The lovely buildings are beginning to crumble and we will be buried if we don't run soon," he shook his head. "She will not listen. She doesn't trust me."

"Do you know where the fire is coming from?" Katya prompted.

"Yes. The mountain. It is a big cloud, grey and hot. Our homes will be destroyed."

"What is the woman doing now?" Katya asked.

"She is holding my hand and I am telling her to come, but she is resisting. I keep telling her we have to go. We have to run."

"Do you know who she is?" Katya waited to see whether he recognised the woman.

"Yes, she is my love. We are to be married. This was to be our home," he hesitated, "But we need to go now."

"Do you know her name?"

"Thalia. I love her" he smiled.

Katya smiled too as she saw the emotion on his face.

"What is your name?"

"Maris."

"What is happening now?" She said calmly.

"The cloud is coming closer, we are doomed. It is getting hotter. There is no escape."

Katya could see that Glen was becoming agitated, "Okay, you can come back to the doorways now if you wish to. That life has nothing more to tell you.

Glen became calm once more and Katya encouraged him to focus on his breathing.

"Do you want to go through another door?" She asked.

"Yes," he nodded.

"Okay, in your own time." She waited as his breathing calmed.

"There are still two doors," he explained.

"Which one do you want to go through?"

"The one on the left."

"Go on then," she said gently.

"There is nothing. I am in a room alone. I am writing with a quill. My hands are old," his face was contorted with sadness and grief. He looked like an old man.

Katya prompted more details. "Is there anything around you?"

"No, just the candle and my writing. My desk. The room is bare," he was silent and his face became sad, "I betrayed her, it was all false. There is nothing for me here now," he paused, then shook his head, "I do not want to stay. She was burned and I am to be hanged anyway despite my loyalty to my master. It is all my fault. I am remorseful. I don't want to be here. It is cold."

"Then come back and go through another doorway if you wish," Katya said softly.

His face relaxed once more. "I have gone through."

"Good, what are you wearing?"

"I am wearing a coat. It looks worn. I have boots and trousers. They look old too," he seemed happy however.

"Do you know where you are?" She asked.

"I am next to a harbour. It is cold and wet," he hugged himself slightly, as if to try to warm up.

Katya struggled to contain her excitement; this was the part she had been waiting for. "And is anyone around you?"

"Yes my friend is here. She loves me," he smiled.

"Do you recognise her?" Katya could feel the warmth of his emotions.

"Oh yes. My dear friend Annette," he was still smiling.

Katya swallowed hard, biting back her emotions. "Do you know your name?"

"Robert, Robbie," he confirmed.

"What are you doing?"

"I am trying to console her," he looked serious now.

"Why?"

"She is crying and I don't want to hurt her. I never meant to hurt her, but I love another." Once again, his face became concerned.

"What is she doing now?" Katya asked.

"She is still crying. It is awful, my heart is so sad. She is running from me."

"Who is the other that you love?"

"Victoria. I am walking up to see her now. To tell her I am about to set sail. I am going to make my fortune and come back. She will not wed me, she says she cannot, as I have little money. I know she wants to but she is scared of her family. She has been ill with a fever." A tear ran down Glen's cheek, but he did not seem distressed, just very sad. "She does not believe I can change my fortune so I have to show her. She says she will wait for me."

"Do you think she will?"

"I don't know. She may meet another while I am gone."

"Then why don't you stay?"

"Because I need to prove to her that I am more than just a harbour boy. That I can return with gold and take her to a new life."

"Which boat do you need to get on?"

"The one that will take me to new prospects. When I return I will have gold and Victoria will be well again." Glen's face was both sad yet hopeful.

"Come forward now in this life and tell me what happens on the boat." Katya urged.

He shook his head. "There is a terrible storm. We have not long set off. It was calm for a while, and safe. Then it just came from nowhere."

"What just came?"

"The storm. The whole boat is tossing and turning, I feel sick. We are all being thrown around. It is so loud," he was frightened.

"Do you want to stop?" Katya asked, concerned.

"I want the boat to stop. I want to go back to Annette. I wish I hadn't come. I am going to die," Glen's face was now becoming distressed.

"What about Victoria?"

"I love her. But I am going to die. I should have listened to Annette," his breathing was too fast and he was agitated, so although she was curious to know more Katya decided to pull him back quickly.

"And now you are back by the doors and you are leaving these lifetimes behind you. They are in the past. You will learn from them what you need to and come gently back into the present when you are ready."

Glen's face relaxed once more as he became calm.

"When you hear the sound of the small bell, you will be back with me in your caravan in your current life as Glen Heathstone. Breathe slowly and deeply. There is no rush."

Katya rang the little bell that she had brought with her, and encouraged Glen not to move too quickly, and to wiggle his toes and fingers as he returned to full consciousness. As he sat up straight, she passed him a glass of water.

"Don't move too suddenly, but stretch and yawn if you need to," she advised.

Glen opened his eyes, which were misty with tears and he gratefully sipped the water. "Thank you," he said. "That was amazing."

"Are you feeling okay?" Katya asked.

"Yes, so much has become clear now," he nodded.

"Such as?" Katya asked, "That is if you want to talk about it?"

Glen stood slowly, gently stretching his tall frame. Walking nearer to the window, he looked out at the harbour that lay to the East of the headland. "Now I am starting to understand," he said quietly, "I have allowed her to slip away three times, and each time brought sadness or death."

"Thalia and Victoria? Are they the same person, the same soul?" Katya asked, hopeful that she had made some progress.

He looked at Katya and she saw tears welling up in his eyes.

"Thalia and Victoria. They were both Daisy. I can't let her go again."

"What about Annette?"

"Annette was a friend, and I should have listened to her."

Katya's heart sank a little. "What about the other life you visited? The one where you were writing?"

"I had nothing, no one, just me. That's how I am now. That's how I am without her." He wore an expression that Katya had not seen on his face before. It was a mixture of realisation and all-consuming grief rolled into one.

"Are you sure it was her?" Katya asked.

"Yes of course I'm sure," Glen replied firmly, "She looked slightly different, but it was her soul, her eyes. I never want to lose her again. I cannot bear that feeling in this lifetime. I never want to feel like that."

Katya was worried. What if she had unleashed a power that could not be controlled? The strongest power of all – love. Had she manipulated events against the will of the universe; or had she stepped in at just the right time, as the messenger that destiny had intended her to be?

"I'm sorry," she said, hardly daring to look at him.

"Why? This is brilliant. You have opened up the truth. I now know why Daisy and I are connected," he looked excited, "I need to tell her."

Again, Katya grew concerned at the difference in him. "But it has pained you so. What if she still won't listen or believe and you have to go through that loss once more?"

"I can't let that happen," he stated clearly, "I will do whatever it takes. I did not think this was about love, but the feeling is like no other I have experienced – other than my vision. The feeling when I am with her is like the golden light I have been searching for."

Katya was exhausted, yet so many answers had come through. She had a past life connection to both Glen and Daisy, but she was the cast off – the unwanted one. Yet he regretted not listening to her. "So what will you do now?" She asked.

"We have to convince her, Katya. We have to find a way to show her the truth." She could see that his determination was now going to be unstoppable.

Katya sighed and rubbed her pretty face in her hands; quietly pleased and amazed that the regression had been so enlightening, but also worried at how this would now manifest. She also wondered why she was always the messenger and never seemed to experience such cataclysmic moments of her own.

CHAPTER TWENTY-FIVE

Seeing the expression on Eliza's face when she returned from her meeting, made Brandon want to punch the walls. He did not even have to ask; her face said it all. He wanted so much for her to follow her dreams, knowing how much time she had invested in her business and how important it was to her. He had offered to help, but Eliza was fiercely independent and cast aside his support. It was almost painful watching her battle on in her lonely bubble.

"Sorry babe," he hugged her tightly as she stood before him, her blue eyes filled with tears.

"It's okay. I knew deep down it wouldn't happen," she sniffed against his shoulder, and his arms gripped her tenderly. He wanted to show her he understood but frustratingly, he never seemed to be able to put it into words.

She pulled away from him, and took off her jacket. "Grr I hate wearing business clothes!" She stormed off to the bedroom and returned quickly in her jeans and a vest top, pulling her favourite patchwork cardigan around her. She slumped on the sofa, appearing tired and relieved at the same time. Brandon was concerned, he had never seen her look this defeated. He opened a bottle of Shiraz and poured a large glass.

"Wine?"

"Yes please!" She took the glass from him and took a large sip, sighing with appreciation.

"So what happened?" He joined her on the sofa.

"I did nothing wrong," she sniffed and he could tell that she had been crying while she got changed, "I did everything right! I presented my case and my plans. My accountant said it would be cost effective in two years and they thought my plan was exciting and achievable,"

"So what went wrong?"

"The competitor for the space is a part of a larger long-running business, but they wouldn't tell me who it was.

Brandon, nothing is about passion anymore, it's all about money. I think it is all signed up already. I don't stand a chance. And even fudging the accounts a bit, it was obvious I couldn't really afford the investment."

He put his arm around her and she nestled her head into him. "So what now?" He asked.

"Just carry on as I am I suppose. The shop is doing well, I can't complain. Perhaps I was getting carried away with bigger ideas?"

"Have you thought about looking for some bigger premises rather than staying in the same shop?"

She shook her head. "No, that building is special, it stands out and it's in the right spot. The last thing I want to do is move. That's why the unit next door would have been ideal."

"Something will come up."

"I suppose."

"On a plus note, I have secured two new contracts for websites," he smiled.

"That's fantastic! Well done!" She clinked glasses with him.

"I didn't want to rub it in, but at least we have one good outcome as a couple today."

Eliza put her glass down. "No, we have two positive outcomes."

"Oh? What's the other one?"

She took his chin gently in her hand, ensuring that he looked at her.

"All that stuff this morning. With the photo and everything. It made me realise how much I love you. I was jealous."

He placed his glass down and reached out to her, his eyes taking her face in fully as he wanted to relish this moment.

"So you finally see that I love you and there will never be another?"

"Yes," she whispered, "I do."

"Thank you," he replied, caressing her cheek and moving a tendril of strawberry blond hair away from her eyes that were again filling with tears.

He felt as though he was drowning in her beauty as he gazed at her and it was overwhelming him. He had never thought that Eliza, his warrior woman, would let down her guard. Now here she was trusting him and loving him as much as he loved her. He pulled her close and kissed her tenderly as silent tears rolled down her cheeks.

· · · · ·

Katya walked into the shop, her face clouded by a crestfallen expression. Sheryl rushed out from behind the counter.

"Oh what's the matter Lovey?"

Katya took hold of Sheryl's hands, and looked into her warm eyes. "I did the regression."

"Well done. I knew you could do it you are…"

"I think I've done more harm than good!" Katya panicked, tightening her grip on the clairvoyant's hands.

"Look, stop panicking. Come on, let's sit down." Sheryl ushered her over to the back of the shop and took her into the small room that Eliza used for readings. "Right, tell me what happened." Sheryl held Katya's hand across the table.

Katya took a deep breath. "He is upset because now Daisy doesn't want to see him," she shook her head, "He was desperate for answers and agreed to the regression. So I did it."

"And?"

"And it worked. Amazingly," Katya half smiled through her angst.

"Why are you so upset when you have achieved so much?"

"Because I am worried about what I have unleashed. And I am also unsure of my motives for doing it in the first place."

"What do you mean? We agreed it was the right thing to do, in the circumstances."

"Yes but was I doing it for him or for me?" Katya cried.

"What are you trying to say?"

Katya took a deep breath, trying to control her emotions.

"Sheryl, I am in love with him."

Sheryl chuckled. "Well I knew that lovey. It's hardly a crime."

"But I regressed him to help him find out about Daisy, and I was looking for answers in his experience to my own questions."

"Which are?"

"Am I a past life connection to him? Did he remember me? Did he once love me? Because if my dreams are anything to go by, he did," Katya wiped a tear away, "for a while anyway."

"And did it answer any of your questions?"

"Yes. He knew me as Annette, here in this town before the storm. He knew I loved him but he chose her and turned away from me!" Katya cried.

"Did he know you were Annette?"

"No, he didn't make the connection, thankfully."

"So was that the only life time he recalled?"

"No, there were two more, and he became so upset I decided enough was enough so I pulled him out. But Sheryl, it was all about Daisy. He is now even more obsessed with her! I don't know what he is going to do?"

Sheryl gave her a hug across the table, then leaned back. "Look, firstly you didn't influence the regression, and secondly you have acted ethically. Thirdly, remember everything happens for a reason. Everything is as it is meant to be in any particular space or time."

"I know," Katya nodded, "I even told Glen about destiny and karma."

"If something is meant to happen then it will. If it is not meant to happen then it won't, no matter how much you try"

"What do I do, if I am never meant to be with him? I don't think I can bear it."

"My dear, you are beautiful, you have a beautiful soul and a beautiful face. I feel you have been misplacing your love for a long, long time. Perhaps that's what this life is about. Remember finding your power and true voice?"

"So am I destined to be alone again, while Daisy enjoys her destiny with him?"

"Not exactly lovey, it's not that simple. Some experiences are about learning."

Katya shook her head. "Well if this is learning, constant love and heartbreak, then I don't know whether I want to learn anymore."

Sheryl pulled her in for another hug.

"We need to regress you Katya lovey."

Pulling out of the hug, Katya looked across at Sheryl. "Me?"

"Yes. It is the only way to find the link."

Katya shook her head. "I'm not sure. I need to think. Glen is now convinced that Daisy is the love of his life. He never wants to be without her again and I am not sure what he will do."

"What do you mean?"

"He is like a man possessed. He is crazy talking. Not by our standards...of course, but to anyone else … everyone thinks he is insane already. What if this pushes him over the edge?"

Sheryl stood and held Katya's shoulders as she began to sob once more. "You have done nothing wrong lovey. You have just speeded up the inevitable, that's all."

"Yeah I saw his aura – his chakras are on overdrive – everything is going in, but nothing is coming out again. He will burn up spiritually if he doesn't unleash the power of this love he feels."

"Daisy and Glen have been brought together for a reason. We don't know what that is but we need to help them understand what it is that needs to be resolved in this lifetime and end this cycle of tragedy."

"Yes. That's a good plan," Katya agreed, sniffing into a tissue.

"Start writing, lovey. Anything you can think of that Daisy and Glen might need to sort out. Unfinished business. Karma, lessons, anything you heard him say." Sheryl took a notepad and pen from the shelf and thrust it in front of Katya. "I'll get you a cup of tea and I can carry on looking after the shop until closing time."

Katya nodded, wiping a tear from her cheek.

"Then, when you have finished" Sheryl smiled, "you might want to think about having a regression yourself?"

· · · · ·

Although the events of the day had sent Daisy into a panic about the guesthouse, she was now fired up, inspired by Penny and Siobhan's enthusiasm and her own refusal to fail. She wondered about calling Eliza to apologise and to thank her for the kick-start, but her pride would not allow her to admit that her friend was right. Instead she took her A3 drawing pad and laid sheets across the kitchen table, loading her favourite playlist on the laptop. She poured herself a glass of wine and moved quickly round the table with a marker pen, jotting ideas onto the sheets. One for the launch, one for the guests, one for the menu and one marked 'other' and soon the ideas were coming thick and fast. This was the way she had worked when she had run the art gallery and a technique she had quite forgotten about.

The doorbell signalled the arrival of her father, who she had also quite forgotten about in her creative burst.

Harry, as always, looked smart in a crisp shirt and a blazer with jeans. Despite his ageing years and grey hair he was still a handsome man, his warm brown eyes twinkling as he greeted his daughter.

"Dad!" Daisy hugged him and kissed his cheek.

"How are you?" He asked returning her kiss.

She sighed. "I need your help."

He followed her into the kitchen, and she poured him a glass of wine.

"Your mother would say it was far too early, but what the hell, Cheers," he clinked glasses with her, looking at the sheets of paper with interest, "So, what's up?"

"I need some guests. Some pretend guests, to stay for a couple of nights so my staff and I can practice and so I can ask them to leave reviews."

Harry nodded. "Yes that makes sense. Like a trial run?"

"Yes. I was wondering if you knew any people who might like a free break at short notice."

Harry thought, rubbing his chin. "Hmm, well there are my friends at the golf club. All retired though, did you want a younger audience?"

"I don't mind. It's feedback on the facilities, food and the standard I am after," Daisy smiled, "I am not catering for families. This is a high quality, art themed guesthouse, I hadn't envisaged kids running around."

"Then the golf club is probably ideal, in fact one of my friends is an art dealer, so he and his wife would be great contacts for you. Leave it with me. When are they invited?"

"Next week, before the launch on Friday next? Monday?"

"Bloody hell Daisy, you don't give me much time!"

"I know, sorry, but things have kind of crept up on me and the launch is next week."

"I will see what I can do. Do you have business cards I can pass on?"

Daisy jumped up. "Yes!" She passed him some cards and kissed him again on the cheek. "Thanks Dad!"

Harry looked at her, smiling. "I am proud of you Daisy, for trying this. Not many people are brave enough to go out on a limb, and I am more than happy to help."

"Thank you," Daisy looked down, "I wish mum understood."

"She will," Harry nodded, "Give her time to get used to the idea. Once you are up and running she will be telling all her Women's Institute friends about you I am sure."

Daisy nodded. "I hope so."

Harry took her by the shoulders and looked into her eyes. "Don't let anyone stand in your way. Follow your dreams and follow your heart. Never let an opportunity pass you by," Harry smiled, "You can do this Daisy. I believe in you."

Daisy's heart filled with love for her dad as did her eyes.

"Don't cry, you'll get red devil eyes," he smiled and Daisy laughed. It was an old joke from when she was a little girl. He gave her what she called a 'dad hug' and then finished his glass of wine. "Look, I have to go. Before I drink any more of this! I have to drive home you know. Your mother will think I have been out gallivanting!"

Daisy walked him to the door and watched as he went out to his car. A black car pulled up as Harry drove off, beeping the horn as he went. Daisy knew who the black car belonged to. It was Glen Heathstone.

He paused and looked at her before walking towards the house. As he neared the doorstep, Daisy was reminded of just how attractive he was, and thoughts of their kiss tumbled through her mind as he approached.

"I need to speak to you," he said.

"I'm busy," she replied, folding her arms, willing herself not to look into his eyes.

"I will only take ten minutes of your time," he stood awkwardly and she felt guilty, knowing that she had given him false hope with her kiss.

"I ...er ... I have a lot to do. My launch is in just over a week and I have guests arriving on Monday."

"Look, I know you are up against it. I can help if you want me to."

"No. Thank you," she saw him shiver in the cold evening air. Looking beyond him it was completely dark. She must get some lighting in the front garden before the guests arrived.

"Please hear me out," he pleaded.

Relenting, Daisy held the door open and stood back allowing him into the house.

"Ten minutes. That's all I can spare."

They stood next to the kitchen table and Daisy moved the sheets of paper out of the way, self-conscious that he may see her workings.

"Go on then, tell me what it is that you have to say that is so important."

Glen hesitated. "It may be hard to get your head around."

Daisy remained silent. The last thing she needed now was mind games.

"I know why we have such a strong connection," he continued.

Daisy's heart was beating fast, she was falling into the abyss again, just from the sound of his voice. It was bittersweet. She wanted him yet feared him too. What was she afraid of? Getting hurt, or that she may just fall in love again? The world around her became blurred.

"We are past life lovers," he stated.

His words seemed to echo past her in slow motion and something similar to, whatever it was that Katya had called it, déjà vu? It was happening again. She knew what he was going to say next.

"Time and time again," she joined in with his words and he froze as their eyes locked on each other. She fought back the emotions that were churning through her: the attraction, the fear, the all-encompassing feeling of intensity. Her heart felt as though it was going to burst as he moved closer and their faces were almost touching. She should move away now, but she did not want to.

He pulled her close and kissed her tenderly on the lips. Her insides melted at his touch as she allowed the kiss to continue, enjoying his proximity and the feeling of safety from his hand at the small of her back. She relaxed as he took her into his arms properly, her body pressing against his quite unconsciously. She was enjoying his warmth, and her hands ran along his back, tantalised by the feel of his flesh pressing against his thin shirt. He smelt like home and the kiss acted as a familiar drug, one she had become addicted to many times before. She could not tear herself away. All thoughts of fear and of her business vanished as a euphoria overcame her, sending her senses into overdrive. Their lips detached from each other and she looked into his eyes, drowning in their allure. Nothing mattered except this. She took him by the hand and led him up to the attic after pausing several times on the stairs to kiss again.

Her bed was not even made from when she had awoken that morning. It had been such a strange day, but one that faded into insignificance as they tumbled onto the sheets. His hands moved gently across her t-shirt, then under her t-shirt caressing her breasts as his lips moved to her neck and she arched towards him, her arms pulling him closer. She undid the buttons on his shirt and ran her fingers over his chest, feeling his heart beating and his body hardening against her. As he kissed her lips again, she wanted to merge into him completely. A world of familiar joy and elation lay at her fingertips and a profound longing coursed through her, an intensity she had never known. As his hands moved to her jeans, unzipping them, his eyes seemed to look into the deepest parts of her soul and she put up no resistance to his hands as they continued to explore her body. She was lost in him, lost in his eyes and his lips as his fingers caressed her, every nerve responding to his touch. Unable to bear the yearning any more, she pulled him towards her, taking him inside her as she crossed over into oblivion. Their souls were finally uniting, crashing together relentlessly as she realised that all she had ever truly known was him.

CHAPTER TWENTY-SIX

Katya had spent the last three days mulling over Glen's regression and her own feelings and dreams, desperately trying to piece it all together, but she was not getting any answers. It felt as though she only had one side of the story.

Daisy and Glen obviously had a past life connection yet she could not see any pattern to their existences other than their inevitable deaths. And where did she fit in? The last encounter that Glen had experienced in his regression resonated with her own dreams but other than his use of the name 'Annette', it offered no proof of their connection, or that she had encountered Daisy before.

She was becoming confused, the spiral growing ever bigger and complicated further by her own imagination. Even her trusted tarot and angel cards were not helping. She frequently turned cards relating to patience and trust. She was trying to trust, but at the same time her patience with the Universe was wearing thin. It was time to take matters in her own hands so she had followed Sheryl's guidance and contacted the colourful clairvoyant for a regression of her own.

Standing outside the charming whitewashed cottage, she was nervous as she knocked the door and turned to look with interest at the small front garden. Lavender, Sage, Basil and Peppermint she spotted quickly, and to any passer-by it would appear to be a normal herb garden, but as Katya spied the holly bush in the corner and a juniper at the side of the house she realised this was a witches' kitchen. She suspected there was probably Valerian and Belladonna growing somewhere around, perhaps even Mugwort. A robin landed on the wall nearby and looked at her, knowingly, and Katya took this as confirmation that she was doing the right thing.

As the door opened inwards, Sheryl's face beamed at her over her blue ensemble and Katya felt instantly reassured.

"Katya, come on in lovey," Sheryl embraced her and kissed her cheek.

"Thank you," Katya bustled in through the narrow doorway, feeling warm as she entered the cottage.

The familiar scent of incense pervaded her nostrils and Sheryl guided her along the hall, gesturing at a closed door to their left.

"That's Jan's sitting room. You don't want to go in there," Sheryl shook her head, laughing.

"Is she in?" Katya was nervous of Jan for some reason, although the woman had been quite supportive during their last conversation.

"No, she has gone away for a couple of days. A course I think. Shamanic drumming or something," Sheryl showed Katya through a door to the right, "This is my sitting room. We are sisters who share a house, but we are very different. We have our own sitting rooms and our own bedrooms and then we share the kitchen and the orangery. It's perfect," Sheryl smiled.

Katya followed her into a most delightful sitting room. Although the walls were painted white, every colour of the rainbow was evident through an array of textiles and ornaments. A large amethyst cave stood next to the fireplace.

"Wow," Katya crouched and touched the sparkling purple stone, amazed by its beauty.

"That is one of the most expensive pieces in this room," Sheryl laughed.

"I don't doubt that. I have always wanted one," Katya stood and admired the rest of the room. There was no single influence. The textiles were a mixture of Indian, Oriental and local hand-made, while the ornaments ranged from Celtic to Norse to Native American.

As if reading her mind, Sheryl spoke: "I can't make my mind up lovey. I like all of them. I never married or had children so I travelled a lot and collected things, as you can see," Sheryl winked at her, "I could tell you some stories!"

Katya laughed, thinking that perhaps filling a room with things you loved, regardless of whether they matched, actually worked very well. She thought that perhaps she should travel now that Liam was grown up.

"Take a seat anyway and I'll put the kettle on," Sheryl invited, and Katya sat comfortably on the sofa.

"I don't think I want any tea just yet," Katya replied, "just water until after the regression."

"Are you sure you want to do this lovey?"

"Yes I have to. My mind is going crazy with questions. This is the only way."

"Okay, then take your coat and shoes off, and make yourself comfortable. You can lie down if you want to. I will go and get us both some water."

Sheryl left the room, leaving Katya alone amongst the mixture of many magical things. Her attention was caught by a ceramic ornament of the goddess, simple and glazed green, round bellied and breasts ripe. Why did she fear witchcraft when this image was so much about the mother and the moon? She thought of the herbs growing in the garden and of Sheryl and Jan themselves. There was nothing sinister about them.

Sheryl returned with two coloured glasses filled with iced water. "Hope you don't mind the ice. I have the dreaded hot flushes."

"Ice is fine," Katya nodded sipping the cool liquid.

Sheryl sat down on the opposite sofa. "Are you ready?"

Katya thought for a moment, visualising Glen and remembering her dreams and the way she had felt when she had been cast aside by him. If it was him.

"I love him and I need to know," she heard herself say.

"Do you want to talk about him before we start?" Sheryl replied.

Katya did, but was unsure how to describe her feelings. It was hard to put into words.

"When I am with him I feel, I don't know, calm. But at the same time my heart beats so fast. I cannot look into his eyes... I feel so much emotion, it hurts so much and yet I want to be near him. I enjoy spending time with him. Everything else seems to fade away when he is with me."

Sheryl nodded. "He may not be the unconditional love we talked about before though. The one your lessons have mentioned."

"Really?" Katya's heart sank with a feeling that was becoming too familiar.

"Only time will tell. You need to be patient."

Not again! Katya thought. She needed answers and here was Sheryl of all people reinforcing what her cards were already telling her. "Won't the regression tell?"

"It may very well, but you don't know what will come up. Are you happy for me to try and empty your mind before we start?"

"Yes. I think so," Katya felt a little helpless, but she had complete trust and faith in Sheryl and wanted to know what the regression would reveal.

. . . . .

After three attempts at meditation Glen gave up, unplugging the earphones that delivered the calming music and changing the track to some rock. He swapped his glass of water for a whiskey and looked out to sea from the window of his caravan. He could not settle. The frustration he felt inside, knowing what felt right, what was right, and not being able to act upon it. It had been three days since Daisy and he had made love, and despite leaving several messages she was not returning his calls. He reluctantly gave her the space and time she obviously needed.

She had been so warm that night; he believed they were deeply in love, feeling so sure she felt the same way. He could not shake off the emotions or the images that replayed in his mind. So many times his fingers had begun to text her or to ring her. But his own sense of discipline and respect had stopped him.

Her business was obviously important to her; he of all people could relate to that, and he did not want to disturb her when she had made it quite clear that the guesthouse was her current priority. Today was the fourth day, however, and his restraint was beginning to crumble. She was obviously having second thoughts. Just a word, a hello would have been enough to keep him from going round in circles. He felt like screaming out loud and almost did.

He checked his emails and apart from the usual junk and one from Stefan thanking him for sorting things out with Helena Sharpe, there were none. He closed the lid of the laptop. He could not stay online, it would be too tempting to contact Daisy. He thought about phoning Stefan, Jayne, his mother – anyone who he might talk to who would understand. He thought of Stefan and how worried he and Jayne must have been about his decision to sell up. *Have I been selfish?* He wondered. *Am I casting an insult at my father's years of hard work?* He felt guilt building up as he thought about Patrick and the long hours he had worked to create his empire. He thought of his mother sitting at home waiting patiently for her husband to return, never complaining. He thought of his own childhood and how he felt his youth was cut short as his father shaped him for a future in business. While his brother Leo was out climbing and trekking around, Glen was studying for exams and being introduced to the business networks. Then, remembering the day they heard news of Leo's death, perhaps it was only fair that he had been allowed such freedom. Leo and Patrick were now in that place that Glen had glimpsed. A place of peace and harmony where time and boundaries ceased to exist. He had his whole life ahead of him and a second chance to make it right. Love. Love of all kinds was the truth. This is what he had been shown, this is what he had felt. Nothing else mattered. Only love.

The image of Daisy's face returned to him as it had appeared in his near-death and he once again felt that certainty and purpose. How clear it had seemed, how easily everything in his heart and soul had fallen into place. In that instant he had changed forever and when he had met her so soon afterwards, by chance, it certainly seemed that fate had engineered their encounters expertly. Katya's regression of him had only strengthened this purpose by showing him the intervention of fate several times over.

He watched the ocean, the relentless movement of the waves. The tide repeating its journey day in and day out, never ceasing. *Was that what each lifetime was?* He wondered. *A tide of destiny? Moving backwards and forwards, pushing and pulling, ebbing and flowing. The same people coming together each time and being torn apart at the end, only to be thrown back together again.* His brain hurt thinking about it and he swigged the rest of his whiskey back, wishing that he could have these silent discussions with Daisy instead.

He had to convince her.

Pouring himself another drink, he sat down and tried to think logically with the business brain that he used to exercise on a daily basis. Logic. He laughed to himself when he realised it defied logic, and not for the first time he wondered whether he was actually insane. Was it the interruption of blood to the brain when his heart had stopped for several minutes after the accident? Was that the true cause of his amazing experience? He had fully expected the memories of the experience to fade with time – like the after effects of anaesthesia. However, they didn't. It was as clear as crystal. How could he ever convince Daisy of its absolute reality and the intrinsic quality it now held over him? She was never going to understand when she had not experienced the same. It was a complete non-starter for a relationship.

Katya, however, did understand and without doubt. Sipping the whiskey and wincing with a dark pleasure each time the taste hit his senses, he thought about Katya. He pictured her face, her beautiful eyes when she removed her glasses and how she seemed to understand both his verbal and emotional language. She could pre-empt him and make him feel calm. She had listened to him, read his cards, regressed him and understood him in a way that no other had ever done. And here he was worrying about Daisy, who would not give him the time of day. Katya's heart was true. He picked up his phone about to call her. She would be able to calm him down, to talk reason and see sense. Then he stopped himself. It was Sunday. The poor woman was probably having a day off, relaxing, and would not thank him for the interruption. No. He had taken enough of her time and energy and needed to give her some space too. This was something he needed to work out for himself.

CHAPTER TWENTY-SEVEN

After a meditation exercise to empty Katya's busy brain and relax her fully, Sheryl hypnotised Katya into a regressive state and began to encourage her on her journey.

"Do you see doorways or paths ahead of you?"

"I see many pathways. There are no doors."

"That means they are all unlocked. Which one do you want to walk along?"

"I am not sure. None of them are intimidating."

"That's good. Ask your higher self to guide you and just talk about what you see and feel. I will record it so you can listen to it afterwards."

Katya could actually picture her higher self. "I am my higher self. I still have long black hair, pale skin and dark blue eyes and I wear a blue dress. A sort of Grecian style dress. I feel beautiful and strong. I want to be this woman," she murmured.

"And so you should. Let her lead the way."

Katya allowed the woman to walk down one of the pathways. "The ground feels warm beneath my bare feet. There is so much foliage and bright coloured flowers. Oh it is beautiful, the flowers smell so lovely. There are butterflies in this woodland, loads of them. Now I come to a clearing and there is a round stone in the middle of the trees."

"Just keep talking lovey. Pretend I am not here."

"It's like an altar and it is where I come to work. I can feel the energy of the woodland all around me. I don't know where it is but it is my home and the trees are tall, but I can see the light at the top. I can hear a rustling sound, someone is coming. I look up to see an old woman. Aw she is so frail and she is in pain so I rush to help her. She wants to sit near the stone. I need to collect leaves and seeds and bark and then at the stone altar I can crush and mix all the things together into a paste. I rub some onto the throat and third eye of the woman and wrap the rest in a leaf for her to take. The woman is smiling and thanking and blessing me, but I don't know her language. Oh someone else is coming now. Ah, it is my husband and my children."

"Do you recognise him as someone in this life?" Sheryl prompted.

"No. He is unknown but I love him so much. He is strong with a beard. We have a boy and a girl. I am a wise woman, but he protects me, the man. It is very equal and beautiful and I can make people better."

"Do you need to stay in this lifetime?" Sheryl asked.

"No, I have seen what I need to. This was my beginning and my true self."

"Then walk another path."

Katya found herself once more at the entrance to the paths, noticing that the one she had returned from was now partly shielded by vines. Following her now much-loved higher self, she walked to find that she was in what looked like a Roman Villa. "I am in a beautiful courtyard. It might be Roman. I work with the apothecaries using herbs to heal the sick and I am content. I am with my friend Maris. He writes poetry and reads it to me first before he reads to others. I am in awe of him because he can read and write. He is my best friend and I love him... We are now at one of his recitals. There are others gathered to listen and he reads so well. Then, Thalia comes along. She always arrives at the end of the recitals, so she never hears the full beauty of his work. She has presented him with a gift. He looks at her differently to me. I feel as though he doesn't care as much for me as he does for her.

"The mountain is rumbling again, so I pull Maris to one side and tell him we have to leave. I have had dreams of being suffocated. There is danger around. He will not listen to me though, all he cares about is Thalia. But I know there is danger, I can't leave him there so I wait.

"It's too late, the dust is billowing from the mountain like a huge thundercloud. It is hot ash and it burns me as I run."

Katya began to cough, and Sheryl gave her some water. "Can you open a window?"

Sheryl did as Katya asked and then returned to her seat. "Do you want to go on?"

"Yes," Katya replied, "I am going back to take another path." As Katya walked along, she became aware of fear. "I am not sure about this one."

"Then come back."

Seeing the image of her higher self facing the path head on, Katya decided to stay.

"No I need to see this," She followed her guide into a house built of dark granite. "Oh it smells awful in here, kind of damp and rotten. It is making me feel sick. I can smell burning in the distance too, but I don't think that is anything to worry about. I am being led quite roughly by a man into another room. There are other women in here. There is little light and it is hard to see them, but it smells in here too. Oh, as my eyes get used to the dark I can see them. They are all thin, dirty and they look at me with frightened eyes. Oh no, some of them are no more than children, and some are old. There must be around twelve women in here. One of the younger ones is crying so I try to comfort her. But then, oh, now the door is opening. A man has come in with what seems to be guards, he has one of those tall hats. Are they cavalier hats? I can't remember what they are called. Like Guy Fawkes. One of the older women is kneeling before him and she is pleading for mercy. Agh! He has struck her across the face! I am trying to protest, to tell them we are all innocent, but they won't listen! Ouch! They have grabbed my arms and they are pulling me out of the room. They will pull my arms out of their sockets if they are not careful. I have no choice but to go. The other women are wailing. They put chains around my wrists. They are so tight they are hurting, I cannot even move my wrists around.

"Now they have thrown me to the ground and a door has slammed shut I have heard them lock it, and it is dark. So dark and cold… I must have slept as they awaken me, kicking my belly. One of them pulls me to my feet and my dress is ripped down one side. He touches my face as though he is going to kiss me, and his hand reaches for my crotch. I cannot move my hands so I spit in his face and bring my knee up. He grabs my hair and pulls a chunk of it from my head before striking me so hard across the face I can taste blood on my mouth. He pulls me out into the open air. It is raining and I am cold. There are crowds jeering and pushing forward to see me. I am exposed from the tear in my dress and my mouth is still bleeding. I feel ashamed to be seen like this. Now they are throwing stones at my face as I am led past them. They are shouting out 'Witch! Witch!' I am looking in front of me and there is a hill before a castle. Oh, there are gallows, I am to be hung.

"I want to come out of this one, I haven't done nothing wrong I am an innocent woman and so are my sisters." Katya's voice began to weaken as she felt the noose being put around her neck.

"Come back to the path Katya, follow your guide, follow the light," Sheryl said quietly.

Katya did as she was instructed and went back to the clearing where the pathways met. The third path had now been bricked up, rather than covered with vines, but the stones could be loosened. None of the pathways she had travelled were fully closed, she got the impression she could revisit any of them if she wished to.

"Now, which path are you going to take? Or have you had enough?"

"I want to take another," Katya determinedly walked down the next path to find herself in a tranquil place. It was a garden. English or perhaps it was French. She tended plants. She was a healer again. She was happy. There was no threat and there were no men anywhere. She was holding a crucifix and she was silent as she attended to her plants. She had food, she had shelter and there was nothing to fear. "There is nothing here except beauty and peace. It is wonderful, but there are no challenges. I am not going to learn anything here."

"Time for another?"

"One more."

Katya returned to the pathways and asked her wonderful and beautiful higher self to guide her. The path she chose smelt of the sea and the harbour. "Oh, I know this place. I am in the kitchen sitting by the fire with Arabella my sister. I don't want to go out into the cold but Mama needs me to run an errand. I have to take a basket to the harbour master's wife. I am walking along. Then, oh there he is. It's Glen. He is looking at me. He is smiling. I cannot stop or people will see. My heart is full of joy... I am on my way back home now and he sees me again... It is another day now, and another errand, and I walk the same way. I have walked this way many times now and each time he looks and smiles. I yearn to speak to him, but I cannot... Oh I am on my way and he is walking behind me. I can hear his footsteps, I am trying not to look round. I am about to turn into the alleyway so I turn quickly and he takes my arm, he pulls me into a nook. He tells me his name is Robbie and I tell him I am Annette, oh he asks me if I want to go for a walk on Sunday... I have to find a way to sneak out, I am desperate to see him. Mama is busy so I run out when she is not looking and run all the way to the cliff path. We walk for a while and talk. He kisses my hand and I run home... It is another meeting, another walk, it is raining and we shelter under a tree. He pulls me close out of the rain and looks into my eyes, I am so close to him now, my heart is reeling. I have never felt like this. He brings me closer still and his lips touch mine and then we kiss deeply, oh it is heavenly. This must be what love feels like. As I leave he passes something into my hand and I look. It is a coin with our initials engraved on it. This must mean we are to be wed one day, perhaps when I am older...

"Oh it is later now, the weather is colder, it is winter and he has not turned up to meet me. I run to the harbour but he is nowhere to be seen. I run to the big house, the nursing house as I saw him there once and he is there. He is walking outside with a patient. She wears a nightgown and fancy robe. Their arms are linked and then... he looks down at her and kisses her. She is beautiful and elegant. I run home crying. I am distraught, my heart is so heavy it feels like it will burst. I cannot bear it. He was to wed me... We meet and he tells me that he is to set sail. I don't want him to go. My heart hurts and my insides are tense, I have that feeling that something will happen. I beg him not to go but to no avail... It is the night of the storm, and it is so frightening. Everyone is screaming and crying, the wind is howling and boats are being wrecked. I cannot bear the thought that he is out there at sea in this terrible maelstrom. I do all I can to help, but I never see him again."

Katya was crying.

"I think that's enough now," Sheryl said calmly, "Ask your guide to bring you back to the pathways and I will bring you back to the present.

. . . . .

"It looks perfect!" Siobhan cried as Daisy hung her painting of the storm in the drawing room.

"The final finishing touch before we open," Daisy said proudly, stepping back to admire the canvas.

"I am so excited," Siobhan grinned.

"Me too!" Daisy hugged her young Irish housekeeper, liking the girl more as she got to know her.

The aroma of home cooking was wafting from the kitchen and Daisy went to see what was so delicious.

"Try this," Penny offered her a steaming spoonful.

Daisy sipped the hot liquid

"Oh my, Penny, that is divine."

"It's my mum's recipe," Penny smiled, "Secret Soup. Despite all my catering experience, this one is the best. Bless my mum she knew what she was doing with soups."

"Why are you making it today?" Daisy asked, "The guests don't arrive until tomorrow."

"Oh, no, this is just a practice to see what you think," Penny laughed, "Everything will be made fresh tomorrow afternoon, ready for their evening meal."

"You are amazing," Daisy smiled, "Both of you."

Siobhan and Penny smiled at each other.

"Now," continued Daisy, "I have hired a couple of agency staff for this week, one to wait tables in the evening, and one to help you with the cooking, Penny, as I want this to run as smoothly as possible. The last thing I want are two frazzled employees running round all stressed. We will know after this week whether we need those staff on a longer term basis or not."

Penny nodded. "Thank you."

"You two are in charge though. Remember that."

"What do you want me to wear?" Siobhan asked. She was wearing jeans, an old t-shirt and sneakers, her brown hair pulled into a pony tail.

"Aha!" Daisy opened the closet in the hallway and presented both ladies with a clothing bag on a hanger, "Your new uniforms."

Siobhan ripped the bag off to reveal a black tailored housekeeping dress with "Hartford's Retreat" embroidered on it. Penny followed suit to find a chef's tunic and trousers with the same logo.

"Ah thank you Miss Hartford!" Siobhan exclaimed, "This is proper smart."

"It's lovely," agreed Penny, holding the tunic up to herself.

"What are you going to wear Miss Hartford?" Siobhan asked.

"Please call me Daisy. I could do with a second opinion. Come up and help me decide."

"Fashion was never my forte," Penny laughed, "I'll leave it to you youngsters."

Siobhan followed Daisy upstairs to the attic, where Daisy began to pull out clothes from her wardrobe area.

"Oh is this more of your artwork?" Siobhan gasped as she stood at the easel.

"Yes, I was trying to finish both pieces for the drawing room. But I haven't had the time."

"It is amazing. You are so clever."

"Thank you, it's still work in progress of course."

"That one in the drawing room reminds me of something I read about that storm here in the harbour. I mean I wasn't there, it was long, long ago. In Victorian times. So sad."

"What storm?"

"The Great Gale," Siobhan replied, turning to face her, "It was terrible. Boats smashed up. So many sailors and fishermen …"

"Oh, now you mention it, I think I have heard of it. Although I never paid much attention to history," Daisy beckoned Siobhan over, "Now do you think the black, or the navy, or this floral dress?"

Siobhan scrutinised the garments as Daisy held each one up to her.

"Definitely the floral for when they arrive as it will be in the afternoon. Save the black one for the evening. The navy is too formal so no, not that one."

"My thoughts exactly," smiled Daisy, "Thank you."

Siobhan looked pleased at being able to help and Daisy decided she liked this girl very much; she was a hard worker and her honesty was refreshing.

"You know, I think I have definitely made a good choice with you and Penny..." Daisy broke off as she saw the girl standing looking at the window, her hand over her mouth, "What is it?"

"I ... I just ... oh my."

"What?"

"Didn't you see her?"

"See who?"

"The lady by the window?"

"What lady?"

Siobhan's complexion drained.

"Miss Hartford ... Daisy, I saw a lady at the window. As clear as day."

Daisy went cold remembering what little Fleur had told her. Eliza had hinted at the same and she herself had felt someone touch her shoulder now and again. She had put it down to tiredness.

"You saw her?"

"Yes. A lady, dressed in white. Like a nurse."

Daisy nodded. "It used to be a convalescent home, back in Victorian times."

"Then you have a ghost Miss Hartford."

Daisy shuddered.

"It's okay. She is not harmful," Siobhan said.

"Do you see things like this often?"

Siobhan flushed red. "Now and then, I have seen. But I am not crazy or anything, please don't think badly of me."

Daisy's heart went out to the girl. "No I don't think you are crazy. I have a friend who also sees. You will have to meet her one day," Daisy felt her eyes fill up as she thought of Eliza.

They had not spoken since their disagreement and it was upsetting Daisy more than she cared to admit.

"Are you okay?" Siobhan asked.

"Yes. Miles away," Daisy smiled, hanging her clothes back up onto the rail trying not to cry, "But, I have plenty to do. As do you." She nodded to Siobhan who smiled uncertainly and left the room.

. . . . .

As Katya made her way home, a mixture of elation, release and confusion was whizzing around her. She could not believe the scenes she had encountered during her regression. She now felt the power of her higher self and felt she had more understanding of what was happening. She loved Glen, she had loved him for many, many years yet he had overlooked her in favour of Daisy at least twice. Back in what seemed to be Pompeii and here in Brixham. There were other paths she had not explored. How many times had he cast her aside? And what of the other lives she had seen? She was a healer, a medicine woman, a nun and a falsely-accused witch. Now, in this current life it was all happening again. Glen was favouring Daisy while she followed a path devoted to spirituality and helping others. It all made sense now. Her gut instinct and feelings about Daisy stemmed from these past lives and she now understood why she so easily slipped into conversation and felt so comfortable with Glen.

Now, she desperately wanted to break the cycle and have Glen choose her for a change, but the past life connection was already working between him and Daisy. It was in motion and it was futile to try and stop it. Despite her answers, she was devastated. Why did the universe keep placing her with this man who clearly didn't care as much as she did?

She had promised Glen that she would help him, and whatever her own desires may be she had to carry through on that promise, no matter how hard it was. There must be a purpose. She must trust that it would all become clear – her oracle cards had been so right.

Fighting back tears as she reached the sanctuary of her apartment, she closed the door behind her in the lobby and heard a familiar squeak behind her.

"Merlin!" She cried, pleased to see the kitten. She picked up his small warm body in her hands as he looked at her, purring with big inquisitive eyes. She began to climb the stairs, a tear rolling down her cheek, when Josie opened the door to her flat and beckoned Katya to come in.

Katya followed Josie in and spying his food bowl, Merlin jumped down from Katya's arms to eat.

"Cats are so fickle!" Josie laughed.

"Yes, they rule their own world," Katya smiled.

"Is everything okay?" She looked concerned.

"Yes, I think so," Katya wiped her eye and chuckled, "I think in my next life I might be a cat."

"Well, before you swap your home for a basket in front of the fire, I have something to show you," Josie gestured for Katya to sit down as she took a folder from the table, "If you want to see it that is?"

Katya sat down next to the window, composing herself. "Yes, yes, forgive me it has been an intense afternoon."

"Here are your two pendants," she passed Katya the coin pendants which were enclosed in small polythene bags and looked more like evidence from a murder case than a couple of old coins, "I had them analysed. Both are from the mid 1800's probably around the same few years although it is hard to tell, with the wear and tear. Both have been carved by the same person as the writing style and the pressure used for the carving is almost identical except for the letters.

"What do you mean the letters?"

Josie showed Katya an enhanced image of the first pendant, printed from the computer.

"R and A, 1865..." Katya gasped as she now recognised the coin as the same one she had been given in her regression.

"Then here is the next one. The second one you gave me to look at."

"R and V, 1865." That must have been the woman at the hospital. The one with the fancy robes who she now knew was Daisy in a previous life.

"Are you sure you're okay?" Josie asked again.

Katya felt a little dizzy. "Yes, I was just a bit taken aback. The R and A, I know what they stand for."

"You do?" Josie looked flabbergasted, "Please tell."

"Katya told her all about the regression, her dreams, and about the whole Daisy and Glen situation. Josie made some hot chocolate which Katya accepted gratefully as Josie joined her.

"So you think R and A stands for Robbie and Annette?" Josie mused, nodding thoughtfully, "Now I have some names to go on, it might be worth me looking at the census records and births and deaths. You say Robbie was killed in the Great Gale of 1866?"

"I think so," Katya replied, "I know I never saw him again after that night."

"Not all deaths from that tragedy were recorded in detail, but I will see what I can find out. You say your home in your dream and the regression was this very building?"

"Yes, I am sure of that! And the nursing home on the cliff top is now Daisy's guesthouse."

"So you have all ended up in the same place at the same time."

"Again," Katya reminded her.

"Leave it with me; I will look tomorrow when I am back at work. I will let you know what I can find out."

CHAPTER TWENTY-EIGHT

She sat with her back against the rocks as the sun shone onto her legs. They looked white and chubby below her baggy denim shorts, unaccustomed to the light. She should not even be sitting here alone, tucked away around a corner, as her family were eating and arguing higher up along the cove. It was supposed to be a family day out. Her brother would come looking for her soon and tell her it was time to go. But for now she enjoyed her solitude, away from his belittling comments, her mother's apathy, and her sister's self-obsessed ways.

Two boys came into view. One about her own age and another who was younger. As they drew closer, she moved self-consciously closer to the rock behind her back, not wanting to be seen. As if hearing her wishes, the world around her seemed to blur and slow down so that they wouldn't notice her. Her eyes were drawn to the taller, and older, of the two boys, and she found she was holding her breath as she watched them paddling in the shallow waves that tickled the shore line. They had long twigs from the coast path and seemed to be prodding the sand beneath the waves. She was curious as to what they were doing. The boys' jeans were rolled up almost to their knees, but were as sandy and wet as their bare feet. She glanced around to see the boys' mother sat further back on a rock, reading a paperback book, a dog lying content at her feet.

Gradually, as she focused and blocked out the outside world, listening intently to their conversation, she realised that the two brothers were using the sticks to dislodge the stones at the water's edge to see what creatures lay hidden beneath.

The day had grown humid following the hot sun. Clouds were descending as the sky threatened to become black with thunder. She looked back at the older boy and, perhaps sensing the fact that he was being watched, he spied her. He stared at her.

For what seemed like an unusually long moment she gazed back at him, captured in an unexpected world of intrigue that knew no end. Her emotions surged in ways that she could not comprehend at her young age. She did not even have names for the mixture of feelings she experienced.

As their gaze remained on each other, the older boy's eyes seemed to speak to her of something hidden; a mystery world that she must surely have knowledge of but could not recall or understand. A longing formed, deep within her, questions unanswered and a yearning awakened for something unknown that would take the heartache away. She felt like crying and singing at the same time. Anger and forgiveness, desperation and release. Joy and despair. These paradoxical compounds flooded her being in seconds and the thirteen-year-old felt that she just might explode with overwhelm. The beach, the sea, and the younger boy disappeared from view and all that she could see was the older boy's eyes. She wanted desperately to go to him, to touch the side of his face, to be near to him and breathe the same air. Not understanding any of what she felt inside, she felt scared and instead became rooted to the spot, her fingers pressing against the rock and making her hands sore. She did not feel the pain until afterwards.

A small girl of pure light, and of a similar age to herself, appeared at her side. The girl stood in between Katya and the boy, and she smiled. The little girl held a finger to her lips.

"Not yet," she whispered. "Not yet."

As emotion got the better of Katya, tears welled and spilled onto her smooth cheeks, her lungs heaving with sobs as the emotional pain that engulfed her craved an outlet. The boy looked away as his dog came bounding over, barking with enthusiasm as the boy called to the animal. The girl of light disappeared from view as the sun finally became hidden by dark clouds, and Katya felt coldness descend around her as raindrops began to fall. A relief from the humidity and pressure, she welcomed the grey and almost dark green clouds; the same colour as the boy's eyes. Her tears mixed with the raindrops dappling her lips with salt and a bittersweet feeling of calm.

Her brother and sister came rushing towards her, calling her name, and as she saw the boy look back towards her she turned away, scared by feelings too painful to endure. However, she did not want to go; she did not want to leave this boy. Her heart ached, her stomach was heavy and her legs would not move. She wanted to stay.

"What's the matter with you now?" Her brother asked impatiently, "Come on, we need to go. There's a storm coming." She refused to move. He yanked her arm until she had no choice but to go with them. Out of the corner of her eye, she could see the boys' mother calling them to return to her and she looked back over her shoulder, her eyes sad and silent tears streaming down her face.

Katya awoke, wiping tears from her cheeks. She had forgotten this memory, but now it had returned with a vengeance. Crystal clear. She had met Glen before in this lifetime, at the cove just down the coast. Why had she forgotten? Was it too painful? Had the spirit girl made her forget and then returned to remind her through dreams? She had to speak to Glen. She had to tell him.

As she quickly showered and got dressed, she felt an urgency. It might not be too late. Perhaps this was the lifetime where they would become united. Perhaps this time he would notice her and realise. After all, his liaisons with Daisy usually led him or both of them to their deaths.

She walked fast, powered by urgency, until she ran out of breath and then, deciding she could not be flustered and tired when she reached the caravan, she slowed right down, her legs feeling like lead after her exertion.

There was no shyness around her now as she boldly knocked on the caravan door.

When he answered the door in an old t-shirt and shorts, he looked as though he had just awoken, his eyes groggy and his normally well-groomed hair dishevelled. It made her love him even more, seeing him in this way.

"Katya."

"I have to talk to you. Sorry if I have woken you."

He took a step back as she walked into the caravan without invitation, taking her glasses off as they had steamed up. Remembering his comment about her beautiful eyes she placed them in her pocket.

"What is it?" He asked, appearing frozen to the spot, concern spreading across his face.

"We have a past life too."

"What?" He frowned.

"You and Daisy have a past life. Well I had been having dreams, and I felt strange around you, so I too have had a regression. We were also connected in at least two past lives."

He rubbed his hair. "Do you want a coffee? I have not woken up yet. I can't think."

"No, tea please. Milk no sugar."

Once he had made their drinks he ushered her over to the lounge area.

"So what are you saying?"

"We have a spiritual connection, we have known each other before. That's why we find it so easy to talk to each other. The lives you experienced in Pompeii and here in Brixham - we were both there... and there may be other lifetimes too."

He took her hand and looked into her eyes.

This was it, she thought, her heart pounding. *This would be the moment when he realised.*

"Actually, that makes a lot of sense."

"It does?"

"Yes, I have been wondering why I find you so... easy to confide in. But why didn't I see you in my regression?"

Katya faltered. "You didn't at all?"

"No."

"Well, maybe you didn't recognise me?"

"No, I would recognise you. You have helped me so much. I can't believe just what a great friend you are turning out to be. But if we have a past life too, then that explains why you are the only one who can understand all this, and why I am so drawn to Daisy. It's fate. Daisy and I are meant to be."

Katya received a fleeting image in her mind, of a helicopter and an ambulance near to the caravan. Her heart sank. It was going to happen again, to one of them.

"But how do you know that Daisy is the one?"

"I just know. You of all people should understand that. There is no evidence, other than I love her and there is not meant to be another. She is my world. I just need to be patient until she has got this launch sorted out."

"Please just stop and think!" Katya raised her voice which was so unexpected it frightened her, "Sorry," she murmured.

"Katya? What has got into you? I thought we were friends?"

"We are friends. But ..."

"But what?"

She looked at him, her heart spilling over with centuries of emotion. Centuries of love, pain and torment. She could never tell him the truth. If she heard him say there was nothing between them, she would give up. It would be too painful. It would crush her soul again, and her hopes and dreams would be shattered. The will to follow her path would crumble before her. She would have nothing except pieces to pick up. She had not thought about the prospect of love for many years, yet here it was ripping her into pieces. Again.

"What did you want to say Katya?"

She fought back the tears. "Nothing. There is nothing I want to say," If they were ever destined to be together it was not at this moment, perhaps not even in this lifetime. Better to keep him in her life and to help him as she had promised. As a friend would, "I'm sorry. I shouldn't have come here."

"Hey, don't cry," he took her hand, "You don't know how much you have helped me. I have been floundering in a world I don't understand and you are the only one who has listened. If I can help you, I will."

She nodded, removing her hand from his as his touch was too intense for her at this moment.

"What are you going to do about Daisy then?" She saw the relief on his face as she gave him permission to talk about his favourite subject, and her heart sank deeply.

He shook his head. "I don't know. Do I go round and tell her that she needs to listen and to follow her heart or do I carry on sitting here waiting for her to work it out for herself? This is killing me."

"Do what your heart tells you. Follow your heart. Trust that all will be as fate intends," Katya felt great power as she spoke these words, as though she was actually wise in some way. Sheryl's advice came back to her about finding her true voice. Had she found it? She was not quite sure, but it was a step in the right direction. "Glen, follow your heart," she repeated and he nodded.

"Believe me I have thought of nothing else," Glen shook his head, "I cannot let Daisy slip through my fingers again."

"Then go tell her," Katya replied, tears rolling down her cheeks.

. . . . .

Daisy was a mixture of nerves and excitement that morning, knowing that her trial guests would be arriving later on in the day. She showered and pulled on her jeans and an old t-shirt. No need for the full ensemble until after lunch when they would be checking in. She heard the post arrive on the doormat and, after switching the kettle on, she ran excitedly to pick it up. There were a couple of items of junk mail and an exciting letter from the Tourist Board confirming her listing. *This is really happening*, she thought, smiling as she tore open the last piece of post, a hand-written brown envelope. She pulled out the contents. It was an A4 sheet folded in half, and when she unfolded it she saw newspaper collage letters, like the sort that featured as ransom notes in murder films of old.

'I know who you are.' It said. That was it, no address, no other correspondence. No photograph. Just that statement. She felt sick and dizzy. Slouching to the floor, she looked at the letter, remembering the night of the damaged windows, and she stared at the front door and the window to its left. Someone was watching her. First the photo, now this. She felt uncomfortable. Not the start she had wanted for her big day. This was not fair.

A knock at the door made her jump and for a moment she was frozen to the spot. What if it was the person who had sent the letter? She looked at the envelope for a postmark. It was indecipherable but at least it had not been hand delivered. Her nerves subsided a little, but she was still feeling on edge as there was another knock.

"Who is it?" She called, her heart beating. This was ridiculous, feeling so jumpy in broad daylight.

"It's me, Glen," replied a familiar voice.

She was filled with a mixture of relief and annoyance. She would certainly feel a lot safer if he was in the house, but she was reluctant to see him for fear of their relationship developing further. The events last time they had met should never have happened. She had let her guard down and she knew that if she opened the door to him, there was a danger it would happen again. Before she knew it she would be too deep and there would be no escape. She would fall in love with him.

He knocked the door again. She looked at the letter in her hand, feeling nauseous again, and decided to open the door.

He looked sad, his eyes clouded with tiredness, and she felt bad for not getting back to his phone calls with some sort of explanation. She had thought of him often but had pushed him to the back of her mind as she focused on the guesthouse. The truth was she did not know what to say to him.

"Sorry," he said as he crossed the threshold, "I know you are busy but I wanted to speak to you."

"I know. It's okay," she walked through to the drawing room and he followed, "I have my first guests arriving later today. Then there is the launch on Friday. That's why I haven't replied to you. I need to stay focused. You distract me."

"The other night. I hope you aren't angry with me."

She leaned against the mantelpiece, the letter still in her hand. She did not want him to see it. "No, I am not angry."

"Have you had a chance to think any more about what I told you?"

She shook her head. "I can't think about it at the moment. I have too much going on."

"But you will think about it? In the future?"

She thought back to his kisses, their lovemaking, how right it had all felt; like returning home to a safe place. That fear in the pit of her stomach was still there, however. To relinquish her independence would be emotional suicide. She could not contemplate a relationship so soon after her escape from

Christophe. She had no doubt that Glen was sincere at the moment. He wanted her, it was all very romantic. But how long before he was making decisions for her, trying to get a hand in on the business and telling her what she could and couldn't do? He was a man used to being in control. He had built a business empire. She had been so resolute in her decision to remain single while she found herself again. No matter how much her heart yearned for him she could not risk becoming embroiled in yet another drama, especially one as deep as Glen promised to be. "I don't know."

"What do you mean, you don't know?"

"I mean, I don't know. I am not ready for a relationship."

"But …the other night?"

"It was a mistake," she dropped the letter as she raised her hands up.

"What's this?" He stooped to pick up the piece of paper from the floor.

"Nothing," she took the letter from his hand and he gripped her wrist. She tensed, scared by his intensity as his eyes looked deeply into hers. She felt her head sway.

"Daisy, what's going on in that mind of yours? I love you!" His eyes were burning into her and she wanted to return his love and kiss him.

She broke her wrist free from his gentle grip and walked back over to the mantelpiece. "You love me now, but how long until that love becomes something else?"

"I don't know what you mean."

"I mean that love becomes an expectation and a form of control. I have just escaped from one prison, I am not about to descend into another."

"Daisy! I would never treat you in that way."

"No one expects that they will ever treat anyone in that way."

"Okay," he sat down on the sofa, "I get that you are scared. I am scared, but I know this is right. We have messed this up in several lifetimes together. I told you the other night that we are past life lovers. This is perhaps our chance to get it right."

"How do you know this?" She asked, annoyed by his constant references to the past lives."

"I had a regression."

"A what?"

"A past life regression. I was hypnotised into a state where I could revisit my past incarnations and view them as though I were there. You were in each one." Daisy could not believe what she was hearing. He was basing his own and her future on a hypnotic encounter. "I know it sounds far-fetched."

"Far-fetched is an understatement," she looked at him, seeing the hurt fleet across his face at her dismissal.

They sat in silence and she began to feel cold.

"When we made love it was…" he began.

"Don't. I told you. It was a mistake."

"How can you say that?"

"Because it was … it was just so …"

"Right?" He looked at her hopefully.

She folded her arms. "What happened in this regression then? Let me guess we were Cleopatra and Mark Anthony or you were Henry VIII and I was Anne Boleyn?"

He sighed. "No. We were not famous."

"So, tell me. I have a right to know about my own previous life."

"We were in Pompeii I think. You wouldn't come with me and we died. Then we were in medieval times and you had already died and I was alone without you and it was unbearable. Then we were here. In Brixham. Victorian times."

"Don't tell me, we died?"

"Well yes of course we did. They are past lives."

"Look, this is all very interesting and bizarre but I have my current life to deal with," Daisy looked at him wishing she didn't long to be in his arms quite so much. The trouble was that his story made perfect sense. It explained everything she felt, and it would be so easy to be swept away by the romanticism and the notion of being time-twisted lovers.

"I wish you would just give us a chance."

She thought about his request and her self-preservation kicked in. "I can't," she replied, "At least not now."

He shook his head.

"And ... "she continued, I don't want you to come to the launch. I know Stella has invited you."

His face contorted into a hurt frown and she felt terrible as she could see how upset he was.

"As you wish," he replied curtly and walked towards the door, "I live in a caravan on the headland," he passed her a piece of paper with an address scrawled on it, "Come and see me if you change your mind. Because my life means nothing without you!" He stormed off and, fearful that she would give in and run after him, she closed the door, slumping against the wall as she broke down in tears.

. . . . .

Katya rushed to the shop. She needed to talk to Eliza. As she burst in, sending the windchime into torrents of melody, she was amazed to see not just Eliza but Sheryl and Jan too.

"Ah! Just the person," Sheryl smiled, "We all need to have a chat."

Katya burst into tears, grateful that her spiritual friends had gathered round just when it mattered. She had never felt so emotional. "I have unleashed something unstoppable," she cried.

"No you haven't lovey, the Universe has," Sheryl corrected her.

"You cannot stop destiny unfolding dear," Jan smiled, "You have just given it a helping hand."

"He is obsessed," Katya sniffed.

"No, he is in love," Eliza said quietly, "But unfortunately Daisy does not know whether she is coming or going at the moment. He has picked a really bad time to act."

"Everything happens for a reason," Jan reminded them all, "What we need to decide is whether we help them both, or whether we walk away and let destiny take its course."

"I promised him I would help," Katya replied.

"And I am worried about Daisy," Eliza said, "Despite the fact that I am not speaking to her at the moment."

The others looked at her quizzically.

"I gave her some tough love, and I was angry," Eliza admitted. She told them about the photograph.

"Do you think she is in danger?" Jan asked.

"I don't know. Whoever sent the photo certainly doesn't have her best interests at heart. And I have my suspicions as to who is behind it."

"Who?" Katya asked.

"Stella Prince," Eliza replied, "She used to be in love with a guy called Rick Rockley at college, a photographer. Unfortunately for Stella, Rick was more interested in Daisy. She has never forgiven her. Now, coincidentally, he runs a business preying on C list celebrities with his camera for cheap, shock magazines. "

"So you think Stella got him to take the photos?"

"I don't know for certain, but she has a weird way of acting when she is jealous."

"But she is not dangerous," Katya argued.

"Maybe not, but I don't trust her as far as I could throw her."

"I had a premonition, I think, earlier on," Katya frowned.

"What sort of premonition lovey?" Asked Sheryl.

"I was talking to Glen and I had this fleeting image of an ambulance parked outside his caravan."

Jan nodded. "Fleeting images don't appear for no reason."

Sheryl picked up a clear quartz crystal from the basket on the shelf display. "Ladies, we are running away with ourselves here, let's focus," she looked at Katya, "I hope you don't mind but I have told both Jan and Eliza about Glen's regression and yours."

"It's okay, I don't mind, I was going to tell them anyway,"

"Okay. Let's think clearly," Jan took a deep breath, "Daisy, Glen and Katya have a past-life love triangle. Glen overlooks Katya in favour of Daisy. Then Glen or Daisy or both of them die."

"And I have been overlooked yet again," Katya said sadly.

Eliza looked at Katya apologetically, "Are you really in love with him?"

Katya's eyes filled with tears again. "It doesn't matter, I have a different path to tread. Again," she paused as a thought entered her mind, "What does matter is the fact that one of them or both of them die when they get together."

"So how do we stop the cycle?" Eliza asked, "Do we stop them getting together?"

"It's too late for that," Jan replied, "They have already met, the wheel of fate is already weaving its web."

"Glen has already died though!" Katya exclaimed, "He died briefly after the accident when he had his near-death experience."

"So, then he is safe. The cycle has broken already," Sheryl smiled.

"No. It hasn't," Eliza became solemn, "It's Daisy's turn to die!"

The women looked at each other and Katya gasped as they realised that Eliza was probably right.

Katya rubbed her head in anguish, "This is all my fault."

"No it isn't." Jan clutched Katya's shoulders, "this is destiny at work. Nothing can stop it. Whatever is meant to be is meant to be."

"Okay, think rationally," Sheryl said, holding her temples and trying to concentrate, "Think back to the regressions, Katya. In Glen's regression why did they die? Remember the notes you made afterwards."

Katya closed her eyes as she thought back. "Well, in Pompeii she wouldn't believe him that they should leave, she wanted to stay and wouldn't trust him. He waited for her and then the volcano erupted killing both of them."

"So she didn't believe him or trust him," Jan pointed out.

"Then, in the life where he had already lost her, he had betrayed her, but he himself had been tricked."

"So he trusted someone and perhaps she trusted him, and that trust was their downfall?" Eliza nodded.

"In the Victorian regression, she would not elope with him, despite him begging her. Because she was gentry and he was a harbour boy, she would not let go and allow him to take her. He went to make his fortune, to prove to her. But he was killed in the Great Gale," Katya explained, "We don't know what happened to her."

"And then he has come back as a wealthy man in this life," Eliza pointed out, "Is that just coincidence?"

"Then the issue must be trust and belief," Sheryl said, "Until she believes in him and is willing to place her trust in his love, they will carry on in this spiral."

"We have to get her to believe in his experience," Katya added.

"Hmm, that will be easier said than done," Eliza shook her head, "Daisy is determined never to fall in love again and she doesn't believe in the spiritual world. And I don't think I have helped the situation. I told her to forget him and focus on the business."

Katya had a thought. "Does Daisy believe in facts and historical reason? If so, I know someone who just may be able to help."

"We have to try something, before it's too late," Eliza nodded.

CHAPTER TWENTY-NINE

"Where are we going?" Jayne asked as she put her seatbelt on.

"We are dropping Leo off at your mum's and going for a few days away at the coast."

"What?" Jayne was flabbergasted that Stefan would think of such a thing.

"We need a break and Glen has left his caravan for a while. He has told me we can use it if we wish."

"Where has he gone?"

"I don't know."

"Why has he gone? Is he okay?"

"I don't know."

Jayne was not sure what to say. Her thoughts went back to when she had visited Glen at the caravan, making him promise not to tell Stefan about the visit. What if he had told him? Stefan had kept plenty of secrets from her. What if she was so obvious that he could see through her subterfuge? What if this trip was a trick? "Did he say anything about me?"

Stefan turned to glance at her briefly as he drove. "No, why?"

"No reason."

They sat in silence. Her mind was wrestling with itself. Did Stefan know that she knew about the emails or not? Was this a ploy to get her alone and then tell her it was over? Perhaps it was a cover up, for Stefan to pretend that there was nothing going on behind the scenes and to pretend to reignite their relationship? Or was it a genuine attempt to say sorry for something he didn't know she knew about? Or perhaps he did. Her mind was running around in circles again.

"You are very quiet," he said

"I am thinking."

"You are always thinking, that's your trouble; you over-think"

"Did you pack everything for Leo?"

Stefan sighed heavily. "Of course I did. I am aware of what our son needs you know."

"I suppose if you have forgotten something, mum will have it. She has some spare stuff."

Stefan's hands tensed on the steering wheel. "Just relax will you?"

"Sorry! I am just not used to leaving him,"

"You used to be so chilled out, now you are obsessed with details. It's so tiring."

Jayne felt her blood burning in her temples. "Tiring! What would you know about tiring?"

"Don't start Jayne. Please. This is supposed to be a happy few days away."

"I am not starting anything. You're the one who started it."

Stefan did not respond and the two sat in silence as Jayne felt her throat rising into her brain and threatening to choke her, holding back the tears and keeping quiet because she did not want to rock the boat. She did not want it to be her fault that the surprise break went wrong. They reached her mother's house, and Leo's carrier was passed to his grandmother as Jayne spoke in hushed whispers so as not to wake her sleeping babe. She looked at his peaceful face and then at the warm face of her mother, wishing she could stay here with her instead of going to the caravan with Stefan.

"Phone me if there are any problems."

Jayne's mother nodded. "Of course sweetheart, but please go and enjoy some time with your husband." The look in her mother's eyes told Jayne that her mother had been in on this before it had happened. Was she colluding with Stefan?

Once they had turned out of Jayne's mother's cul-de-sac, Stefan turned the music up loud on the radio. Jayne put her hands over her ears. "Oh my god, why have you turned it up so loud?"

"Because we can!" He grinned at her, "We have time to be us again, without worrying about disturbing or waking Leo."

"You speak of him as though he is an inconvenience!" Jayne cried, "Turn it down."

Stefan turned the music down again. "I love my son with all my heart. Stop misinterpreting everything! There is nothing wrong with being a couple now and again rather than parents. For god's sake Jayne, will you just chill out? Please!!"

He was angry now and it was her fault. Again. *No wonder he's having an affair*, she thought. If she was him, she would probably have an affair too. What was this break going to be like with just the two of them?

They sat in silence for the rest of the journey, eventually pulling up outside Glen's caravan. *It looks different in the daytime*, Jayne thought. It had been dark last time she had come. She stood next to the car, taking in the view and the sea air, and as she inhaled she did start to feel relaxed. Maybe this was what she needed after all? She walked right to the edge of the cliff, feeling the wind buffeting against her. It rekindled memories of their more adventurous days. Stefan put his arms around her.

"Don't go jumping off now," he murmured against her ear, and for a moment she felt alive. It could have been anywhere in the world.

She took a step back away from the edge as she realised just how close she had been standing.

"Come on and look round," Stefan took her hand and led her to the caravan. He was smiling, looking like his old self. She must make an effort to enjoy this break. He was right; she needed to relax. This was what their marriage needed.

He showed her round the caravan and brought their bags in from the car. She was about to put the kettle on when he presented her with a bottle of gin and got two glasses out of the cupboard, smiling at her.

"Today, you are my wife and not Leo's mum. Enjoy."

She smiled at him, realising that she was not a bad mother for taking some time out. For the first time in months she could actually relax and have a drink. Leo was safe with her mother. She had a couple of days of freedom.

"Tonight we will drink a little, go out for a meal," he kissed her, "Tomorrow we go for a hike."

"I haven't brought my boots," she replied.

"They are in the car," he smiled.

"You really have thought of everything," she returned his kiss, enjoying the attention from him and the knowledge that she might just be able to relax.

He pulled away from her, and poured two measures of gin into their glasses.

"I haven't thought of everything." He replied, "I forgot the ice. I will be back shortly," he kissed her again and she smiled at him as he left the caravan and started the car up. She sipped her gin without the ice, enjoying the sharp taste of the liquid on her tongue and, taking her coat off, she curled up on the sofa to watch the sea from the panoramic window.

. . . . .

Siobhan and Penny were busy preparing for the arrival of the guests, but Daisy was standing watching the sea from her attic window, the place where she always found herself after the intense dreams. She once again had a sensation that there was a cool hand on her shoulder, and she felt peace and calm. She had been so excited about the arrival of her first guests, and she knew she should be getting ready. Her clothes lay on the bed, pressed and ready to change into, but she still wore the jeans and t-shirt she had put on earlier. She could still feel his hands upon her. She could feel his lips upon her. She could hear his voice in her mind, tugging at her heart strings. But she had told him to go. Was she to end up bitter and sad, forever watching the ocean as her dreams predicted?

She turned around, taking a deep breath and preparing herself to take control and go and prepare for her guests, when something caught her eye. She looked up to see a shining woman before her. It was the nurse that the others had seen. Despite being caught off guard, she felt no fear as the woman smiled at her. The apparition's mouth did not move, but Daisy heard her say:

"It's time. This time."

She faded before Daisy's eyes and Daisy sat on the floor, wanting to cry with a mixture of sadness and relief. She wanted to understand what was happening. The dreams, the déjà vu, and the intensity she felt with Glen. Her tears spilled over and she felt small and cold as she hugged her knees into her body, rocking as her sobs took over.

She looked at the clock. It was only two hours until her guests arrived. She must pull herself together. Today marked the culmination of her plans becoming reality. Yet today of all days was one where she could have easily gone back to bed and immersed herself in the dreams.

The dreams of him waiting for her beneath the window. She would put her fine silk robe over her nightgown and the nurse would help her down the stairs, knowing that his visits and the fresh sea air were good for her patient's health. She would sit on the chair that the nurse would bring out and read poetry to him. She was not sure whether he really liked it or understood it, but she enjoyed the feeling of his eyes watching her as she read. He absorbed every word. Every breath. Every movement of her face.

She wished she were strong enough to go with him. It was her own fault. She had provided him with knowledge. He was a simple harbour boy, yet she had filled his mind with ambition, attempted to educate him and promised him a world beyond his reach.

She was weaker than she had let him know. She was about to die, and yet she wanted to die remembering his eyes upon her face, his adoring gaze, his attention unwavering as her educated voice read to him the words of love sonnets, capturing his heart and his imagination. She could inspire him, he was worth so much more than she. She did not want him to watch her wither and die, better that he took his chances at sea, and made something of his life, formed memories and grew while she passed through the veil of death without him knowing.

The dreams were so vivid that when Glen spoke of their past life, she knew deep down that he was telling the truth; but, reluctant to walk into another relationship and reluctant to admit that the connections made sense, she held back.

A knock on her attic door disturbed her.

"Miss Hartford?" Siobhan's voice rang through the door.

Daisy managed to climb to her feet and walked towards the door, opening it slightly.

"Miss Hartford, there are some ladies in reception. They say they are your friends."

"I don't want to see anyone," Daisy said less clearly than she wanted to.

"Miss Hartford, are you alright?"

Daisy opened the door fully and let the young housekeeper in; she looked smart and proud in her new uniform and Daisy knew she could trust her.

"I saw the lady. The nurse."

"Oh Miss Hartford, that is wonderful so it is."

"Please call me Daisy."

"Daisy, you have seen a wonder. It is a gift it is. I didn't know you believed."

"I didn't," seeing the elation on the girl's face made Daisy wonder if she had been missing out on something all these years, "Who are these friends in reception?"

"Eliza, Katya, and Josie."

"Josie? I don't know a Josie."

"Do you know the other two?"

"Yes," Daisy cried, rushing out of the room and running down the stairs. She fell into Eliza's arms as she reached the hallway and Eliza hugged her tightly.

"I'm so sorry Daisy. I shouldn't have got so mad with you,"

"No, I am glad you did. I have got so much done since that day. You were right!"

Katya was hovering awkwardly behind the reunion. "Daisy, we need to talk to you."

Eliza nodded. "Do you have a few minutes to spare before you need to get ready?"

"Yes. I do." For the first time, Daisy smiled at Katya sincerely, seeing genuine concern in the woman's eyes. She led them through to the drawing room.

"Is it okay if we sit down?" Eliza asked, "I don't want to mess the cushions up."

"It's fine."

"This is Josie," Katya introduced the kind looking woman with long brown hair and spectacle, "She lives in the flat above me and she is a historian."

Josie looked embarrassed. "I wouldn't say I am a historian – I'm not that clever! Let's just say I have an interest in the past, and I work in a museum."

"Pleased to meet you," Daisy smiled.

"Josie has found out some information that may help you," Katya continued.

"Well, Katya found this," she passed Daisy the coin pendant with "R and V' carved into it, "It's a love token from Victorian times."

Daisy looked at the coin and as she touched it, something stirred. "I feel as though I have seen this before. Where did you find it Katya?"

"Under the tree outside," Katya replied.

Daisy went cold; it was the tree she could see from her window, the one where, in her dreams, Robbie stood and watched for her.

"It would have been given as a gesture of love from one who could not afford to buy jewellery," Josie continued.

Daisy nodded, a tear rolling down her cheek.

"Show her what else you have found," Katya nudged her friend.

"These are records from the home that this building used to be. There was a Victoria Armitage convalescing here. She was being nursed for TB but she died on 14th January 1866," Josie passed Daisy the document.

"Four days after the Great Gale of 1866, when many sailors and fishermen lost their lives," Katya was looking deeply into her eyes and, not for the first time, Daisy wondered whether she could see into her soul.

"He went to sea…" Daisy murmured.

"Who did?" Eliza prompted.

"Robbie." Daisy replied, "I sent him away because I knew I was dying. I did not want him to see me weaken."

"There are no records of a Robbie losing his life in the Great Gale, but many men were unaccounted for," Josie explained.

"I know it was him," Daisy stroked the edges of the coin pendant, tracing the letters with her fingers, "I should have listened to him," She jumped to her feet, feeling an urgency. All she could think about was Glen. He was not a fake like Christophe. He was so truthful it hurt. He loved her and she loved him. What was more important than that? "I have to go and see him!"

"What about your guests?" Eliza cried.

"I will be back before you know it. He is waiting for me to go to him. If I don't go now I never will," Daisy ran towards the door, rushing past a surprised Stella as she left the house.

"Oh My God!" Stella looked shocked as Daisy ignored her and carried on running. "Daisy? Daisy!" Stella shook her head, "What on earth is the matter with her? I have the press arriving in an hour!"

Eliza stormed up to her looking her straight in the eye. "I think you have some explaining to do."

"Eh?"

"What's with the photos Stella?"

Stella was clearly surprised. "What? What photos?"

"The photo of Daisy kissing Brandon? That you kindly posted to me. Or was it something to do with Rick Rockley? I know he works on the seedier side of his art now," Eliza squared up to the diminutive Stella as Brandon himself appeared on the doorstep.

"I haven't got a clue what you are on about," Stella replied, holding her hands up.

"Oh come on, I'm not stupid. You would do anything to get back at Daisy over Rick and you always hated me at college. What better way than to get your slimy ex to spy on everyone and send a photo?"

"Eliza, I really do not know what you mean. Seriously. I haven't seen Rick for two years."

"Oh yeah right."

"Look. Rick is a mess. He is hooked on coke and he has lawsuits against him from some high up people because of his photographs. He only contacts me when he wants money," Stella's facade cracked, "That was all he was every interested in! My family's money. So I would never liaise with him, especially if it involved one of my clients."

Katya's phone rang. "It's Glen," she answered the call, "What do you mean you're going up north? Where are you?"

Eliza turned to Brandon. "We have to go and get Daisy. She has run to Glen's caravan but he is not there and her guests will be arriving in less than two hours! If she waits for him she will miss it all."

Heather, Daisy's sister, arrived on the doorstep with a big smile on her face. "I've come to help. What needs doing?"

Katya was worried: "I have one of those odd feelings like something is going to happen," she looked at Eliza.

"Yes, Katya, so do I. Come on Brandon let's go."

"What's going on?" Asked Heather.

Siobhan appeared in the hallway. "Is everything okay? Where is Miss Hartford?"

"Slight change of plan." Stella clicked her heels into action. "I'm in charge now until Daisy gets back. Show me what needs doing,"

Siobhan nodded and took her through to the kitchen where Penny was busy preparing the food for the guests' arrival.

"Do you have a location on your phone from Glen's call?" Eliza asked Katya as she left the house."

"Where is Daisy?" Heather asked.

"She has gone to find her true love," Eliza smiled.

"What? But …"

Eliza turned to Katya. "Go and see Sheryl, she is minding the shop. Jan can drive you to him. If you can find where he is. We will go and get Daisy!"

"I'm coming too! I want to know what's up with my sister!" Heather added, and followed Eliza.

CHAPTER THIRTY

Daisy was out of breath as she approached Glen's caravan, and despite the chill of the winter air she had pulled off her jacket, feeling far too warm. She had never felt such a sense of urgency. She could not wait to tell him that she believed; that she finally accepted his whole story that had sounded so far-fetched. She imagined the look on his face as he heard her words. The way his face would break into a relieved smile and his eyes would look into hers. She visualised him taking her into his arms and kissing her, their bodies becoming united again as they were meant to be. They had always been meant to be. Oh this was going to be blissful.

She stopped when she saw his car was not there. He had probably popped into town for something. She hovered awkwardly, the fire taken from her as she had reached a dead end. Her love and desire were spilling over, but with nowhere to go. She felt foolish. She realised her heart was beating too fast. She was nervous for goodness sake! Taking a deep breath, as Eliza always advised, she tried to think rationally. The car may be in for repairs, or he could have left it somewhere. He may still be home. Tentatively, she knocked on the door of the caravan. There was no answer, but she thought she saw a movement through the window. Trying the handle she was surprised to find it unlocked and almost fell through the doorway as it swung open.

Daisy stumbled into the caravan, clutching the door which swung too quickly; she hurtled into the compact kitchen worktop. Looking up, expecting to see Glen, she stopped in her tracks as she saw a young woman sitting on the sofa. The woman appeared as startled as she did, and for a long moment they both stared at each other.

"I am looking for Glen," Daisy broke the silence.

"He's not here," replied the woman.

Daisy felt that the woman was looking at her with a hostile expression. Was she Glen's new lover? Had he lost patience with her and moved on to another? Surely not so soon.

"Do you ... er ... do you know when he will be back?"

The woman shook her head, and simply stared at Daisy as though she was not sure whether to cry or speak. The woman was becoming quite red in the face. She must be a lover or she would surely not appear so upset. Daisy's mind was reeling with panic.

"Do you know where he is?"

"No," the woman replied.

Daisy was beginning to feel unnerved; surely it was normal to ask a visitor who they were, and to at least provide some sort of polite response to reasonable questions. Daisy then recognised her as the woman who had been sitting with Glen in the restaurant when he had spilt the drinks over her.

"Are you a friend of his?"

"I have known him for a long time," the woman said, staring at her as though she had seen a ghost.

"Well, okay, I'll be off then. I'll try ringing him." Daisy turned her back and moved towards the door. Before she could reach the handle, she felt her hair being almost tugged from the back of her head as the woman moved swiftly. She yanked Daisy back by her hair, and pushed her against the worktop.

"What the ...?"

"You bitch!" Hissed the woman. She slapped Daisy hard around the face.

Daisy was horrified and her hand moved automatically to the side of her face in disbelief.

"I have been waiting for weeks to do that!" The woman cried.

"I ... I don't understand," Daisy shook her head.

"Oh, you don't understand? How convenient for you! Don't tell me – you didn't know he was married?"

"He is widowed ... his wife died?"

"Oh is that what he told you?" The woman began to cry hysterically. "Did he also fail to tell you about his son?"

"Glen doesn't have a son."

The woman stopped and laughed. "Oh, sorry, I think we are at cross purposes. I am not talking about Glen. I am talking about Stefan. My husband."

"Sorry?"

"Don't deny it. I know you have been having an affair. And now it seems you are interested in Glen too? Of course he is obsessed with you. Did he tell you he was prepared to ruin us financially, all because he had seen your pretty face?"

The woman was coming towards her again, and she was angry and volatile. Daisy backed away into the small kitchen.

"I don't know what you mean, I don't know anyone called Stefan…"

"You are a liar as well as a bitch then. Is one man not enough for you? First Stefan, then Glen, and there is your friend's man as well. I saw you kissing him. Well you can't have my husband!"

"The photos …" Daisy murmured as she looked around for something to pick up in defence as the woman approached. Spying a gin bottle, Daisy began to edge around, the space. If she could get to that in time …

"Yes, I took the photos. It made me feel sick watching you," The woman moved up close to her and took Daisy's jaw, squashing it between her fingers, "Just because you have all your airs and graces and your pretty clothes … just because you are perfect. Just because of everything!" The woman raised her other hand as though she was about to strike Daisy's face again when Brandon walked in, taking hold of the upset woman and pulling her away.

"Get off me!" The woman cried struggling.

"Daisy what's going on?" Heather appeared with Eliza.

"I don't know!" Daisy cried, running towards her sister, "This woman is crazy, accusing me of having an affair with her husband."

"Don't deny it. I've seen the emails, from Daisy Hartford!" The woman had escaped from Brandon's grip and was sat on the sofa crying.

Eliza approached her slowly, Brandon hovering nearby and Daisy staying close to Heather.

"What emails?" Daisy cried. "I don't even use the name Daisy Hartford on emails. They are still set up as Daisy Dupont. And I don't even know Stefan or whatever his name is!"

Heather gasped. "Oh!" She turned quickly, moving towards the door.

"What is it sis?" Daisy followed her.

Heather walked out of the caravan and stood looking out to sea. Daisy placed a hand on her shoulder.

"Heather?"

Heather turned round, facing the woman who now made her way to the door, closely tracked by Brandon and Eliza. "Jayne, it was me," Heather said clearly.

"What?" Jayne shook her head.

"It was me who was emailing Stefan."

"I don't understand?" Daisy was confused.

"I used an old email account from when Daisy and I were teenagers. I couldn't risk Simon seeing the emails."

"You?" Jayne looked from Heather to Daisy and back again, shaking her head.

"What is so surprising?" Heather smiled, "Good old sensible Heather, perfect wife, the plain and sensible sister. Always well-behaved. Well, there's fire in the old girl yet!"

Jayne launched towards Heather and Daisy intervened, pulling the emotional woman away from her sister. As the weight of Jayne fell against Daisy, Daisy's heel caught on a stone and she fell backwards, over the cliff, her fingers clutching the edge painfully and her eyes wide with terror.

"Daisy!" cried Heather rushing to her sister.

Jayne began to wail.

"I can't hold on!" Daisy cried.

Brandon and Eliza rushed over to assist, just as Daisy's fingers slipped from the edge and she landed on a piece of rock jutting out several feet below.

The crowd stood looking down at Daisy's body, lying on the ledge beneath them, a trickle of blood running from her head.

"Oh my god Daisy!" Eliza knelt down on the cliff edge, her hands gripping the rocks, "Remember to breathe! Deep breaths! We are getting help!"

Brandon was calling an ambulance as Stefan pulled up and got out of his car.

"What's going on?" he said.

. . . . .

Katya burst into the shop, running up to the staunch Jan as Sheryl watched with wide eyes from behind the counter.

"We have to find Glen!" She cried, tugging at Jan's sleeve.

"Katya lovey, calm down dear," Sheryl cooed, waving her hands like a magician.

"I can't! Glen's gone! Daisy's gone running off to the caravan, and both me and Eliza have one of those bad feelings! It's all happening. She has finally realised he is telling the truth … and …one of them, probably Daisy is going to die. It's all my fault!"

"Sshh!" Jan took hold of Katya's shoulders, "Stop panicking. You won't do anyone any favours getting in a silly tiz about it."

"Sorry. I know, but …"

"Do you know where Glen has gone?" Jan asked calmly.

"No! He just said he was going north! Let me try phoning him," Katya fumbled in her duffle bag, for her phone and clicked on Glen's number, "Its gone straight to voicemail."

"Well it will do if he is driving," Jan commented.

"Do you have something that belongs to him?" Sheryl asked.

Katya crouched down, fumbling in her duffle bag again and scattering its contents until she pulled out a crumpled business card, "I have this." She passed it to Sheryl.

The clairvoyant reached into the pocket of her red cardigan and pulled out a dowsing pendulum. She held it over the business card, focusing on it as it swung from side to side, and then round in circles.

"Right, he is definitely heading north and he is only two hours ahead. Jan, if you put your foot down you can catch him up. Katya do you know his car?"

Katya nodded, scooping up the contents of her bag.

"Come on then," Jan led the way out of the shop and they got in her car.

Katya was amazed at Jan's skill behind the wheel. She was in total control, accelerating, overtaking, and Katya was holding her breath as they sped along.

"If I get a speeding fine I'm sending Glen the bill," she muttered as she overtook a van in order to better see the road ahead.

They were soon onto main roads, which were fairly clear, and making good time. Eventually reaching the motorway, Katya wondered how they would ever find him in the midst of fast moving cars.

"What if we don't find him?"

"Try phoning him again. I can't drive like this all day."

Katya tried his number again, and again it went to voicemail.

"Glen, it's me Katya. You have to phone me back. It's important. It's about Daisy," she hung up.

Jan was forced to slow down a little as they met some traffic approaching a junction. "What are you going to say when you find him?"

"If we find him. I just need to tell him Daisy wants to see him. That she believes him," Katya's eyes filled with tears. It was so hard helping someone she had such deep feelings for to get together with someone else.

"Sometimes it's hard to do the right thing, Katya," Jan said without looking at her as she concentrated on driving, "But you know when it is the right thing."

Katya nodded, amazed at Jan's wisdom as her heart filled up with something she had no words for. The intensity of the last few weeks was building to a crescendo. She just hoped that both Daisy and Glen would survive this time. Her phone rang in her lap and she jumped, expecting it to be Glen. It was Eliza.

"Have you found him yet?" Eliza asked.

"No. We are on the motorway."

"Daisy is in a bad way. It's a long story, but she has been hurt. Tell him to get here fast if you reach him."

"What … what's happened to her?" But Eliza had hung up. Katya felt a flutter of palpitations and concentrated on her breathing. She turned to Jan, "Daisy's been hurt. It doesn't sound good."

Jan cast her a quick glance and then put her foot down. "Spirits and angels guide us please!"

Katya tried Glen's number again only to get the answer machine and she sighed heavily, trying to control her breathing.

Eventually they reached a service station and Jan began to pull into the entrance lane.

"What are you doing?" Cried Katya, "We can't stop."

"Sorry, but I have to stop for a while, if only to use the lavatory."

CHAPTER THIRTY-ONE

Despite Jayne's emotional state, the sense of emergency she felt as they waited for the ambulance triggered something within her, and she remembered Glen's brother, Leo, along with other friends who had been injured through adventurous pursuits. This was her fault. She had gone off the rails and lashed out at a woman who had done nothing wrong. All because her excuse of a husband had cheated with the woman's sister. *Daisy's plight was an accident*, she told herself, but she felt a sense of responsibility. The whole series of events had been due to her outburst. She must do something.

She looked down at the beautiful woman lying on the rocks below, blood pouring out of her head. If she could stop the bleeding it may help. She knew that even a few minutes of blood loss from the brain could have serious consequences. She turned to Stefan, anger rising through her as she tried to look him in the eyes.

"Do you have any ropes in the car?"

"What?"

"I need to get down there and help her!" Jayne wanted to slap him harder than she had slapped Daisy. She shook her head, feeling remorseful at her loss of temper. "This is my fault … no! It's your fault! Get the ropes!!"

Like a small child being told off, he rushed to the car and opened the boot as she followed him, her hands reaching into the backpack.

"Don't do this Jayne. Let me, please."

"No!" She cried, taking the ropes, tying one firmly around her waist and clipping another to it, "I have to do this!" She walked towards the cliff edge, as Stefan grabbed the other end of the rope.

"Jayne! Stop, you are not thinking straight."

"Oh I am thinking very straight! A woman's life is at stake because of you, and because of me. Hold the damn rope and concentrate!" She sat on the edge of the cliff, scanning for secure footholds before turning around and lowering herself over the side and finding rocks to cling on to, "Okay, I'm good to go. Lower me down slowly."

The adrenalin was buzzing through Jayne's body as she began to move down the cliff face, her feet touching the rock here and there to steady her descent. She felt alive, like she hadn't done for months. She was in control and pacing herself, encouraging herself to take it slowly. She was out of practice, but the skill never went away. Feeling at one with the face of the rock and the breeze gently swaying the rope she felt peace. For the first time in ages she was Jayne again. Brave, adventurous, fearless Jayne.

Stefan's face was watching her over the edge of the cliff. Her life was in his hands but she was in control. She was timing her pace, signalling when he should lengthen the rope and he was obeying. It felt good.

Eventually she reached Daisy and signalled to Stefan to relax the rope as her feet landed firmly on the rocks. Daisy was still breathing and had a pulse. Jayne stripped down to her vest top, glad of the cold air as she wound her shirt tightly around Daisy's head, taking care not to move the woman's neck. She stroked the side of Daisy's face.

"I am so, so sorry."

"Cold," Daisy whispered.

"Hang on in there Daisy, help will be here soon," Jayne lay close to her to keep her warm and as the sun came out from behind a cloud she felt a rush of pride. The old Jayne was still in her soul, she had not lost herself.

Hearing the sound of helicopter blades, she sat up waving. The paramedics worked quickly, safely moving Daisy onto a stretcher and lifting her into the air ambulance, hoisting Jayne in too.

. . . . .

In the service station, Katya was becoming impatient waiting for Jan to return from the toilets. She turned to look at the coffee bar queue, wanting a cup of tea, when she saw him. He was too far away to shout and he was heading towards the door of the service station. She ran, a flurry of fake fur coat, duffle bag, and clanking crystals, pushing past people and accidentally spilling someone's cup of tea she skidded across the floor nearly losing her balance.

"Sorry, sorry!" She cried as she weaved her way through, trying not to lose sight of the tall figure that was walking away from her. Eventually she decided she must be within earshot.

"Glen!" She called.

There was no response; he kept walking.

"Glen!" She called again.

He stopped. She raced as fast as she could, ignoring her phone ringing in her pocket. She had never been able to run and talk at the same time. As she neared him he turned round, his phone pressed to his ear as she became level with him.

"I was just phoning you," he said, hanging up, "I got your message."

"Daisy has been hurt. You have to come back," she replied, trying to catch her breath as she adjusted her glasses.

"Hurt? How?" His face was panic-stricken and he grabbed Katya's arm, pulling her along.

"I don't know," she gasped, "She ran to your caravan. Eliza just said she was in a bad way."

"Come on!" He cried, dashing to the car.

"What about Jan?" Katya asked.

"Who's Jan? Just get in the car!"

"My driver," Katya tried to explain as he started the car while she was still getting her seatbelt on.

"What's going on?" He asked, as he drove – even more quickly than Jan. Katya was beginning to wonder if she was going to survive the day.

"Daisy believes you."

"She does?"

"Yes, she believes in your experience. She was rushing to the caravan to tell you."

"But today is her first proper day at the guesthouse?"

"I know. She dropped everything and ran to the caravan."

"What changed her mind?" Glen turned to glance at her.

"I have a friend, Josie who works at the museum. I found two old pendants carved with initials. One of the pendants has initials that match yours and Daisy's names in your previous life. And Josie has also found census information that corresponds. It was enough to prove to Daisy that you were telling the truth."

"What about the other pendant? Why were there two?"

"That one was different," Katya replied, "Not important." She fought back the urge to tell him that it was of great importance. That it represented his betrayal to her and that she was devastated.

"So that alone was enough to persuade her that I am not completely off the rails?"

All he cared about was Daisy, she thought. "I suspect that something else may have triggered it, or added to it, as she was already emotional when we arrived this morning."

"But now she is hurt. Why did I leave?" He punched the steering wheel and accidentally sounded the horn.

"Can I suggest driving a bit more sensibly? You don't want to get hurt too." Katya sighed.

He was quiet then, concentrating on the road.

Katya's mind was jumping from one scene to another. The man she loved was sitting next to her, taking her at break neck speed to reunite with the past life love that he had forsaken her for. Again. She shook her head, almost laughing to herself at the irony.

. . . . .

The corner of the waiting room felt isolating as Eliza sat alone waiting for Brandon to return from the guesthouse. Heather sat with Felicity and Harry, Daisy's parents, and they had that family thing going on - she felt like an intruder if she attempted to join in with their muted conversations. Harry's brows were furrowed, his eyes staring blankly at the floor as Felicity sobbed into her handkerchief telling Heather how proud she was of both her daughters.

Stefan and Jayne were sitting in silence and there could have been an icy wall between them as unspoken words were being exchanged in their minds, those which could not be said in front of the concerned family. Heather totally ignored the couple, and the couple totally ignored her. Eliza wondered how Jayne must be feeling, knowing that she sat in between her husband and his married lover, unable to vent her anger or ask the many questions that must be going through her mind. Jayne had come through though. Jayne's bravery had outshone her outburst as she had risked her own life to help Daisy. No one had known how long the ambulance was going to take and Jayne's selfless actions may have given Daisy a fighting chance of survival. Eliza was strong and loyal to her friends, but she would never have been brave enough to do what Jayne had done. She watched the woman's face as she sat almost frozen to the spot, her eyes glazed over, holding a hospital blanket around her tired body. She had been checked over and given some painkillers while Daisy was rushed into A and E as she had lost consciousness in the helicopter. Stefan sat fidgeting, tapping his foot, his arms folded. He was frowning and looked like he wanted to escape. Eliza hoped Jayne left him for good.

She looked over at Heather, wondering how this adulterous union between her and Stefan had happened. Heather was certainly doing a good job of keeping it together in front of Harry and Felicity. She had no doubt that the affair would never be mentioned and that Heather would carry on as usual for the sake of the family.

Then what of Glen and Daisy? The whole reason Daisy had found herself in this drama was because she had impetuously decided to run off and tell him she loved him after all. Typical Daisy. Always the artist, the damsel, and the centre of attention. Without actually trying, Eliza realised. Daisy was just herself; she couldn't help her temperament and her need for dramatics. It was not engineered, she was a romantic, creative soul with a feisty nature. Nothing false and nothing manipulated, Daisy followed her heart but did not like to be tamed. True to her Leo astrology and a true friend.

Katya had dashed off to find Glen, and Eliza now wondered how her lovely assistant was coping with the enormity of her own emotional burden. To experience unrequited love was hard enough. To experience it several times over, only to be stuck in the spiral still, must be torturous. Eliza silently vowed to herself to be more supportive to Katya in future and to give her predicament some real sympathy. Poor Katya, she had come on in leaps and bounds. Eliza had enjoyed watching her grow in confidence. She had gathered through snippets of conversation that Katya had been misunderstood, mistreated, and misaligned throughout most of her life. Her only shining light was her son, Liam. Eliza asked the angels to help Katya in discovering her truth and her answers. She could not allow this Glen thing to break her again.

She was disturbed from her thoughts as Brandon walked into the waiting room and her heart filled with joy at the sight of him. Unusually, she felt on the brink of tears as she noticed the look in his eyes towards her, one of warmth, trust and love. She jumped out of her seat and flung her arms around him, breathing in his familiar scent and enjoying the solid and safe feeling of his body next to her. She need never feel alone again.

"Any news?" He whispered into her ear.

"No," Eliza buried her face into his shoulder, "Is everything at the house okay?"

"Yes, I have left Stella in charge."

Eliza gave him a quizzical look and he smiled.

"Trust me, she will not let Daisy down. Stop worrying."

Eliza buried her face in his shoulder.

"I love you," she whispered, "So much."

A member of the medical team walked through the room swiftly towards Harry and Felicity, and they all turned their heads expectantly.

"She's going to be okay," The male nurse confirmed, smiling, "She has extensive concussion and is in and out of consciousness and she has a broken leg. But no lasting damage is indicated."

"Oh! Thank god!" Felicity swayed against Harry as Heather squeezed her mother's shoulder and Harry dabbed his eyes with a tissue.

"Where is the lady who abseiled down the cliff?" The nurse asked. Jayne turned around to face him, her face dazed.

"That was me,"

The nurse came over to her and smiled.

"You have probably saved Daisy's life. If she had lost any more blood from the head wound she would be in a much less stable condition."

Jayne was lost for words and appeared to be between somewhere between elation and numbness. Stefan reached for her, but she pulled away. Eliza went over and hugged her, allowing the woman to shed tears she could not show to her husband.

Heather and Stefan looked across at each other with no affection, but simply an awkwardness that hung like barrier between them.

"It's over," Heather mouthed at him as Jayne was safely hidden on Eliza's shoulder.

Stefan nodded solemnly as Heather followed her parents swiftly down the corridor.

Jayne pulled away from Eliza.

"I want to go to my mum's. I want to see Leo," she said to Stefan, "I don't want to be on my own with you."

Stefan nodded, avoiding eye contact with Eliza and Brandon as they walked out of the hospital.

Eliza and Brandon finally found themselves alone and they sat down on the cold, plastic waiting chairs. She nestled her head into his shoulder and his hand took hers, pulling her towards him.

"Will you marry me?" Brandon asked.

"Umm, what?" Eliza looked up at him with glazed eyes.

"Will you marry me?" He said again.

"What? Are you being serious?"

"Yes," he laughed and got down on one knee, taking her hand, "I love you Eliza, and I want to spend the rest of my life with you."

"Oh. Yes," she laughed at him, her heart filling with joy, "Yes!"

"I have no ring yet, as I didn't plan to do this today but I mean it. Eliza I mean every word."

Ignoring the amused glances from onlookers, Eliza took his face in her hands and kissed him passionately, tears rolling down her cheeks.

The movement of people rushing in through the automatic doors interrupted their kiss as Katya and Glen appeared in the waiting room.

"What's happening?" Asked Katya, her braided hair spilling out at the sides and her glasses slipping as she wrestled with her duffle bag. She looked tired.

"Is Daisy okay?" Glen was agitated, hovering next to Katya.

"She's going to pull through, it's okay," Eliza smiled, still holding onto Brandon. It was the first time she had ever seen Glen face to face yet she felt unsurprised. There was something about him that belonged in her group of people. She hoped that he and Daisy would work it out and Katya could heal her heart.

"Sshh, don't tell them yet," Brandon pressed his finger gently to her lips.

"I won't," she kissed his fingertip.

The male nurse reappeared. "She has come round and is asking for Glen?" He looked from Brandon to Glen, confused by the sight before him.

"That's me!" Glen exclaimed.

"Follow me sir," The medic ushered him along the corridor.

· · · · ·

As Daisy watched the goings on around her, she wondered if it was an illusion when Glen walked through the door. She was relieved as he approached, blurring in and out of focus. She tried to lift herself up from the bed but wires caught her and she felt disorientated. What the hell had happened to her? She did not like this feeling.

As Glen sat at her bedside, he moved his face closer and kissed her cheek, his face filled with concern as his hand smoothed her forehead. She could sense that she wore a bandage around her head. It was comfortable and safe, better than the open wound, but it was foreign and she wanted to shake her hair free and feel his fingers running through it. He wore a look of deep seriousness making him look older than his years and she wanted to lighten the mood but she did not have the energy.

"I ... I wanted to see you..." She murmured.

"I know. That's why I am here."

"You are ... you were ..." She faltered as her breath ran out.

"Sshh. It doesn't matter. I'm here."

"Sorry..."

Glen clutched her hand tightly and brought it to his face, pressing his lips against her fingers. "Daisy I love you."

"You don't even know me."

"Does that matter?"

"Huh?" Daisy was tired.

"If I feel it in my heart, then does it matter how long we have known each other?"

"It does in a way ... the future ..."

"What of the future? The place I went to had no time – no past no future; just the now. And the love I felt in that place was like no other."

Daisy's eyes were blurring again as she looked at him, but his voice felt like a soothing gentle melody to her racing heart as she stopped trying to fight the effects of the painkillers.

"You are that love," he murmured.

She tried to nod and smile but it was too much for her. She commanded her eyes to tell him and she could see from the reaction on his face that he had understood her unspoken words.

"Let's just live in the moment Daisy. Let's love each other for as long as we both want. No promises, no shadows. Just love," he looked at her and for a moment she saw his eyes clearly, no longer feeling threatened by their intensity, simply reassured.

She allowed herself to swim in the blur, the unreality of the chemical and technological world she was placed in. The beeps slowed down and the fog around her brain increased as she let the feeling of delightful numbness and euphoria take over. She could sleep now, she was safe, feeling the warmth of his hand, the only real thing touching her. She allowed herself to drift into nothingness, enjoying the way she could just slip into it so easily.

CHAPTER THIRTY-TWO

Leaning on the edge of her dressing table, Daisy scrutinised her appearance in the mirror. She felt confident to meet and greet the guests at her launch. She looked good and, from her outward appearance, no one would know of the accident. Her face fell as Siobhan passed her the unsightly crutch that she relied upon to get about.

"Damn this leg," Daisy muttered as the walking aid appeared alongside her reflection.

"Miss Hartford, you still look beautiful," Siobhan reassured.

"Thank you. For god's sake though Siobhan, will you call me Daisy?"

"Sorry Miss… I mean Daisy," Siobhan flushed, "I am so thankful for this opportunity. I love working here."

Daisy hobbled over to her housekeeper's side and touched her arm. "Siobhan, I am grateful to you for keeping this place running. Which is why…" She hobbled back to the dressing table and took out a sheet of paper, "I am giving you a new contract and a new job title." She passed the paper to the young woman.

Siobhan's face lit up as her eyes scanned the page and she gasped. "Oh thank you so much! You don't know what this means to me!"

"It's only what you deserve," Daisy smiled, "You are now hostess and manager over the two housekeeping staff I have hired this week. It was foolish of me to think that one person could look after the whole house. Except you have… but you cannot continue to work fourteen hours a day. It would be against employment law for a start!"

"Thank you Miss Hart... I mean, Daisy," Siobhan's eyes filled with tears.

"From now on, you greet and host the guests and manage the house in the daytime, and I host and manage in the evening. Is that okay with you?"

"Oh it most certainly is … Daisy."

"Then sign it!" Daisy laughed, sitting down on the end of the bed as standing and laughing while leaning on the crutch was something she still hadn't mastered.

Siobhan took a pen from her pocket and scrawled her signature across the page, beaming.

Daisy linked arms with her.

"Are you ready to help me down the stairs again?"

"Of course… Daisy," Smiled Siobhan.

As Daisy leant on the younger woman she cursed her own decision to have the guesthouse lift only go as far as the guest rooms and not her own attic. She had never considered at that point that she would be in need of a lift.

She turned to smooth her hair in the lift mirror, relieved that the scar from her head wound was not visible and enjoying the way her black, halter neck evening dress sparkled in the lights. She looked stunning, crutch or not, she told herself.

The lift doors opened onto the hall and she walked out to a round of applause and cheers from the crowd before her. All her friends and family were gathered here. Her father stood next to the lift, his arm ready to escort her and a proud twinkle in his eyes. Even her mother was beaming with joy.

Daisy spotted Eliza, surprised to see that she was wearing a dress. Even Brandon had made an effort, wearing a black suit and bow tie along with his customary waistcoat, this one in a deep red silk. Heather and Simon were applauding, while her young niece, Fleur, watched her aunt emerge with sparkling eyes. Daisy paused to blow a kiss to the little girl as she made her way towards the drawing room.

Stella was in full flow, directing the press photographers to snap Daisy as she emerged from the lift, and standing behind them was Glen.

He walked effortlessly through the crowd, dressed simply in a black suit and white shirt. Every time she laid eyes on him, he grew more attractive. She fought the urge to fall against him so she could breathe in his skin and hear his reassuring voice murmuring in her ear. Instead she waited as he walked towards her, linking her arm and taking her weight so that she could pass him the crutch and walk between him and her father more elegantly to the front of the room.

They posed for photographs and Daisy felt as though she had finally arrived. The reviews from her trial guests had been excellent despite her being indisposed in hospital – Siobhan, Penny and Stella had taken care of everything. This was real. This was her launch. Her moment was finally happening and she felt jubilant.

As the cameras stopped flashing, she paused for a moment, leaning against one of the armchairs in the bay window as Glen passed her a glass of champagne.

"Well done," he smiled reassuringly.

"This is not down to me," she replied, "It's everyone else. My friends, my family and my new staff. I was foolish to think I could do all this on my own,"

"You were not foolish, just idealistic," he stroked her arm tenderly.

Harry and Felicity walked over, each kissing Daisy on the cheek.

"Mum, Dad, I need to officially introduce you. This is Glen Heathstone."

Glen stepped forward and shook Harry's hand firmly, then kissed the back of Felicity's hand gracefully. Daisy could tell her mum was already smitten.

"It's a pleasure to meet you," Harry smiled at him, "I hear you used to be in the property business."

"Yes, but that is now the past, I have different plans now."

"Oh, what would those be then?" Harry asked smiling.

"I can't say just yet, there are still two people I need to speak to before I finalise. But it is a local investment opportunity and close to my heart."

Daisy eyed him curiously. "What are you up to?"

"You will see," he smiled.

"Well, I admire you for following something you believe in," Harry nodded.

"So, Glen," Felicity smiled with a glint in her eye, "Do you have any other plans that are not business related?" She nodded towards her daughter.

"Just helping Daisy get back on track and trying not to interfere with the guesthouse," he laughed, "She is very independent you know."

"Oh I know! You don't have to remind me. But ..."

"Sorry I'm late," A voice said next to them, and Daisy looked up to see Jayne.

"Jayne!" I am so glad you could come," Daisy stood, leaning on Glen's arm, and kissed Jayne on the cheek.

"I am so sorry about what happened in the caravan. I nearly didn't come tonight, I am so embarrassed!"

"Oh please, there is no need to worry about that. You saved my life!"

Jayne blushed. "I don't know about that. I just did what seemed right."

Harry and Felicity moved away to speak to some of Harry's golf friends who had been trial guests and, as Heather weaved her way towards them, Glen excused himself. "I need to go and speak to Eliza about something."

Daisy nodded, tensing as her sister joined Jayne and herself. The two women had not met since the day of the accident. She had no idea how Heather or Jayne were going to react.

Jayne was visibly defensive, watching Heather as she joined them.

"I'm sorry." Heather said sincerely. Jayne looked down. "I mean it. I am truly sorry. You have every right to hate me. I never set out to hurt you and it was all over weeks ago. It actually only lasted a matter of weeks."

Jayne looked up at her. "I forgive you."

"I was bored. I mean, I was unhappy. I needed to feel like me again, instead of just Simon's wife and mother to his daughter."

"I forgive you," Jayne repeated, "And I totally understand."

"You do?" Heather looked surprised.

"Yes. The whole thing, in a roundabout way has done me a favour."

"What do you mean?" Asked Daisy.

"Well," Jayne smiled to herself, "The first breakthrough was abseiling down the cliff to help you Daisy. I realised I was still Jayne. In here," she pointed to her heart, "The second thing was that I actually had something to yell at Stefan for. I let rip at him. I didn't care whether he left me or not. I told him I was unhappy, depressed, and that I needed more out of life. I told him that either things changed or that I would leave him."

"And then what?" Daisy asked.

"We have decided to sell the house, and move nearer to my family. We are going back to the suburbs. We can go to the pub like a normal couple and my mom will be nearby to help with Leo."

"And you as a couple?" Heather raised an eyebrow.

"One day at a time. I need to trust him again," Jayne nodded solemnly. She leaned forward and hugged Heather tentatively, "I hope you can find happiness again too."

Heather's eyes filled with tears and she hugged Jayne back. "Thank you. Not many women would be so understanding. You are an amazing woman."

. . . . .

Katya was disturbed by the intercom from the front door. She was not expecting anyone to visit; she listened for Josic's footsteps up above but there was nothing. The intercom sounded again. She got up and picked up the receiver.

"Hello?"

"Katya Lovey, it's us; Sheryl and Jan."

"Oh, come on in!" Katya released the door lock and opened her own door into the hall to see the two sisters bustling in from the cold night.

As they entered her flat, Sheryl took one look at her and frowned.

"Why aren't you ready?"

Katya looked down at her fleece pyjamas. "I'm not going."

"Told you so!" Jan said to her sister.

"You must go!" Sheryl insisted.

"What for?" Katya cried, "So I can watch him ignore me again?"

Jan went into the kitchen and put the kettle on. "Look, I know it's hard, but your relationship with Glen in this life might not be about romantic love?" Sheryl sat down, removing her scarf and coat. For once the colourful lady wore black, and with her red and blonde hair it worked well.

"You look lovely," Katya stared at her.

"Thank you. And so would you if you got changed out of those pyjamas."

"Into what? I don't have fancy clothes. I never go to anything as grand as a hotel launch."

"It's a guesthouse, not a hotel," Jan chipped in as she poured cups of tea.

"Let's go and look through your wardrobe," Sheryl suggested.

"But I don't actually want to go."

"You are instrumental in this whole story. Daisy and Glen would not be together without you. Or us. Or if you want to put it another way, Eliza would not have had time to help Daisy so much if you hadn't looked after the shop."

Jan walked through with three cups of tea. "Are you going to tell her?"

"Tell me what?"

"We turned some cards over for you; there is a great opportunity ahead of you."

"What? What has that got to do with Daisy's launch?"

"Perhaps nothing, but opportunity doesn't happen when you are sitting around in your pyjamas does it?" Jan chided.

Katya sipped her tea and looked at the sister's expectant faces. She had grown to love these two very different women. Sheryl with her warm enthusiasm and her colourful charisma, and the stern but protective Jan with her common sense. She could not help but smile at them. "Aren't you supposed to ask someone's permission before you pull cards out for them?"

"Technically, yes. But this was different," Sheryl replied.

"How?" Katya asked.

The sisters looked at each other.

"We just had one of those feelings," Jan said as Sheryl nodded.

"Okay. I'll go, but I need some help with what to wear."

"That's my girl," Sheryl beamed.

. . . . .

As Katya wound her way through the crowded guesthouse, she found Eliza and Brandon outside on the rear terrace, smoking. She was about to venture out through the French windows off the dining room, when Glen appeared from the kitchen door. Katya hung back and listened.

"Eliza, Brandon," he smiled.

"Glen, it's so good to finally meet you properly," Eliza replied, "I heard all about you from Daisy and from Katya but we didn't actually meet until the hospital and that was all a bit …"

"Crazy?" Glen asked.

"Yes," Eliza cast a warm glance at Brandon, "It was a strange yet memorable afternoon."

Glen looked awkward as Eliza scrutinised him with what Katya recognised as her protectiveness over Daisy.

"So, are you going to move in here with Daisy then?" Brandon asked.

Katya watched Glen relax at the conversation opener. She wanted to hear what he had to say. He was probably about to propose to Daisy in front of everyone. In his suit and shirt he seemed aloof and inaccessible. She thought back to the regression when she had seen him at his most vulnerable, in a hypnotic state. The day when she had called in unannounced, about to tell him she loved him, and he had just got up. The *real* Glen that she knew seemed a million miles away from this smart business man that stood with Eliza. He was out of her league. Who was she to think that she had ever been anything more than the messed-up girl who had got pregnant at seventeen, and now, when she should know better, had run away to the seaside? Why would Glen even think of her in any other way?

"I have no plans to move in with Daisy. Not yet. We have decided to see how things go first. I will stay at the caravan for now."

Katya was surprised and wondered if it were Glen's decision or Daisy's?

"I like that," Eliza nodded, "Daisy is quite impulsive sometimes – I would hate to see her rush into another relationship disaster."

"I hope it won't be a disaster!" Glen laughed, "But we want to enjoy the getting to know each other part of it. You know the dates and the holidays, before day to day life kicks in."

Eliza smiled uncertainly.

"I admire the way you are so protective of her Eliza. She has a good friend in you," Glen smiled.

"We go back a long way. We are like sisters."

"Which is why I want to talk to you about something," Glen said, "But I need to speak to Katya too. Where is she? I haven't seen her here?"

Katya gasped as she stood in her hiding place, then covered her mouth in the darkness, just as she had back on the cove that day when she was a child. Why was she always hiding? She was supposed to be finding her true power and her voice.

"She is supposed to be here, I don't know why she is so late," Eliza shook her head.

"I'm here," Katya stepped out of the French windows in a dark blue dress, her long, thick hair styled into an up-do and fastened with a jewelled clip.

"Wow, you look amazing!" Eliza gasped.

"You do," Glen agreed, looking into her eyes. Katya blushed. He actually looked as though he meant it.

"What took you so long?" Brandon asked.

"Well, you know, I wanted to be fashionably late… But no, actually, I wasn't going to come, but then Sheryl and Jan came round and …"

"Your timing is impeccable, Katya as I was just about to tell Eliza about something that involves you as well," Glen smiled.

A waiter brought glasses of champagne out and Glen took one for them each and passed them around.

"What did you want to say?" Eliza asked, looking puzzled.

"I have a business proposition for you."

Eliza rolled her eyes a little and looked at Brandon. "It's no good asking me about business. I wanted to expand, but the Universe appears to be against me at the moment."

Brandon put his arm around her and kissed the top of her strawberry blond head.

Glen turned to Katya. "This proposition involves you too."

"Me? How?" Katya felt the chill in the air. She was totally sober and not used to going without a coat. She sipped her champagne quickly, hoping that the alcohol may take the edge off.

"You want to learn and train and research yes?" Glen looked at her. His eyes were smiling.

"Well, yes, but… I don't have… "

"How hard are you prepared to work on your quest Katya?"

"My quest?"

"The secrets of the Universe, the healing, the truth?"

"Oh my, well it is my whole life. You know that," Katya was confused and looked at Eliza's face for reassurance.

"So, if I were to invest in you and your learning, Katya, and I was to invest in your shop, Eliza, we could all work together?"

"I don't know what you mean?" Eliza looked suspicious.

"Well you know you were out-pitched for the shop next door?"

Eliza nodded.

"Yes…?"

"It was me. I outbid you."

For a moment Eliza's face was full of fury. "How could you?"

"Because I wanted to," Glen replied smiling.

"But… I had all my plans, if you hadn't come in and done that I could have got it? I don't believe this!" Eliza looked angry.

Brandon laid a hand on her shoulder. "Hear him out."

"I also know that Katya has a special gift and that she could do great things, with the right financial backing," Glen continued.

"So what are you suggesting?" Eliza placed a hand on her hip, "Get to the point!"

"I have bought out the shop next door for *you*. I am prepared to … No, I *want* to invest in Katya's training and education – and yours if you wish, so that you can follow your dreams and run that holistic centre you have been dreaming about."

Eliza stood staring at him defensively. "Why? What's in it for you? And how did you know about my plans?" She glared at Katya.

"I would not interfere. I don't need money. This is an investment from the heart because I believe in you and Katya," he touched Katya's shoulder and she gasped, unprepared for the touch, "Katya thinks the world of you, and I think the world of Katya. If it wasn't for your shop, I would not have met her and I would still be in a sea of confusion. This is my way of saying thank you."

Katya swayed a little, but luckily no one noticed. He thought the world of her?

"But I am a stranger to you?" Eliza continued to argue, "You haven't even seen my business plans."

"It doesn't matter. Your shop and Katya's empathy have been like an anchor to me and I want to learn more. Perhaps by investing in you and Katya, I will find my own answers. Daisy is the beginning, but I was brought back to life for a reason – and property is not that reason."

"So you would let me have free reign to run it as I wish?" Eliza asked.

"Yes. It would still be your business. I would be a sleeping partner. I pay the money and you run the business. In the meantime I will fund any training courses and materials that Katya needs to progress her own purpose."

"This seems too good to be true," Eliza looked sceptical.

"We will get everything drawn up by a solicitor stating what I have just said. You are shrewd Eliza, and I would expect nothing less from a business partner."

"What about a return on your investment though? Won't you want an income from it?

"My income, and my return, will be giving something back to the spiritual world I was privileged to see a glimpse of. I vowed to myself that any business dealings I made would be to help that along. All you two need to do is to make it work."

Eliza nodded. "I need to pinch myself. I never thought that shop next door would be mine. I still need something in writing. There is no handshake tonight."

"As soon as you agree to meet me at the solicitors and sign the paperwork that handshake can take place. The ball is in your court," Glen smiled.

"Eliza! Just say yes! For once in your life just stop being so self-sufficient!" Katya cried.

"She has a point," Brandon smiled.

Eliza rolled her eyes and shook Glen's hand. "Okay! This is more than I could have ever asked for. Thank you. I will see you at the solicitors. That wasn't an official handshake though – not yet."

Katya could not help herself, she flung her arms around Glen clumsily and squealed into his jacket. He squeezed her and then as she stood back and looked up at him tears in her eyes.

"You don't know how much this means, that someone believes in me."

"Hey I believe in you," Eliza play-punched her arm.

"Me too," Brandon joined in, "You are awesome."

Katya did not know whether to laugh or cry, so she did both. "I need some time alone," she said by way of apology, walking away quickly; such was the effect of being in an embrace with him. She could not look at him, or at any of them. Again, she wanted to hide.

. . . . .

The sound of Stella tapping the side of a glass and calling for hush over the microphone, gathering everyone's attention, told Daisy that this was the moment. This was her moment. The final launch.

Glen appeared at her side and held her arm so that she could pass the crutch to Siobhan and at least walk to the front of the drawing room without it. Stella stood next to the Mayor and the Dean of Daisy's old college, and Daisy sat in one of the beautifully upholstered Victorian armchairs.

"Ladies and gentlemen," Stella spoke out loud and clear, "Thank you for attending this evening. We are gathered to celebrate the grand opening of Hartford's Retreat. A high quality guesthouse catering particularly for the creative soul."

The crowd applauded, and Daisy felt more alive than she had done in years. Glen stood next to the chair, and she felt glamorous and beautiful in her elegant gown. Stella passed her the microphone.

"Well, yes, thank you all for coming. Thank you to the Mayor and to Dean Avery, for making time to attend at short notice. As some of you know, this event nearly didn't happen and the reason for my being seated is due to an accident I had a couple of weeks ago. So I have to pass on a big thank you to Stella Prince and Siobhan O'Malley for pulling all this together for me. Would Siobhan please step forward?"

Siobhan came to stand next to her, her face blushing a bright red as the Mayor presented her with a bouquet of flowers. Stella was also presented with one as the crowd applauded again.

"I also need to thank my friends and family for supporting me through all of this. I could never have done this without you. To Brandon for the website, Eliza for giving me the push I needed, and to my parents and family for all their support. Between them they have helped me to decide how this guesthouse should operate; as a creative retreat. We all lead busy lives, and for those of us who enjoy art and creative pursuits, what better place to stay than this amazing old building, with its sea view? I hope that as well as a guesthouse, Hartford's Retreat will also run workshops and events, encouraging local and visiting artists to become involved. Thank you."

Daisy passed the microphone to the Mayor. She stood awkwardly to shake his hand, holding the pose for a photo, smiling through the pain that throbbed through her leg. She would not allow it to spoil her grand moment.

"Thank you Daisy," the Mayor said, "I now declare Hartford's Retreat, officially open."

The crowd applauded and raised a toast to Daisy and her new beginning. She turned to look up at Glen, who held her hand and looked at her with those deep eyes that had at first unnerved her so much. They still unnerved her, but now she knew why. As well as her business being up and running, she was looking forward to getting to know him. Slowly. There was no rush. They had spent centuries rushing, avoiding, and betraying each other only to die. Now, it was time to enjoy and relish him. To learn about him and learn about herself. They had made no promises to one another; just to be forever honest. That was the way she liked it. No frills, no front, and no commitment. Not yet anyway.

Brandon was making his way over and he bent down to her. "Is it okay if I borrow the mic please?"

"As long as you don't swear," Daisy smiled, passing him the microphone.

"Ahem," Brandon cleared his throat, "A few days ago I sat in the waiting room in A and E, waiting to hear whether Daisy, here, was going to be alright, and something quite monumental in my own life happened. Over the past two years I have got to know a very special lady. Many of you may know her as a shop owner and a little eccentric at times. However she is a fighter, a worker, a great friend and if I ever have an ounce of her strength I will consider myself lucky. Eliza, would you come here please?"

Eliza blushed brightly and made her way self-consciously to the front of the room.

Brandon kissed her on the cheek and held her hand. "When we were in the hospital, I asked Eliza a question, and her answer was positive. But you can't ask a question like that in a waiting room. So… " Brandon reached into the pocket of his waistcoat, taking out a small box, got down on one knee, and held the ring out to Eliza, his eyes wide as he gazed at her. "Eliza, my warrior woman, will you marry me?"

Eliza looked totally embarrassed, but managed to utter the all-important 'Yes' into the microphone as Brandon pulled her close and kissed her passionately.

The crowd applauded yet again, this time a bit louder, and Katya was in tears as she stood in the background next to Sheryl.

"Oh how romantic," she whispered.

"Yes, beautiful, absolutely beautiful," Sheryl agreed. She turned to Katya, "Are you feeling better now?"

"Not quite. Can we talk in the other room?" Katya whispered.

. . . . .

It was easy for the two empaths to slip away as they made their way onto the terrace. They sat down at a table.

"What is it lovey?" Asked Sheryl, her eyes sparkling in the moonlight.

"What do I do about him? I don't think I can bear this."

"There is nothing you can do Katya," Sheryl squeezed her hand, "At the moment."

"I don't understand; why do our paths keep crossing in all these lifetimes if my feelings for him are completely futile? What is the point?" Katya felt her words blocked in her throat; she was choked and over-emotional.

"The familiarity from your past lives together has brought you together once more. That doesn't mean it is a romantic union. You may be destined for someone else?"

"I couldn't possibly ever feel this way about anyone else. I have never felt this way in my entire life!"

"So why does he overlook you? Why does he not see your beauty? What are *you* missing in each of these lives by waiting for *him*?"

"I don't understand? I love him. It's as simple as that."

"Listen Katya. You are beautiful, you are wiser than you give yourself credit for, and you have so much potential. I have so much belief in you and your future."

"He believes in me too Sheryl. He is investing in me."

"Investing?"

"This is top secret, but he is buying the shop next to Eliza's so that she can expand and create a mind, body, spirit hub."

"Oooh!" Sheryl squealed. "That is amazing!"

"Sshh," Katya whispered, "He is willing to finance all the training courses and workshops I want to do so that I can qualify in all the treatments I want to do."

"This is brilliant," Sheryl squeezed Katya's hands tightly, "You see. Perhaps this is the reason why you met? This is the opportunity your cards told me about."

"I know and I am excited. But, I don't know how I am going to stay in his life when I feel so much for him? I don't know if I can watch him with Daisy – again. Part of me wants to run away. I can't even look at him without getting upset."

"Lovey. Let's get this straight. You are not going to run away when you have been presented with such an amazing opportunity. I won't let you do that. This sort of thing doesn't happen very often. In addition, you don't know whether it will work out between Glen and Daisy. This is the first time, that we know of, that they have both cheated death and been given a second chance. We don't know whether their relationship will develop or flounder. However lovey, you cannot live your life with baited breath waiting to see what happens. Yes, you and he have a bond, and I feel that will only strengthen, but you, Katya my love, are destined for greater things, bigger things, and stronger feelings. This is just the beginning," Sheryl placed her palms on Katya's cheeks, and for an instant she was reminded of her grandmother.

"Destined for bigger than this? I think my heart would burst."

"I know lovey, I know. I was in love once. Years ago."

"What happened?"

"He overlooked me. I waited. Jan told me I was a fool."

"You are not a fool."

"I was then lovey. I put off others, I turned down opportunities, so convinced was I that he would come to me when he was ready. Because I believed he was my soul mate."

"What happened?

"He did come back to me. His wife left him and he came back into my life. It was spontaneous and unplanned. Fate. It all fell into place and I believed it was the real thing," Sheryl's eyes filled with tears and her face became twisted with bitterness "He stayed with me for six months. The best six months of my life. Until I woke up one morning to find my bank books gone, and my jewellery and my car taken."

"No!"

"In those six months, he persuaded me to share a lot with him. Including adding his name onto my savings account. It was before the days of pre-nuptial agreements and digital banking. It was all on paper. But I was in love. I knew he was the one. I waited for ten years for him. I missed out on having children, my biggest regret. I passed up several relationships because of my obsession with him."

Katya shook her head in disbelief.

"What I am trying to say, is that no matter how much you feel for someone, don't let it stop you doing what is right for you. Love will come for you if you open your heart and make the most of life. You have to love yourself first. At the moment, Katya, you are building up to something. Don't be surprised if you end up stronger than he is and less in awe of him."

"You really think so?"

"Yes. You can't make your feelings for him go away. Accept them, enjoy them, feel the emotion, but don't let it become bitter. Don't let it sour your life and your purpose as it did mine."

"I am so sorry."

"What for lovey?"

"For you… And your tale. You are so lovely, you did not deserve that."

"I know that. Now," Sheryl smiled, "But look at me! I bounced back. I love my life. I wear all the colours I wish to and no one can tell me what to do. I am the ultimate free spirit! You have your Liam, your son, and you will always cherish him I know, but now it is your time Katya lovey. Take it with open arms and an open heart. You have no idea where the future will take you."

"I am going home," Katya replied quietly as she stood up.

"Let me drive you back then," Sheryl nodded, understanding her desire to be alone.

"Thank you," Katya hugged her friend tightly.

Katya sneaked out quietly, casting an eye out for Glen and seeing the now-familiar image of him with Daisy. His hand protectively at her waist as she talked to her guests, an image of beauty and glamour. She wanted to move away from the sea of faces and voices, the noise and the activity.

She avoided Eliza, who she could see chatting to Brandon, animated, probably about the new business proposal. Brandon stood gazing at Eliza's face, smitten and brooding. Siobhan was pink-faced, rushing around doing her work with a smile, while Jayne stood quietly in a corner, alone but together again with herself. Even Josie was in a deep conversation with an intellectual type, his face looking at her with interest as she waved her hands while talking. Stella was in her element, passing her business cards and flashing her smile.

Katya wanted to go home and put her pyjamas back on. She wanted to hear nothing except her favourite music, and cry. She wanted to feel all this emotion that was bubbling up like a huge ball inside her chest. She wanted to let it explode and sob until her heart was relieved of its burden. Then she would get her books out and curl up in her favourite armchair with a hot chocolate. She wanted to make notes in her special journal and plan ahead. She just might, she thought, get the cards out and see what they came up with.

She felt excited.

This was her new beginning.

About The Great Gale of Brixham

I would like to pass on thanks to Laura J, of The South Devon Players, Theatre and Film Company, who kindly shared with me, her own research on the Great Gale of Brixham. This has not only been fascinating but also a great help to me in writing the historical sections of this book. The following text is an extract taken from the South Devon Players Blog, written and maintained by Laura

"On the night of January 10 – 11th 1866, a southeast gale blew up, and the storm is widely remembered in Brixham to this day. Much of the towns fishing fleet, as well as other ships sheltering in Torbay were destroyed, with a large loss of life. The fishwives of Brixham built a bonfire of their household effects on the end of the breakwater (half the length of the current breakwater, although in the same location) to try to guide their husbands home safely, while the men on shore in the town did all they could to save people from the ships which were wrecked along the Brixham and Churston coastline, and all those saved, both locals, and those from other parts of Britain, and indeed mainland Europe, were shown great kindness by the residents of the town who in many cases offered them lodgings in their own homes, even as they waited for news of their own loved ones.

It is said, however, that after the storm one could walk along the coastline from Brixham to Paignton, upon the wreckage of all the wrecked ships. Over a hundred bodies were identified, and records to this day also list many other unidentified seamen who were found torn apart by the fury of the storm and unidentifiable. A mass grave and memorial exists at St Marys Church in Brixham to this day. The full death toll from the storm will never be known – for example it was reported that two passenger steamers had been seen in Torbay, and some sailors, later rescued from the wreck of their own ship, reported that in the chaos of the night, in the bay, their ship had crashed into an unknown steamer which then sank, as far as they knew, with all hands.

In the 19th century, at the time of this storm, Brixham was one of the foremost fishing ports in England, and it was due to this storm that the people of Exeter, the county capital, raised funds for Brixham to have her first RNLI lifeboat; named The City Of Exeter, and the town has always had a lifeboat since."

To find out more about the South Devon Players Theatre and Film Company visit https://www.southdevonplayers.com/

About Near Death Experiences

I would also like to pass on thanks to Dr Penny Sartori, whose book
"The Wisdom of Near-Death Experiences" assisted greatly in my research on this subject, and was a fascinating and enlightening read.

The book, based on over twenty years of study, research and experience working in critical care, balances the scientific with the spiritual, presenting evidence to support the existence of the Near-Death Experience and the life-changing effect it has for many people who have witnessed it.

If you are interested in Near-Death Experiences and would like to read
Dr Sartori's books and learn about her work visit

http://www.drpennysartori.com/

Website links correct at time of publishing

Printed in Poland
by Amazon Fulfillment
Poland Sp. z o.o., Wrocław